ALL OUR WRONG TODAYS

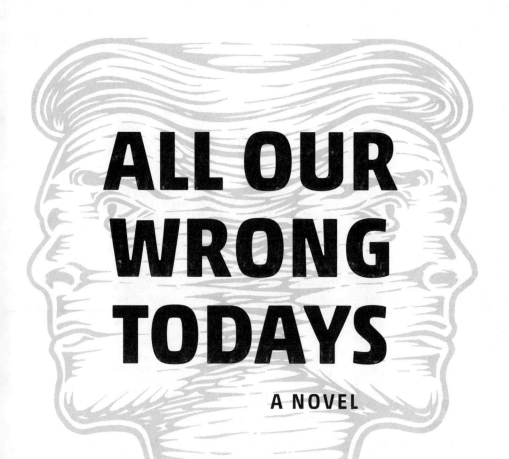

ALL OUR WRONG TODAYS

A NOVEL

ELAN MASTAI

DUTTON

DUTTON

An imprint of Penguin Random House LLC
375 Hudson Street
New York, New York 10014

LIBRARY OF CONGRESS CATALOGING-IN-PUBLICATION DATA
Names: Mastai, Elan, author.
Title: All our wrong todays : a novel / Elan Mastai.
Description: New York : Dutton, 2017.
Identifiers: LCCN 2016013073 (print) | LCCN 2016024489 (ebook) | ISBN 9781101985137 (hardback) | ISBN 9781101985151 (trade paperback) | ISBN 9781101985144 (eBook)
Subjects: LCSH: Young men—Fiction. | Reality—Fiction. | Utopias—Fiction. | Time travel—Fiction. | Self realization—Fiction. | Psychological fiction. | BISAC: FICTION / Literary. | FICTION / Family Life. | GSAFD: Fantasy fiction. | Utopian fiction.
Classification: LCC PR9199.4.M3745 A35 2017 (print) | LCC PR9199.4.M3745 (ebook) | DDC 813/.6—dc23
LC record available at https://lccn.loc.gov/2016013073

Printed in the United States of America
1 3 5 7 9 10 8 6 4 2

Set in ITC Galliard Std
Designed by Alissa Rose Theodor

This book is a work of fiction. Names, characters, places, and incidents either are the product of the author's imagination or are used fictitiously, and any resemblance to actual persons, living or dead, business establishments, events, or locales is entirely coincidental.

For my wife

ALL OUR WRONG TODAYS

1

So, the thing is, I come from the world we were supposed to have. That means nothing to you, obviously, because you live here, in the crappy world we *do* have. But it never should've turned out like this. And it's all my fault—well, me and to a lesser extent my father and, yeah, I guess a little bit Penelope.

It's hard to know how to start telling this story. But, okay, you know the future that people in the 1950s imagined we'd have? Flying cars, robot maids, food pills, teleportation, jet packs, moving sidewalks, ray guns, hover boards, space vacations, and moon bases. All that dazzling, transformative technology our grandparents were certain was right around the corner. The stuff of world's fairs and pulp science-fiction magazines with titles like *Fantastic Future Tales* and *The Amazing World of Tomorrow*. Can you picture it?

Well, it happened.

It all happened, more or less exactly as envisioned. I'm not talking about the future. I'm talking about the *present*. Today, in the year 2016, humanity lives in a techno-utopian paradise of abundance, purpose, and wonder.

Except we don't. Of course we don't. We live in a world where, sure, there are iPhones and 3D printers and, I don't know, drone strikes or whatever. But it hardly looks like *The Jetsons*. Except it should. And it did. Until it didn't. But it would have, if I hadn't done what I did. Or, no, hold on, what I *will* have done.

I'm sorry, despite receiving the best education available to a citizen of the World of Tomorrow, the grammar of this situation is a bit complicated.

Maybe the first person is the wrong way to tell this story. Maybe if I take refuge in the third person I'll find some sort of distance or insight or at least peace of mind. It's worth a try.

2

Tom Barren wakes up into his own dream.

Every night, neural scanners map his dreams while he sleeps so that both his conscious and unconscious thought patterns can be effectively modeled. Every morning, the neural scanners transmit the current dream-state data into a program that generates a real-time virtual projection into which he seamlessly rouses. The dream's scattershot plot is made increasingly linear and lucid until a psychologically pleasing resolution is achieved at the moment of full consciousness . . .

I'm sorry—I can't write like this. It's fake. It's safe.

The third person is comforting because it's in control, which feels really nice when relating events that were often so out of control. It's like a scientist describing a biological sample seen through a microscope. But I'm not the microscope. I'm the thing on the slide. And I'm not writing this to make myself comfortable. If I wanted comfort, I'd write fiction.

In fiction, you cohere all these evocative, telling details into a portrait of the world. But in everyday life, you hardly notice any of the little things. You can't. Your brain swoops past it all, especially when it's your own home, a place that feels barely separate from the inside of your mind or the outside of your body.

When you wake up from a real dream into a virtual one, it's like you're on a raft darting this way and that according to the blurry, impenetrable currents of your unconscious, until you find yourself gliding onto a wide, calm, shallow lake, and the slippery, fraught weirdness dissolves into serene, reassuring clarity. The story wraps up the way it feels like it must, and no matter how unsettling the content, you wake with the rejuvenating solidity of order restored. And that's when you realize you're lying in bed, ready to start the day, with none of that sticky subconscious gristle caught in the cramped folds of your mind.

It might be what I miss most about where I come from. Because in this world waking up sucks.

Here, it's like nobody has considered using even the most rudimentary technology to improve the process. Mattresses don't subtly vibrate to keep your muscles loose. Targeted steam valves don't clean your body in slumber. I mean, blankets are made from tufts of plant fiber spun into thread and occasionally stuffed with feathers. Feathers. Like from actual birds. Waking up should be the best moment of your day, your unconscious and conscious minds synchronized and harmonious.

Getting dressed involves an automated device that cuts and stitches a new outfit every morning, indexed to your personal style and body type. The fabric is made from laser-hardened strands of a light-sensitive liquid polymer that's recycled nightly for daily reuse. For breakfast, a similar system outputs whatever meal you feel like from a nutrient gel mixed with color, flavor, and texture protocols. And if that sounds gross to you, in practice it's indistinguishable from what you think of as real food, except that it's uniquely gauged to your tongue's sensory receptors so it tastes and feels ideal every time. You know that sinking feeling you get when you cut into an avocado, only to find that it's either hard and underripe or brown and bruised under its skin? Well, I didn't know that could even happen until I came here. Every avocado I ever ate was perfect.

It's weird to be nostalgic for experiences that both did and didn't exist. Like waking up every morning completely refreshed. Something I didn't even realize I *could* take for granted because it was simply the way things were. But that's the point, of course—the way things were . . . never was.

What I'm not nostalgic for is that every morning when I woke up and got dressed and ate breakfast in this glittering technological utopia, I was alone.

3

On July 11, 1965, Lionel Goettreider invented the future.

Obviously you've never heard of him. But where I come from, Lionel Goettreider is the most famous, beloved, and respected human on the planet. Every city has dozens of things named after him: streets, buildings, parks, whatever. Every kid knows how to spell his name using the catchy mnemonic tune that goes *G-O-E-T-T-R-E-I-D-E-R*.

You have no idea what I'm talking about. But if you were from where I'm from, it'd be as familiar to you as *A-B-C*.

Fifty-one years ago, Lionel Goettreider invented a revolutionary way to generate unlimited, robust, absolutely clean energy. His device came to be called the Goettreider Engine. July 11, 1965, was the day he turned it on for the very first time. It made everything possible.

Imagine that the last five decades happened with no restrictions on energy. No need to dig deeper and deeper into the ground and make the skies dirtier and dirtier. Nuclear became unnecessarily tempestuous. Coal and oil pointlessly murky. Solar and wind and even hydropower became quaint low-fidelity alternatives that nobody bothered with unless they were peculiarly determined to live off the main grid.

So, how did the Goettreider Engine work?

How does electricity work? How does a microwave oven work? How does your cell phone or television or remote control work? Do you actually understand on, like, a concrete technical level? If those technologies disappeared, could you reconceive, redesign, and rebuild them from scratch? And, if not, why not? You only use these things pretty much every single day.

But of course you don't know. Because unless your job's in a related field you don't need to know. They just *work*, effortlessly, as they were intended to.

Where I come from, that's how it is with the Goettreider Engine. It was important enough to make Goettreider as recognizable a name as Einstein or Newton or Darwin. But how it functioned, like, technically? I really couldn't tell you.

Basically, you know how a dam produces energy? Turbines harness the natural propulsion of water flowing downward via gravity to generate electricity. To be clear, that's more or less *all* I understand about hydroelectric power. Gravity pulls water down, so if you stick a turbine in its path, the water spins it around and somehow makes energy.

The Goettreider Engine does that with the planet. You know that the Earth spins on its axis and also revolves around the Sun, while the Sun itself moves endlessly through the solar system. Like water through a turbine, the Goettreider Engine harnesses the constant rotation of the planet to create boundless energy. It has something to do with magnetism and gravity and . . . honestly, I don't know— any more than I genuinely understand an alkaline battery or a combustion engine or an incandescent light bulb. They just work.

So does the Goettreider Engine. It just works.

Or it did. Before, you know, *me*.

4

I am not a genius. If you've read this far, you're already aware of that fact.

But my father is a legitimate full-blown genius of the highest order. After finishing his third PhD, Victor Barren spent a few crucial years working in long-range teleportation before founding his own lab to pursue his specific niche field—time travel.

Even where I come from, time travel was considered more or less impossible. Not because of time, actually, but because of space.

Here's why every time-travel movie you've ever seen is total bullshit: because the Earth moves.

You know this. Plus I mentioned it last chapter. The Earth spins all the way around once a day, revolves around the Sun once a year, while the Sun is on its own cosmic route through the solar system, which is itself hurtling through a galaxy that's wandering an epic path through the universe.

The ground under you is moving, really fast. Along the equator, the Earth rotates at over 1,000 miles per hour, twenty-four hours a day, while orbiting the Sun at a little over 67,000 miles per hour. That's 1,600,000 miles per day. Meanwhile our solar system is in motion relative to the Milky Way galaxy at more than 1,300,000 miles per hour, covering just shy of 32,000,000 miles per day. And so on.

If you were to travel back in time to yesterday, the Earth would be in a different place in space. Even if you travel back in time one second, the Earth below your feet can move nearly half a kilometer. In one second.

The reason every movie about time travel is nonsense is that the Earth moves, constantly, always. You travel back one day, you don't end up in the same location—you end up in the gaping vacuum of outer space.

Marty McFly didn't appear thirty years earlier in his hometown of Hill Valley, California. His tricked-out DeLorean materialized in the endless empty blackness of the cosmos with the Earth approximately 350,000,000,000 miles away. Assuming he didn't immediately lose consciousness from the lack of oxygen, the absence of air pressure would cause all the fluids in his body to bubble, partially evaporate, and freeze. He would be dead in less than a minute.

The Terminator would probably survive in space because it's an unstoppable robot killing machine, but traveling from 2029 to 1984 would've given Sarah Connor a 525,000,000,000-mile head start.

Time travel doesn't just require traveling back in time. It also requires traveling back to a pinpoint-specific location in space. Otherwise, just like with regular old everyday teleportation, you could end up stuck *inside* something.

Think about where you're sitting right now. Let's say on an olive-green couch. A white ceramic bowl of fake green pears and real brown pinecones propped next to your feet on the teak coffee table. A brushed-steel floor lamp glows over your shoulder. A coarse rug over reclaimed barn-board elm floors that cost too much but look pretty great . . .

If you were to teleport even a few inches in any direction, your body would be embedded in a solid object. One inch, you're wounded. Two inches, you're maimed. Three inches, you're dead.

Every second of the day, we're all three inches from being dead.

Which is why teleportation is safe and effective only if it's between dedicated sites on an exactingly calibrated system.

My father's early work in teleportation was so important because it helped him understand the mechanics of disincorporating and re-incorporating a human body between discrete locations. It's what stymied all previous time-travel initiatives. Reversing the flow of time isn't even that complex. What's outrageously complex is instantaneous space travel with absolute accuracy across potentially billions of miles.

My father's genius wasn't just about solving both the theoretical and logistical challenges of time travel. It was about recognizing that in this, as in so many other aspects of everyday life, our savior was Lionel Goettreider.

5

The first Goettreider Engine was turned on once and never turned off—it's been running without interruption since 2:03 P.M. on Sunday, July 11, 1965.

Goettreider's original device wasn't designed to harness and emit large-scale amounts of energy. It was an experimental prototype that performed beyond its inventor's most grandiose expectations. But the whole point of a Goettreider Engine is that it never has to be deactivated, just as the planet never stops moving. So, the prototype was left running in the same spot where it was first switched on, in front of a small crowd of sixteen observers in a basement laboratory in section B7 of the San Francisco State Science and Technology Center.

Where I come from, every schoolkid knows the names and faces of the Sixteen Witnesses. Numerous books have been written about every single one of them, with their presence at this ultimate hinge in history shoved into the chronology of their individual lives as the defining event, whether or not it was factually true.

Countless works of art have depicted *The Activation of the Goettreider Engine*. It's *The Last Supper* of the modern world, those sixteen faces, each with its own codified reaction. Skeptical. Awed. Distracted. Amused. Jealous. Angry. Thoughtful. Frightened. Detached. Concerned. Excited. Nonchalant. Harried. There's three more. Damn it, I should know this . . .

When the prototype Engine was first turned on, Goettreider just wanted to verify his calculations and prove his theory wasn't completely misguided—all it had to do was actually *work*. And it did work, but it had a major defect. It emitted a unique radiation signature, what was later called *tau radiation,* a nod to how physics uses the Greek capital letter T to represent *proper time* in relativity equations.

As the Engine's miraculous energy-generating capacities expanded to power the whole world, the tau radiation signature was eliminated from the large-scale industrial models. But the prototype was left to run, theoretically forever, in Goettreider's lab in San Francisco—now among the most visited museums on the planet—out of respect, nostalgia, and a legally rigid clause in Goettreider's last will and testament.

My father's idea was to use the original device's tau radiation signature as a bread-crumb trail through space and time, each crumb the size of an atom, a knotted thread to the past, looping through the cosmos with an anchor fixed at the most important moment in history—Sunday, July 11, 1965, 2:03:48 P.M., the exact second Lionel Goettreider started the future. It meant that not only could my father send someone back in time to a very specific moment, the tau radiation trail would lead them to a very specific location—Lionel Goettreider's lab, right before the world changed forever.

With this realization, my father had almost every piece of the time-travel puzzle. There was only one last thing, minor compared to transporting a sentient human being into the past, but major in terms of not accidentally shredding the present—a way to ensure the time traveler can't affect the past in any tangible way. There were several crucial safeguards in my father's design, but the only one I care about is the *defusion sphere.* Because that's how Penelope Weschler's life collided with mine.

6

Nearly every object of art and entertainment is different in this world. Early on, the variations aren't that significant. But as the late 1960s gave way to the vast technological and social leaps of the 1970s, almost everything changed, generating decades of pop culture that never existed—fifty years of writers and artists and musicians creating an entirely *other* body of work. Sometimes there are fascinating parallels, a loose story point in one version that's the climax in another, a line of dialogue in the wrong character's mouth, a striking visual composition framed in a new context, a familiar chord progression with radically altered lyrics.

July 11, 1965, was the pivot of history even if nobody knew it yet.

Fortunately, Lionel Goettreider's favorite novel was published in 1963—*Cat's Cradle* by Kurt Vonnegut Jr.

Vonnegut's writing is different where I come from. Here, despite his wit and insight, you get the impression he felt a novelist could have no real effect on the world. He was compelled to write, but with little faith that writing might change anything.

Because *Cat's Cradle* influenced Lionel Goettreider so deeply, in my world Vonnegut was considered among the most significant philosophers of the late twentieth century. This was probably great for Vonnegut personally but less so for his novels, which became increasingly homiletic.

I won't summarize *Cat's Cradle* for you. It's short and much better written than this book, so just go read it. It's weary, cheeky, and wise, which are my three favorite qualities in people and art.

Tangentially—Weary, Cheeky, and Wise are the three codified reactions I couldn't remember from the Sixteen Witnesses to the Activation.

Cat's Cradle is about a lot of things, but a major plot thread involves the invention of ice-nine, a substance that freezes everything it touches, which falls out of its creator's control and destroys all life on the planet.

Lionel Goettreider read *Cat's Cradle* and had a crucial realization, what he called the "Accident"—when you invent a new technology, you also invent the accident of that technology.

When you invent the car, you also invent the car accident. When you invent the plane, you also invent the plane crash. When you invent nuclear fission, you also invent the nuclear meltdown. When you invent ice-nine, you also invent unintentionally freezing the planet solid.

When Lionel Goettreider invented the Goettreider Engine, he knew he couldn't turn it on until he figured out its accident—and how to prevent it.

My favorite exhibit at the Goettreider Museum is the simulation of what *could've* happened if the Engine had somehow malfunctioned when Goettreider first turned it on. In the worst-case scenario, the unprecedented amounts of energy pulled in by the Engine overwhelm its intake core, triggering an explosion that melts San Francisco into a smoldering crater, poisons the Pacific Ocean with tau radiation, corrodes 10,000 square miles of arable land into a stew of pain, and renders an impressive swath of North America uninhabitable for decades. Parents would occasionally complain to the museum's curatorial staff that the simulation's nightmarish imagery was too graphic for children and, since the experiment obviously *didn't* fail, why draw attention away from Goettreider's majestic contributions to human civilization with grotesque speculation about imaginary global disasters? The simulation was eventually moved to an out-of-the-way corner of the museum, where generations of teenagers on high school field trips would huddle in the darkness and watch the world fall apart on a continuous loop.

I'm not a genius like Lionel Goettreider or Kurt Vonnegut or my father. But I have a theory too: The Accident doesn't just apply to technology, it also applies to people. Every person you meet introduces the accident of that person to you. What can go right and what can go wrong. There is no intimacy without consequence.

Which brings me back to Penelope Weschler and the accident of us. Of all of us.

7

Penelope Weschler was supposed to be an astronaut. In early-age evaluation matrices, she indicated the necessary mental aptitude, physical capability, and unwavering ambition. Even as a child, Penelope immediately knew this was the correct path for her and wanted nothing else. She trained nonstop, both in and out of school. Not to walk on the moon. Anybody could walk on the moon. Anybody could go for a monthlong orbital cruise. Penelope would cross the next frontier—deep-space exploration.

It wasn't just the studying, the training, the constant testing. It was social. Or, really, antisocial. For long-term space operations, the recruiting agencies want you to grow up with parents and siblings so you have empathy models to apply to fellow astronauts on missions that last years, sometimes decades. They want you capable of caring about other people. But they don't want you to actually miss anyone back home *too* much, so you don't have a breakdown six months into a six-year mission. It's a sliding psychological scale—self-assured loners whose parents never divorced are good, shark-eyed sociopaths less so.

From junior high on, Penelope maintained amicable but purposefully limited personal relationships, so she wouldn't have anybody tethering her to Earth.

And she was utterly kick-ass. Top of her cohort across all categories. Universally recognized as a natural mission leader. She'd be a pioneer. She'd see the storms of Jupiter with her own eyes and surf the rings of Saturn on a space walk. And that was worth not having close friends or romantic relationships or a loyal dog.

Everything was going according to plan. Until the first time she went to space.

The launch was flawless. Penelope performed her functions with such precision they would've used it to teach incoming recruits how gloriously capable an astronaut can be. She was prepared. She was ready. She was perfect.

Until she passed through the top layer of Earth's atmosphere and her mind went completely blank.

There's a small subset of people whose cognitive functions get scrambled in outer space. Something about how the pressure change of the vacuum affects the bonds between molecules in the neurons of their brains. No one's even sure why it happens. But Penelope was one of that subset. Somehow this fact eluded the years of rigorous screening. One moment she's deftly guiding the launch vehicle through the final atmospheric layers, seeing the gaping expanse of space for the first time, her heart beating in measured but ecstatic bursts, the happiest she's ever felt. And then . . . nothing.

She doesn't know who she is. She doesn't know where she is. She doesn't know what to do. Something in her basic constitution keeps her from having a panic attack, as most people would if they suddenly woke up piloting a goddamn spacecraft with the planet receding behind them. But she can't remember anything. The instrument panel she'd spent years mastering means nothing to her, inscrutable acronyms printed over lights flashing in seemingly random patterns. She stares out the viewing dome at the radiant vapor of stars smeared across the black canvas of space, like the pollen clouds that would rise from the cedar trees in her grandparents' backyard when the squirrels jumped from branch to branch, although she can't understand why she's thinking about something she hasn't seen since she was eight years old when there are these *voices* in her earpiece getting loud and insistent.

"I'm sorry," she said, "but I'm not really sure where I am right now."

Her copilots, just as well trained and keening with tiny flames of envy at how far ahead of them she'd always ranked, relieved Penelope of her duties. They had to abort the mission, at no small expense, because her unpredictable presence endangered everyone. Just like that, Penelope, the best of the best of the best, became a threat.

Strapped into an observation seat for the abrupt return home, she watched the Earth loom below her, lacquered blue and swirled with meteorological haze. Her eyes burned with tears. It was the most beautiful thing she'd ever seen and she would never see it again, even if she didn't know it yet.

Back on Earth, her mental capacities returned to normal, she understood her career as an astronaut was over. She'd planned to spend decades off planet. Instead, she got to experience less time in space than a tourist who splurged for a Sunday afternoon jaunt through the thermosphere on a discount shuttle. The same brain that made her the perfect astronaut made it impossible for her to do the job.

This would've crushed most people. But Penelope wasn't most people. After a few months swimming deep into a gravity well of spiraling depression, and refusing any pharmaceutical intervention in case it affected medical qualification for another endeavor, she found a new ambition to fuel her talent for punishing rigor.

If she couldn't be an astronaut, she'd be a chrononaut.

8

I leave my condo on the 184th floor of a 270-floor tower connected to seven other towers by a lattice of walkways, with a transport hub at the base of the octagonal complex. My father pulled some strings because the building is owned by the same property conglomerate that manages my parents' housing unit, so at least my place faces away from Toronto's densest building clusters and I have a decent view of Lake Ontario and the Niagara Escarpment biosphere preserve in the distance, the spires of downtown Buffalo glinting morning sunlight along the arced horizon.

A lot of people take their own vehicles to work but, seriously, three-dimensional traffic sucks. Whatever the cool factor of a flying car, it's mitigated by the gridlock hovering twenty stories above every street.

I prefer to catch a transit capsule on one of the layered tracks that run through the city. Each capsule is a sleek metallic pod that opens like a clamshell, and inside is a padded bench, with screens and speakers to jack in your entertainment interface. The capsule takes you wherever you need to go on the citywide transport system, although each capsule also has a retractable hover engine to travel short distances off grid.

I get to work twelve minutes late, which is typical for me. My boss is too soured on pretty much every aspect of my life to get worked up about chronic tardiness. Because my boss is my father.

The sign outside the building says THE CHRONONAUT INSTITUTE. I find this unbearably cheesy but, since all my father's employees revere him, I'm clearly in the minority. Nobody else would even consider rolling their eyes at that stupid sign when they come to work at the lab. They're way too busy rolling their eyes at me.

One thing I should make clear—just because I work at a lab, that doesn't make me smart. Where I come from, everybody works at a lab.

All the banal functions of daily life are taken care of by technology. There are no grocery stores or gas stations or fast-food joints. Nobody collects garbage from a bin at the curb or fixes your car with, like, tools in a garage. The menial and manual jobs that dominated the global workforce in past eras are now automated and mechanized, and the international conglomerates that maintain those technologies keep busy tinkering with minor refinements. If your organic waste disposal module malfunctions, you wouldn't call a plumber, even if plumbers still existed, because your building has repair drones at the ready. A lamplighter with a jug of kerosene and a wick on a pole has as much relevance to contemporary life as tailors and janitors and gardeners and carpenters.

Places like bookstores and cafés still *exist*, but they're specialized niche businesses aimed at nostalgia fetishists. You can go to an actual restaurant and have a chef prepare your meal by hand. But the waiter who serves you is essentially an actor playing a role on a set in which you're also a performer, an immersive live-action narrative spooling out around you in real time.

In the absence of material want, the world economy transitioned almost exclusively to entertainment—entertainment is both the foundation and the fuel of modern civilization. Most of us now work in labs imagining, designing, and building the next cool innovation in entertainment. It's the only thing you really need in a world where almost nothing is asked of you. Other than *paying* for that entertainment. The newer and shinier and wilder it is, the more it costs.

If you're a scientist driven to crack uncrackable codes and break unbreakable ground, nobody beyond a few chronically underfunded

government agencies is all that motivated to finance that code cracking and ground breaking. But if you can somehow frame it as the
newest, shiniest, wildest entertainment around—there's no limit to
the financing you can rake in.

Which is why my father, widely considered one of the world's top-
tier geniuses, has devoted his career and reputation to, basically, time-
travel tourism.

"Time travel" is not an investment draw. But you add the word
tourism to it, the promise of a ceaseless flow of customers lining up to
pay to visit whatever era of life on planet Earth they want to see with
their own eyes, well, then the money pours in. And so—*chrononauts*.

9

My father's experiment, set for July 11, 2016, will send the first human beings back in time to witness the moment the original Goettreider Engine was switched on, using the Engine itself as an anchor in time, its tau radiation signature tracing the Earth's trajectory through space to July 11, 1965, fifty-one years earlier.

The year 2015 was the fiftieth anniversary of the Activation of the Goettreider Engine, which was obviously a big deal—every city on the planet competed to outdo the others with their local celebrations. The collective blood pressure of the Danish people ratcheted dangerously high as they seized the opportunity to remind the world that even though his great scientific discoveries were made in the United States of America, Lionel Goettreider was born in Denmark. But the marquee event happened at the Goettreider Museum, built up around the original San Francisco State Science and Technology Center, its drab cement walls and squat windows preserved inside a modern edifice—a spectacular crystalline whorl that refracts sunlight in the day and moonlight at night.

On the morning of Saturday, July 11, 2015, standing on a dais with the Goettreider Museum perfectly poised behind him for every media report, Victor Barren kicked off the semicentennial celebration by publicly announcing that the world's first time-travel experiment would occur *exactly* one year from that moment—at 10:00:00 A.M. on Monday, July 11, 2016. He gestured to a large clock on the dais and began the countdown: 31,622,400 seconds, 527,040 minutes,

8,784 hours, 366 days. It would be the greatest experiment since, well, the Activation of the Goettreider Engine. And once the appropriate government safeguards had been satisfied, the technology would become commercially available to the public, with licensed chrononaut facilities allowing anyone and everyone the chance to safely travel in time. People *freaked out* in anticipation. My father's time machine was assured to be among the most successful products ever launched.

This is how Victor Barren made himself the star of the Goettreider Engine's fiftieth anniversary.

Transported to the Chrononaut Institute in Toronto, the big clock continued its countdown, as if the precise moment my father would take his place among the giants of science was a mathematical inevitability. All that was required was for that clock to run out of numbers.

By the way, the fiftieth-anniversary thing had no scientific significance. It was a bit of theatrical razzle-dazzle to build public anticipation and impress the financiers who bought into my father's supposedly game-changing new form of high-end entertainment.

But for it to be a viable business, my father had to actually *prove* people can safely time travel. Enter the chrononauts.

For security and safety purposes, the prototype time machine is programmed for a single, fixed destination: Lionel Goettreider's basement laboratory in San Francisco, California, on July 11, 1965. The tau radiation trail leads there and only there. This *should* prevent a miscalculation that sends the chrononauts to the wrong era. The prototype is like a gondola strung between two alpine peaks—you can't just use it to go wherever or whenever you want. Once the experiment is successful and the path between 2016 and 1965 is accurately mapped both in space and in time, further exploration will be possible. But until mission launch, it's still just a very expensive untested theory—so the chrononauts need to be ready for anything.

It's a six-person team, apparently the ideal number for this kind of mission. Psychologically, it's large enough to feel like a unit but small enough to cultivate reasonably intimate individual bonds. Each of the six is painstakingly trained in multifaceted survival. Not just physical, but cultural. Let's say something does go wrong and instead of five decades in the past, they travel back five centuries, or five millennia. The whole team needs to be acutely familiar with the on-the-ground conditions of whatever era they may find themselves in.

There's an abort protocol to slingshot them back to the present, but it takes crucial seconds to engage regardless of mortal threat. There is of course an automatic rebound function that activates in the event of a catastrophic systems failure so, even if the whole team dies, the technology itself isn't lost in the past, wreaking unknowable consequences on history.

Obviously it makes more scientific sense to send back an inanimate object or a trained animal. But there are two problems with a more cautious approach. First, my father wants to knock everyone's socks off right out of the gate, and sending a team of people back in time is way cooler than, like, a robot drone or a bunny rabbit. Second, the margin of error is so minute when you're mucking about in space-time that you want nimble human minds making considered decisions, so if anything unexpected happens nobody accidentally triggers a calamitous change to the timeline. That would be bad.

Almost anything could go wrong. You need people who are resolutely calm under pressure and can survive in unpredictably lethal situations. Six chrononauts, each among the most impressive individuals alive.

Which is why it was totally absurd that I was involved in this mission.

10

I guess now is as good a time as any to mention that my mother, Rebecca Barren, died four months ago in a freak accident.

Yes, despite the many technological marvels of my world, people still got killed for no good reason. People also acted like assholes for no good reason. But, sorry, I'm trying to tell you about my mother, not my father.

Like a lot of high-impact thinkers, my father needed everything that didn't involve his big brain managed for him. Of course, most of these functions could be automated, but my mother embraced a handmade quality to our family life that could be seen as tactile and quaint and also could be seen as neurotic and sad. Like, if she didn't personally fold my father's clothes, clean his study, serve his food, he wouldn't be able to unlock the mysteries of time travel. And it's entirely possible she was correct. Because he *did* unlock the mysteries of time travel, and within a few months of her sudden death, everything was a total disaster.

They met at the University of Toronto. My father's parents had emigrated from Vienna to Toronto when he was nine years old, and he never lost an Austrian clip to his vowels. My mother came from Leeds on an international exchange program to continue her undergraduate degree in literature and never lost her British ability to reflexively vector herself within rigid class dynamics.

My father was a graduate student in physics and my mother noticed him around campus, always wearing mismatched socks. She wanted to know if it was a fashion choice above her station or the mark of someone with more important things on his mind. One day, she walked up and handed him a gift—a box of one hundred identical socks. He had no idea who she was. They were married within a year and slotted themselves into their respective lifelong roles—my father was the lighthouse, my mother the keeper who wound the clock-work, polished the lenses, and swept all those rocky steps.

My father had a wife who was more like a mother. And I had a mother who was more like a sister. My father's reputation propelled him up through the scientific community, but it cocooned my mother from any honest, vulnerable friendships. She had a role to play—midwife to my father's genius—and she couldn't admit to anyone that she felt hollow, lonely, full of dread.

Except me. My mother would tell me everything. I was her confidant, her simpleton therapist, a forever ready ear to her bot-tomless reservoir of anxious chitter-chatter. My father's job was to change the world. My mother's job was to create a warm, soft nest for him to preen in. My job was to listen to my mother talk, end-lessly, so she didn't have a nervous breakdown while suppressing anything consequential about herself in case it spoiled my father's expansive mood of cosmic contemplation.

My mother's comfort was books. Not the immersive virtual story-telling modules the rest of us enjoyed—actual books, the paper-and-ink kind that nobody made, let alone wrote, anymore. Her leisure time was spent reading words written in a previous era. Before she met my father, she'd imagined a career surrounded by books, teach-ing them, editing them, maybe even writing them.

I should clarify that my father never *requested* any of this. Part of his blissfully unaware state of grandiose self-importance is that he noticed none of it. He somehow found a spouse who would natu-rally wear herself down into a ball of gray wool. She became the comfortably downy socks that were always clean and ready in his drawer whenever his feet felt cold. As far as he knew, the house just made them to order.

And then, four months ago, while she sipped a coffee and read a novel on a patch of grass outside my parents' housing unit, a malfunctioning navigation system caused a hover car to break formation, careen out of control, and smear half of my mother across the lawn in a wet streak of blood and bone and skin and the end of everything.

When someone dies they get very cold and very still. That probably sounds obvious, but when it's your mother it doesn't feel obvious—it feels shocking. You watch, winded and reeling, as the medical technicians neutralize the stasis field and power down the synthetic organ metabolizer. But the sentimental gesture of kissing her forehead makes you recoil because the moment your lips touch her skin you realize just how cold and just how still she is, just how permanent that coldness and that stillness feel. Your body lurches like it's been plunged into boiling water and for the first time in your life you understand death as a biological state, an organism ceasing to function. Unless you've touched a corpse before, you can't comprehend the visceral wrongness of inert flesh wrapped around an inanimate object that wears your mother's face. You feel sick with guilt and regret and sadness about every time you rolled your eyes in annoyance or brushed off a needy request or let your mind wander when she told some inconsequential anecdote. You can't remember anything thoughtful or sweet or tender that you ever did even though logically you know you must have. All you can recall is how often you were small and petty and false. She was your mother and she loved you in a way nobody ever has and nobody ever will and now she's gone.

When I was born, my mother planted a lemon tree on their property and once a year she would make lemon tarts, her grandmother's recipe, for my birthday. That tree, thirty-two years old, same as me, was just strong enough to stop the hover car from smashing right through the large window of my father's study, where he was considering matters of lofty import and absentmindedly eating the grilled cheese sandwich that my mother had prepared for him as she made herself a mug of coffee to drink while sitting out in the sunshine to read a chapter of *Great Expectations* before it was time to do some other incredibly thoughtful routine thing that made my father's life so pleasant and that he would realize she'd done for him for more than thirty years only once she was gone.

Without that tree, my father would be dead too. I would be an orphan. And everything would be much, much better for everyone.

I remember, as a kid, when I first understood that only half of every tree is visible, that the roots in the soil are equal to the branches in the sky, that a whole other half is underground. It took me a lot longer, well into adulthood, to realize people are like that too.

11

The funeral was on a crisp, sunny morning. A few dozen of my father's employees, their spouses and bored kids, my mother's relatives from northern England, my father's relatives from Austria, several of the families from my parents' housing subsection, some close friends of mine, and three ex-girlfriends gathered at the spot where my mother died to listen to a bunch of eulogies spoken by people who quickly revealed they knew nothing about her internal life.

I should've spoken, I wanted to, but I couldn't get any words out that day.

After the vacuous eulogies that, to be clear, still made me cry like hell, everyone watched, solemn, as my father sprinkled her ashes at the base of the lemon tree that was planted on the day of my birth and prevented his death, and I wanted to scream that this was a repulsive commemoration of a kind, brittle woman who collapsed into herself for her husband. Except it wasn't. It was in fact a perfectly appropriate commemoration. Her final living act was to slow the malfunctioning hover car just enough that the lemon tree could stop its deadly momentum. In death as in life she was there for my father.

So, he scattered her ashes and, after the reception, I slept with one of my ex-girlfriends in my childhood bedroom.

In full disclosure, I subsequently slept with the other two ex-girlfriends who came to the funeral, as well as one of my closest friends from high school, whom I'd never made a play for because she was so cool that I didn't want to screw up our camaraderie by inevitably disappointing her as a boyfriend.

I'm not bragging here. I mean, I could be more discreet about it, but I'm trying to do that by not mentioning their names. Out of respect. Or, I don't know, maybe not mentioning their names seems sleazy.

All four encounters followed more or less the same script. She would ask to talk in private, *really talk,* she'd say. I got the wary sense she felt some shudder of excitement at me so openly expressing my grief to her, to her alone, as if she were the only one who could coax it out of me before it rotted right through my skin.

Looking back, it's like the grief was an offering I made to them in exchange for their bodies and, for reasons I'm not insightful enough to understand, my tears turned them on. Or maybe it was just a simple thing that each of them decided I needed and they could do for me and I should be grateful, because it helped. At the time it felt like an honest moment of sadness and want. I was flailing out for something alive. Sex was basically the first thing I could think of to knit back together my unspooled heart, and if those four women had declined I guess I'd have come up with a second idea. But their gentle willingness and my lack of imagination led to four nearly identical encounters.

We'd be alone, late at night, and I'd tell them about sitting with my mother at the hospital in the hours between the accident and her official time of death, while the stasis field kept her alive from the waist up because she'd been obliterated from the waist down, and how all she could do was repeat the same phrase over and over, like the trillions of neurons in her brain had cooperated in a final slurry of consciousness to make sure her last thought was transmitted to whoever might listen.

"He's lost, my love, so you must help him be found," she'd say, again and again.

And I'd cry and say she's right, I am lost, but I don't think I can be found. I knew saying it like that, sobbing and jagged, instead of shrugging it off with a self-deprecating joke or a snarky dismissal, would resonate with the woman I was speaking to, because three of them had ended things with me for the same reason, which is that they got sick of my bullshit and realized I wasn't going anywhere in my life, except for my friend from school, who knew me well enough to discount a romantic relationship before one could even start, no doubt aware she'd eventually end it with me because she'd get sick of my bullshit and realize I wasn't going anywhere in my life.

So I'd cry and they'd hold me and we'd look at each other and I'd kiss them.

"I don't know if this is a good idea," they'd say.

"It's the only idea I have," I'd say.

They'd kiss me back. We'd take off our clothes. I've lived in a world of infinite amazement and technological marvels, but none of it was worth a damn to me compared to those four nights.

I doubt they felt the same about me. Maybe I just seemed pitiable and pity is a strange aphrodisiac. It definitely screwed things up with my friend from school. She insisted she didn't regret it, but that I was obviously in a difficult place and it was a mistake to consider anything more right now, and she hoped in time things would get back to normal between us. And I said I hoped the same, but after that we only hung out one last time, surrounded by our other friends, who tried to keep it light and airy around me, unsure how to behave with someone whose mother died and so acting like it didn't happen, even though they were all at the funeral. Except her, my friend, more quiet than usual, smiling sadly at my dumb jokes, as if she thought that's what I needed to feel better, her sad smiles at my dumb jokes.

Just because we could holiday on the moon or teleport to a shopping mall or watch a fetus gestate in a celebrity's uterus or regenerate body parts from a plasmic soup or any of the countless things that sound like science fiction to you but were documentary to me, it doesn't mean we had everything figured out. We were still just people. Messy, messed-up people who didn't know how to act when one of our lives came undone. So my friends cracked jokes and squirmed in my presence and I slept around, and whether or not it was right or wrong it helped for an hour or two at a time. And I'll never know if my friend and I would've figured out how to be friends again or if I would've gotten back together with one of my exes. I'll never know if one of those nights of sadness and want could've turned into years of happiness and plenty.

My friend's name was Deisha Cline and she was funny and smart and mischievous and sweet. My ex-girlfriends were Hester Lee, Megan Stround, and Tabitha Reese and they were funny and smart and mischievous and sweet too. And it doesn't matter if I mention their names because none of them exist anymore.

12

My father's interpretation of *"He's lost, my love, so you must help him be found"* was to offer me a job.

We sat in his study, the lemon tree that saved his life outside the window, fat lemons hanging heavy on its branches, ripe for lemon tarts that would never be made for a birthday that he would forget and I would ignore. My father has given countless public lectures about the future, but this was the only one I can remember that had anything to do with *me*. The gist of it was that his father gave him the freedom to find his own way in the world and he'd wanted to do the same for me, to respect that even if it *seemed* that I was meandering through a dispiriting procession of pointless endeavors, maybe an actual direction would eventually emerge, as if by sorcery, from the haze of randomness and caprice. But after thirty-two years, my father thought it was time to reassess that judgment. After all, my grandfather was a pharmacist, not a visionary inventor, so it stands to reason that I, as the progeny of greatness, might require firmer parenting.

To sum up—he's a genius, I am not, I am a disappointment, he is not. He didn't need me to tell him he was a genius, and I didn't. I didn't need him to tell me I was a disappointment, but he did.

It's interesting that neither of us, for even a moment, thought my mother might not have been talking about *me*. *"He's lost, my love, so you must help him be found,"* she said. We both assumed I was the lost *he* and my father the *my love*. Even though I was the one at her bedside, holding her hand in those final hours, feeling the papery skin against my fingers, trying to ignore that everything below her rib cage was gone, a grim magic trick. But the idea that he might be the lost one wasn't worth considering, let alone that I could be the one to help.

All the chrononauts had understudies—*contingency associate* is the official term—who trained alongside them, learning everything they did, ready to take their place on the historic mission in the unlikely event they were somehow incapacitated. When my father appointed me as Penelope Weschler's understudy, he presented it as a vote of confidence, letting me train next to his very best chrononaut.

This was obviously bullshit. I was made Penelope's understudy for two reasons. One, the condescending side of my father hoped if I worked closely with someone as impressive as her, some of her focus and drive might rub off on me. Two, the pragmatic side of my father recognized that, of all the chrononauts, Penelope was by far the least likely to *need* an understudy. She was the most instructive and also the safest choice.

On a petty, sad, adolescent level, I still get a tiny shiver of pleasure at how seriously, for all his towering intellect, my father misunderstood Penelope.

But not me. He had me pegged just right.

This is how someone of my wildly limited capacities was granted a key—although clearly incidental—role in the planet's most sought-after scientific experiment.

You could see it as my father dutifully honoring my mother's deathbed wish. I prefer to think that she had to die for him to pay attention to anything she said.

13

Death is slippery. Our minds can't latch onto it. Over time, you learn to accommodate the gap in your life that the loss opens up. Like a black hole, you know it's there because it's the spot from which no light escapes. And there's the sinewy exhaustion, the physical toll of grief that you just can't seem to sleep away. If I'd been thinking clearly I never would've accepted the job with my father.

My mother drove me crazy a lot of the time, but the idea that she's never coming back makes no sense to me. She birthed me. Half of me is made of her. She was shaping my consciousness before I was a self-aware entity. Whatever her faults, she was a warm place no matter how cold a day might be. But she's never coming back.

When you're young, you think of your parents with the simplest adjectives. As you get older, you add more adjectives and notice some of them contradict each other. He's tall. He's tall and strong. He's tall and strong and smart. He's tall and strong and smart but busy. He's tall and strong and smart but busy and aloof and judgmental. She's safe. She's safe and kind. She's safe and kind and caring. She's safe and kind and caring but sad. She's safe and kind and caring but sad and lonely and brittle. Maturity colonizes your adolescent mind, like an ultraviolet photograph of a vast cosmic nebula that turns out, on closer examination, to be a pointillist self-portrait.

In a world of negligible crime, police services were combined with actuarial functions—cops were federally empowered security and insurance operatives who assessed damage, allocated blame, and assigned reparatory figures. Within hours of the accident that killed my mother, the circumstances were analyzed, the appropriate funds transferred, a diagnostic patch relayed to all linked navigation systems, a letter of apology issued by the liable companies, and the assembly robot that constructed the faulty code box disabled and melted into repurposable scrap.

My father arranged the funeral, tied up some legal matters, and was back to work within the week. After all, he had his arbitrary deadline to hit—mourning makes the days seem both longer and shorter, but July 11, 2016, was fixed on the calendar, and nothing, not even his wife's death, would stop my father from making history. And if any small part of me considered, even for a moment, that he might not be thinking clearly either, it was a small, silent minority too disenfranchised to raise its voice.

14

I mentioned there are two reasons I was assigned to be Penelope's understudy—my father's condescension and pragmatism. Plus the deathbed promise, which I guess makes three reasons.

But there's a fourth reason too: Penelope and I were genetically compatible for the defusion sphere. It's a machine that infuses your body with a molecular immateriality field, allowing you to physically move through objects and vice versa. So, if you launch back in time and accidentally land in the middle of some object, large or small, it'll pass harmlessly through your body or you through it. Chrononauts remain immaterial the whole time they're in the past. They can touch nothing and nothing can touch them.

The immateriality field lasts a maximum of fourteen minutes. Beyond that, your molecules drift apart and, well, you die. From the moment you're decorporealized, you have fourteen minutes to return to the defusion sphere before you come fatally unglued.

Because the fourteen-minute window is so strict, the six chrononauts all require their own defusion sphere, so they can be simultaneously rendered immaterial prior to engaging the time-travel apparatus. But it's extremely complicated to calibrate a device that requires precision at the molecular level. It's also very expensive.

What helps with both calibration and cost is if you put only genetically compatible people into the same defusion sphere. Recalibrating to accommodate major genomic inconsistencies takes several days. When my father's invention is brought to market, they'll need a more efficient way to make time-travel tourists immaterial in the past—but that's a problem he doesn't need to solve just yet.

As it happened, Penelope Weschler and I were highly genetically compatible. It's the kind of thing that might come up on a cell-donation program if your fetal stem cells had accidentally been corrupted during cryogenesis and you developed some eukaryotic biomolecular illness. Or on a dating profile if you were looking to start a family but faced reproductive challenges. Our respective chromosomes naturally lined up like zipper teeth. It made it quick and easy for the technicians to recalibrate Penelope's defusion sphere when her contingency associate needed to use it.

They told me that, of all the understudies, I required the least recalibration to my assigned chrononaut. It was without a doubt the only criterion at which I excelled, because of course it was the one that didn't require me to *try*. I simply had to . . . exist.

15

The actual experience of being immaterial is totally bizarre. You strip off all your clothes and put on these skintight, well, skin tights. Like, tights made out of skin. Fortunately not someone *else's* skin. The suit is genetically engineered from your own harvested skin cells. Don't think about it too much—it's super-gross. Because the defusion sphere codes to your genetic sequence to ensure your molecules can be properly knit back together on reconstitution, it's either wear the skin suit or time travel naked.

So, you're wearing basically a leotard made of your own skin, but dyed blue-black to look cool. You've got skin boots and skin gloves and a skin cap that covers your head to prevent loose hairs from accidentally materializing inside your brain. You look like you're about to do a luge run.

There are around seven octillion atoms in a human body. That's a lot of goddamn atoms to disassemble, shoot back through time and space, and reassemble in perfect order. But biological entities have a major advantage over inanimate objects. They're not discrete particles. Those 7,000,000,000,000,000,000,000,000,000 atoms are spinning around in the thirty-seven trillion cells of the human body and each of those cells comes with its own architectural blueprint. Unlike stone or metal or plastic, a person is made of 37,000,000,000,000 maps of themselves.

You just have to program a quantum computer to read the map.

If you're my father, you realize that when sending a person back in time, your best bet is to have everything you send with them actually made of the *same genetic material* as that person. That means employing a cutting-edge bioengineering team to forge some dark, dark magic in their plasmic vats and grow a personalized organic computer to integrate into every skin suit. A central operations node links via wires made of neural axon fascicles to a dozen coordination points, each a microscopic bundle of repurposed brain cells firing off simple electrical impulses.

Yes, when you travel back in time it's wearing a suit of skin threaded with nerves to a dozen tiny brains. An organic computer system built for one purpose—to return you from the past to the present, safe and whole.

You step into the defusion sphere, a pearlescent white orb with a hatch that closes seamlessly, and the machine powers up with a low-gauge basso profundo hum. You get goose bumps everywhere. Your orifices dilate. Your nose and mouth feel dry and smoky, like a phosphorescent match got struck inside your throat. Your bones feel hollow, the blood frothy in your veins and arteries. Your eyeballs seem more buoyant in their sockets, as if they might float up out of your skull like helium balloons if they weren't tethered in by your optic nerves.

And then you're a ghost. People can see you, but you can pass through anything solid. You can't talk—immateriality does something wonky to your vocal cords—but you can see and hear just fine. Scent is weird. Even if you're smelling something right in front of you it seems like a faint whiff caught on a breeze from miles away.

I never really got to do anything cool while immaterial. It was only for experimental training purposes. I'd spend on average twelve minutes going through a routine series of tests and then, when I hit the two-minute red zone, hurry back into the defusion sphere to be reconstituted. You're sluggish for a couple of hours afterward, like your molecules need to get familiar with gravity again, but other-wise you feel fine.

Not that it mattered how I did on my immateriality tests. There was zero chance I'd be going back in time. Penelope was too good at her job to even need an understudy.

I was there for four reasons, but really it was one reason—pity.

16

Why am I going into such detail about the defusion sphere? Because it's how I saw Penelope Weschler naked for the first time. It's also how she saw me naked for the first time. I was way more interested in the former, but the latter turned out to be way more significant.

Penelope and I are doing a routine training module, this virtual simulation on how to walk when immaterial so you don't, like, sink into the ground or float off into the air and can actually put one foot in front of the other. It requires lining up the intangible molecules in your feet with the coherent molecules of the floor, sort of like strolling across a pond that's frozen over with a thin layer of ice and trying not to fall through.

I do what I usually do, which is to try to imitate what Penelope is doing to the best of my ability and falling dramatically short. And she does what she usually does, which is to excel at the given task beyond all previous metrics while ignoring me completely.

And then . . . something goes wrong. Alarms honk, red lights flash, Penelope and I get hustled into a locked decontamination chamber. A voice, too loud, the speaker giving a tinny buzz on the vowels, tells us the security system flagged an unidentified pollutant that exceeds medically safe radiation levels. They have to follow protocol.

We're told to remove our clothes. I'm a bit numb, because someone just told me I may have been contaminated with a lethal dose of radiation, so not really registering that I'm in a small room alone with Penelope Weschler and we're both undressing. I take off all my clothes and she takes off all her clothes and we place them in a container that's withdrawn into the wall by robotic arms.

I'm standing there, naked. She's standing there, naked. They spray this mist onto us from nozzles in the ceiling and it smells metallic but it looks, basically, like glitter. You know, the kind that kids sprinkle on glue for craft projects. I'm sure there's a sound medical reason for its appearance, but it makes my possible death by radiation poisoning seem awfully *festive*.

We're six feet apart, glitter clouds whirling around us. I do my best to avert my eyes, because I don't want her to catch me looking at her, but I also know this is almost certainly my one and only chance to see Penelope naked. So I dart a furtive glance at her.

She's staring right at me.

Physiologically, it's not exactly a surprise what happened next, but still—and I'm telling you this next part only out of full disclosure, so you'll believe this is the whole truth, because if I admit something this mortifying and weird, what else is there to possibly conceal?— standing there naked with Penelope in the swirling glitter, both of us looking at each other, I can't help it. I get an erection.

Penelope looks, you know, surprised. Since we're being doused with an emergency antiradiation treatment. And I know it's ridiculous. I might be about to die, horribly, lesions waffling my flesh, my organs liquefying, my bones ropey and gelatinous. But I don't feel like I'm dying. It's stupid, I know, but what I feel is vividly alive.

And Penelope, well, she looks at me like she just noticed me for the first time.

To clarify, it's not that my penis is so magnificent she was overwhelmed with desire. It's more that I'd never done anything notable in her presence before and this was such a demented response to the situation that it couldn't help but stand out.

There's a jarring buzz and the glitter spray stops. The voice on the speaker tells us they ran all the requisite tests and there was no radiation leak—the alarm was triggered by a malfunction in the security system that monitors contaminant levels, but all precautionary protocols were followed, we performed admirably in a high-stress situation, and we can resume training as soon as we get dressed in the clean uniforms already waiting for us outside the decontamination chamber—but I'm not really listening because I'm trying to memorize every contour of Penelope's body in the last few seconds we have together.

The air lock pops open with a depressurized hiss, and without a word, Penelope turns to exit ahead of me. And I think that would've been the end of it, I would've stuffed my febrile crush down into the fertile self-loathing I keep watered in my guts, and the rest of it never would've happened. Except as she bent over to squeeze out of the air lock, Penelope looked back at me. It wasn't to confirm that I was okay after the scare or that I was following protocol. She was checking to see if I was staring at her ass on the way out. Which I was. By the time I understood why she'd even care it was much too late.

17

As the boss's son, my introduction to the chrononaut team inspired some initial curiosity. A few of the understudies even flirted with me. But it didn't take long for them to lapse into resentment and contempt. It was like my new colleagues took the same emotional journey my father did from the day I was born, except it took them only a month instead of thirty-two years.

The actual front-line chrononauts were mostly nice to me. Not, like, *interested* in my thoughts on the issues of the day or my taste in popular culture or my most endearing personal anecdotes, but they were basically polite. People with that level of focus and drive don't spend much time thinking about anything other than the incredibly challenging tasks they're facing. Bland friendliness is easier than spending even one joule of energy formulating an opinion on someone fundamentally irrelevant to you. Same with the scientists who worked on the theoretical models and the engineers who had to actually build the outlandishly complex technology. I was, after all, the boss's son.

But the other understudies *hated* me.

To put this in perspective, even though they were not the front-line chrononauts chosen for the primary mission team, they were all highly accomplished top-tier professionals who would, in all likelihood, embark on subsequent missions.

And then there was me. They all knew I was there only because my father waived every possible qualifying requirement. Every task I messed up, every training module I failed, every cognitive analysis I couldn't quite parse, not only made my presence more of an insult, but also pulled down their cumulative scores. To stay at an acceptable average, these hardworking men and women had to work even harder.

It was terrible. I would've quit after the first month. If it wasn't for Penelope.

All of my father's employees had felt obligated to attend my mother's funeral, so when I started at the lab there was this awkward ritual where the first time I met anyone they immediately expressed sympathy for my loss. I'm sure they meant it, but I'm also sure that what they really wanted was for me to mention to my father how *thoughtful* they were if they ever came up in conversation with him, which they didn't because my father and I barely spoke. Once our strained dynamic became common knowledge, the compassion seeped away, along with the intermittent flirtation and ambient curiosity.

The first time I met Penelope Weschler, it wasn't that I was intimidated by her reputation or desperate to impress her, although I was both of those things, or even how she looked, lean and coiled and ready for anything at a time in my life when I felt qualified for nothing. The thing I noticed about her right away was what she *didn't* do: mention my mother at all.

I assumed she was too immersed in her training to care about social niceties, but then, two weeks after I'd been assigned as her understudy, I showed up for a seminar on how the original Goettreider Engine prototype operated—the internal machinery was exceptionally complex, but to activate the device required just a single lever that was pulled up to turn it on and pulled down to turn it off, although it was designed to never switch off except in an emergency—and the technician giving the talk, whom I hadn't yet met, took me aside for the ritualized expression of sympathy. I mumbled some socially mandated gratitude and sat in my assigned seat next to Penelope. In two weeks she hadn't said anything to me that wasn't a technical instruction about tolerance ratios or grid diagnostics. So I wasn't expecting her to speak, in a low voice only I could hear, her gaze never wavering from the presentation happening in front of us.

"Sympathy is a transaction," Penelope said. "If you let your grief be for sale, it'll end up worthless."

I was so shocked she'd spoken to me that I couldn't muster a reply. But I knew exactly what she meant.

Like those little medical hammers that test reflex amplitude, a lifetime of paternal distance and maternal neediness had primed me to bond instantly, like an abandoned duckling to a passing swan, to a specific frequency of phatic empathy—genuine understanding stripped of pity.

I was in love with her, even though she didn't know or care or want it. Her not knowing or caring or wanting it was intrinsic to her allure. I would've claimed, had anyone asked, that if Penelope actually liked me I'd probably be repelled. But as usual I was wrong.

18

When you've never really known what you want in life, spending a lot of time in close proximity to someone like Penelope Weschler is mesmerizing. She understood that my presence at her side for concurrent training was a requirement of her job and accepted it without question. Like the uniforms we wore at the lab, I was just part of the gig.

At least that's what I figured. When you jump off a cliff, falling can look a whole lot like flying, for a while anyway.

I spent hours scrolling through dating algorithms trying to embroider my profile so the system would match me with Penelope, but her name never came up. A few of the other understudies overlapped with my appeal spectrum because profession is considered high yield for romantic compatibility, but by the expansive standards of artificially intelligent data correlation, Penelope and I were not a match. There was no math for us.

I spent three months training next to Penelope. She kept her hair bound in a tight ponytail, but sometimes wisps escaped and they'd dance in the breeze from the air-conditioning system. It's the only thing about her that could be described as even borderline whimsical. Otherwise, she was relentless in her focus, determination, and grit.

It was clearly inappropriate and sort of creepy to ogle her when she had no choice but to train with me, so I willed myself not to look at her unless there was some reasonable professional justification for doing so. The exception was her hands. Since I was supposed to be learning from her, it was okay to watch her hands on the simulator controls. Her long, tapered fingers and peaked knuckles, wrists oddly delicate, somehow too thin for the tensile strength on display, muscles taut and wiry. I studied her dermatoglyphs like an antique palmist.

Penelope would display total mastery of whatever task she was given and when it was my turn she'd watch, patient, impassive, as I flailed around trying to imitate her moves. I felt ashamed, but the shame was wrapped around something else, like insulation—I knew the longer I failed, the longer she'd look at me.

Yes, this makes me sound like an unbelievable loser. But my mother was dead, my father was distant, my colleagues were dismissive, my friends were awkward, my exes were even more awkward, and Penelope Weschler was the best part of every day.

She never treated me with disrespect. She was polite but perfunctory. Of course, she was polite but perfunctory with *everyone,* but compared to the overt derision of the understudies it almost qualified as warmth. I shadowed her as she excelled at everything and she diplomatically ignored me. Until the day we saw each other naked in the decontamination chamber. After that, she still mostly ignored me. But there was something else, hard to pin down exactly, a *charge*—this magnetic pheromonal buzz that hung between us like a spider's web, generally invisible, but at a certain angle, flecked with morning dew, it could sparkle for just a moment.

We were never alone together, but I'd catch her glancing at me by the simulators or during one of the daily medical scans or in a workshop on 1960s cultural references. If our eyes met, she'd flush along her collarbones. I didn't believe someone like Penelope Weschler could be *attracted* to me. I figured she was just embarrassed by what happened in the decontamination chamber. But then there was the way she'd looked back at me when she was climbing out of the air lock—what did that look *mean?*

Here I was, finally invited into my father's inner sanctum, poised to play a minor but not wholly irrelevant role in a groundbreaking scientific experiment while grieving my recently deceased mother, and all I could think about was Penelope.

19

On Sunday, July 10, 2016, the evening before the experiment's official launch, there was an elegant reception at the sleek, opulent headquarters of one of the conglomerates that funded the project. Everyone put on formal outfits and mingled with the corporate executives, government officials, and scientific advisers my father had assembled to back his initiative.

Before we arrived, my father listed off all the important people who would be in attendance. The implication was clear—this is a list of people you should absolutely not speak to in case you embarrass me.

I applied a pharmaceutical patch to my abdomen, right over my liver, that let me set my preferred blood-alcohol ratio, like cruise control for booze. If I exceed my fixed limit, my liver is flushed with toxin filters. I went with light-headed and garrulous without careening into impaired motor function or loss of social inhibition. That sweet spot between confident and arrogant, loose but not sloppy.

So, I drank a few glasses of champagne and made small talk with people at least two degrees of separation away from anyone on my father's list and did my best to play the proud but humble son. Eventually I drifted off to look around the building, which wasn't that interesting because anything interesting was sealed behind locked doors.

That's how I ended up in an open-air courtyard dotted with sculptures, the life's work of some artist shoved in an obscure corner to bolster the company's cultural credibility index. The sculptures were stylized human figures looking up at the sky with polished glass eyes.

The moon was bright, and the glass eyes played a nifty visual trick with the moonlight, refracting it through the sculptures' hollow insides, giving them a pale interior glow.

That's how I noticed her. She was the only figure that wasn't lit up from within.

It was Penelope. We were alone together.

20

She stood there, staring up at the black sky in the blue moonlight. I wasn't sure if I should approach or retreat. At the reception, the other chrononauts were awash in fawning crowds. She'd chosen to have a moment by herself and I couldn't imagine a scenario in which I'd be welcome. But then, without looking away from the night sky, Penelope spoke to me.

"I still think about it all the time," she said. "Being up there. Everyone says this is so much more important. I would've been the millionth astronaut but I get to be the first chrononaut. So why do I wish I was out there instead?"

I came up next to her, shoulders almost but not quite touching, and mimicked her pose, peering up at the sky. Of course we'd had conversations before, but mostly just about technical matters and training protocols. Not like this—personal, confiding. I knew if I didn't say something right away I'd lose my nerve.

"Maybe because we already know everything about where you're going," I said. "There's no mystery to the past. It's all about how you get there. You didn't want to go to space to test a rocket ship. You wanted to see things no one's ever seen before."

I don't know where any of that came from. I just kind of said it. Penelope didn't reply, so I worried I'd said the wrong thing and too much of it. But when I looked at her, she was staring at me. Somehow I managed to keep my mouth shut and hold her gaze.

She kissed me.

As many times as I'd imagined it, I wasn't prepared for this kiss. I don't mean, like, emotionally. I mean its tactile quality. The emphatic pull of her lips on mine. It may have been the first time our bodies deliberately touched, my mouth pressed to her mouth, surrounded by glowing sculptures, standing on the hard surface of a 200,000,000-square-mile ball of rock and ore and water protected from the endless void by a 300-mile cushion of atmospheric gas.

It was both the greatest kiss of my life and also made me feel like until that moment I'd been kissing all wrong.

Penelope broke the kiss, glanced back up at the sky, and walked away. For a moment, I didn't think I'd be able to take it, the heartbreak, if I had to spend the rest of my life trying to re-create what that kiss felt like with other people.

But then she looked back at me.

"Come on," Penelope said.

21

When I was growing up, I used to threaten to run away a lot. There was only the most hackneyed, blunt reason for it—I wanted my parents to pay more attention to me, or a different kind of attention, more expansive and impressed with my meager adolescent achievements. I'm not saying this made me special. I've never thought I was special. That's why I wanted to run away.

But one time, and this is maybe the key moment of my childhood, my father actually responded to my threat. He was stuck on the thorny question of how the unpredictable path of a magnetically charged asteroid might affect a time traveler's reverse trajectory if they came into near contact, which was enervated by the fact that the asteroid might have long since ceased to exist. So he was looking for something else to focus on and, for what felt like the only time in my life, he chose me.

I told him I was going to run away.

"You should," he said.

I had no frame of reference for this reply. My father was always too busy to deal with me. But now he looked me in the eye like he'd picked this random moment to take my measure. He noticed I was there and so he wanted to know who his son really was.

What could I do? I packed a bag and ran away from home.

I was twelve years old. I was gone for nineteen days.

22

Before I went to work for my father, I had a few other jobs. It was always the same. The company would get in touch with me because whatever proprietary employment algorithm they used spat out my name and a ripple of interest would shiver through them when they realized who my father was. They'd wonder if maybe I was also a genius and could revolutionize their product or service or system. In the meetings, they'd mistake my sheepish ambivalence for cocky nonchalance. I'd get the job—I always got the job—and it would take them a couple of weeks to realize their error. I was not a genius. I was just a guy with a last name.

Most recently, I worked for this advertising agency that specializes in perceptual marketing. They ensure that whatever ads you see in your everyday life are geared to your specific taste, style, demographic, purchasing history, and countless other interwoven criteria. If you walk by a billboard, it shows you something you actually want or an upgrade to something you already have. They use real-time rolling data feeds, so you might see a different ad depending on your mood before versus after lunch, if you were running late or had time to linger, whether you had sex that night or argued with your spouse that morning. Following a negative experience with some company's wares, they'd give a competitor a shot at shifting your brand loyalty.

My big idea was that clients could pay a monthly fee to see no ads at all. Instead of individualized niche marketing, you could experience a world blissfully emptied of promotional clutter. It was a total failure.

Because it turns out people *like* ads. Especially when they're targeted to warp the visual environment around you to emphasize *your*
needs above all others, as if you're the indispensable center of the
global economy. Nobody wanted to pay for the privilege of being
irrelevant to commercial interests. Except me. I essentially got my
employer to launch an expensive new product solely for my use. An
industry of one.

Before that, I worked for a company that dealt in microtrends—
fashion fads that can emerge, spike, and dissolve within a day, even
within a few hours. Sometimes they'd be global, but usually hyperlo-
cal, thousands of people in a certain neighborhood sporting identical
shoes or jackets or haircuts on the way to work, and by lunchtime,
none of them would be caught dead wearing that style.

With portable clothing recyclers, the frequency of fashion evolu-
tion is dizzying. You can deconstitute and reconfigure your apparel
at will or whim. But if you care about that kind of thing, and billions
did, it can be stressful to keep your appearance protocols constantly
updated. Some people found it easier to wear a uniform-tone bodysuit with marking dots and have their outfit digitally projected onto
them, so they could keep their look as fluid as possible.

The company I worked for crunched tremendous amounts of
data to predict and manage accelerated fads for the major design
labels, and they hoped I could help amplify their business. The problem is I don't like to stand out, so fashion makes me testy. I set my
home clothing recycler to generate minor random adjustments to my
outfits just so people who notice that kind of thing will leave me
alone, but otherwise I wear pretty much the same thing every day.
My employers initially thought I was being deliberately inscrutable
with my appearance to keep them off-balance, but by the end of my
first week they became suspicious.

I actually managed to boost profits almost immediately, until
they clued in that all I'd done is the same thing I did at home—set
their prediction algorithms to random. Millions of people were wearing

a certain style of pants or cut of shirt or thickness of belt because the system told them to. But it was chance, not aesthetics. I had a contract, so they couldn't fire me. I got transferred to a side project involving pets.

Unfortunately, the company didn't particularly care about profit. When you live in a world of universal plenty, people genuinely aspire to make things that work well. They didn't want to trick their customers. They wanted to help them be happier.

Whereas it turns out my specialty is disappointment and ruin.

I spent my postcollegiate decade coasting, resenting the opportunities that came my way because of my father while simultaneously not pursuing any other opportunities. I'm aware that this isn't an endearing quality in an adult human—my ex-girlfriends each repeated this point with varying levels of intensity on numerous occasions. When you have a healthy relationship with even one of your parents, it's hard to understand what the hell the problem is—just, you know, *grow up*. But blaming my father feels so *good*, an itch that always wants to be scratched.

If you could peel away everything about me and Penelope except what made us tick at the most essential level, that's what we had in common—like a clock with a broken oscillator, some people can't keep time no matter how often they're wound.

23

The time I ran away from home, I made a crucial and in retrospect pretty sharp decision—I wouldn't speak to anyone who looked older than sixteen. I packed a bag with a food synthesizer, a clothing recycler, and an entertainment interface, disabled the embedded tracking protocols, and walked out the front door.

I made my way via transit capsule to one of Toronto's outer boroughs and approached the first kid I saw. I told him I'd run away from home and needed somewhere to crash that night. He immediately decided that was badass and let me sleep at his place. His parents never even knew I was there. We hung out in his room and played virtual immersion games deep into the night. The next day I moved on, caught a capsule to another borough, and did the same thing—found a kid, told him the truth, crashed at his place without his parents ever finding out, and moved on the next day.

At first, I approached only boys because I was twelve and girls were intimidating. I expected at least some of the kids I encountered would rat me out, but not one did. After two weeks, I approached a girl. She was even more into it than any of the boys. She'd been waiting her whole life for a total stranger to walk up and propose an adventure, but one that didn't require leaving the safety of her bedroom. We didn't play games that night, unless you count making out for four hours a game. It was the first time I'd ever kissed a girl. Her name was Robin Swelter.

I stayed with Robin for five nights, until her older brother caught us in her bedroom wearing nothing but underwear. He yanked me off of her while she covered her semi-formed chest and he punched me in the face. Their parents blundered in and they were too mortified that I'd been living in their home for five days without their knowing it to get properly angry. They called my parents while their home medical drone iced my black eye. My mother came to pick me up with a grim look on her face.

Over those five nights of adolescent fumbling, Robin and I learned enough about the organics of our complementary physiques to propel us into the top ranks of sexual experience at our respective schools. I walked down the halls a newborn legend. Every girl that had resolutely ignored me suddenly took note. And thanks to Robin and her bony, generous curiosity, I knew a little about what to do with that attention.

Robin and I kept in touch, but we both knew the spell between us had broken. I can't say I loved her, but I've never *appreciated* another human being more.

My mother convinced herself I ran away *because* of Robin, not that I'd met her on my travels. Youthful romance was acceptable. My father's thoughtless challenge was not.

As for my father, he was mildly concerned, mostly because my mother's panic and worry over those nineteen days had colonized his normal routine. When he found out that I could've survived indefinitely if I hadn't been seduced by Robin Swelter's pillowy embrace, he decided that he'd completed his job as a father. If sent out on my own, I wouldn't die. I could even get to third base.

24

Returning to school after I ran away, I made the most important discovery of my adolescence—it doesn't matter if you're smart or skilled if you can somehow be *first*.

My five days with Robin Swelter made me a pioneer in the high-status field of adolescent sexuality. The boys were halting and gruff, desperate to hear about my discoveries yet insistent they already knew whatever I might say. I soon learned another important lesson—nobody likes a know-it-all. Envy soured into resentment and the boys closed ranks on me. But I didn't care because I had the girls. And the girls didn't want description. They wanted *evidence*. For once, my appeal had nothing to do with my last name. Where I come from, it's actually kind of hard to be a bad student. Every kid's education plan is tailored to personalized learning methods that are routinely evaluated and updated to ensure nobody falls behind. So it was particularly wayward of me, the only child of the great Victor Barren, to neglect my studies and devote myself to a sole extracurricular activity: hooking up with anyone who wanted me.

For a while, anyway. I had no sense that the currency of my early experience would be radically devalued with oversaturation. By age fifteen, wrung dry of my secret knowledge, I collided with an impenetrable obstacle. The girls wanted it to *mean* something. They wanted to count on me. They wanted me to confide in them. Sex wasn't enough anymore. They wanted love.

I felt like a runner who discovers he is not, in fact, racing in a marathon—it's a triathlon, and not only did he forget to bring his bicycle but he never learned to swim.

Fifteen, friendless, a mediocre student with no real hobbies, I don't know how I would've turned out if I hadn't sat next to Deisha Cline on a field trip to the Goettreider Museum in San Francisco. I'd never paid her much attention because she gave off a standoffish asexual vibe that I appreciated only after I became a social outcast. Deisha was remote with the other girls and suspicious of the other boys, except her elementary school best friends Xiao Moldenado and Asher Fallon. The four of us spent the whole day in the gallery with the simulation of the malfunctioning Goettreider Engine, watching the world end again and again. We became a tight pack that lasted well into our twenties.

Most experiments fail. Most theories fail. But you'd never know it by my father. If he ever failed in the decades he worked on time travel, he never discussed it. Unique in all of scientific history, Victor Barren didn't make mistakes. In my childhood home, failure felt shameful. And so I was ashamed everywhere I went.

Until I met Deisha, Xiao, and Asher and I learned to be *amused* instead. Our peers were all so enthusiastic about even the slightest technological innovation, so we became connoisseurs of failure, obsessed with the inventions that didn't work out as intended. Holographic tattoos that accidentally turn your skin translucent. Backyard weather generators that glitch and create pinpoint tornados encircling your house with 250-mile-per-hour winds. Buildings encased in landscape emulators to give you the view you'd have if no other structures existed to block it, but that malfunction and project thousand-foot images of whatever the residents are doing in their bathrooms.

After high school, we staved off growing apart by attending the University of Toronto together and then squeezed out a few more years of postgraduate closeness with occasional weekend day-trips to the nearest biosphere preserve. But biannual became annual and annual became biennial and biennial became never as they moved away and got real careers and I stayed home and got increasingly dissolute.

Asher lived with his fiancée, Ingrid Joost, in Auckland, where they were both engineers at a company developing *antipodals,* vehicles that can bore right through the subterranean layers of the planet and come out the other side. They were deep into planning their wedding, which was apparently just slightly less complicated than drilling an 8,000-mile-long tunnel through iron and lava. Xiao married his college girlfriend, Noor Priya, and they had a baby girl named Fae who was arguably the cutest thing conceivable by the human mind. His lab in Mexico City was assessing what can legally be done with teleportation data following a recent scandal where this employee hacked the biometric scan archives for men she liked and grew DNA-accurate sex surrogates out of a plasmic model synthesizer. Deisha, inscrutably single as always, did who knows what for a secretive think tank that she implied but never admitted outright was exploring the viability of a Martian colony by running equipment tests out of a biodome in Antarctica. Which was a tiny bit ironic since Deisha was notoriously icy to our girlfriends over the years, although she melted considerably with Noor once Fae was born.

The last time the four of us even hung out as a group was at Xiao's wedding three years ago. But two weeks after my mother died, my friends all had a day suspiciously free of responsibilities and they teleported in from their far-flung homes. Since the funeral, my major activity had been sleeping with my three ex-girlfriends and subsequently eradicating whatever vestiges of affection they had for me by not returning their messages, so seeing Deisha, Xiao, and Asher sounded like a pretty great break from being a grief-stricken, self-absorbed idiot.

25

Asher piloted the hover car, Xiao up front next to him, me and Deisha in the back, flying above the Niagara Escarpment biosphere preserve—25,000 square miles of wilderness straddling the American-Canadian border, one of a global chain of environmental sanctuaries mandated to grow unmolested by human ingenuity. Nobody's lived there since the mass urban migrations of the 1970s, when accelerating technology rendered industrial manufacturing and resource harvesting unnecessary, and from overhead we spotted the occasional town now reclaimed by nature, buildings threaded dense with foliage. I hadn't been in a hover car since one killed my mother two weeks earlier, but either nobody realized that or it was a really intense form of exposure therapy.

After an hour in the air we decided to check out one of the abandoned towns—Ubly, Michigan, although nobody had called it that since the last people left in 1978, judging by the newspaper still preserved in a rusted box on the town's Main Street. It was a chilly April day, but thermal strands in our clothes warmed us as we poked around.

In its own mossy, squalid, eroded way the derelict town was a kind of monument to the past we'd left behind, back when humanity felt like it was locked in a perpetual race against the muscular entropy of the planet itself, always just one step ahead of being consumed by nature. Most of the buildings had collapsed, enveloped in branches and vines, meticulously disassembled by the elements. As the wood rotted and the brick crumbled, all they needed to become trees and soil again was to be left alone by people.

As sardonic kids, we would've howled at the obsolete technology and primitive materials—homes made from wood and brick instead of synthetic polymers and recombinant alloys. But the whole mood of the trip was strained, no inside jokes or nostalgic anecdotes or even much everyday catching up between longtime friends. To defuse the percolating tension, I brought up a recent scientific fiasco, the sort of thing we would've laughed about endlessly as teenagers.

"Did you hear about the zero-gravity weight-loss clinic?" I said. "Okay, so, they put a medical facility on an orbital station to run experimental procedures on people who can't seem to burn fat in regular gravity. But something goes horribly wrong and the clients sprout fat-filled growths as big as cantaloupes under their armpits and behind their knees that have to be drained and cosmetically reconstructed."

"I think I saw that, yeah," said Xiao.

"I must have missed it," said Asher. "But it sounds, you know, hilarious."

"No, it doesn't," Deisha said. "It sounds upsetting for the people it happened to."

"Come on," I said, "you used to find this stuff funny."

"When I was a kid," she said. "Before I actually tried to do anything and found out how hard it is. If the project I'm working on fails, will you laugh at me too?"

"Let's go back to the hover car," said Xiao. "We don't need to talk about this."

"Sure, let's never talk about it," said Deisha. "Let's just keep getting together without him and discussing how worried we are about what he's doing with his life."

"Deisha, his mother just died," said Asher.

"That's right. So let's talk about that. Instead of acting like we're still those kids who sat around making fun of all the losers who actually care about things. Because guess what? They were right and we were wrong. Caring about things feels good. And you know what feels even better? Contributing in some small way to the world. That's all I'm saying, Tom. Do something. Be something. Make something."

"How?" I said. "I'm not *anything*. And it's only going to get worse. My father tests his prototype in July. And when it works, because of course it'll work, he'll be even more of a genius and I'll be even more of a . . . nothing."

Nobody knew what to say to that. The problem with knowing people too well is that their words stop meaning anything and their silences start meaning everything.

26

The four of us shuffled back to the hover car, past the decrepit buildings engulfed in flora, Xiao and Asher pulling ahead to talk discreetly about the wedding—Xiao was set to be the best man. I could tell Deisha was anxious to say more, but I didn't feel like hearing it because I was busy thinking about how the three of them had been hanging out without me so they could discuss what a colossal screw-up I'd become.

What remained of the sidewalk was steadily disintegrating, every crack stuffed with knee-high weeds, so I kept my eyes on the ground to avoid tripping. That's the only reason I saw the glint of metal half-buried underfoot. It was an antique pocket watch. The gold-plated case was scuffed and mottled but because the cover was clasped shut the glass face inside wasn't too badly scratched. The main clock had arrow-pointed hands for hours and minutes and a smaller, inset clock below it with a thin, delicate hand for counting seconds. On the porcelain dial it read—HAMILTON WATCH CO., 1909.

When you invent the train, you also invent the derailment. In the early twentieth century, railroad accidents were commonplace because trains running on the same tracks weren't accurately synchronized. Keeping time was actually a matter of life or death. A watch like this was made to protect people. Every piece of technology in my world shared a global chronometer, coordinated to the microsecond, a planet of people all living in unison. But this pocket watch was from an era of temporal isolation, a planet of people each inside their own definition of time.

That's how I felt too. Deisha, Xiao, and Asher lived in literally different time zones but they found a way to keep time between them, while I was falling away.

"Tom," Deisha said, "you have to see this."

Upset, I was ready to say something shitty to her in reply, but she was standing outside a two-floor redbrick building, the wood trim streaked with flakes of cream-colored paint, peering into a window. The glass was cracked and filthy and when I looked through I saw it was once a library. Hundreds of decomposed books littered the floor, and out of the rotting mulch of paper grew a dozen spindly pine trees, reaching for the sunlight that beamed down from the half-collapsed roof. Deisha goggled her eyes at me in a playful way I hadn't seen in probably a decade. She'd hardened over the years and I had no idea if it was a natural progression or provoked by human error. We weren't as close as we used to be. The frantic intimacy of teenage friendship was long gone.

"I shouldn't have said all that stuff," Deisha said. "But I don't know when I'll get another chance. We never see each other anymore."

"You live in a secret base in Antarctica," I said.

"We have a teleporter," she said. "We could talk. *Really* talk."

My friends and I used to debate our adolescent relationship dramas, but other than occasional dirty jokes, we didn't talk about sex. And we *never* discussed Deisha that way. There was a mutual understanding, unspoken but of quarriable density, that we wouldn't cross that line with her. But standing next to her, our shoulders touching, looking through a grimy window at trees rising from a pile of moldering pages, I started to think about just how uncrossable that line really was. What is a line, after all, if not for crossing?

Back at the hover car, Xiao and Asher were synthesizing sandwiches and beer. We flew back to the city in silence, Asher switching off the autopilot to steward us home himself, Deisha staring down at the treetops below us, Xiao napping on my shoulder in the back, me trying to focus on my grief to keep from imagining what it might feel like to kiss my closest female friend. Is there a word for a thing you know you absolutely shouldn't do, that would be wrong in every way that matters to you, but that you're pretty sure you're going to do anyway? Or is that just—human?

I suddenly realized the antique watch was in my pocket. I hadn't intended to take it with me. By international law, you weren't allowed to remove anything from a biosphere preserve. I'd accidentally committed my first crime. There were more to come.

After we said good-bye to Asher and Xiao, I told Deisha we could *really talk* now, if she had time. I'd already had my funereal nights with Hester, Megan, and Tabitha, so I can't pretend I had no idea where it could go. Back at my place, I told her about my mom's last words, I cried, she held me, I kissed her, we slept together. Could I have found another way to alienate someone that cared about me? Probably. But I like to stick with the classics.

The next day I took the job at my father's lab. Three days later I met Penelope Weschler. I only ever saw Deisha, Xiao, and Asher one last time and then never again—a bar, dumb jokes, and sad smiles, Deisha keeping her distance, tensing when we hugged good-bye, old friends drifting apart because that's what old friends do.

27

Life is defined mostly by how you handle failure. I've never succeeded at anything, so for me failure is pretty much synonymous with life itself. But for other people, people who more or less succeed at everything they attempt, people like my father and Penelope, their reactions to failure can be unpredictable.

For example, after washing out as an astronaut, Penelope had a lot of unprotected sex with strangers. She'd meet them wherever, go back to their homes, and if the question of contraception came up—and hilariously few of them even broached the subject, assuming if she didn't mention it she must be on an appropriate gametic suppressant—she'd never lie. She'd just say she didn't use protection, and if they wanted her, they'd roll the dice and see what happened. Most of them went for it without hesitation, too caught up in being desired by this hungry, beautiful woman to fret over the implications, and the few who did hesitate were easily seduced by her hunger and beauty.

Why have unprotected sex when it was so easy to avoid conception? Because, you know, fate or something. Penelope figured that fate had wired her brain to make her the perfect astronaut while also giving her an undetectable neurological flaw that ensured she'd never be able to soar through the cosmos. Fate had fucked with her. And so she would fuck with fate. She'd wager her body, and every morning she didn't wake up pregnant was another day she'd kept a step ahead of destiny.

She told herself if it happened, she'd keep the baby. Whoever the father was, she'd try as hard as she could to make it work with him as parents. She'd focus her prodigious ambitions on motherhood. She might never travel between planets, but she'd be the best mom who ever lived.

Except Penelope never actually got pregnant. No matter how many men she went home with, she couldn't screw away her destiny.

Of course, I didn't know any of this when we slept together. I thought I was special. That maybe because she was about to embark on a pioneering experimental mission through space and time from which she might not return, she wanted to get laid one last time. And, for some inexplicable reason, she liked the look of me.

When she didn't mention anything about protection, well, I was one of those guys who just assumed she was taking care of it. Nobody ever expected me to take care of *anything*. Let alone something as obvious as ensuring my sperm didn't fertilize her egg.

If any of this sounds like I'm moralizing, then I'm not expressing myself clearly enough. It doesn't bother me at all that Penelope slept with a bunch of strangers. I was one of them. What bothers me is that I was too dumb to realize it didn't matter to her. At least not the way I wanted it to.

28

Penelope and I spent the night together and it's possible I'm an adequate enough writer to convey something of its giddy eroticism. But I don't want to. I'd seen her naked before, but sight really is the least alluring sense. The way she *felt,* her skin on my skin, the weight of her on top of me, my body inside her body, taste and scent, the sounds we made, the density of all that sensory experience makes the way she looked kind of beside the point. Although I remember everything about the way she looked because she told me to leave the lights on.

I've already said too much. I want it to be private, *that* if nothing else. I know it doesn't matter, it didn't matter, but it did matter, it still does matter, to me.

Let me try this again—we slept together.

Afterward, lying in my bed, because she came to my place so she could leave whenever she wanted, we talked.

That's what I want to say about it, that it wasn't just thirty-eight minutes of aerobic thrusting and a strained good-bye. She stayed for almost three hours. We lay curled up in each other and talked about our lives. Mostly she talked about her life and I listened, tried to ask the right questions and memorize her answers in case this wasn't just a one-off, in case it became something more.

I *know* it's adorable and sad that I thought it could be the start of a relationship.

She told me about her childhood, her astronaut training, her failure, her depression, her sexually irrational phase. All the things I've told you about her are what she told me about herself that night. At the time, I was spellbound. If she was sharing these intimate personal revelations, I had to mean something to her.

Now it seems more likely that telling me all of that was a direct example of Penelope's brutal self-sabotaging streak. I mean, I was her boss's son. Her boss's son, who everyone knew was a screw-up. Sleeping with me, confiding her problems, staying up half the night when she was due at the lab first thing in the morning to be launched on a trillion-dollar experimental time-travel mission—I was too head over heels to appreciate what was really going on.

And the truth is, I still don't care. Even after everything that happened . . . I loved her. I don't think that justifies my subsequent actions. But it explains them.

At one point, so late at night it was early morning, Penelope told me why she decided to trade space for time and become a chrononaut.

"I spent my whole life trying to be the best astronaut there ever was," she said, "and all I'll be remembered for is a cautionary case study in safe abort procedures. I was depressed about that for a long time. Until one day it hit me. It doesn't matter if you're the best, as long as you're the first."

Of course I understood. It was the lesson I'd learned at age twelve— your mistakes, your wounds, your compromises, your failure and pain and rot, it all blows away like dead leaves if you get to be first.

29

At some point I fell asleep wrapped up in Penelope and at some point she unwrapped herself and slipped away. For once, I wasn't late for work. The place was aflutter with activity. A crowd of scientific, corporate, and government overseers checked their communications devices at fifteen-second intervals. Today was the culmination of my father's life—humanity's first mission back in time.

Everything was ready to go. All that was left were the routine medical checks to ensure the primary chrononaut team was fit for duty. But since they'd been testing them every morning for the past month, what could *possibly* have changed since yesterday?

I walked into the medical center, trying to appear nonchalant as my eyes darted around searching for Penelope and wondering what the look on her face would be when she saw me. It felt like the rest of my life would pivot on that initial expression, before any emotional barriers locked down her nonverbal reactions. I wanted to see her before she saw me, so I'd catch whatever flashed across her face—excitement, regret, embarrassment, hope, love.

I'm such an idiot.

I guess that's the problem when you're used to waking up into your own dreams. It makes it easy to mistake romantic delusion for reality.

I did see Penelope first. She was surrounded by a jittery cluster of medical technicians. The room was weirdly hushed, like after snow falls or when someone's launched into the sucking vacuum of outer space. No one spoke. They just waited for Penelope to say something while staring anywhere but at her. The only one looking right at her was me. And when she saw me, it was nothing I expected.

She looked grim. Nobody had looked at me that way, that grim, since I was twelve years old, my mother at the front door of Robin Swelter's home nineteen days after I'd run away.

And then Penelope Weschler did something inconceivable. She burst into tears.

30

She was pregnant.

Not by much. Fertilization had barely occurred. My most ambitious spermatozoon had bonded with her secondary oocyte somewhere in the outer third of her uterine tube. At this point, six hours in, the zygote hadn't even cleaved once. It was still a single-celled organism. Mitosis was around eighteen hours away. Twenty-three of my chromosomes and twenty-three of her chromosomes had coiled together into a cleavage spindle, migrating to opposite ends of the microscopic globule pulsing inside her. Human life doesn't get any more provisional.

There are about 37,000,000,000,000 cells in the human body. Not counting microorganisms in your digestive tract. Thirty-seven trillion cells comprised of your specific DNA. At that moment, six hours after I ejaculated inside her vaginal canal like a fucking moron, unnamed Weschler-Barren zygote was only one cell—36,999,999,999,999 to go before it was anything you might legally name.

I mean, you lose 30,000 to 40,000 skin cells every hour, almost 1,000,000 per day, eight pounds of yourself a year, a flurry of dead cells peeling off and floating away.

What's one cell in all that?

Enough to end Penelope's career as a chrononaut.

It didn't matter that the zygote—our zygote—was a unicellular organism. It modified her genetic composition in an untenable way. The purpose of the daily medical scans was to model out a hyper-accurate predictive map for all physiological cycles in the chrononaut team. Even one extra cell deformed that predictive map and corrupted Penelope's unique DNA matrix.

Penelope insisted she would immediately terminate. There was hardly anything *to* even terminate—one lousy cell. A ten-second procedure administered by a pharmaceutical drone could wipe her clean of any trace of me.

Irrelevant. Protocol is protocol. This is time travel. The human body is so complex, so thorny, the instruments so finely tuned, the energies at play so powerful—it's all too complicated, too dangerous, too important. Even if Penelope terminated right away, her body had already undergone minute but detectable biological changes. Her system would have to be cleansed of the toxins used to end the pregnancy. They'd have to run diagnostics and correlate the new medical scans with the old ones to ensure this trillion-dollar mission couldn't be thrown off track by something unexpected.

You know, *unexpected* like the lead chrononaut having unprotected sex with the idiot son of the genius who came up with the whole idea and convinced multiple corporate, governmental, and scientific interests to invest vast sums in his grand plan.

Even if they *could* delay for the two months it would take to confirm Penelope was mission ready—it wasn't going to happen. This was both a publicly and privately financed initiative. Full transparency was mandated. My father couldn't hide this from his investors. Nobody would approve Penelope after a lapse in judgment like this.

No, for Penelope, it was over. She would never go back in time.

The whole point of having a backup team is to ensure mission continuity. If anything happened that required a primary team member to be removed from duty, a contingency associate was trained, vetted, scanned, and ready to step in.

Penelope was no longer on the primary team. And I was her contingency associate. Which meant, according to protocol, I would take her place on the mission.

31

I don't remember Penelope attacking me. I just remember the look
on her face. I'd fantasized she might fall in love with me, but the
only thing in her eyes was hate, ice-cold, white-hot. She screamed
that I'd done this on purpose. That I wanted her place on the mission. That this was some sick plan and they couldn't let me get away
with it.

Is it weird that I was kind of flattered? That she thought I was
cunning enough to concoct such a brilliantly sordid scheme. Did
that mean she was, like, *impressed* with me and eventually some sort
of emotional alchemy could spin hatred into love? We made a whole
new life together and even if it was an accident there had to be something meaningful and connective in that literal bond . . . right?

The fact that I was having these inane thoughts while Penelope
tried to beat me to death with her bare hands and the medical technicians flailed about trying to restrain her was *ample* evidence that
I was not cunning enough to concoct, let alone execute, a plan like
seducing and impregnating her so I could supplant her on the mission.

Didn't she understand that I could care less about the mission? I
hated time travel. It was my father's obsession, not mine. I'd only
stuck around as an understudy to be near her. I guess neither of us
really knew the other.

Biology doesn't require soul mates to do its business.

Security rushed in, pulled Penelope off of me, and carried her out

of the room. The medical technicians swarmed over my minor abrasions with their skin-regeneration lamps, and as I sat there, my eyes
caught a screen on the wall. The image showed a fuzzy-edged circle
with a slight dimple on top.

It was the cell inside Penelope. Our cell.

32

Penelope and I sat in my father's office as she explained to him, using indelicate clinical terms, what had happened last night, the steps she would take to resolve it, and why she was absolutely still the most qualified person to lead the mission team.

Hearing the person you slept with the night before describe the whole experience to your father while you sit there like a scolded child was horrifically uncomfortable, but *much worse* was morbidly witnessing Penelope try to turn the humiliating situation around. The veneer of calm rationality in which she'd somehow veiled herself since getting hauled out of the medical center kicking and yelling by the security team ten minutes earlier was so painfully brittle it was hard to be in the same room as her.

It was a remarkable turn of events, considering that eleven minutes ago all I wanted in the world was to be in the same room as her, any room, anywhere.

My father listened, his back to us, staring out the wall of windows that overlooked the main platform where the Chrono-Spatial Transport Apparatus—the *time machine*—sat. The big clock was almost out of numbers, forty-seven minutes until the moment my father had announced with such fanfare one year ago. A crowd of technicians stood around awkwardly waiting for instructions when they should've been running final preparations for mission launch.

I remember thinking how bullshit the whole thing was. I knew for a fact my father designed the apparatus so it could be operated by just one person. The technicians were all for show. So the investors felt they got their money's worth. Sure, each person on the platform had a specific task, but all functions were automated. When the calculations are this precise, human intervention is a hazard. The plan was always for my father to run the control interface himself. He was the only one he trusted to do it right.

These are the things you think about when your future is coming apart right in front of you.

My father interrupted Penelope's scattershot monologue. He said he understood her point of view but it didn't matter. Chrononauts required lucid judgment under intense pressure, where even a seemingly inconsequential lapse could have cataclysmic results. The simple fact that she could make such a disastrous personal error on this of all days terminated her involvement. She couldn't be trusted, he said. She was not trust*worthy*.

Rattled, Penelope said it was very convenient I'd be taking her place—his own son. At which point my father looked just, like, *completely* disgusted. He said there was no way he'd send me on the mission. The experiment was now on indefinite hold.

Today was the day my father had been working toward for three decades.

I didn't even say anything. But I guess the expression on my face was enough to set him off. After thirty-two years of cool disinterest, I felt the heat of his anger. As a kid, all I wanted was for him to care enough to get mad, but now his genuine rage just washed over me. His eyes had a watery quality I'd never noticed before. His skin was paunchier under the chin. His voice went up an octave when he yelled and it kind of undercut the thunder of his fury.

The gist of what he said is he wished I was never born.

That everything would've been better if I didn't exist. Listless, aimless, useless, my life had no value. Worse, I'd ruined the lives of my betters. Namely, *him* and to a much lesser extent Penelope. That my mother was lucky she died before the true immensity of my failure was revealed.

All of a sudden it sunk in—my father thought that what I did with Penelope was all about *him*. An act of patricidal aggression. Penelope Weschler was his anointed one, our mission leader, the chrononaut to whom all others were compared and found wanting, and the night before the experiment that's supposed to cement his scientific legacy not only do I have sex with her but I get her pregnant. Like I was *claiming* her.

To be honest, I'd never considered that there might be a thorny root of vengeance burrowed deep inside my longing and desire. No, that was too messed up even for me. So I was totally goddamn outraged. Like, *of course* my arrogant, egocentric, cheerless father would try to take this from me and make it his. Maybe we find the most offense in the truths we can't admit.

I decided it was time to ask the fundamental question of my life.

"Why did you even have me?"

"Because I had work to do," my father said, "and your mother was lonely."

Today was supposed to be a day unique in human history. And it was. It was the day my father was finally honest with me.

Listening to him rant, while the woman I loved sat there calculating how to turn this to her advantage, I felt like I *was* time traveling, back to every moment in my life when my father could've gotten angry at me, could've gotten *anything* at me. It was a glimpse at what it might have been like if I'd grown up with this father, the honest one, instead of the liar, the genius, the ghost.

The time I ran away from home for nineteen days, *this* is what I wanted. Instead, my mother made me a grilled cheese sandwich and refused to discuss any of it. My father wandered into the kitchen and, without even acknowledging I was back, picked up the sandwich, assuming it was for him, and trotted back to his study to eat it behind the heavy closed door. My mother cried and I held her and apologized over and over.

Eventually my father's venom tapered off and Penelope tried to steer the conversation back to how crucial she could still be to the mission.

"You slept with my son," my father said. "You'll never be part of this or any other mission. Everyone will know what you did. It's over for you."

"This mission means everything to me," Penelope said. "Please, Dr. Barren . . ."

"By all means, call me Victor," he said. "Since you don't work for me anymore."

I don't know if he was trying to hurt her or it was just that the outer halo of his anger for me was corrosive to all who ventured near, but something inside her switched off. She went numb, her face pale and loose, eyes glassy, opaque. She understood.

My father told her to submit a final report while he informed his investors that, due to an unfortunate personnel issue, the experiment was postponed until further notice.

He was really doing it. He was canceling the first mission back in time. The best day of my life followed by the worst day of my life. Everyone would know. Everyone would know about this forever.

Penelope left without another word. I stood to go too, but he said he wasn't done with me yet. He wasn't even mad anymore, like his last jab at Penelope expelled the poison and he could go back to being detached and superior. My father droned on, cataloguing the many cascading disappointments I'd subjected him to over the years—my unimpressive academic record, lack of personal interests, listless career track, inability to foster a single socially, culturally, or even politically meaningful relationship—and, honestly, I was surprised he remembered any of that stuff since he rarely even acknowledged I was in the same room with him.

And that's when I realized something that made me just about explode.

Penelope wasn't going to file a report. She had nothing left to say. She was going somewhere else and she was going there right now.

33

For all my father's genius, he had no clue why I lunged for the door. He hadn't figured out what Penelope was about to do.

I raced down the hall, twisting my ankle as I took a corner too fast, bounced off a wall hard enough to leave a bruise, and skittered down the stairs, my foot flaring hot with pain. I knew I was right because I heard that familiar basso profundo hum as soon as the door seal cracked open to the high-ceilinged room that housed the defusion spheres.

One of the spheres was active.

I was rooted to the floor, my mind as blank as it's ever been. Maybe this was what Penelope felt like when she went to space. I heard people skid into the room behind me, technicians yelling at each other about how the security protocols were overridden. The alarms blared just like the day Penelope and I first saw each other naked. But that was the beginning of something and this was the end.

Penelope came out of the defusion sphere. Except the entry hatch was still closed. She walked right through it. Which is supposed to be impossible because the defusion sphere is constructed from a high-density compound that suppresses immateriality. Or at least it does within safe dosage parameters. Nobody's ever seen what happens at unsafe dosage.

Which is why everybody went silent when she stepped out. Stepped *through*.

Penelope didn't seem any different. She had that weird shimmer you get when you're immaterial, like the intangible molecules on your outermost layer of skin can't properly interact with the coherent molecules of the air around you. But other than that, she looked like she always did.

Except that nobody could touch her or grab her or pull her back into the defusion sphere. It didn't matter how much anybody screamed or cried or begged her not to do this. It didn't matter how much, in that moment, somebody might realize that everything he never knew he wanted was coming apart at the seams. It didn't matter that at least one of the cells in the ghost that used to be her body was half someone else.

It didn't matter because what I wanted was immaterial.

We could've done so many things. We could've brought a life into this world of wonders and that life could've changed us both, made us better, fixed the broken clocks inside our brains that wouldn't let us be happy when happiness was within reach. It wasn't just a *who* inside her. It was a *where,* a place both of us could've finally been free of the people we never meant to become because that's the magic trick of creating life—it takes every bad decision you ever made and makes them necessary footsteps on the treacherous path that brought you home. For just a moment I had a home. It was the size of one cell but that was enough to fit in all I ever wanted.

I slumped to the floor and just stared at her. Penelope stared back.

She touched her stomach. I like to think that's the moment she changed her mind and decided to have our baby and become a family.

But of course it was too late. Even if she wanted to run back into the defusion sphere and reverse the process, she couldn't move anymore. She'd come unglued. Her neurons no longer able to fire to her muscles, her muscles no longer able to wrench her bones, her bones no longer bones at all, her heart, its heart, our baby's heart, will never beat in what was no longer her womb.

She floated apart in front of me. They. They floated apart in front of me. Her hand on her stomach. Her eyes frozen in terror, regret, grief. Mine too.

I wanted to memorize every contour of her while she still held her form, but it was impossible to look away from her eyes. Her molecules drifted away, carried off in all directions, through the walls, the ceiling, the floor, until there was nothing left.

34

It's not like everything in my world was perfect. People still got screwed up by anxiety and stress and off-kilter neural chemistry. Pharmaceutical use was rampant. So was status panic. Power still corrupted, infidelity still hurt, marriages still collapsed. Love went unrequited. Childhood could be a playground or a dungeon. Some people are just constitutionally bad in bed and no amount of interactive pornography can fix that.

But in the world built on the limitless energy of the Goettreider Engine, oil was irrelevant, basic resources were plentiful, and everyone had access to all manner of technological enhancements, major and minor. Not everyone chose to live in our global techno-utopia, and it wasn't like countries never had tense disagreements and diplomatic posturing, but weaponry was so sophisticated and life so comfortable that there hadn't been a real geopolitical conflict in three decades. What was there to fight about?

I'm sorry if that sounds wide-eyed or heavy-handed, but it is what it is.

Scientific discovery was the dominant social motivator, since even the most arcane theories could be enacted by vast resources. Religion had little place in the public sphere. Hundreds of millions of people were still religious, but as more of a cultural affectation. Like folk dancing and pierogies.

Morality did not collapse into nihilism. People were kind, people were rude, people were generous, people were greedy, people were courageous and cowardly, insightful and dull-witted, self-sacrificing and self-destructive, willful and easygoing, happy and sad. You could still get into a fistfight if you said the wrong thing to the wrong person at the wrong bar. Damaged people sometimes made bad decisions. Smart people sometimes did stupid things. But everyone who wanted it had a place in the world.

What is religion? What is philosophy? What is art? It's a question—*why?*

When you live in a miserable world of systemic inequity and toxic want, the answer is elusive and dissatisfying. And there's always a blameworthy *because*. Because of human nature. Because of money. Because of the government. Because of magical puppet masters manipulating us from their celestial lair. The because can never really answer the *why*.

The existential difference between my world and this world is that where I come from the *because* is self-evident—just look around. No one needed to ask *why*. The answer was obvious. We were happy. Our purpose was to keep it going and, if we had some way to contribute, make it incrementally better for those who would follow us, just as those who preceded us had.

Yes, I understand that's a pretty good working definition of ideology—a belief system so immersive that it renders questions unquestionable.

It wasn't perfect. Mistakes got made. Accidents happened. Ambitions were thwarted. People got hurt. Mothers died. Sons couldn't figure out why their fathers didn't love them. Women got pregnant and didn't want the babies. Suicides were committed.

But it was a good world, a sane world, billions of people with worthwhile lives, some selfish, some selfless, most a bit of both. None of them deserved what I did to them.

35

I woke up in a hospital, my thoughts sludgy and scattered. At first I thought I'd gone deaf, but it was just the sound dampeners in the sterile recovery cube. My eyes took a long time to focus, like the light waves undulating up my optic nerves were getting frayed in transit. I must have freaked the hell out for them to dope me up so heavily. Maybe everything that happened afterward was because the doctors got the dosage wrong. Maybe the neural scanners misgauged my endocrine levels. Maybe none of my subsequent choices were choices at all.

Then again, are any of our choices actual choices? The brain is a soupy lightning storm swirling and crackling in three pounds of wet meat. Do conscious decisions even exist, or is everything an instinctual response gussied up with malformed logic?

These are the kinds of questions I assuredly was *not* asking as the chemical haze dissipated and the leaden truth returned. Penelope gone. Our cell gone. My father's genius in ruins. His lab abandoned. The mission indefinitely postponed. The entire team, chrononauts, technicians, advisers, my father, all sequestered in communication-proof suites as the lawyers massed for the required inquiry, auguring a swarm of legal sanctions, blackened reputations, government crackdowns, corporate audits, the entire field of time travel set back a generation.

It's amazing how much damage one penis can do.

36

Where I come from, people have a different relationship with the authorities. Food synthesizers, clothing recyclers, and vast interlocked housing towers meant no one lacked for food or cover or shelter. Property crime wasn't really a thing because everything was encoded and tracked, so even if you stole something you couldn't use it or take it anywhere. Mental illness and substance abuse existed, but they were managed as health care issues. Drugs were self-synthesizable in a local treatment facility, so you could develop a foaming-amp or binary-sweet or morphocaine addiction and go sleep under a bridge if you really wanted to, but no one ever did it.

It just wasn't a rebellious world. Maybe that sounds lame and not, like, punk rock enough, except punk rock never happened in my world. Punk rock wasn't required.

That isn't to say entropy never warped the system into disarray, just that when it did most people patiently waited for the authorities to get their shit back under control so we could all return to security and comfort and plenty. All of our material needs were managed by attentive corporations with excellent customer service, so elected governments were mostly there for legal oversight, public safety, international trade agreements, and disaster preparedness. People trusted the system.

Which is why it was easy to just walk out of the hospital even though I was technically supposed to remand myself into police custody on release. No one stopped me because it wasn't the kind of society where people deliberately violate protocol.

Lying in the soundproof recovery cube was supposed to feel velvety and tranquil. Except, alone with my own thoughts, it was more like being buried alive inside a coffin. My brain was rejecting any orderly assessment of my situation, like the organ itself had seized shut to prevent contamination. Can your brain scab over a memory like your flesh does a wound? My brain was sure as hell going to try.

I opened the cube and looked around the narrow, windowless room where it was stationed. There was no guard. Nobody would think that I'd need to be guarded. I reconstituted my clothing and strolled down the hallway. The medical technicians were all busy with patients, and those who did see me assumed if I was leaving the hospital I was allowed to do so. My nonchalance wasn't cool under pressure. It was acute shock. My blood was lava. My heart poured flame. But whatever pain ignited my nerves couldn't quite find its way to my numbed mind.

In front of the hospital was a wide plaza with hover-car landing slots, transit-capsule docks, and teleportation platforms. Hundreds of people moved this way and that, going to work, visiting patients, getting tests, dropping off spouses, picking up family, gossiping with colleagues, chatting with friends, flirting with strangers, a fractal knot of daily life. In the afternoon sunshine, nobody knew my annihilation.

I watched the mesh of hover cars swoop by overhead. Because they're seen just as often from below as from above, the undersides of hover cars are designed to be as pleasing as their hulls, sleek ribs of iridescent piping and the round shells of the antigravity engines shimmering with languid force. I realized I couldn't remember what happened to the driver of the hover car that killed my mother. I couldn't picture their face or recall their name. Were they injured too? Admitted to the same hospital I just left? Did they come to the funeral, awkwardly hanging at the back of the crowd, unsure if they should express condolences in person or remain mute and abashed in the periphery? How do they feel about what they did to my family? Their presence was like a shadow cast from a trick of light, this person who changed everything about my life but whom I'd utterly forgotten.

I smiled amiably at everyone I passed as I crossed the plaza and stepped into a transit capsule.

I couldn't explain what I was doing. I had no plan. I was twelve years old again and I was going to run away. Someplace no one could ever find me.

37

I went back to my condo. I wasn't worried about the police coming after me, so I kept to the surveilled public grid and walked through the front door in broad daylight. I wasn't hiding. I was running away. There's a difference.

There was nothing for me to pack, but I wanted to have a body cleanse and reconstitute my clothing. It was in my bedroom that I saw it—a strand of Penelope's hair. It was enough to have a genetically accurate android sex doll incubated, with supple skin and warm insides and an indulgent artificial intelligence. It would do anything I wanted whenever I wanted and it would look just like her.

And if that route proved too pliant, not spontaneous enough, I could log on to a hookup site and find a willing stranger to come over wearing digital makeup—a real-time image projection virtually applied to her face. She could look like anyone I wanted, she could look like a tiger or a dolphin or a goose if that's what turned me on, but she'd be a living, unpredictable human being who found this role-play fulfilling for her own curious reasons.

Or I could scan an image of Penelope into one of the countless dating algorithms and find a woman who looked as much like her as possible and say whatever I needed to say to get her to fall for me and use black-market pheromone supplements to hormonally bond us and maybe even steadily undercut her self-confidence to the point where she'd think the cosmetic surgery was her idea and I could marry her and we could have a kid and I could live to old age with a simulacrum of the life that dissolved before me.

What I'm saying is, there was a moment there where other options presented themselves. Not wise options. Unwise options. Weird, twisted, self-destructive options. But options with consequences limited to my immediate emotional radius. I could've kept it personal.

But I didn't.

Maybe, with enough time, I would've just moved on. Dug a hole and buried it and built something new on top. But that's not the kind of time I had in mind.

38

It was eerie in the lab. Since I typically arrived late and left early, I was used to it being conspicuously busy. But now the place was empty.

My father conceived his time-travel apparatus to be elegant in design and simple in operation. Even an idiot could use it. Or a profoundly disappointing son.

If you build a machine that requires fifty people to make it work, what happens if something goes wrong during a trip to the past? Let's say the team is incapacitated and their lives, the future of the project, the future of *everything,* depends on an injured or disoriented survivor clumsily firing up the emergency boomerang protocol to return them to the present? No matter how ornately complex the machinery and absolutely precise the calibrations, the apparatus itself is easy to use because it might have to be.

No alarms went off when I was scanned for entry. Like I said, authority didn't work that way where I come from. No one would break into the lab for nefarious purposes. We didn't have corporate competitors or scientific rivals. My father was a pioneer in a field with few peers. And those he did have, he hired to work for him.

Even outside the arching hangar-like room that housed the time-travel apparatus, there was no extra security. The assumption was that no one would choose to pass through the sliding doors into the cool, antiseptic air and stand in front of this machine that cost trillions to construct and was expected to generate quadrillions in revenue unless they had a good reason. When the facility was built, the current circumstances—the project on hold, the team leader dead, my father's legacy in tatters—were not among the long-term projections.

And yet here I was.

The Chrono-Spatial Transport Apparatus isn't that big, considering what it does. A central axial construct linking six oval berths hung with shiny metallic rigging and flanked by glowing instrument panels, thrumming with possibility.

I powered it up.

A machine that's never used is like a baby that will never be born.

39

Lionel Goettreider didn't live to see the future he invented. He and the Sixteen Witnesses to the original experiment were dead within three months, killed by the unexpectedly massive amounts of tau radiation that surged from the Engine when it was first switched on. Goettreider didn't anticipate just how powerful his invention would turn out to be. Or how lethal for those in attendance.

It didn't matter what expressions were on those famous faces at the moment the future erupted from Goettreider's device—skeptical, awed, distracted, amused, jealous, angry, thoughtful, frightened, detached, concerned, excited, nonchalant, harried, weary, cheeky, or wise—they were all fatally irradiated. Hematopoietic degradation leading to aplastic anemia, irregular cell division, genetic warping, gastrointestinal lique-faction and vascular collapse, catastrophic neurological damage, coma, prayer, death.

Goettreider himself was the first to die. Moses on the border of the promised land. The others followed, one by one, martyrs for science.

If there's a religion where I come from, it's self-sacrifice at the altar of discovery. Lionel Goettreider gave his life so the world could blossom into a paradise beyond his imagining. The fact that his sac-rifice was accidental is considered poetic.

Going back to July 11, 1965, was pragmatic, because the radiation trail left by the original Engine is a tether to our past, bread crumbs made of semidegraded atoms tracing a connect-the-dots path to the ex-act coordinate in space and time at which my world was born. But that same atomic string is also a trail of blood, or poison, or poetry, because it's the same radiation that killed Goettreider and the Sixteen Witnesses.

That's what makes the original Goettreider Engine different from any other, why it's the one we can follow through time and space, the one with the fatal flaw, fixed in subsequent models thanks to the unwitting sacrifice made by those seventeen people in the holy temple of our glorious future.

Time traveling to see the creation of my world isn't just a scientific experiment or a historical curiosity. It's also a murder investigation. It means witnessing the birth of the future and the death of the person who made it possible.

I've always appreciated the fact that this towering visionary died because he underestimated himself. Had the Engine not proved to be so epochal, Goettreider would've been a catastrophic failure.

What makes an artistic depiction of the Activation interesting isn't the reactions of the Sixteen Witnesses—they've become formalized over time—it's the expression the artist chooses to put on Lionel Goettreider's face in the moment he unleashes his invention on the world. Skeptical? Awed? Distracted? Amused? Jealous? Angry? Thoughtful? Frightened? Detached? Concerned? Excited? Nonchalant? Harried? Weary? Cheeky? Wise? The artist's choice in this telling detail says everything about the piece.

The real reason my father wanted to visit this specific moment was to observe Goettreider's face right *before* he switched on his invention—to see if he recognized that expression from the mirror. Basically, to find out if Victor Barren and Lionel Goettreider are as alike as he thinks they are.

I'm curious too. Because they turned out to be more similar than my father anticipated. Geniuses who miscalculated something essential, with unforeseen consequences that ended everything they knew and changed their world.

For Goettreider, the tau radiation that killed him was the fatal flaw. For my father, it was me. I was the fatal flaw.

40

I walked through the empty lab to the chrononaut changing area, where there were private vestibules for disrobing and lockers for our personal items. I opened Penelope's locker. There wasn't much inside. Her skin suit was sealed in its sterile gel pack to ensure nothing contaminated it prior to the trip back in time that she would never take. A spare uniform was folded neatly on the shelf next to a pouch of extra hair elastics for her usual ponytail. And something else—an antique pocket watch.

I don't know how long I stood there, but eventually my body shook so hard with coarse sobs that I had to sit down. I held the pocket watch in my hands, rubbing the cool metal with my fingers.

About six weeks ago, we were doing a training simulation on the time machine's emergency boomerang protocol, establishing how fast we could engage it manually if a calculation error stranded us in outer space. Penelope successfully rescued the whole team on every try. I managed to get everyone killed, several times. In the debrief, Penelope told me that instead of thinking of it as a single mortally important procedure, she'd break it down to a series of individual tasks, one per second, and count them down in her head while she did them, each second a discrete unit of time, like an old watch ticking out the moments in a steady rhythm.

The next day, I brought in the pocket watch I'd found in that abandoned town with my friends and showed it to her, like a puppy bringing its master a ball. I explained that it didn't work but maybe I could get one of the technicians to repair it for me.

"Don't do that," Penelope said. "Either they'll be pissed off that an understudy is wasting their time or they'll be worried that if they say no you'll tell your father."

"Oh," I said. "Right. Yeah, of course."

"Give it to me," she said. "If I tell them to do it they won't even think of it as a favor."

I handed her the pocket watch and never mentioned it again. I figured if she even remembered this conversation, it would hardly be a priority for her.

The pocket watch ticked in my hand, seconds into minutes into hours, as I sat there thinking about what it meant that Penelope had gotten it fixed but had never returned it to me. I put it back in her locker and shut the door. I opened my locker, took off my clothes, unsealed the gel pack, and put on my skin suit. I knew what I had to do.

I would be what she could not—*first*.

41

There's still so much about where I come from that I haven't told you.

The air. It's not like here. It has this buoyant, effortless quality, like being on a boat in a vast lake, not the ocean with its seaweedy tang, just a clean, sweet emptiness. No one bothered burning carbon past about 1970, so there was no acrid, oily residue in the atmosphere. It's the kind of thing you notice only when you're used to something else, like a freshwater fish dropped into the sea, its gills ragged with saline burns.

Botanical engineering, I mean, you have no idea. Homes made entirely of trees that organically filter your air, generate electricity through natural breakdown cycles in the soil, and grow fresh fruit and vegetables on your kitchen walls. They weren't exactly commonplace, but you could rent one for a vacation. Some people lived in them all year.

So many social anxieties were gently eliminated because whenever you met someone new you could just run a quick scan and get correlated data on whether you'd be better suited as friends, lovers, spouses, or strangers. And it's not like you had to do what the data suggested. Lots of people ignored it with sometimes lovely and sometimes fraught results. You could even find out if the person you were considering had a history of ignoring the assessment data and if it had worked out for the better or for the worse.

I could go on indefinitely, listing stuff that may seem quasi-cool or terrifyingly technocratic depending on your personal slant—but you get the point.

Or maybe you don't get the point: the banal everyday wonder of it all. I never thought about the air I breathed. I never vacationed in one of those tree houses. I found the data profiles helpful, but my favorite gadget was this pheromone detector that emitted a soft *ping* when the woman you were interacting with gave off a puff of attraction hormones, so you knew she was at least interested enough to keep talking to you . . .

Even *this,* composing a narrative one word at a time and pretending that I don't know how it ends—it's weird for me. Unless you're a bespoke novel enthusiast like my mother was, someone who enjoys being led by the hand like a child through a hedge maze, where I come from most narrative entertainment is at least passively interactive, using the same neural tracking technology that lets your virtual environment simulator ease you out of your dreams in the morning. Every story is uniquely personalized, your desires, fears, anxieties, quirks, and kinks shuffled into the prestructured plot, like a skeleton around which your own weird little brain grows a one-of-a-kind body.

Déjà vu is crucial to the narrative palette, the uneasy sensation that you've heard the story before but can't quite place it. That strange, vibrating discomfort is one of the richest pleasures of our storytelling and it's almost entirely absent here. Here, people complain when they think they know where a story is going. As if plot is what really matters. In this world, the same words are always in the same order, set there according to the personal eccentricities of the author. I don't *like* the feeling that this story is about me. In my world, every story is always about *you.*

I'm sorry, I know, I'm like a bad date who spends the whole time talking about their ex and insists it's so you can get to know them better, rather than that they just can't let go. I don't want this part of my story to be over, but it's time.

42

The countdown clock read—00:00:00. It was all out of time.

There were six berths in the Chrono-Spatial Transport Apparatus, one for each member of the standard chrononaut team. Wearing my skin suit, I settled into the berth predesignated for Penelope or her contingency associate—me. I could lie and say I had a moment of remorse or at least pause, but I was way too deep in shock.

I was operating on instinct, but not for self-preservation. I wanted revenge, I see that now, although at the time I would've called it justice. Which is hysterical and melodramatic, I know, but I was in a hysterically melodramatic state of mind.

If I could have, I would have gone back just far enough to save Penelope's life. Half a day was all I needed. Unfortunately, the time machine doesn't work like that. It may be the single most advanced piece of technology engineered by the human mind, but it's still just a prototype. Even if I knew how to reprogram its spatiotemporal navigation code, which I *don't*, the apparatus was deliberately built with only one destination.

So, no, I couldn't save Penelope. But I could finish what she started.

I was going to do something my father couldn't take away from me. I would be the first human being to travel back in time. Even if I was sued or arrested or, I don't know, executed—I mean, is it *illegal* to time travel?—it would be a permanent achievement. No matter who else did it, I'd always be the first.

Considering these were possibly my last moments alive, I didn't linger the way I might have if I'd been thinking rationally. But I wasn't thinking rationally. I wasn't *thinking* at all. I was conducting a practiced series of tasks, initiated in sequence without hesitation, counting them down by the second, in a steady rhythm, just like she taught me. It turns out, during those hundreds of hours of training simulations, I had been paying attention to more than just Penelope.

The time-travel apparatus has a three-part access procedure—genetic scan, elaborate pass code, and a big red button. Biological, intellectual, physical.

I activated the time machine.

There are no specific visual or auditory phenomena associated with time travel. But my father was concerned that the early adopters of the technology would feel let down if there wasn't some sort of razzmatazz. It was scientifically pointless, pure showmanship. As if just going *back in time* wouldn't be cool enough for the high-end consumers my father's financiers planned to attract.

So, a team of psychologists was commissioned to figure out how to make people feel emotionally engaged with the experience, and what they came up with was a melodious hum and a softly oscillating glow of warm light.

Those psychologists were good at their jobs. When that hum and glow started, all my grief and anger and shock lifted away. I felt grounded and hopeful and free.

And I realized with absolute clarity that this was a terrible fucking idea.

But it was too late. The stupid goddamn hum and stupid goddamn glow would've been a fantastic thing to have experienced, like, right *before* I engaged the device, instead of right *after* . . .

I felt a tightening in my brain, as if it was contracting like a snail into its shell. I had the ungainly sensation of slipping on ice, freefalling to a hard landing that never came, suspended in the moment when balance loses to gravity. My blood felt heavy, thick, the veins and arteries bowing like wet towels on a clothesline. My fingernails and toenails tingled and flexed like they were growing at a shocking rate, curling into loops of chalky keratin. My eyeballs pulsed, filling up with the wrong kind of light, the viscous syrup inside them starting to boil. Strange tastes flickered across my tongue—sour tea, rotten lemon, sweet grass, Penelope's lips. The hairs on my head seemed to burrow inward, piercing my skull and knitting into the dendrites. Or maybe the dendrites were burrowing out, worming from my scalp like the delicately fibrous skin of a starfish.

It felt deeply, deeply weird.

And then I was gone.

43

SUMMARY—Chapters 1 to 42

Tom Barren lives in the world we were supposed to have. The technological utopia envisioned by the optimistic science fiction of the 1950s became possible when, in 1965, a scientist named Lionel Goettreider invented a radical new kind of energy production—clean, robust, boundless. Fueled by the Goettreider Engine, scientific advancement massively accelerated. In 2016, everyone has everything they need to live happy, comfortable lives. With all everyday functions automated or synthesized, most people work to develop the only thing that matters anymore—entertainment.

Like almost everyone else in the world, Tom works in a lab. His boss is his father, Victor Barren, a genius pioneer in a cutting-edge field—time travel. The science itself is radical and brilliant, but to secure the corporate financing and government authorization to realize his experiments, Victor has packaged it as high-end tourism.

Following the accidental death of Tom's mother, Rebecca Barren, Victor offers Tom a job out of guilt and pity. Their father-son relationship has long been strained because Victor was always so busy with his important research and Tom was always so busy being a chronic disappointment.

Tom is assigned to train alongside Penelope Weschler, the team leader of the first mission back in time, so he can take her place in the unlikely event that something insurmountable goes wrong with her.

Tom soon falls head over heels for Penelope. He assumes she has no interest in him because she generally ignores him. But Penelope is much more troubled than anyone realizes. She's just very good at hiding it.

The night before the mission, Tom and Penelope have a quiet encounter at a reception hosted by the project's financiers. They sleep together. It's kind of the best night of Tom's life.

But the next morning turns into the worst day of Tom's life. At the routine pre-mission medical screening, Penelope finds out Tom got her pregnant, which automatically takes her off the roster. Since Tom is her official replacement, she accuses him of doing it on purpose. Victor, furious and embarrassed that his life's work has been threatened by his own son's irresponsible actions, lashes out at both of them and postpones the mission. Humiliated, her hard-fought professional accomplishments in tatters, Penelope does something horrible—she kills herself.

The project is indefinitely shut down. The lab is abandoned until the legal mess can be resolved. In shock from grief about Penelope and churned up with anger at his father, Tom decides to complete the mission himself. He sneaks into the lab and activates the time machine.

44

Materializing in the past, there's this initial synesthesia, my senses scrambled, touch into taste into scent into sound into sight into touch, and then everything contracts in on itself, like gelatin setting in a mold. Although my father's invention makes time travel feel instantaneous, it comes with a visceral kick that makes a routine teleport to the moon seem like a foot massage. I just became history's first time traveler, but I'm not really feeling the grandeur of the moment because I'm trying so hard not to throw up 2016's breakfast onto 1965's floor.

I take a few seconds to get steady on my feet and orient to my surroundings, and that's when it hits me—I'm in the actual laboratory where the future was born. The whole building has of course been maintained as a permanent museum exhibit, with the original Goettreider Engine still in operation in the windowless 500-square-foot basement lab in section B7 of the San Francisco State Science and Technology Center. But visiting it in my time is not the same, obviously, as *being here.*

I can smell the industrial cleaner wafting up from the chipped tile floor. The lighting, incandescent bulbs under metal cages, warm and steady, casting every surface with a coppery glow. The machinery is state-of-the-art for the time period but looks adorably archaic, like watching heart surgery conducted with sharp sticks.

And there's the Goettreider Engine itself. It's thick and clunky compared to the sleek, refined iterations that, in the last weeks of his life, Goettreider designed to be constructed posthumously. The housing is dull steel, hand-tempered by Goettreider to fit his specifications. The absorption coils are wound up in thick rolls of springy filament. The gauges have actual arrows wobbling in their dials and the indication counters have tiny numbers punched into metal rings that revolve around an axis point. The gears look comically large and cumbersome and the venting stacks might as well be Victorian-era chimneys belching smoke. The key component, the Radiometric Pulse-Field Emitter, is the only thing that looks remotely modern—because its innovative form, with the graded angles and undulating petals and interlocked segmentation, became so influential on contemporary style, spilling from the lab into architecture, industrial design, fashion, art, cuisine, everything really.

Standing in the room looking right at it, the machine that changed the world looks hilariously handmade. It's a miracle Goettreider got any reaction from the assembled observers other than eye-rolling condescension.

Goettreider's work was considered vaguely interesting from a theoretical perspective but not exactly promising. A bureaucrat with just enough authority to approve minor grants had taken a shine to Goettreider because he'd filled out the administrative funding forms in fastidious detail and the bureaucrat was a man who appreciated neat paperwork above all other virtues.

The Goettreider Engine itself is quite compact, but the venting shafts and thick clusters of coolant tubes fill up the space, ready to gear down the device if it malfunctions and safely release any accumulated energies—so the Engine doesn't erupt in, for example, a fury of global destruction.

As I get my bearings, I realize I'm not alone in here. Someone is hunched over a notepad, scribbling equations with a pencil. I recognize the notepad before I recognize the man because I've seen it in an impenetrable display case in the Goettreider Museum—it's the notepad in which Lionel Goettreider wrote his final calculations before he switched on the Engine.

Which means the person currently writing down those famous figures with a half-chewed yellow pencil is Lionel Goettreider.

45

ionel Goettreider wasn't famous when he died, his cremated remains scattered into a high wind off the Golden Gate Strait and blown out to the Pacific. So, initially, nobody thought to record his opinions on anything beyond technical specifications for the Engine itself. Later, of course, a magnificent global industry of assertion and abstraction sprung from every utterance remembered by his few social acquaintances and professional peers, people who wanted to be known to have known him.

Born in Aarhus, Denmark, in 1923—in my world there are, like, fifteen different Danish holidays devoted to him—Lionel Goettreider grew up in a middle-class home with a Danish mother, a Polish father, and two younger brothers, a warm and pleasant childhood marred only by his father's occasional spasms of delusional paranoia. When the Germans invaded Denmark in 1940, his father's paranoia became rather less delusional—someone really was out to get him. But life continued, as it does. At age seventeen, Lionel received a scholarship to the Institute of Theoretical Physics at the University of Copenhagen, and so, while the Danish government submitted to Nazi rule and his father's mind went septic with fear, Lionel moved to Copenhagen to live with his aunt and study under the institute's founder, Nobel-winning physicist Niels Bohr, his scientific idol.

On September 29, 1943, Bohr got an early warning that the Nazis planned a mass raid of Denmark's Jews on October 1, assuming they'd all be home for the Rosh Hashanah holiday. Bohr immediately left for Sweden, where, legend has it, he convinced the Swedish king, Gustaf V, to coordinate with the Danish king, Christian X, to rescue Denmark's Jews. Among the more than 7,000 Jewish people spirited across the Oresund Strait in fishing ketches, rowboats, and kayaks to Sweden was Lionel Goettreider. His rescue was a boundless gift to the world, but a bitter personal tragedy.

Five months earlier, his father heard from friends in Poland that Jews had been rounded up and promised asylum if they cooperated, only to be interred at concentration camps. His father convinced his mother that the family had to escape Denmark before it was too late. Lionel, busy with his studies and convinced the Danish king would protect him because Bohr insisted it was true, refused to join his parents and brothers when they paid fishermen to smuggle them across the North Sea to Scotland. Lionel never heard from them again. After the war, he found out a German patrol intercepted the boat and his family was sent to the Chelmno extermination camp, not far from his father's birthplace in Lodz, Poland. And so Lionel Goettreider was saved by trusting a man in a crown.

A few days after arriving in Sweden, believing his family was safe in Scotland rather than already buried in a mass grave in the Rzuchow forest, Lionel Goettreider lay in a field outside the farmhouse where he was staying, staring up at the stars on a cold, clear night. He thought about how the war seemed like the end of the world but, in fact, no matter what people did to each other the Earth's movement through the solar system was entirely unaffected, its orbit unchanged and unchangeable, constant, forever. He felt utterly powerless, alone in a foreign country, but he took comfort in that eternal spin. Not just comfort—*power*.

And in that moment Lionel Goettreider had an idea.

After the war, he did his master's degree at Oxford and his doctorate at Stanford, remaining in San Francisco until his death in 1965. That's where the Goettreider Institute for Advanced Physics was founded in 1972 and began training the world's most brilliant and ambitious young scientists to become even more brilliant and ambitious, including Victor Barren, who completed two of his three PhDs there. If I had to pinpoint the moment my father wrote me off completely, it was the day my application to the Goettreider Institute was rejected. He was considered among their most esteemed alumni and yet an exception would not be made for his only child. I moved out of my parents' housing unit into the 184th-floor condo and attended the University of Toronto instead.

When asked about his wartime experiences, all Lionel Goettreider would say is that Niels Bohr saved his life. He returned to Denmark only once, for Bohr's funeral in 1962. And it seems he never really trusted anyone else again. His few friends were just polite colleagues. He lived by himself. He never married or had children. What he had, instead of other people, were the infinite possibilities of his own mind and a relentless drive to build a better world.

At least that's what they teach at every school on the planet.

46

In 1965, Lionel Goettreider was forty-two years old. He wasn't some wizened High Priest of Science. He was a man, not young, but not all that old either.

He had a long, angular face, sharp cheekbones, a crooked nose that looked like it had been broken in a long-ago fistfight, full, bow-shaped lips, thick curly brown hair, and wiry eyebrows that bristled above his glasses, each lens smudged with fingerprints around the edges. His eyes had three-colored irises: a ring of blue, a ring of green, a ring of brown. He had long eyelashes and a permanent ridge of glabellar creases. He stood just over six feet tall, broad shouldered but gangly, arms and legs too long for his torso.

These are some of the things you notice when you're standing right in front of the most important person in human history and he can't see you because you're cloaked with a disruption field that warps photons around your body, rendering you invisible to camera and eye.

But here's something I hadn't considered: scent.

Lionel Goettreider's nose crinkles. He inhales sharply, his eyes darting around the lab. He *smells* something out of place. I take a step back, jarred, because what he's smelling is—me.

It's inconceivable that my father could've neglected something as elemental as smell, but then I remember—I'm supposed to be immaterial. My molecules should be disembodied, intangible, and, consequently, *unsmellable*. But I neglected to go into the defusion sphere before coming back in time. That means, despite my invisibility, I can touch things. Not even deliberately. The molecules of my body can interact with the molecules around me. If I was immaterial, the volatilized airborne compounds swirling off of me would safely pass right through the olfactory receptors in Lionel Goettreider's crooked nose. But I'm not immaterial.

My whole life, everyone waited for me to do something spectacular. To prove I was my father's son. Well, I finally did it—it just turned out to be spectacularly stupid.

I have made a very, very bad mistake.

As I step away from him, I bump into a console, jostling the mug of coffee sitting on it. The oily black liquid inside sloshes over the rim. A runny finger of coffee slides down the white porcelain, trailing onto the console's green-gray metal surface.

Goettreider sees it too. The crinkle in his nose spreads to his eyebrows, those glabellar creases folding even deeper. Coffee pools around the base of the mug. He picks it up, wipes away the liquid with his hand, and dries it on his starched white lab coat. He looks around, troubled.

I don't know if the emotional trauma of Penelope's suicide kept me from facing the defusion sphere or if I'm just a total goddamn idiot—and the fact that the time-travel apparatus could even *be* activated without confirming my immateriality points to a major oversight on my father's part, the realization of which would give me much more enjoyment if I wasn't trying so hard not to freak out.

I look for a spot I can stand where there's no chance I'll touch anyone or anything. But the problem isn't just deliberate action. My body is a maelstrom of autonomous responses, heat, hormones, gases, chemicals, radiation. I try to formulate a plan but my thoughts are a toxic fizz of regret, panic, and self-loathing, as if someone shook up a bottle of carbonated soda and uncapped it inside my brain. My mind feels weirdly doubled, trebled, quadrupled, like some sort of cognitive stutter or echo or—I guess this is what *fear* feels like. I've clearly led a sheltered life because it's hard to muster the focus to put one foot in front of the other.

My mind was failing me, as it had so often in my life, but this time there was nobody to rescue me from myself. No grim-faced mother knocking on the door to steer home her sexed-up runaway. It was very much like the moment you realize you're no longer dreaming, that you're awake in your bed and it's time to get ready for work. Except in this case my job is to get the hell out of the past.

There's a nook to one side, created by two consoles that don't quite meet in the back corner. Moving as silently as possible, I wedge myself in there to catch my breath before this all spins even further out of control. I step over a leather rucksack with its brass buckles left unlatched, shoved out of the way. Inside it is a gift-wrapped box with a satiny bow on top. I recognize the rucksack as Goettreider's own bag—the association with him ensures they'll never go out of style. But the present inside is a detail I've never noticed in any of the simulations. It's good to focus on the little things instead of the big picture. Which is that I just came very close to total disaster.

47

The main problem with effectively modeling the cognitive impact of time travel on a human subject is nobody's ever done it before.

You might wonder why my father couldn't just do a trial run, you know, send the chrononauts back a minute, or an hour, or a day, take some readings, crunch some numbers, confirm it's at least moderately safe? It would still be *time travel*—isn't that dazzling enough?

Well, no, obviously not. A few of my father's more prudent advisers brought up these questions from time to time. But they were curtly dismissed as lacking the boldness necessary for such a groundbreaking endeavor and encouraged to peddle their caution at someone else's lab.

I come from a world where the impossible is commonplace. So my father's legacy-defining experiment can't just be successful. It has to be dramatic. A showstopper. The kind of confident, visionary statement no one will ever forget. It's a mission to witness the most important scientific experiment in human history, because that's the kind of direct comparison my father wants made to *him*. His goal is to ensure the names Barren and Goettreider are mentioned in the same sentence as often as possible.

And here I am, actually witnessing history, fulfilling my father's self-aggrandizing dream—but my disappointing catastrophe of a brain is spoiling even this, my one big chance to make a permanent mark, getting lost in cul-de-sacs of tangent and memory and jargon. It's hard to believe I spent months training for this, side by side with

Penelope, close enough to smell the lilac and orange blossom in her hair because we sat downwind from the overcranked air-conditioning vent. My thoughts loop into themselves, adrift and hollow, a mal-functioning navigation system, like the one on the hover car that killed my mother.

I came here to do something nobody else ever has. To be first. To make history by witnessing history. Somewhere in the fractal fog of my muddled consciousness comes a loud, clear imperative drilled deep from my chrononaut training—*focus*. Focus on concrete infor-mation. What you see. What you hear. What you smell. What you taste. What you touch. What you *feel* doesn't matter. Pain doesn't matter. Grief, anger, humiliation, love, awe, none of it matters. Focus on what's real.

What's real is you're in trouble. What's real is you've made a mis-take. What's real is this is an opportunity to rise to a challenge, even if it's a challenge caused by your own stupidity.

48

Lionel glances around, weirded out by the phantom movement. But before he can investigate any further, a woman comes in through the lab's only door, thick steel with a heavy lock that she clunks into place. I immediately recognize her—she's Cheeky.

Her name is Ursula Francoeur, a physics professor at Stanford University, the first tenured female physics professor they ever had, if I'm accurately recalling my high school history seminars. She's one half of the only married couple among the Sixteen Witnesses. Her husband is Jealous, Jerome Francoeur, the bureaucrat who approved Goettreider's funding. Why a federal science-and-technology funding administrator would be jealous of an obscure scientist, even in his moment of unexpected triumph, is one of many enduring mysteries of this endlessly fascinating moment in time.

I'm just registering it's a bit weird that Ursula Francoeur locked the door—history asserts they barely knew each other—when Lionel Goettreider looks at her with a very odd smile. Anxious. Careful. Charged. There's a lot going on in that smile.

And then I witness something I've never heard mentioned in any of the countless biographical analyses, scientific discussions, artistic flights of fancy, or virtual representations, something evidently no one has ever even *considered* before it happens right in front of me.

Lionel and Ursula kiss.

49

It's not a first-time kiss. It's a grasping, clenching, yearning kiss between two mouths that know each other well.

Holy shit. I know this doesn't mean much to you out of context but it's blowing my mind. Nobody, I mean *nobody,* knows that Lionel Goettreider and Ursula Francoeur were having, what, I guess it's an affair? Is that why she looks Cheeky? Is that why her husband looks Jealous? What would this have meant for Goettreider if his experiment had failed, if he had lived, if any of them had survived?

Even in their final weeks, when Goettreider and most of the other witnesses had died from the radiation, neither Francoeur ever mentioned anything that might suggest Ursula was romantically involved with Lionel and Jerome knew about it.

But here they are, sharing a secret moment just minutes before the experiment is scheduled to begin. And it's not a quick peck either. They're *making out.* I feel like a bit of a pervert standing here staring at them, but it's too crazy to look away.

If this is the only thing I see in the past, I've already changed Goettreider scholarship forever. The look on his face when they break the kiss, I mean, every schoolkid has seen thousands of images of Goettreider's face, but I can say without hesitation none of them ever looked *carnal.*

"They'll be here any minute," Ursula says. "I'll unlock the door."

"Are you coming over tonight?" Lionel says.

"I can't," she says. "I think he knows something's going on."

"With us?"

"No," she says. "With me. I can't help it. I can't go home and touch him after I've been with you. It's making me distant. Mean. He doesn't deserve that."

"He doesn't deserve you," Lionel says.

"You know I hate it when you talk like that. This isn't a soap opera. It's my life."

"It's my life too," he says.

"It's not the same," she says.

"You're right. I'm sorry. I know you have much more to lose. But if this experiment works . . ."

"You don't think it's going to work?"

"I don't know," he says. "My calculations, the yields I'm showing, they seem impossible. But your husband says they'll pull my funding without some concrete results. Something I can publish. Even if it fails, at least I'll have some real findings instead of a bunch of theories scribbled on paper."

"You know Jerome has Donald Hornig's ear . . ."

"Hornig was Kennedy's appointment. Everyone says Johnson doesn't listen to his science advisers because they're all against Vietnam."

"This isn't about Hanoi," says Ursula. "It's about the moon. If you can generate even a fraction of the power you're projecting, it could be a tremendous contribution to the Gemini and Apollo programs. That's the legacy Johnson wants, the one every man, woman, and child on Earth can see just by looking up at the night sky."

"Ursula, why would your *husband* help me get to the president?" says Lionel.

"You really don't understand politics at all, do you?"

"It's not how my mind works," he says.

"I love how your mind works," she says. "That and other parts of you."

They stand close together, their bodies like complementary magnets. Ursula looks at the locked door. She knows she should open it.

"A lot of people have been asking him what you're doing down here," she says. "He's bringing a few associates."

"How many is a few?"

"I don't know," she says. "A dozen or so."

"So if this thing fizzles, I'm going to look like a goddamn idiot."

"Just try not to blow up half the city," she says.

"More like half the continent," he says.

"Please tell me you're joking."

"I'm mostly joking."

"Well, if this is the end, I'm glad we had last night," Ursula says.

"Me too," Lionel says.

They kiss again.

The doorknob rattles. Ursula's eyes flash with alarm. Lionel gestures to her mouth, her smeared lipstick. She digs a tube out of her purse and reapplies it, checking her appearance in the reflective surface of the Engine's steel casing. Lionel wipes his mouth with the back of his hand.

Lionel opens the door, makes a sheepish comment about the lock being sticky. Jerome Francoeur comes in, a polite smile on his face that flickers when he sees his wife already in the lab, welcoming the others, talking up how excited she is for them to see what Goettreider's been working on.

They file in—Skeptical, Awed, Distracted, Amused, Angry, Thoughtful, Frightened, Detached, Concerned, Excited, Nonchalant, Harried, Weary, Wise. Cheeky props herself next to Jealous, takes his arm in hers as she chats with the others.

It's Sunday, the building otherwise empty. A reminder of how little was expected of the experiment that changed the world— nobody wanted to waste time in their busy workweek on this obscure display by an unknown scientist. The historical record says those in attendance came out of professional curiosity and loyal devotion to the grand ideals of scientific discovery. But from their general manner, polite but impatient, and Ursula's host-like friendliness, the real reason is clear—they're all here as a favor to the wife of the man who signs the checks that fund their research.

That man, Jerome Francoeur, squints at Lionel, a look on his face like the one you get when you can't quite think of a word on the tip of your tongue.

Lionel avoids eye contact with anyone. He scribbles on his note-pad, studious, brow furrowed. And then he notices the lipstick stain on his shirt cuff, where he wiped his mouth. He looks at the stain and reflexively looks at Jerome, who looks at Lionel and sees the stain. Lionel Goettreider may be a genius, but he's not exactly smooth.

Lionel looks away, tries to focus on his calculations. Jerome squeezes Ursula's arm tight enough to distract her from her small talk. When she looks at her husband, he won't meet her gaze.

50

ionel ignores the crowd, temples prickling with sweat, and peers at a series of gauges. And that's when he sees something . . . strange. He taps a dial. Frowns.

"Is everything in order, Mr. Goettreider?" says Jerome.

"Of course," says Lionel. "I just need to check the readings one last time."

"Everyone's excited to see what your contraption can do," says Jerome. "We're ready to be dazzled."

"Jerome, please," says Ursula, "be patient."

"The American people paid for all of this," says Jerome, "and it's my duty to ensure their investment is returned."

The assembled observers exchange awkward looks, although it's hard to tell if they're embarrassed for Lionel or uncomfortable about Jerome's noisy dickishness.

Lionel plugs a device into the console, a modified Geiger-Müller tube of his own design, built to assess the half-life frequency of radiation wave forms—the notion being that the Engine may generate previously undiscovered types of radiation and he'd need to identify and catalogue them. The primitive colored bulbs on the device light up and its sensors emit sharp squeaks and scratches, detecting a radiation signature of unknown provenance. Lionel scrawls out some hasty calculations and, tense, he asks Ursula to come take a look. They murmur to each other, too low to overhear from where I stand, but then curiosity seems to best Ursula's discretion.

"How is that possible?" she says. "You haven't even turned it on."

It's an excellent question. How *could* an undiscovered kind of radiation be emitted when the Engine hasn't yet been activated? And the answer is—me.

Too late, I remember that immateriality isn't just to keep chrononauts from knocking over coffee mugs. It's to make sure nothing from the future can be physically present in the past. Things like, you know, undiscovered kinds of radiation.

51

'm torn between the panicky need to return to the present before I irrevocably screw anything up in 1965 and my incendiary fascination with everything I'm witnessing, both of which are soaked through with the realization that I may have *already* irrevocably screwed something up in the past, in which case my present may no longer exist.

But, no, the fact that I *exist* in 1965 means 2016 has to still be there, because I had to be sent back from somewhere . . . right? You know you're having a seriously fucked-up day when *ontology* becomes a life-or-death proposition.

My father embedded several technical safeguards into the time-travel apparatus to ensure an automatic return to the exact point in space and time from which I was flung—what the chrononauts call the "boomerang protocol" because . . . actually I don't know why. Maybe it just sounds cool. The safeguards should cause me to rematerialize in my father's lab one minute after I left. I mean, assuming the Goettreider Engine doesn't malfunction when it's turned on, maybe because I accidentally corrupted its wonkily calibrated inner workings with whatever unpredictable energy glommed onto me during my space-time travels, and vaporize half the continent, including the parcel of Toronto real estate on which my father's lab will be built.

So, I guess I should at least wait to see what happens when Lionel flips the switch before boomeranging back to a future that may not be there.

52

Lionel seems hyperaware that the mood in the room is shifting from curiosity to impatience. Someone asks Jerome how long this is going to take and he shrugs, hammy, smirking, enjoying the ozone tang of looming failure.

I expected to witness a momentous fault line in human discovery, dense with portent and grandeur, but it's scuffed up with careless infidelity and lame office politics and clammy sweat beading on the forehead that houses history's greatest mind.

"It's fine," Lionel says. "The readings aren't at significant enough levels to affect the experiment."

What Lionel doesn't realize is he just discovered *tau radiation*—the very trail I followed back in time, the unique energy signature of the Goettreider Engine itself, wisping through my molecules and paradoxically announcing its presence minutes before it would first be introduced to the world. So, yeah, huge screw-up on my part.

Ursula hesitates but takes her seat. It's unclear if it's the radiation readings troubling her or the rigid, marauding fury in her husband's eyes as she sits next to him. Lionel faces the assembled observers and offers a tight smile.

"Thank you for attending what I hope will be an illuminating display," Lionel says. "I believe Mr. Francoeur has explained the essential nature of my work to you all and you've already been patient watching me fiddle with the equipment, so I'll just say that if, and I realize it's a substantial *if,* but if my theory holds and the constant rotation of the planet can be harnessed to produce an efficient and robust energy source, it could be of great value to our technical endeavors. Of course, I don't expect much of today's experiment. But it should at least indicate that there's something to my theories worthy of further pursuit."

There is no record of what Goettreider said before switching on the prototype. He wrote no notes, spoke off the cuff. The gist of it was conveyed by the various witnesses in the subsequent weeks, before they all died, but they were scientists and none paid his words much mind before the device was turned on and stunned them all with what it unleashed. In the decades that followed, thousands of writers have taken a crack at imagining this speech, imbuing it with pomp and prophecy, politics and philosophy. Scholars have dissected its possibilities. Poets have made it vast and uncanny.

And I just heard it, his actual statement, cautious and modest with an undercurrent of self-regard. It's always been a subject of intense argument whether or not Goettreider suspected what he was about to achieve—but as I stand here, hearing his words, seeing the way he carries himself, he clearly had lofty ambitions but grounded expectations. He looks like a guy mostly hoping to avoid public humiliation.

Ursula gives Lionel a sweet nod of encouragement and he stands up straighter. His eyes survey the console to ensure everything is as it should be. He takes a deep breath, playfully cocks an eyebrow at the observers, and pulls up the activation lever to turn on the Goettreider Engine.

53

I'm still tucked in the nook behind the observers, so I have about thirty seconds before the Engine begins its operation cycle to reposition myself if I want to see the faces of the assembled witnesses and catch their celebrated reactions.

There's a tickle in the back of my mind that tells me I'm safe where I am, even if I don't have the best view of the experiment and its observers, the best way to ensure I have no material interaction with the unfolding events is to stay put. Unfortunately, reason is no match for vanity and wonder.

As the device gears up and the absorption coils start to crackle, I slip out of the nook and position myself on the other side of the room from where Lionel stands with his hand still on the activation lever, so I have a clear view of the observers. Everyone has a similar expression, vaguely interested, vaguely unimpressed. Except Ursula, her face knit with apprehension, jaw muscles flexing as she grinds her teeth.

The Engine gets up to speed and emits a rumble that makes my internal organs wobble gelatinously. Loose objects like the coffee mug I bumped jiggle in place. A few observers flash nervous half smiles, but everyone's definitely paying attention now. Lionel stares at his invention, his hand on the lever, ready to switch it off if things take a wrong turn, but fascinated by what might happen next.

What happens next is a glittering, radiant plume leaps from the absorption coils and pitches across the lab, enveloping the observers in a silvery whorl of light.

A few people scream. A few raise their hands to protect themselves. The rest just stare in mute shock. Ursula laughs, bright, delighted. The plume doesn't hurt them, although everyone's hair rises in the air like the strands have lost their tether to gravity.

Another glittering energy plume spirals harmlessly through the room.

And that's when I see the sixteen faces. They're not exactly as advertised. Skeptical simply doesn't understand what he's seeing, Awed is probably an exaggeration, but his eyes do go pretty wide, Distracted reaches out to touch the energy plume while Amused recoils from it, Angry is just spooked by the light show, Thoughtful realizes she's witnessing something unprecedented, so does Frightened but he doesn't like what it suggests, Detached is more like taken aback, Concerned is more like curious, Excited would be overstating it, Nonchalant would be understating it, it's hard to tell Harried from Weary, Wise is more like impressed, and, while Jealous is entirely accurate, Cheeky is nowhere to be seen—that's Pride.

Another bright silver plume leaps from the Engine, and this one hurtles right at me. It's mesmerizing. Up close, I can see that within the energy whorl—the mollusk lick curling in on itself that's come to symbolize everything Goettreider's genius gave us—the glittering effect is because the larger whorl is made up of countless smaller whorls, which are in turn comprised of tinier and tinier whorls, an infinity of them spiraling into themselves beyond the subatomic, each a spinning thread of pure power unlocking a door to a future the assembled witnesses have seen only in the cheap stock pages of the science-fiction pulps they read, three-quarters embarrassed and one-quarter thrilled, wondering what it might take to make their vivid dreams a waking life. Like the virtual environment projector that ushered me to consciousness every morning, in this moment they were all launched into a floating limbo between the half-awake past and the half-asleep future. They didn't know it yet, but the Goettreider Engine was the means by which their most outrageous dreams would be mapped onto the world.

"Jesus Christ!" Lionel says.

Everyone looks at him. I look at him. And I realize he's looking right at me.

He can *see* me.

Because that magnificent glittering plume I was marveling over disrupted the invisibility field that cloaked me from view, rendering me translucent but visible—and I'd rejoice at yet another colossal error in my father's grand plan if I wasn't too busy having a panic attack. Lionel Goettreider stands rigid and pale, staring at the ghost gaping at him from across his lab.

It turns out I'm the Seventeenth Witness—Idiotic.

54

I fumble with the emergency reset toggle on my wrist panel. It wipes me invisible again before the Sixteen Witnesses fling their heads in my direction.

"Did you see that?" Lionel says. "Did anyone see that?"

"See what?" Ursula says. "Lionel, what?"

"So he's Lionel now?" says Jerome.

Another plume hurtles out of the Engine. No one knows where to look. The most important experiment in human history is happening in front of them and they're all staring at the empty space where I'm standing, about to engage the emergency boomerang protocol and get the hell out of the past.

Everyone knows what happens next.

After the initial pyrotechnics, the Engine stabilizes. With a flourish, Goettreider plugs in a light bulb to prove it's generating power. The light bulb glows brightly, too brightly, surges, and bursts. Wiry fingers of electricity spew out, singeing the concrete ceiling. The power to the whole building goes out, then the block, then the neighborhood, then the city, then the continent. But in the darkness and confusion, the Engine keeps spinning, sucking up unfathomable watts, quickly filling up the high-yield battery Goettreider had set up in the unlikely event his invention actually worked. Once the furor over the blackout dies down, the device is evaluated by multiple teams with overlapping jurisdictions, and when the vetting process is completed, first the United States, then Canada, then Mexico and Central America, then most of the world is patched into the prototype, running off its ceaseless turn until a network of dedicated Engines is constructed in relay centers around the planet. A few countries insist on maintaining their own power generation, but on his deathbed, chalky and emaciated from radiation poisoning, his teeth and hair and fingernails gone, his eyes pulpy and blind, his organs a black and murky soup, Goettreider releases any legal claim on his design, allowing anyone to build their own Engine. He died without wife or heir, his parents and brothers and most of his relatives were murdered in the Holocaust, he had nobody to give the money to, and so he gave the world the gift of limitless power and the world gave him the gift of immortal stature. The future began.

Here's what isn't supposed to happen.

Goettreider isn't supposed to panic after seeing a translucent stranger in a sleek bodysuit standing in his laboratory.

He isn't supposed to yank the activation lever and shut down the Goettreider Engine midstream.

The Engine isn't supposed to shudder and spark because the outrageous amounts of energy it's generating have nowhere to go.

The harmless pulses of silvery light aren't supposed to glint into a fiery blue.

A blue pulse isn't supposed to rip into the control console, melting the metal and glass, burning right through the concrete and licking flames up the wall.

Ursula isn't supposed to scream at Lionel to get away from the machine.

The next blue pulse isn't supposed to shoot right at her, like it's been aimed that way on purpose.

Jerome isn't supposed to shout something incoherent, lunge forward, and push Ursula out of the way.

The blue pulse isn't supposed to shear the skin and muscle right off his arm, just below his elbow, and punch through the far wall as Jerome clutches his skeletal limb, the blood cauterized on impact, squealing in terror and agony while the exposed bones disintegrate into a powdery ash.

Ursula isn't supposed to open her mouth to make a sound that never comes as her husband sinks to his knees, flailing his smoking stump.

The other fourteen observers, all sharp and cogent scientific minds, aren't supposed to snap into a seizing mob of weeping, scrambling, chittering fear, knocking over chairs and thrusting toward the only door, tumbling over each other, fingers breaking, hard teeth crunched into soft lips, as another blue pulse whirls into the ceiling, slicing up to the floor above, a steel joist melting on contact, flames swooping up along the jagged cracks that spider across the ceiling as the heavy concrete slabs sag ominously.

Lionel isn't supposed to raise his hands in futile self-defense, heat sluicing off the Engine's intake core as it convulses into meltdown, blisters bubbling and popping on his palms, the downy hair of his eyelashes and eyebrows catching fire, but too mesmerized by the calamity before him to blink.

But mostly I'm not supposed to be here. So everything that isn't supposed to happen is happening.

The truth is, everyone in this room is destined to die. But *after* they make history, bronzed into the future as martyred visionaries. Not like this, crying and shoving and skittering for cover on their hands and knees, Ursula cradling a mutilated cuckold and the world's greatest mind staring at the wreckage of his genius while the tip of his nose burns away to raw cartilage.

In this moment of chaos and horror, I discover something kind of nice about myself—I'm reasonably calm under pressure. Instead of devolving into a blubbering amoeba of terror, I charge across the lab, invisible, and shove Lionel away from the Engine with as much force as I can muster, sending him slamming into the far wall, at least a couple of feet closer to safety.

Another fiery blue plume bursts from the Engine, washing over me. I should be incinerated, but my skin suit was designed to be remarkably resilient to physical damage. What it *does* do is send a catastrophic surge through its organic circuitry, causing a cascading system failure. Fortunately, my father and his engineers built in a fail-safe—in the event of a total and comprehensive malfunction, the emergency boomerang protocol automatically triggers.

In one second, I'll be going home.

Against all odds and for possibly the only time in my life, my brain is operating at peak efficiency. One second is just enough time for my nervous system to convey a simple message to the muscles in my shoulder, arm, hand, and fingers. The message is this: Switch the Engine back on so it doesn't destroy half the continent.

I pull up the activation lever with my invisible hand.

And then I'm gone.

55

SUMMARY—Chapters 44 to 54

Fueled by shock, grief, anger, and idiocy, Tom Barren uses his father's prototype time machine to travel from 2016 to 1965, just a few minutes before Lionel Goettreider first activates his world-changing invention—the Goettreider Engine.

Invisible to both eye and camera, in his agitated state Tom neglected to render himself immaterial as well, so he's able to physically interact with his environment. Which he soon does, accidentally, drawing the confused attention of Lionel Goettreider.

Lionel's curiosity is interrupted by Ursula Francoeur, one of the celebrated sixteen observers who witnessed Goettreider's experiment. They think they're alone and so Tom learns something no one has ever discovered—that Lionel and Ursula are having an affair.

The other fifteen observers arrive, including Ursula's husband, Jerome Francoeur, the government bureaucrat who approved Lionel's research and oversees his funding. Nobody in the room expects anything amazing to happen.

Lionel runs some final calculations and notices something odd—a trace of a previously unidentified type of radiation. Tom realizes the radiation is coming from *him*. Because he's not immaterial, the energies he brought back in time with him are showing up on Lionel's instruments.

Fortunately, the social pressure of the moment overrules Lionel's concerns. The future of his research rests on the experiment he's about to conduct, and any show of hesitation could fuel an already suspicious and resentful Jerome.

He pulls up the lever to activate the Engine.

At first, all goes as it should. The device gets up to speed and starts pulling in massive amounts of energy. Swirling plumes of glittering silvery light arc wildly through the room, dazzling but harmless.

And then one of the plumes hits Tom and disrupts his invisibility field. Only Lionel sees him. But of course it's shocking to see a ghostlike figure standing in his lab.

In a panic, Lionel yanks the lever down, abruptly switching off the Engine just as it hits full speed, unleashing torrents of energy. The device shudders into meltdown. The harmlessly sparkling plumes erupt into fiery blue spires of destruction, punching through the concrete walls, melting the steel support beams, nearly collapsing the ceiling onto them. Jerome bravely pushes his wife, Ursula, out of the way of a plume and has his arm seared off below the elbow. The rest of the observers try to claw their way to safety but there's no escape. Lionel, closest to the overheating Engine, starts to blister and burn. If it's not stopped, the meltdown will vaporize half of North America.

Tom has no choice but to take action, shoving Lionel to safety. As the immense heat radiating off the device fries the circuitry of the time-travel apparatus—activating the emergency return function that automatically propels him to his own time—he pulls up the lever to turn the Engine back on before it's too late.

Not knowing if his desperate final act worked, Tom disappears.

56

*F*uck. Fuck fuck fuck fuck fuck shit fuck. Fuck fuck fuck. Shit. Fuck fuck fuck. Fuck fuck shit shit shit shit fuck. Fuck fuck fuck fuck shit fuck shit fuck shit shit fuck fuck fuck fuck fuck fuck fuck fuck fuck fuck fuck fuck fuck fuck fuck fuck fuck fuck fuck fuck fuck fuck fuck fuck fuck fuck fuck fuck fuck fuck fuck fuck fuck fuck fuck fuck fuck fuck fuck fuck fuck. *Shit.* Shit shit shit shit shit fuck. Fuck fuck fuck. Shit shit fuck shit. Fuck fuck fuck fuck fuck fuck fuck fuck fuck fuck fuck fuck fuck fuck fuck fuck fuck fuck fuck fuck fuck fuck fuck fuck fuck fuck fuck fuck fuck fuck shit fuck fuck fuck fuck fuck fuck fuck shit fuck fuck fuck fuck fuck fuck fuck fuck fuck fuck fuck fuck fuck fuck fuck fuck fuck fuck fuck fuck fuck fuck fuck fuck fuck fuck fuck fuck fuck fuck fuck fuck fuck fuck fuck fuck fuck fuck fuck fuck fuck fuck fuck fuck fuck fuck fuck fuck fuck fuck fuck fuck fuck fuck fuck fuck fuck fuck fuck fuck fuck fuck fuck fuck fuck fuck fuck fuck fuck fuck fuck fuck fuck fuck fuck fuck fuck fuck fuck shit shit fuck fuck fuck fuck fuck fuck fuck fuck fuck fuck fuck fuck fuck fuck fuck fuck fuck fuck shit shit shit shit shit shit shit shit shit fuck fuck fuck fuck fuck fuck fuck fuck fuck fuck fuck fuck fuck fuck fuck fuck fuck fuck fuck fuck shit. Fuck fuck shit fuck fuck fuck shit. *Fuck.*

57

You wake up in a hospital.

You wake up in a hospital and they tell you that you collapsed at a building site.

You wake up in a hospital and they tell you that you collapsed at a building site and they're not sure what exactly went wrong with your brain, but whatever it was involved you twitching and writhing on the poured concrete floor and saying "fuck" and occasionally "shit" over and over again.

They say your name is John Barren.

They say your name is John Barren and they don't know why you think your name is Tom Barren.

They say your name is John Barren and they don't know why you think your name is Tom Barren, but it's probably connected to the collapsing and twitching and writhing and cursing.

You do your best to stay calm.

You do your best to stay calm and explain to them that you don't know why they think your name is John instead of Tom.

You do your best to stay calm and explain to them that you don't know why they think your name is John instead of Tom, but you've just seen some pretty remarkable things that will forever change the way we think about arguably the most important ten minutes of all time and if you could just see your father, even if he's furious with you, which you understand is justified, but if you could just tell him what you saw, you know he'll recognize how important it is and help you explain to them why the very fact that you're even alive, that *any* of them are even alive, proves you didn't screw up as badly as you could've, since against all reasonable odds you somehow managed to turn around a situation that was escalating at a rapid pace into some truly abject chaos and, look, while you realize there's no, like, prize for *not* irrevocably warping the basic through line of human history, under the circumstances a simple *thank you* wouldn't be an unreasonable thing to expect.

They look at you.

They look at you and you realize.

They look at you and you realize they're your parents.

Your mother is alive.

Your mother is alive and you start to cry.

Your mother is alive and you start to cry and you can't stop.

58

I'm not great with suspense, so I'll skip the narrative subterfuge and explain what the hell is happening—I am here. As in, *here*. The here that *you* are in. The here I'm not supposed to be in.

It's 5:57 P.M. on Monday, July 11, 2016. Apparently I've been unconscious for nearly three hours.

When the emergency boomerang protocol on the time-travel apparatus got triggered by the incipient meltdown of the Goettreider Engine, I was automatically launched back to my own time, specifically to sixty seconds after I'd left—my father could've programmed the return to be instantaneous, but he thought the drama of a full minute's bated breath would excite his investors.

Except I didn't reappear in his deserted laboratory. Because *here* that laboratory was never built. Because *here* my father never invented time travel. Because *here*, July 11, 1965, was not the pivot of history. Because *here* it was just another day.

Do you understand? I'm in the same world you're in. The world you think you've *always* been in. Dull, vapid, charmless, barely evolved from the 1965 I just left.

I know you think it's changed a lot since then, because of iPhones and drone strikes and 3D printers and, I don't know, gluten-free pretzels. But to me that stuff feels like the early 1970s. The hospital I woke up in might as well have been a medieval torture chamber, everything looked so clumsy and barbaric.

I managed to keep the Goettreider Engine from destroying half of North America—but the Goettreider Engine itself and the world its boundless power manifested . . . it never happened.

It never happened and you think my story up to this point has been semicoherent science fiction.

I tried to explain all this to my parents and they were kind about it, careful, concerned, compassionate, hoping this was temporary crossed wires and not an incurable neurological calamity. The doctors weren't much help with their archaic medical scanners. I knew I wasn't going crazy, but I could also tell where this was going after a battery of tests revealed nothing tangibly out of order with my brain—psych consult.

And then I'm rescued, sort of, by the intervention of an unexpected party.

My parents are in a heated, hushed conversation with a pack of doctors when the door to my room opens.

She has sharp eyes and a wide mouth and a permanent furrow between her arched eyebrows due to a general penchant for skeptical glares. She seems weirdly familiar for someone I've never seen before.

My parents hug her and she squirms at their clinginess. She comes up to my bed, squinting at me like she half expects this is an elaborate practical joke.

"What the fuck, dude?" she says. "You're freaking out Mom and Dad."

Apparently, I have a sister.

59

My sister's name is Greta Barren. She's three years younger than me. She immediately takes charge of the situation, asks the doctors to excuse us so we can talk as a family, tells my dad and my mom—who, to repeat, is *alive*—to take a seat. And my parents do what she says, cowed, squeezing together on the threadbare orange couch under the window, while Greta—who, to repeat, is my *sister*—leans against the wall by my bed, arms crossed, brow knit, and asks me to repeat my story.

So, with as much lucidity as I can muster—considering I'm in a reality that shouldn't exist talking to a sister that was never born while my dead mom holds hands with my dad, something I never once saw them do in my entire life—I explain what happened. Greta listens, nods, doesn't interrupt. But about halfway through my story, her brow unknits and her lips press together like she's trying hard not to smile. Which starts to piss me off. But I press on, describing the events that occurred in Goettreider's lab on July 11, 1965, and how they resulted in me turning up here, with them, instead of where I should be, there, without them.

When I finish, Greta looks me in the eye and bursts out laughing. She turns to my confused and worried parents, holding hands on the orange couch.

"Guys," she says, "it's his *novel.*"

60

My mom and dad have no idea what my sister is talking about.

"You don't remember those stories he used to write as a kid?" Greta says. "About how he lived in, like, the future or whatever? And those drawings he'd do, you know, the weird buildings with all the swirls? Flying cars, robots, jet packs, that kind of crap?"

"Of course we remember," my mom says. "But what does that have to do with a novel?"

"I guess it was a few months ago," Greta says, "he told me he found a bunch of his old stories and drawings and thought they'd make a good book or even a movie or something. He said he was going to write it and ask that producer to read it. You know, the one who commissioned the house in Malibu?"

"We saw that producer's last movie," my dad says, "the one that won the Golden Globe. It got the science all wrong. I mean, I had half a mind to write the man and explain that the actual science is *fascinating* and you don't need to gussy it up with all that nonsense to make the plot work."

"Focus, honey," my mom says.

"Sorry," says my dad.

"I'm still not sure I understand," my mom says. "When did he write a book?"

"I don't think he did," Greta says. "But what he just said, that whole time-travel thing, that's the plot of his novel. When he told me about it, I figured he was joking. Because, I mean, like he has time to write a book. But, whatever, the point is, whether or not he actually wrote it, he hasn't had a schizoid break or something. He just got a little screwy and mixed up real life with his story idea. He's going to be okay."

My mom and dad look at Greta with gratitude. They're still holding hands.

I'm propped up in the hospital bed, frustrated, insulted, annoyed, because I know she's wrong, it's not a goddamn *plot*—it's my life.

Except, I mean, what if she's right? Am I so sure of myself because I'm correct . . . or because my brain's gone wonky for as yet undetermined reasons and my reality principle is in stupendous existential flux?

"Hey, idiot, snap out of it," Greta says. "I have a date tonight."

61

Apparently, my name is John Barren. Apparently, I have the same birth date, October 2, 1983. Apparently, I'm an *architect*.

I finished my master's degree in architecture at the Massachusetts Institute of Technology five years ago, did a postgraduate year at the Royal Danish Academy of Fine Arts in Copenhagen, and got a job at a top firm in Amsterdam. I contributed to a variety of projects around the world, including that producer's house in Malibu, an office building in Kuala Lumpur, another office building in Boston, a ski resort in Switzerland, a bank tower in Singapore, and a convention center in Dubai.

Nine months ago, the firm was approached to do a condo tower in Toronto, my hometown. After clashing with my bosses over the design, I made what sounds like a super-rash decision to quit and go out on my own. For reasons I don't understand but that supposedly involved an impassioned speech to the board of directors of the development company about how this tower won't redefine just the Toronto skyline but the way the world understands what a building can be, launching a new vanguard of modern architecture—I have no idea what any of that means—I was given full control of the condo project and returned to Toronto six months ago to open my own firm. I quickly booked several high-profile commissions, hired a bunch of junior associates with slim-fit black clothing and eccentric eyewear, and have been the subject of several fawning media profiles on my visionary design philosophy.

This is madness because I don't know a goddamn thing about architecture.

Except, impossibly, I do. Tumbling around my brain are years of studying and considering and experimenting and failing and failing and failing and coming up with something not totally horrible and failing and failing and failing and glancing on a not completely embarrassing notion and failing and failing and failing and failing and then achieving a minor success and then achieving a slightly less minor success and then clearly descending into narcissistic self-delusion by striking out on my own with some hazy but confidently articulated pronouncements on the future of architecture.

Still, I must be a total sham because how could I—who never had an original thought or created anything of value, who only ever disappointed and underwhelmed—accomplish anything other than unpredictable new ways to screw up not just my own life and the lives of those I love, but the fundamental integrity of the space-time continuum.

And then I see some photos of the buildings I worked on. And I get it.

After I'm released from the hospital, I insist my mom and dad and sister take me to the building site where I collapsed. It's a big square hole in the ground with a poured foundation and the first few stories framed in steel. Inside the on-site trailer, there's a detailed model of the building-to-be and I stare at it for a long time. Because it's the way things are supposed to be. It looks like home.

Whatever contradictory memories are surging through my mind, I know I'm Tom Barren, from the real 2016—but John Barren is in me too, his memories and thoughts and preferences and opinions sticking to my own memories and thoughts and preferences and opinions like the gunky residue on your skin after you peel off a bandage.

By the way, I only know that because I pulled off the bandage that was on the crook of my elbow, covering the spot from which they drew blood—where I come from, trying to protect a wound with a piece of adhering fabric would seem cluelessly vintage.

But I'm starting to understand. Until this afternoon, when my consciousness somehow seized control, John's consciousness was the dominant one. I—me, Tom—was in there too, tucked away like a bill in the pocket of a pair of jeans that went through the laundry, another analogy that would've made no sense to me before I found myself in a place where clothes are made of processed vegetation or animal hide, instead of recombinant molecules.

There was a barrier between us, me and John, but it was porous. From his earliest moments of awareness, John drew off my earliest moments of awareness. He saw what I saw, but he perceived it as his imagination. His childhood drawings of vast, weird cityscapes—I dug them up from a box in my parents' basement and they're eerily accurate depictions of the cities from my world. The cutting-edge ideas he introduced to his designs at the Dutch firm, the bold concepts that marked him as one to watch by his employers and one to envy, loathe, undermine, and imitate by his peers—they're typical of even the most basic and functional buildings where I come from.

All his supposedly innovative design concepts, the brash structural effects, the sleek but organic interiors and modern but majestic exterior embellishments, the integration of material and environment, the complexity masquerading as simplicity, and of course the *whorls*, everywhere with the whorls—it's cribbed wholesale from the architecture of my reality. The designs he's currently developing, including the condo tower in Toronto that's creeping its way up to the sky on skeletal steel fingers, they're rip-offs of buildings from my world, the world we're supposed to have. The Toronto project looks almost *exactly* like the building that sits on the same lot in the other world. He re-created what should've been there and called it his own.

I'm not a visionary. I'm a plagiarist. Only I'm plagiarizing buildings that never existed, designed by architects who were never born, in a world that never happened.

62

My dad, Victor Barren, is a tenured professor of physics at the University of Toronto with a specialty in photonics—the replacement of conventional electronics with exponentially faster and more capacious photons instead of sad and puny electrons, enabling aspirational projects like quantum computing with the power they need to effectively function. He teaches undergraduate and graduate courses, he publishes in arcane scientific journals, he spent seven years as his department's representative on the campus union council, he applied twice and was twice rejected to be department head, and he's occasionally a talking head on local news when some development in the world of physics is buzzy enough to catch the fleeting attention of the general public, in large part because he has a deep, commanding voice that's offset by his entertaining tendency to make deadpan comic references to popular science-fiction movies when explaining complex scientific principles.

He is not considered by anyone, including himself, to be a genius. He's not even all that successful. His one attempt at a mass-audience science book was a flop, a brief, peppy, pun-heavy work called *The DeLorean and the Police Box—The Art and Science of Time Travel*.

So, yes, my dad retained his fascination with time travel, but not in a professional context. With his colleagues at the university, he sheepishly referred to his book as a lark, an amusing childhood interest buoyed by a scientist's frustration with the ridiculous technical chicanery of time-travel stories by half-assed writers who'd rather deform hard science to their shaky plot machinations than engage in the tough but rewarding challenge of actually conveying the subject with clarity and precision.

My dad is jovial, long-winded, occasionally scattered, generous with his time and his advice, admired by his students, devoted to my mom, patient and kind with his children, a good, caring, exceedingly pleasant person.

This man is not my father. It is not possible that my father and this man share the same DNA.

63

Despite the widespread political chaos, social dysfunction, technological incompetence, and putrid toxicity of this world, one thing *is* way better here—the books.

Where I come from, nobody reads novels unless they're like my mother—fetishizing the artistic media of a bygone era, probably because it was the last time she was happy. But regular people don't read books there. That quasi-telepathic pact between author and reader held little interest for a general audience. Because the dominant storytelling medium of my world involved the seamless integration of an individual's subconscious wiring into the narrative, evoking deep personal wonder and terror, familiarity and delight, yearning and fury, and a triggering catharsis so spellbinding and essential that the idea of sitting down to page through a novel that's not even *intended* to be about the secret box inside your mind—why would anyone want to do that for, like, fun? Unless, of course, you were constitutionally inclined to sublimate yourself to a stronger personality, in which case reading a book where every word is fixed in place by the deliberate choices of a controlling vision, surrendering agency over your own imagination to a stranger you'll likely never meet, is some sort of masochistic pleasure.

At least, that's how I always felt about novels. Except coming here, I have to admit there are a lot of good ones. People in this world consider the novel a moribund art form. But where I'm from it's a mummified corpse clutching the wisps of its long-gone wealth in desiccated fists, so here the shelves of even a meagerly stocked book-store are overwhelming in their splendor and variety.

My mother, Rebecca Crittendale-Barren, is a tenured professor of literature with a specialty in the serialized storytelling of the Victorian age—Wilkie Collins, George Eliot, Elizabeth Gaskell, Thomas Hardy, Robert Louis Stevenson, and of course Charles Dickens. She was department head for ten years and three years ago became the University of Toronto's dean of arts and science. She is collegial and open-minded, but firm in intent and sometimes prickly. She has a nimble mind for political calculation and disarming intellectual opponents, up front with her ambitions and never one to shy away from a necessary fight. Philosophically, she considers everyone who disagrees with her to be merely uninformed, assuming that when they have the facts they'll understand she was right all along.

She has a wry appreciation for tacky gift-shop ornaments that convey homespun but acute insights. On the wall of her office hangs an embroidered cloth in a frame that reads, in looping, folksy letters—WE MUST SUFFER FOOLS GLADLY, OTHERWISE HOW CAN WE HELP THEM TO STOP BEING FOOLS?

This woman is my mother. She's my mother unshackled from my father's genius.

64

Maybe right now you're wondering—if he altered history, how is he even alive? How could he exist? How could so much change, practically everything, but somehow the *exact same* sperm entered the *exact same* egg at the *exact same* moment and created the *exact same* idiot?

Well, it couldn't, it can't, it shouldn't have. By changing history before I was born, I shouldn't be able to have *been* born. But I did, was, am.

Basically, I'm what's called a *temporal anchor*. The fact of my existence warped chronology to ensure my existence. Whatever the trajectory of events might have been without me, subsequent events aligned to produce me here, the same as I was there. The technical term—sorry, the theoretical term that I've unintentionally proven—is *temporal drag*.

Whatever happened between July 11, 1965, and October 2, 1983, quantum probability required my father and my mother to be exactly who they were and mate exactly when they did to make me exactly as I am.

Other people, more or less everyone *else* born after July 11, 1965, weren't so lucky. The domino effect started slow. Millions of people were born on schedule, unaffected by my warping effect. But by 2016, billions of people have been born who were never meant to live and billions who should be alive were never conceived.

I've personally caused not just the death but the *nonexistence* of billions. That I also caused the lives of billions doesn't make it feel better. My emotional loyalty is with the ones that never got to be because of me.

Not to be monstrously glib, but there isn't even a name for my crime. *Chronocide?* Cooking up a fancy sci-fi term for it only obscures its immensity. There are some acts beyond label or measure.

Four billion human beings were born between 1965 and 2016. Actually, where I come from the number was more like three billion because we had more effective birth control, less religion, and better entertainment. Still, that's a lot of lives to swap in and out of existence, particularly since the extra billion are stuck on this dank blister of a world. And it's been a goddamn catastrophe for the ecosystem. It's like the planet can only sustain a specific tonnage of life, so for every human born something else has to die, another species ground into sewage.

I didn't mean to do any of this, but there's no one else to blame. Not even my father. And clearly I've lost the plot because I've *always* been able to blame my father for whatever went wrong in my life—blaming my father is basically my superpower.

But I can't pin this on him, not the horror of what I did, not the guilt I feel for my inability to really process it. Whatever the karmic weight or moral consequence that is my due, I'll have to accept it when it comes, as it must. Existence is not a thing with which to muck around.

65

By the way, there's no novel, okay? John never wrote down anything that formal. But there are notes, pages and pages of handwritten notes in a moleskin sketchbook, which frankly I find kind of pretentious. Although maybe I just feel defensive because my handwriting is garbage. Nobody where I come from handwrites anything. It's not considered an essential skill to teach in school. I mean, I'm *capable* of it, but I never need to do it.

This led to a total disaster at the hospital. The doctors ran a standard cognitive test, asking me to handwrite certain words and comparing the results to examples of my past handwriting. Which of course didn't look remotely similar. My erratic scrawl was so different from John's steady architect's line that they were convinced I'd had a stroke.

I had to submit to a battery of cognitive tests and medical scans, but nothing turned up, which led to another battery of tests and scans, but still nothing turned up, which led to a lot of hushed conversations and medical jargon and worried looks, until finally I came up with an excellent solution, which was to take a day to teach myself how to handwrite like John. The next time they tested me, my mimicry was good enough that they dropped the whole thing.

Something I've realized about doctors here—they mostly have no idea what's going on in your body unless it precisely lines up with standard presentation. Anything just a little bit off course and they're clueless. Obviously they'd never admit it. They must teach a med school class on carrying yourself with absolute conviction when you have zero idea what's really happening. The clinical lingo helps maintain the fog of expertise, as does the ambient panic of the patients and their families. Once I could imitate my own handwriting, they were so relieved they didn't have to keep searching for an answer that was clearly beyond their medieval capacities that they were quick to announce me cured.

After I get discharged and we visit the building site, my parents drive me to my condo. In a car that rolls on pneumatic tires along roads made of bitumen and stone, propelled by an internal combustion engine fueled by refined petroleum. My condo is in a spindly tower with a cramped view of Lake Ontario between the dozen or so other spindly towers squeezed around mine, high enough up that the elevated expressway swooping past our cluster of buildings doesn't seem grotesquely intrusive.

The place has a lot of glass windows—you know, *melted sand* instead of a polymorphic resin—and they don't *do* anything cool other than let in light and let you see outside. There's a device that looks like a Victorian steam engine but is apparently an espresso maker. The whole place is done up in gray hues and dark-toned wood, sharp-lined furniture slung low to the floor to emphasize the ceiling height. I guess the decor is supposed to impress women but it seems cheesy to me. I'm becoming increasingly concerned that John Barren is kind of a douchebag, which is upsetting.

On one wall is a massive frame around a hundred or so old magazines mounted in symmetrical rows and columns—they're all 1950s pulp science-fiction anthologies, lurid painted covers with square-jawed adventurers and bosomy scientists, robots and ray guns, spaceships and jet packs. I stare at this wry shrine to my lost world and it makes me want to punch John in the face. Except it's *my* face.

I don't really care about exploring my supposed home, I just need to find this "novel" Greta mentioned and, if it's real, see what it says. The confounding swirl of impulses that comprises John's memory sends me to the moleskin sketchbook on his bedside table and it's exactly what I'm looking for.

Here's my sense of it—for his whole life, John has been dreaming about my life. When he was a kid, it was chalked up as his imagination, encouraged by his supportive parents and amused teachers, expressed in drawings and scenes played out with action figures for an audience of one, his little sister, Greta, her own private sci-fi soap opera. The visions of my life seemed to come to him simultaneous with when I actually lived them—I'd experience something and he'd dream about it. There's a raft of drawings stuffed in a box on a closet shelf, moments of my life rendered in crayon and construction paper. There's a whole series, like a comic book, with panels and dialogue bubbles, about the time I ran away from home at age twelve. Kissing Robin Swelter. Getting punched by her brother. My mother's grim face.

As he grew up, John continued to have the dreams but rarely mentioned them to anyone. From time to time he'd tell Greta, but she was busy being a teenager and not giving a shit about her family. Greta abides by the reasonable philosophy that there is nothing in the universe more boring than someone else's dreams.

The dreams never stopped, but John didn't think much about them as he moved from adolescence to adulthood. The extent to which the cityscape of his recurring dreams inspired him to pursue architecture and fixed his design aesthetic is obvious—*a lot*. But John didn't know he was ripping off my world. He just thought he was a genius.

Four months ago something changed—John had a terrible nightmare that his mom had died in an accident, hit by a flying car. He woke up in a panic, called her, disoriented, upset. Of course she was still alive. But the memory, so vivid, stuck inside him, aching, unreachable.

He started writing down his dreams in the sketchbook. He kept it next to his bed so, when he woke up, he could get down whatever he'd dreamed about before it faded from conscious grasp. There are pages and pages of semi-lucid scribbles, details, observations, insights, things I said and things said to me, thoughts I had but never spoke. It's all true.

John decided his subconscious was telling him a story he needed to write. This was his "novel"—my life in the months since my mother died.

He didn't actually start writing it. But he did compose a summary of the "story" on his laptop. In fact, he was working on it during a coffee break at the building site, moments before he collapsed in a fit of curse words and frenetic seizing.

You've already read what he wrote: I included it as chapters 43 and 55.

So.

66

grew up as an only child, so it's *really* weird to suddenly have an adult sister who appears to know me—or the me she thinks I am—better than anyone else in the world. All my bullshit seems to drive her nuts and yet she also seems wholly at ease with my bullshit. I've never hung out with a woman around my age and not worried in the slightest that something I say might render me unattractive. Even with women I wasn't interested in, I still wanted them to find me attractive.

But with Greta, yeah, nothing. I know that sounds *obvious*, but I have no frame of reference for the sibling dynamic. I was an only child. I've never felt unconditional affection for anyone who didn't biologically spawn me.

Sorting through this flood of John's memories, Greta's there, my sister, in all of the experiences that made me who I am, who *he* is, and I can't help but wonder if maybe my whole life I've been kind of sexist.

I mean, rereading some of my earlier chapters, the way I wrote about seeing Penelope naked for the first time and sleeping with my exes after my mother died—I'd feel embarrassed if Greta read that stuff. I'm not trying to dismiss any retrograde blunders in the way I talk about the women in my life . . . it's just hard to recognize your own blind spots, you know?

Part of the problem is this world is basically a cesspool of misogyny, male entitlement, and deeply demented gender constructs accepted as casual fact by outrageously large swaths of the human population. Where I come from, gender equality is a given. I'm not talking about absurdly fundamental things like pay equality. I mean that there is no essential difference in the way men and women are perceived in terms of politics or economics or culture. Your genitalia are considered no more pertinent to your status than the color of your eyes.

Of course, that also means some stuff that's considered normal where I come from would be super-weird here. Like, okay, in my world, when you break up with someone, it's considered gracious to offer the person you dumped a lock of hair so that, if they want, they can get a genetically identical surrogate grown for whatever purposes they need to get over you. It has no consciousness, but it looks exactly like you and can be used for rudimentary physiological functions. Like, you know, sex. The expectation is that when your ex feels ready to move on they'll have it deconstituted into a biological goop and returned to the manufacturer for disinfection and recycling. Describing it, yes, I realize it sounds bizarre, but it's a fairly everyday thing.

It's why my mother's abject devotion to my father rubbed me the wrong way. It's not just that *I* wanted to be the center of her attention—it's that her self-abnegation was so unnecessary. He didn't even notice most of what she did until she was gone. There was no reason to live that way except as a deliberate choice. It was actually *harder* for someone like my mother to do nothing but service my father when there were so many options open to her. To *anyone*.

Except maybe I'm still being sexist. Her choices are her choices.

I went back to chapter 11 and cut out a few indiscreet comments about my ex-girlfriends' private lives. With my friends, I knew them for seventeen years and feel okay revealing personal stuff about them, but I can't honestly say Hester or Megan or Tabitha would've given me permission to include details about their lives. And if it seems *more* disrespectful to their memories to elide them from my story, well, you can't possibly appreciate just how annoying I was to date. Their privacy was earned.

It's like with John's condo. My immediate impression was it's all a sham to impress women. But the more time I spend in his head, the more I realize—it's just his *style*. I thought of it as a cheesy seduction ploy because that's what *I* would've done if I had any confidence in my own taste. Every accomplishment in my life that meant anything to me involved impressing someone who wasn't naturally inclined to find me attractive. I make my mother's death a story about sleeping around. I make the end of my reality a story about my broken heart.

I feel superior to John because I come from a more technologically and socially advanced world. But none of that has anything to do with *me*. I was just born there. I contributed nothing to it—except my sense of entitlement.

67

I'm doing this all wrong. I shouldn't be rambling on about my inchoate gender epiphanies, I should be developing the "characters" of my mom and dad and sister instead of just cataloguing the ways they're not like who they were or, in the case of Greta, who they weren't.

I had dinner at my parents' house with Greta, and I found myself slipping effortlessly into conversation along the various narrative strands of the infinitely dense soap opera that is our family life—my mom's department politics, research projects, interesting and/or inane comments made by colleagues in her meetings, my dad's department politics, research projects, interesting and/or inane comments made by students in his classes, something a neighbor said, something a neighbor did, something a neighbor plans to do, lunch with an old friend who told an amusing and/or sad anecdote that made them laugh and/or cry, frosted with sarcastic comments by Greta and punctuated with intermittent jokes by me that my mom and dad laugh at way too hard.

It's comfortable and easy. It's terrifying how comfortable and easy it is to sit around the dinner table with these strangers, and I have to keep reminding myself it isn't real. This is not my family. The comfort and ease are a lie. Only the feeling that I don't belong here is true.

My parents live in the same overheated Victorian row house where Greta and I grew up, in a neighborhood called the Annex, half a dozen blocks from the university campus where they both work. My mom believes there is no better decoration than a shelf of books, and the house is a testament to that. The rooms are organized by category—contemporary novels in the dining room, the kitchen for cookbooks, the bedroom for non-antique editions of Victorian novels, what used to be my bedroom and is now my mom's office for literary criticism, the bathroom for my dad's collection of spry pop-science books, my dad's serious science tomes in his study, the living room colonized by well-preserved early editions of Victorian novels, the rare first prints in a glass case that hangs in an awkward spot on the wall, not quite in balance with the rest of the room, but necessary to keep it both prominently displayed and shaded from natural sunlight. It makes every room feel cramped and still, because the thick wood shelves make the walls feel two feet closer and the volume of paper absorbs most ambient sound.

I'm in my dad's study, trying to appear casual as I scan for books on time travel, when Greta leans in the doorway.

"You're acting weird," she says.

"No, I'm not," I say.

"You're making a lot of jokes," she says.

"They're not funny?"

"They're okay. But you never make jokes around Mom and Dad. You're always so serious around them."

"Maybe I'm trying to develop, you know, an adult relationship with them."

"Bullshit."

"What do you want from me, Greta?"

"You had a major neurological who knows what and told everyone you're a time traveler," Greta says.

"And you made fun of me," I say.

"Because you're *not* a time traveler," she says.

"Yeah."

"And now you're being weird, man. You're all, like, cracking jokes as if you didn't just have some babbling seizure three days ago. If you and Mom and Dad want to be in denial, fine, pretend nothing happened. But something happened. So I call bullshit. You're not acting like yourself."

"Because I made a couple of jokes."

"Yes. My brother is a lot of things. But funny isn't one of them."

"Maybe I save my best material for my friends," I say.

"What friends?" Greta says. "You don't have friends. You have work people and you have me."

She punches me in the shoulder, harder than necessary.

"I have friends," I say. "You think I don't have any friends?"

"Do you honestly think you're from the fucking future?"

"No. I'm not from the future."

This is, of course, true. I'm not from the future. I'm from an alternate timeline. It's still today. It's just a different today.

68

I wake up stiff and groggy and annoyed that my virtual environment projector has malfunctioned, until I remember I'm in John's condo bedroom. I assume the searing headache must be another neurological spasm, like the one I had at the construction site four days ago, but then a single word pierces the mental fog—*coffee*. I manage to manipulate the steam engine until it squirts out an oily jet of espresso. Headache cured.

Finally, something in this crappy world that actually does what it's supposed to.

I wish I had more of a sense of humor about all the, like, fish-out-of-water hilarity as I try to fit into this backward mess you call a civilization. Of course, there's something absurd about an adult human who doesn't know how to open a jar of peanut butter or work an elevator or use a credit card. To an outside observer, I probably look like I'm suffering from some debilitating cognitive trauma.

Conscious decisions are hard. It takes forever to choose an outfit and I end up in a pair of suspiciously tight denim pants and what I later learn is a pajama top.

Calling up something from John's memory works only when I stop trying to think about it, like how to use his laptop or his cell, which are both beeping with insistent messages from his architecture firm that I'm definitely *not* going to answer.

I recognize the kitchen appliances from elementary school history classes and get excited when I find a food synthesizer, until I realize it's a microwave. John eats out a lot, so the refrigerator is empty except for a tub of yogurt and an avocado. I *know,* it's so poetic. You probably think I'll cut into the avocado because it looks ripe but inside it's all brown and mushy, like a metaphor. Except I *do* cut into it and it *is* brown and mushy, but I don't care about poetry because I'm hungry so I eat it anyway. It tastes thin and watery. I swallow a few spoonfuls of the yogurt before I realize it expired two weeks ago. Not knowing what an *expiration date* is doesn't feel like fish-out-of-water hilarity when I'm vomiting into the sink because I just ate bad yogurt.

It's the little things that get to me, like not knowing how to work a shower, because to me a shower seems like what an outhouse probably seems like to you—a quaint and kind of gross throwback to an age you're very happy is long gone. And it's the big things that get to me, like the framed photo on the desk of my sister, mom, and dad smiling next to a stranger with my face.

I scrutinize photos of John and try to get my hair to look like his, but I have never once washed with shampoo and conditioner—I have to read the fine print on the bottle to find out what conditioner even does—let alone smeared my hair with something called *sculpting mousse.* In my world, you lower a grooming helmet over your head and it cleans, trims, and shapes your hair for you. Here, when my hair grows too long I apparently have to pay another grown-up to cut it with *scissors,* like a day-care craft.

I wash, dress, and eat all on my own and I'd be proud of myself except these are the accomplishments of a precocious child. But that's what I feel like—a kid waking up in an empty home, unsure if his parents arc asleep or gone or dead, going through the normal morning routine because it's the only thing that keeps the panic at bay.

69

I can't stay here. It's wonderful that my mom is alive and my dad isn't a distracted asshole and Greta is, I mean, she's awesome. Scabrous, incautious, and sharp. She deserves to live, much more than I do. Clearly John has his act together in a way I never did. He's successful, driven, and impressive. Even if all his best ideas are ripped off from his dreams of my world, even if he's limited his life to work and convinced himself it's enough, even if I know why—because he's always had this steady, bleak, overwhelming sense that none of this is the way it's supposed to be, that everyone he meets, everywhere he goes, every thought in his head is inexplicably but irrevocably *wrong*. He holds everyone at a remove because, on a level he could never articulate but could also never shake, he knows they shouldn't exist. The one exception is Greta, but only because she refused to be pushed away and fought a pitched, merciless, never-ending battle to keep John present in this world. I spent my life wanting my parents to pay attention to me. John has their rapt focus and chronically shrugs them off. He has everything I wanted, but it can't fill the void that opens up every night in his dreams. And now the void has overtaken him—me, I'm the void.

But I can't let them in either. Not Greta, not my parents, not this version of my life. I have to keep John's consciousness tamped down, locked up, swallow whatever affection he feels for the individuals who comprise the lattice of his life, because this world is a dank, grimy horror and I *can't stay here*. I have to figure out how to get the timeline back on track and return us all to the future we're supposed to have. I'm the only one who can do it, and, as pleasant as this interlude has been, it's monumentally selfish to condemn the rest of the world, reality itself, to this wrong existence just because my little life has been improved. I'm not important, not compared to the billions who have never known how things should be.

70

So, how do you go about changing the last five decades of history in a world where time travel is considered an amusing thought experiment? Even if the science existed, in the absence of crucial advances in related fields—teleportation, immateriality, invisibility, even simple component manufacturing—the whole endeavor is futile. And, of course, my father's plan depended on following the radiation trail emitted by the original Goettreider Engine. Without that, even if I somehow solved the technical issues, I'd still have no way to get to the exact spot in space at the exact moment in time.

Plus, I don't know how any of this stuff actually works. I have some insider lingo picked up from my months working at the lab and mingling politely with my father's acolytes, but I can't build a time machine from scratch any more than I can build John's espresso maker from scratch.

And there's a Pandora's box waiting to be opened—my dad. After all, he did write a book about time travel, even if it's considered an eccentric blemish on his academic reputation. No matter how sweet and considerate this iteration of him appears to be, I'm not ready to ask him for this kind of help, not yet.

I need to find out what happened to the Goettreider Engine. Everything stems from that, all that went wrong and all the ways to possibly set it right. I use John's laptop to search "Goettreider Engine" online—but the computer tells me nothing matches that entry. I try "Lionel Goettreider"—nothing. A billion websites and not one mentions the most important person who ever lived.

Before giving up, because it's the Internet, I look up ex-girlfriends. Hester Lee, nothing. Megan Stround, nothing. Tabitha Reese, nothing. Robin Swelter, nothing. I try my friends, but there's nothing for Deisha Cline or Xiao Moldenado and Noor Priya or Asher Fallon and Ingrid Joost either. No trace of them online, no social media pages, no blogs or articles or tags of any kind. They don't exist. They never existed.

I do find the official website for Ubly, Michigan, that abandoned town we visited. Except here it's not abandoned. My friends are gone but around 830 people currently live in Ubly. John's cell estimates the drive would take five hours, up the Don Valley Parkway to the 401 until it splits into the 402, then across the Blue Water Bridge onto the 25 alongside Lake Huron to East Atwater Road, which becomes Ubly's Main Street when it runs right through the center of town. The library I saw, with the trees growing from the rotting books, is still standing. I could knock on every single door in town to search for whoever owned that pocket watch. If they're alive, if they still have it, I could make them an exorbitant offer, pay any price they asked. I could hold the exact same watch in my hands, just like I did that final day at the lab.

But what would be the point? It's just a watch. It didn't have a life. It didn't have a career like Deisha or a fiancée like Asher or a child like Xiao. It wasn't my friend, even if I wasn't that great a friend in return. It didn't love me, maybe a little, the way Hester or Megan or Tabitha sort of did, briefly and without much benefit. It didn't alter the trajectory of my life like Robin did over five gawky, glorious nights. It's a thing.

And then, because I can't help myself, I look up "Penelope Weschler" online.

For at least thirty seconds, I just stare at the screen until my eyes water, and it's not because I can't seem to blink.

It's because there she is—Penelope Weschler.

She exists.

Except she's *not* Penelope Weschler.

71

Penelope Weschler lives right here in Toronto. She goes by *Penny*. She owns a bookstore, in a neighborhood called Leslieville, on the east side of the city just past the ribbon of murky gruel known as the Don River. There are a lot of effusive write-ups about the bookstore online. It hosts reading series with authors and weekly book clubs. It's called Print Is Dead.

I click around until I find a photograph of her.

I stare at it, woozy and jittery at the same time.

She is not Penelope Weschler. Or, no, she is, but she looks like someone else. She *is* someone else.

It will turn out that despite the changes I caused to the timeline, her father, Felix Weschler, and her mother, Joanne Davidson, still become high school sweethearts and still decide to start a family shortly after college, and Felix still wants to name his first-born daughter after his beloved grandmother Penelope, and Joanne still agrees. The Penelope Weschler I knew was never born on January 12, 1985. But another Penelope Weschler was, on June 9, 1985, just under five months later.

Instead of *the Penelope Weschler I knew* I originally wrote *my Penelope* and deleted it—as if she *ever* belonged to me, as if she ever could.

This Penelope looks like her in some ways, different in others. Like they're sisters. Except they're not. She's a genetic variation conceived five months later by the same parents, the identical combination of chromosomes with an alternate result. Her freckles are all wrong, like a map of the night sky on another planet. The shade of her hair, the color of her eyes, the shape of her jaw, her optometric prescription, the epidermal ridges of her fingerprints.

The way she kisses.

I'm getting ahead of myself. As with everything in my life, both my lives, all my lives, things go awry when Penelope Weschler is involved.

72

I stand on the sidewalk outside Print Is Dead. I haven't called ahead, she probably isn't even here, and maybe that's for the best because I can't think straight, the mesh of my thoughts knotted up into oceanic noise. I just had to come here right away. I have no plan.

The hours are printed on the glass front door. The store closes in twelve minutes. It's the ground-floor shop front of a speckled brick building, apartments on top, a dingy law office on the right with its dust-caked blinds shut, a coffee shop on the left with a bearded barista in overalls hissing out foamy drinks for the customers squatting on mismatched chairs at a pale-wood communal table, their faces glowing blue-white from the cell screens propped before them. A streetcar rumbles along Queen Street East, squealing against the metal rails laid in the asphalt.

I go inside. It's warm and bright and smells like ink and glue. Rows of shelves made from reclaimed barn board, knobby and pleasingly asymmetrical. Covers and spines of every hue and font. Displays of signed copies by local authors. Framed prints of vintage editions on the walls.

And Penny Weschler on a stool behind the counter, reading a novel. The place is empty. She hasn't looked up. I could still leave without her seeing me.

I'm not going anywhere.

I pretend to browse, so I have something to stare at other than her. Most of these authors should never have been born, but here are their books in neat little rows, millions of words that weren't supposed to be written, saying things that weren't supposed to be said. In the *V* section are eight novels by Kurt Vonnegut that shouldn't exist. I run my fingers over their spines.

Every step feels heavy, like my heart is exerting its own gravity, trying to drag me to the floor with a pulverizing force, so I'm liquefied against the clean herringbone tiles.

She looks up at me. Propriety dictates I nod or smile or avert eye contact, *anything* but stare right at her like a lunatic. I resolve to play it cool. My resolve doesn't even make it to the first syllable.

"Penelope Weschler," I say.

"Hey," she says. "Sorry, do we know each other?"

Her voice is different because her larynx and tongue and teeth and lips are different. But the way she looks you right in the eye when she talks to you is the same.

"Yes and no," I say. "I'm from an alternate reality."

Penny closes her book without marking the page.

"So, we know each other in another reality, but not in this one?"

"Yeah," I say.

"How did you get here? To this reality?"

"It's a long story."

"I bet," Penny says.

"I can tell you about it, if you'd like."

"You're John Barren," she says.

"How do you know that?"

"I've seen your picture. You designed that tower that's going up downtown. People on the Internet say you're maybe some kind of genius. And not just the Internet. Real people too."

"Well," I say, "I stole all my ideas from another reality."

"The reality you come from," she says.

"Yeah. You're taking this pretty well. You don't think I'm demented?"

"I don't know," she says. "You might be demented. But there are security cameras recording us and you're sort of well-known. Not, like, famous. But semi-recognizable to people who pay attention to local city stuff. If you do something violent or crazy or whatever, they'll find you right away."

"I'm sure they will."

"Why are you here? I mean, here in my store."

"To see you," I say.

"To see *me*," Penny says.

"I realize everything I'm saying sounds extremely weird. I'm sorry. I should've come up with an actual plan. But as soon as I saw you, I couldn't lie to you."

"About how you're a quasi-famous architect who is secretly pla-giarizing his brilliant ideas from another dimension?"

"I didn't know I was doing it until a few days ago," I say.

"What happened a few days ago?"

"I'd like to explain it to you," I say, "but it involves time travel and I'm concerned that even telling you that much is going to irre-vocably freak you out. I don't know why I feel compelled to be hon-est with you when I know I sound kind of insane. But it's a pretty good story. Even if you don't believe it, I think you'll be entertained."

"Okay," she says.

"Okay what?"

"Okay, I close in a few minutes," she says. "Go outside while I text a bunch of people that I'm going for a drink with you and if I turn up missing you definitely murdered and possibly ate me."

"Great."

"You don't mind me telling people that?"

"I'm just happy you're willing to spend a few more minutes with me after what I just said."

"Pretty much everything you said sounds crazy," Penny says. "But you know what's crazier? I think I might have been waiting my whole life for you to walk in here."

73

I decide to tell Penny *some* of the truth but omit the more off-puttingly painful details. I promise myself I'll reveal those things later, maybe, if it seems like she trusts me enough to hear the whole story . . .

But as soon as I'm sitting across a wobbly bar table from her and she's looking at me, the singular object of her full attention, it all spills out. I tell her everything.

It takes a few hours. We're in a peaty, underlit dive bar up the block from her bookstore, a holdover from the neighborhood's rundown past that's being co-opted by its gentrifying present, much to the delight of the proprietor, who is discovering how much she can charge for a glass of booze if she cultivates just the right air of alluring disrepute. Our table for two is propped up against the front window, separated from the rest of the bar, perfect for two people to talk until closing time over several overpriced bourbons.

Penny has a lot of questions about the other Penelope, how she became who she did, her failure as an astronaut, her reinvention and self-destruction, my role in it. She cries when I tell her how Penelope died, and why, our cell. I tell her about breaking into the lab, traveling back in time, screwing up the world, ending up here, as John—she doesn't totally get how temporal drag works, but then again neither do I—deciding I need to put things right but not knowing where to start.

After I'm done, Penny is quiet for a long time. The bar's empty and we're getting sharp looks from the bartender. She finishes her fourth bourbon, drops some cash on the table, and stands up.

"Come on," Penny says.

74

We walk to her condo a few blocks away in an old factory that's been hollowed out and fitted with floor-to-ceiling windows and poured-cement floors and stainless-steel appliances for two hundred or so urbanites to call home. Her place looks down on a few building sites deconstructing similar factories and replacing them with towers that will soon colonize what's left of her view of downtown's jagged gray-and-turquoise skyline and the vast spread of Lake Ontario.

She's invited me into her home. That seems like a good sign. Although a sign of what I'm unsure.

Penny kicks off her shoes, goes to the kitchen, pours us both some water. She doesn't turn on the lights, but there's enough ambient city glare through the windows to give her a soft, glowing outline as she looks at me.

"Look," Penny says, "you're either amazingly nuts or the most interesting person I've ever met. If you told me that story to score with me, I'm going to be forthright and admit it's working pretty well, although the four bourbons are playing an important role in that. I have a pretty well-tuned Spidey sense for the bullshit men say to get your clothes off. And if that's what this is, well, *bravo*, motherfucker. There's no reason to believe you. Except that I've felt, like, forever, that my life isn't what it's supposed to be. That even though the bookstore is going well and I have a nice, tidy, comfortable little life where I've rarely got to leave my neighborhood and my customers seem to, like, genuinely appreciate that my store exists in an area that's in the process of devouring and regurgitating itself into who knows what and they see me as, you know, a symbol or whatever that maybe what it's becoming won't be so bad, it might even be better than what was here before, something genuine and particular instead of a bunch of dreary shit-box chain restaurants and logo shops. But I've never felt like this was it, the right life for me. I read a lot of speculative fiction, I mean hard-core nerd stuff, I love it, I've always loved it, even when it made me weird and the only boys who dug me were way too scared of girls to do anything about it, which meant I always had to make the first move, well, not just the first move, *all* the moves, and they were so petrified of rejection that they'd seriously rather get angry and call me a skank than risk being lousy in bed. What I'm saying is, my imagination is *trained*, okay? I've considered many other lives that I could be living instead of this one. I've *luxuriated* in what seemed at the time to be outrageously improbable possibilities for who I could be instead of who I am. And now you show up, telling me all the dopey, delusional fantasies I harbored as a frustrated adolescent and sheepish adult were, what, *unambitious*? That the life I'm supposed to lead is so far beyond anything I was even capable of imagining for myself? That I'm a fucking lioness living like a mouse?"

"Yeah, I guess I am," I say.

And Penny kisses me.

75

Later, Penny asks why I think I'm an accidental plagiarist—I skimmed over it in my initial explanation because I'd drank a lot of liquor and wanted to get to the part where I found out she still existed—so I go over it again.

"Okay," she says, "but what if every creative idea that someone has is unconsciously borrowed from that person's experiences in another reality? Maybe *all* ideas are plagiarized without us knowing it, because they come to us through some cryptic and unprovable reality slippage?"

"Does that mean, like, the version of you that had the idea in the other reality also stole it from *another* version of you in yet *another* reality?" I say.

"I don't know," she says, "maybe we can only access a limited number of, like, adjacent realities and we're constantly shoplifting ideas from different versions of our world and mistaking them for our own insights."

"Although some realities are going to be superior to others in terms of quality ideas," I say. "Not to be a dick about it, but there doesn't seem like a lot my reality can learn from this one."

"Yeah," she says, "but for all you know, the best ideas from your reality were stolen from this reality, except *here* we could never properly execute them because we didn't have access to the . . . what's it called again?"

"The Goettreider Engine."

"Right," Penny says. "We didn't have the resources to actually make the stuff we came up with, so we stuck them in our science fiction. We kept them safe in our dreams. And then you assholes raided our imaginations, took credit for our ideas, and built yourself a paradise."

"That's actually . . . a not unreasonable point," I say.

"Or maybe we're giving individual human beings too much credit. Maybe a vast alien intelligence is seeding original concepts into our minds to test if they can pass through whatever boundary separates us from other dimensions. Like, some ideas are porous, while others are impermeable and can't escape their root reality. Maybe the best ideas are the ones that travel freely and don't really belong to any one person."

"You're not like the other Penny," I say.

76

She *was* different. The other Penny—it already seems strange to call her *Penelope*—had a taut hardness to her, physically and emotionally. Her body practically whirred when she stepped, so calibrated were her movements, muscles in harmony with gravity, not a joule of wasted energy. She was reserved in a careful, feline way, like she'd speak only the minimum number of words necessary to state her core point, not because she didn't have more to say, but because she knew that in unsavory circumstances every word she spoke could be used against her, so the more precise and guarded her sentences, the less likely her verbal history might undo her. She was all determination and dread that determination wouldn't be enough. A life spent with a white-knuckle grip on herself, so as to appear without guile or rot, unfouled.

This Penny *talks,* the words tumbling out of her, gesturing wildly in emphasis. She has slightly rounded shoulders, a loose-limbed walk, an easy laugh. She doesn't seem at all cautious. She has her issues, like all of us, but that sense of a shameful wrongness that Penelope trained herself to conceal, except when it gushed out like water from a burst pipe, this Penny has no trace of it. It's not that she lacks murky personal contradictions—she has her fair share of those—it's that she doesn't think of them as wrong and they don't cause her shame. Like everyone, she carries around a suitcase of troubles everywhere she goes, but she leaves it unlocked, for anyone to rifle through if they care enough to be curious.

There are other differences, physical ones, but it seems irrelevant, and impolite, to catalogue them. They had the same name and the same parents, but with markedly distinct results.

One thing they had in common—their hands. I knew Penelope's hands well from all those hours at the simulators, and Penny has the same long, tapered fingers and thin, delicate wrists, even if the lines and creases and swirls on her palms are her own.

And there was the way they both looked at you. Penelope rarely made eye contact, but when she did you felt like the center of the universe. Penny is like that too. Her attention seems to pour from her eyes into yours, like there couldn't possibly be anything anywhere as interesting as what you're saying to her right there and then.

I mean, admittedly, I was either a time-traveling emissary from another reality or a damaged maniac in the midst of a radical schizoid break, so maybe I was interesting regardless. But Penny didn't need a crazy story to hold my attention—she had it, it wasn't going anywhere, and as soon as I met her neither was I.

77

The truth is, there are no alternate realities. At least not the way Penny describes them. Maybe an infinite multiverse is born from every action, whether it's two atoms colliding or two people. Maybe reality is constantly fluctuating around us, but our senses aren't equipped to detect those quantum variations. Maybe that's what our senses *are*, an ungainly organic sieve through which the chaos of existence is filtered into something manageable enough that you can get out of bed in the morning. Maybe the totality of what we perceive with our senses is as clumsy a portrait of reality as a child's chalk drawing on a sidewalk compared to the face of the woman you're already falling in love with lying next to you in a mess of sheets and blankets, her lips still pursed as they pull away from your mouth.

But in terms of our actual experience, there's just one reality, this reality. The other reality, my reality, is gone. I erased it when I interacted with the past—*interacted*, that's a nice way of saying *catastrophically broke*. Nobody in my world is wondering where I am because that world no longer exists. This world is all there is now.

I say all this to Penny. Except the part about falling in love with her. I somehow manage to keep that to myself. Since we just met last night and I'm attempting to appear *less* like a lunatic around her.

"The *truth* is," she says, "you don't know what the hell you're talking about. All this crap about alternate realities and time-travel contradictions and consciousness transferring, you don't actually *know* anything. You're speaking with authority because it's calming to feel in control of the unknowable. So chill out, man, and enjoy what you *do* know. Which is that in this reality, you get to make out with me."

And I do. But I also know I'm right—because I'm starting to forget.

When I got out of the hospital and found John's sketchbook, I wrote down a lot of things that I knew for sure had happened, trying to sort out the jumble in my overtaxed brain. It was only a few days ago but when I look through those notes now I can barely remember most of it. The memories have gotten wispy, threadbare, curled up to sleep in some cognitive fold I can't access. Maybe the brain heals wounds too, grows over the tip of the splinter that broke off when you pulled the rest out with tweezers, leaving a fragment of something foreign to rot inside you.

When I wrote those hasty notes, it felt pretentious to describe it all in too much detail. I wrote out the basic events, and, of course, my narcissism kept derailing the story toward my anxieties and doubts and guilt and regret. But if I'd known I would start to lose all those memories, I would've spent every day writing and writing and writing down everything I remembered about my world, no matter how irrelevant or banal or obvious. Because now those pages of scattered, sheepish description are almost all I have left. It might as well be fiction. I might as well be fiction. A life, a world, a whole universe, reduced to twenty-seven pages of scrawled handwriting.

I'm feeling less and less like Tom every day. I can feel it happening. I'm becoming him. Becoming John.

78

We spend the night and the day together. We walk around her neighborhood with take-out coffees. We eat breakfast at a place she likes. She decides to close the bookstore for the day, so we just keep walking, heading west toward downtown. Penny wants to show me her city, the place I've lived most of my life but barely recognize.

I talk about how the buildings are all the same. The skin and hair varied but the skeletons and muscles and nerves and organs are virtually identical. Good for making people, boring for making cities. Like with people, you need to manage the inevitability of gravity and decay. Unlike with people, your materials aren't limited to bone and flesh. Where I come from, there wasn't much by way of architectural nostalgia. The past was thought of as an unsightly skin tag, kind of embarrassing, mostly benign, but with an implicit warning about how bad things can get if you don't keep an eye on it. There were landmarks, of course, the Taj Mahals and Eiffel Towers and Washington Monuments of postcard history, but otherwise the charitable thing to do was raze it away.

And I talk about how the buildings are all so different. My world long ago embraced *macroarchitecture*—designing individual buildings as interlocked parts of an overall municipal whole, fusing cultural precedent, local taste, global trends, environmental context, and geographic specificity. Dubious macrodesigns would occasionally emerge, like how Beijing looks like a dragon from above and San Antonio is shaped like a giant version of the Alamo and Brasília's grid replicates the map of Brazil. But macroarchitecture mostly spares cities from the aesthetic incoherence of this world.

Penny disagrees. Walking streets lined with mismatched buildings, what she sees isn't visual clutter—it's history made vivid, the juxtapositions that narrate the city. Every original detail, every date-stamped renovation, every brick and shingle and window and door and staircase have something to say about the city they made together. And every city has hundreds of these blocks, thousands, pages in its never-ending story.

I think about the other Penelope and the likelihood we ever would've spent a day like this. We had only the one night together and then . . . the parallel hits me, hard and blunt: This is the morning after the night before. Standing here on the sidewalk with Penny, it's almost the exact time of day that Penelope stepped out of the defusion sphere and floated apart in front of me. But here she is, this version of her, the past razed away, sipping a coffee while traffic roars around us. This world is so blaringly, grindingly, screechingly loud, and in moments like this it's hard to think straight.

"Are you okay?" Penny says.

"Yeah," I say. "I was thinking about the, uh, other world."

"The other world," she says, "or the other me?"

"There is no other you anymore."

"But there is. In your memory. I've dated enough boys with ex-girlfriend issues to understand. Women get to be perfect angels or naggy bitches in the memories of the men who loved them. And I'm guessing she never nagged you. She was probably hotter than me too. It's cool, I promise I won't be jealous of myself. I mean, maybe a little . . ."

She comes up close, smiling, playful. But I feel flimsy and unsettled.

"I don't think I'm ready to joke about it yet," I say. "Even if I seem okay."

"I'm sorry," Penny says. "Honestly, I keep expecting you to drop the act and admit this time-traveler thing is totally a bit you do to hook up with chicks and, once you've had enough of me, you'll be going back to your own dimension forever, which basically means you fully ghost me and I never see you again."

"I can't go back even if I wanted to. I don't know how to invent a time machine."

"But if you did, that would mean I'd never be born, right? Me and everyone else."

I think about that thing Penelope told me, how she'd break down tasks into seconds. Does that work with everything? Would it help me forget all the people I erased? Could the steady ticktock rhythm clean away a whole world?

"By the way, I noticed you still haven't said which one of us is hotter."

"You," I say.

"Good answer," she says. "Kiss me a little and maybe I'll even believe it."

We kiss and we walk and we talk. We eat a late lunch, head back to her place, and fall asleep until the afternoon.

It's my favorite day I've ever had. I mean, it's not even close.

When I wake up, Penny lies curled up next to me, still asleep.

She's not Penelope. She's not going to float apart.

79

We lie in bed meandering our way to a decision about dinner when my cell rings. I don't want to answer it, because there's nobody I want to talk to that isn't already lying in Penny's bed, but she gets up to go to the bathroom so I do. I've been avoiding calls from my office for days. I figure maybe if I confirm I'm at least alive, they'll stop bothering me.

But it's a panicky programming assistant on the line, asking where I am. She says they've been trying me for hours and only just discovered that they'd been mixing up my office and cell numbers. She tells me dinner is almost over and my keynote address is scheduled to begin in thirty minutes.

The International Conference on Architecture and Urban Design is this weekend, hosted in Toronto for the first time, and as the local wunderkind I'm supposed to give a speech to open the conference. I agreed to it months ago and I don't know why it wasn't canceled after my hospitalization, but no one told the conference organizers and they're freaking out that I didn't show up to the dinner before-hand, because five hundred architects, urban designers, cultural critics, graduate students, and, well, I don't exactly know who, but five hundred of them are milling around outside the auditorium waiting to hear my talk.

I have *nothing* to say to five hundred architecture nerds. But some pushy rattle in my subconscious tells me this is important to John, so, even though I don't want to be John, I tell the person on the line

that John will be there at the scheduled start time. I explain the situation to Penny and I can tell she suspects this might be a ruse to
disappear now that I've slept with her four times in the past eighteen
hours, so I invite her to join me and we have our first shower together
and, yeah, I *really* don't want to leave that shower stall, but she's
suddenly all business, slipping on a lovely little dress and fixing on
makeup while I shave with the razor she uses on her legs and armpits.

We catch a taxi to my place and leave the meter running while I
hurl myself into a suit and let her look around a bit. She ties my tie
and it feels so intimate I almost cry. She smiles at me, warm and
curious at the same time, and I think it's that smile that gives me the
balls to do what I do next.

80

I have nothing planned for this crowd of probably very smart, very talented people who are no doubt wondering if the fuss about me—him, John—is remotely worth it and of course it definitely is not.

Conference organizers cluster around me as I walk into the auditorium holding hands with Penny, asking if I brought any audiovisual aids. I look around the venue with its five hundred full seats and its tiny lectern set before curtains closed over massive floor-to-ceiling windows and my mind is devoid of human thought. Every molecule of liquid in my body squeezes out of my sweat glands. There's a flittering, sooty sensation in my throat that feels like I swallowed a cloud of moths.

I notice a crack between the curtains, like whoever shut them neglected to give the cord a last tug. The auditorium is on the top floor of a tower by the lake and through the crack I see a sliver of the city skyline. I ask for a marker, something I can sketch with, and pull open the curtains, revealing the view of the city. A programming assistant scrambles over with a thick felt-tip permanent marker. I uncap it and, with the full-bore gaze of five hundred people on the back of my head, start to draw right onto the window.

What I draw is the city as I remember it, not as it looks here. My skyline, not this skyline. It's a strange cognitive experience because I *can't* draw, but John can, so I'm teetering between the two of us, his talent and my memory. I sketch out the city as it should be. The room is quiet, some soft murmurs and throat clearing, but no one calls out, like, *stop drawing on the window, idiot.* So I keep going until I've completed the skyline that's supposed to be there. Only then do I face the crowd.

"We are failures," I say. "We've failed ourselves and we've failed the world. Architecture is the art we live in. And we could be living in miracles. Instead of dull boxes. Instead of geometry. We, in this room, make the frame that the world looks through to see its own reflection. And if the world has not provided us the materials we need to unbind our imaginations, we must demand it. Everything that we need to reimagine this city, every city, to redefine how human beings live on this planet, it's all possible. No idea is impossible. All we need is infrastructure. But are we inspiring the material world to chase our grand visions? Or are we letting infrastructure shackle us? You fail yourself, you fail the world, you fail the future, you fail whoever looks out the window to see what we as a civilization are capable of. Look out that window at the story we've told. Is that a story you're proud to tell? Think about what you tried to build today and ask yourself if it will change this world into the one we need. If not, why not? Start again. These are not buildings. They are monuments to the future we deserve."

I'm supposed to talk for an hour, and that's, like, maybe two minutes. But it's all I've got, so I put the cap on the marker, throw it to the wide-eyed programming assistant, take Penny by the hand, and walk out of the auditorium, letting the heavy wood doors swoop closed behind me.

As we wait for the elevator, it sounds like they're destroying the auditorium, ripping out the seats bolted to the floor with their bare hands and hurling them against the walls. Later someone tells me that's just the sound of five hundred people applauding.

81

Just to be clear, I don't think my speech was all that applause-worthy. My wild skyline drawing was dramatic, and people were surprised I called them all failures, and everyone likes to be told their profession sets the tone for the whole world, but I can't tell if people applauded because they were inspired or provoked by what I said, or if mob logic just peer-pressured the rest of them into joining in once the first person clapped.

Whatever the reason, the speech made the cover of the *Toronto Star* newspaper the next day, with my window drawing reproduced above the fold. Countless hastily posted online think pieces followed in prompt succession, pro-and-conning me, the speech, the skyline, architecture as a profession, and various tangential subjects cooked up by journalists needy for something to write about so they can get paid, late and badly.

I got a lot of interview requests and my office fielded a flood of calls looking for me to bid on new projects, and apparently I only boosted the swirl of intrigue by refusing to say anything more. This wasn't a public relations strategy. I was in bed with Penny and I never wanted to leave.

So. Maybe right now you're thinking—okay, why isn't this story over? Everything kind of worked out for this jackass. His mom is alive, his dad is nice, his sister is cool, his career is on fire, and he's actually involved with the woman he obsessed over in his other life—why would he want to go back to a world where his mom's dead, his dad's an asshole, his sister never existed, he has no professional accomplishments, and the woman he loved killed herself?

And I get that, trust me, it's more or less *all* I'm thinking about. Despite an edgy sense of loyalty to my timeline and compassion for humanity as a species being stranded on this sad, broken planet, *my* life is much better.

Except that it's not my life. It's *his* life, John's. The longer I stay here, the less I'm me and the more I'm him and I understand it's hard to relate to what it feels like to have your consciousness subsumed into its own warped mirror, but let me tell you—it's goddamn horrifying. It's burning to death in the flames of your own mind. It's being eaten alive by alien memories that have taken root inside you, devouring everything that makes you who you are and spitting out someone else right into your own brain. Think about the mass of information packed into the dense, wet folds of your mind, every memory and opinion and impulse, uncountable coiling trails of identity both grand and trivial. Now double them in the same humid box and shake them together and force them to fight. John's mind is like a sickness that my mind is trying to ward off with the antibodies of what I know to be true, my memories, my opinions, my impulses, my grand and trivial humiliations and delights. Except the truth is—*I'm* the cancer. I'm the virus trying to colonize John, not the other way around. He's waging a desperate battle to regain control of his own thoughts and I'm the interloper who somehow escaped his dreams and perverted his consciousness.

Maybe this is what it feels like to go crazy. Every happy moment is compromised by cold fingers around my ankles, trying to drag me into a yawning maw of loss and fear and shame. It would be easier to let go and be John. And I've always been one to take the easy way out.

It feels like I've been rewarded for destroying the world. The only reason I still feel like myself, like Tom, is a throbbing low-grade ache that says—you should be *punished* for what you did. You're not allowed to be happy. Everything you touch will turn to ash. Everyone you love will be swarmed with darkness. You must be held accountable for your crimes, even if the only one capable of passing judgment is you.

82

The staff of Barren & Associates waits for me in the conference room. After I ignored their messages for another week, while Penny and I cloistered ourselves in each other, they threatened to convene the meeting at my condo if I didn't come to work today. I step up to the glass door and wait for it to slide open, like doors are supposed to, but it doesn't because there's a handle to turn, even though the technology already exists for doors to just open automatically. Do you have any idea of the germ count on the typical doorknob? Your exposure to microorganic pathogens would be no worse if you wiped your hand all around the inside of a public toilet.

My fifteen employees start applauding and flexing their zygomaticus muscles to bare their teeth and gums, which makes me recoil until I realize they're *smiling* at me. On a conference table made from a slab of maple tree encased in a cube of transparent epoxy are stacked several copies of the *Toronto Star* with my sketch on the cover. I'm getting better at plucking information from John's memory, so I recall the one guy who isn't clapping, a decade my senior, is named Stewart and he's the firm's operations manager.

"We've had so many calls about your speech that I had to put the interns on the phones to keep up," Stewart says.

"That's, uh, good," I say. "Isn't it?"

"Look, we all knew what we were signing up for when we came to work for you," Stewart says. "You are the Barren. We are the Associates. But we spent weeks on that speech. As a *team*. Not just on the visual presentation. On the text. The references. The research. This was supposed to be the *firm's* introduction to the international community. You didn't use a word of what we all agreed you'd say. You didn't even acknowledge us sitting there in the audience. It was supposed to be a big night for the rest of us too. And, by the way, the conference is making us pay to replace the glass you defaced."

I get the impression this is a huge moment for Stewart, a boil that needs to be lanced. *My* immediate reaction is to get the hell out of here and never come back. I'd rather throw myself through that window I drew on and plunge to my death than deal with office politics. I've never been in charge of anything before and it's a measure of the grasping alarm I feel that the only thing I can think to ask myself is—what would my *father* do in this situation?

"Tell the conference organizers we're happy to pay for the window as long as it's removed without damaging my sketch," I say. "We're going to hang it right here in our office, so it's the first thing anyone sees when they walk in. Now, there were five hundred people at the speech, right? And how many people read this newspaper?"

One of the associates pulls up the information on her cell and shows it to Stewart.

"Three hundred thousand on weekdays," he says. "Five hundred thousand on weekends."

"Tell them I'll expand on my speech in an exclusive for their weekend edition. They can publish what I was supposed to say with all the images I was supposed to show. Five hundred people in a room versus five hundred thousand people in a city. Even more online."

"With your name on it, of course."

"With all our names on it. They can say Tom Barren in the headline, but we'll insist everyone who worked on the material is credited."

"Did you just say . . . *Tom* Barren?"

"No," I say. "Did I? I don't think so. Anyway, I'm sorry if I screwed up."

"You're . . . apologizing," he says.

"Yeah," I say.

"I've never heard you apologize to anyone. Has he ever apologized to anyone?"

The associates all shake their heads, mute, riveted.

"John, we're *worried* about you," he says. "You were in the hospital. One minute you're ordering around the foreman and complaining about the client's lack of vision, the next you're writhing around in the mud. I'm the one who called the ambulance."

"I'm fine," I say.

"All of us left very good jobs at very good firms to work for you because we believe you see the future of architecture the way nobody else does. But that means we can't do this without you. If you're having health issues, we respect your privacy. We're just asking you to trust us with what's going on."

"I don't know," I say.

"You don't know," says Stewart. "Okay, well, that's the other thing I've never heard you say. You *always* know. You're the most arrogant know-it-all son of a bitch I've ever met."

My brain feels swollen, like it's trying to push out of my ears and find a more hospitable residence. I press my forehead against the table's cool, epoxied surface. I can feel the sweat trickling from my armpits down along my rib cage. I've spent my whole life deliberately avoiding situations in which anyone looks to me for answers.

"You're right," I say. "I do know. I know what every building in this city should look like. What every city on this planet should look like. We're so far away from where we should be. But it's too much. I can't fix the whole world."

"John, nobody expects you to," Stewart says.

"I'm taking an indefinite leave of absence," I say. "Starting today."

"What are you talking about?" Stewart says. "We've got half a dozen projects in process. Hundreds of commission opportunities have come in since your speech. The concert hall in Chicago. We promised to deliver your initial concept next week."

"I'll come in on the weekend and finish the design. Put anything that needs my signature on my desk and I'll sign it. After that, you're on your own."

On the way out, I forget the door doesn't open automatically so I smack my nose against it, hard enough to rupture blood vessels in my anterior nasal septum. I leave a streak of blood on the glass and don't look back. My head throbs with pain and something else—a slithering coil of anger buried too deep to slow me down. I know I'm destroying everything John built, but I don't care because it's all a lie. I'm not a genius or a visionary or a leader or whatever else these people have deluded themselves into believing. I'm not and have never been anything at all.

83

Penny actually gasps when she walks into my parents' house and sees their elaborate, fetishized book collection. My mom immediately recognizes a kindred spirit and in less than sixty seconds they're debating the merits of various Victorian binding procedures and I accept that I'm done for—I won't say anything anyone finds remotely interesting for the rest of the evening.

It gets worse over dinner, some eccentric ratatouille recipe my dad picked up at a conference in Toulouse, when Penny asks about his book on time travel. Greta groans like a teenager and my dad flushes, trying to parse if she's making fun of him. Penny tells him she's a lifelong speculative-fiction fan and would love to know more about his views on the topic.

That's all my dad needs—that and two glasses of pinot noir—to launch into his adolescent obsession and secret shame, prone to whispering key terms as if saying them at full volume would bring the Science Police crashing through the front door to arrest him for Crimes Against Serious Physics. In the other world, my father spoke with arrogant bombast and squinty, patronizing boredom, like he knew everything he said was fascinating and important but the mental energy required to dumb it down enough for anyone other than him to understand wasn't really worth the effort. Here, my dad is delighted to even be asked, since his colleagues continue to rib him about his book years after it was published to zero acclaim and total neglect by the general public.

My dad's book was a breezy analysis of why time travel, as depicted in mainstream entertainment, doesn't make scientific, technical, or logistic sense. But tucked between the zippy puns and pop-culture references was a sincere exploration of how it possibly *might* work, which was of course the thing my dad continued to ponder even though he knew it could lead only to professional embarrassment and academic censure if he dared to speak his theories aloud in distinguished company or, worse, commit them to publication.

But around the dinner table—while I sop up the remains of the ratatouille with crusty spelt bread and my mom takes the dessert she baked out of the oven and my sister opens another bottle of pinot noir and Penny listens to my dad with guileless interest while her foot occasionally presses down on mine under the table—he can speak openly without fear of any ridicule more acrid than the exasperated sighs Greta doesn't bother to conceal as she accidentally splits half the cork into the bottle because her fine motor skills decrease exponentially with each glass of wine. I watch, amused, as Greta pours herself a glass flecked with bobbing cork bits and picks them out with her thumb. She looks at me and shrugs and I feel blown through with love for her.

I catch my mom's eye as she glances over from the kitchen, sprinkling powdered sugar on the dessert. She gives a little nod of approval in Penny's vicinity.

This is what I'm talking about. This is the happiness I don't deserve. Not after what I did. This pleasant family moment is a piece of cork floating in a sea of blood.

84

My mom comes out of the kitchen with an antique porcelain platter that belonged to her grandmother, the border an azure geometric pattern laced with gold filigree.

On it are a dozen lemon tarts.

"I made your favorite," my mom says.

My internal organs clench, a cold, sick sweat worming from my pores. I must look visibly stricken, because my mom hesitates before placing them on the table.

"Wow," says Greta. "The fancy platter."

"What's wrong?" says my mom.

"Nothing," I say.

"They look delicious," says Penny.

"It's my grandmother's recipe," my mom says. "I make them every year for John's birthday. Right before he turned five he announced he *hated* birthday cake . . ."

"At which point you should've used corporal punishment till he came to his senses," says Greta. "How can a human being not like birthday cake?"

"So, I started making him lemon tarts," my mom says. "One for every year."

"Which was an adorable tradition when he was five," says Greta, "but less so at age thirty-two. He probably eats one and throws the rest away."

"He does not," says my mom. "You don't throw them away, do you?"

"John, are you feeling okay?" my dad says. "You look pale."

My mother was dead, torn in half by a flying car, and now she's alive, looking exactly the same except her posture is better, holding a platter of the lemon tarts I was never going to taste again.

"I'm great," I say. "Thanks for making them."

I pick up a lemon tart. It tastes the same as the ones from my world. Collapsing the sensory boundary between realities is too much for any pastry to bear. I reach for the wine bottle. And I drink.

I drink because of course I like perfect avocados and waking up into my own dreams and jet packs being a completely reasonable teenage birthday gift and clean air and global peace but I am in no way selfless—I'm happier here with my mom and dad and Greta and Penny than I ever was back there, a place that's already getting gauzy and frail in my memory. Except there's Deisha. And Xiao and Asher. And Hester and Megan and Tabitha. And the chrononauts and understudies from my father's lab and my coworkers and classmates and Robin Swelter and her parents and her brother who punched me and the kids who helped me that time I ran away and the girls who hooked up with me when I came back to school and the billions of unborn strangers I never even met and if I ever forgive myself for taking their lives away from them it'll be the exact moment they're all lost forever.

85

My dad's opening gambit is to explain why most time-travel models in popular culture don't work: because the Earth moves.

I already summed this up in chapter 4, but if you skipped that part, okay, the Earth spins on its axis—we call that a *day*—while also rotating around the Sun—we call that a *year*—which is also moving through the solar system, which is also moving through the galaxy, which is also moving through the universe, which may well be moving through the multiverse. We have no words for those movements because the patterns are too vast to calculate with our current tools. It's immanently probable there's a clockwork charm to the whole mess but all we can see is the lonely tip of the smallest hand on the infinite watch face of reality.

The Earth travels through space, really fast, nonstop, every day. In the three and a half seconds it takes you to read this sentence, the planet spun a mile on its axis. Time travel isn't just going back in time—it's also leaping vast distances of space and landing in a hyper-specific location so you don't materialize *inside* something. Either the time traveler must be immaterial or the location must be empty at a molecular level, because one stray particle in your brain could kill you.

Penny delights my dad by knowing way more about this stuff than anyone could reasonably expect. They spend dessert discussing the merits of creating a vacuum-sealable pod, powered by a nuclear engine that emits a trackable half-life frequency, so if time travel is ever mastered in the future there would be a safe place for time travelers to arrive and a direct path for them to follow. Theoretically, it could prove time travel is possible because if such a pod were built presumably someone from the future would immediately appear as soon as it's activated—the ultimate *if you build it, they will come* according to my dad.

Feeling festive, my dad digs out a dusty bottle of small-batch bourbon from a kitchen cupboard and pours glasses for everyone. My mom looks oddly jealous, like she assumed that after dinner she'd get to drag Penny away to show off more gems from her book collection, but somehow my dad got his hooks in and won't let go. She makes a few attempts to steer the conversation back to nineteenth-century literature via H. G. Wells's *The Time Machine*, but my dad keeps a firm hand on the conversational wheel. It's a character trait my mom's not used to over here, but I recognize it as the softest possible iteration of the man he's supposed to be. I feel an uncomfortable pang of homesickness.

Greta's had a few too many glasses of wine and she lies down on the couch, while Penny and my dad discuss Novikov's self-consistency principle—that there's only one causally rigid reality and anything a time traveler might do in the past has always already happened, so there's no way to change the present timeline. I snort into my second glass of bourbon, because clearly Novikov didn't know what the hell he was talking about.

Penny and my dad work their way through branching universes and timeline corruption, causal loops and the self-healing reality hypothesis. Greta naps. My mom does the dishes. I drink too much bourbon. I feel like I haven't spoken in hours, although it's probably more like twenty minutes. But when they segue into temporal merging, I make the catastrophic decision to pipe up.

"What about temporal drag?" I say.

"Sorry, what?" my dad says, squinting at me.

"I go back in time to before I was born," I say, "and, I don't know, accidentally change the past. What if I'm never conceived? What if

I'm born but I'm not the same person, even at the most minute genetic level? Wouldn't I *have* to exist in the altered reality in order to have gone back in time to cause the change?"

Penny looks unsure, like maybe she should be tense or maybe she should be glad I'm engaging with my dad on the thorny topic that hangs over my life, and now hers.

"Well, yes," my dad says, "that's sort of what temporal merging suggests. There aren't multiple simultaneous dimensions, just one coherent reality, so causal changes in the past ripple through the timeline to resolve paradoxes. But the mechanisms that might make such a thing possible are hazy. Is there a kind of chronal energy that accumulates and releases in the event of a paradox, like a nuclear reaction? And, if so, why would it be oriented to resolving temporal paradoxes here on Earth, when we exist in a cosmic metasystem far grander than the inconsequential life of one particular human being? This kind of thing quickly descends into some vast intelligence guiding events and unknotting conflicts, which gets a bit theological for my taste."

"I'm not talking about god," I say. "I'm talking about what actually happens."

"I didn't know you were interested in this stuff," he says. "When did you even read my book?"

"This has been such a lovely night," Penny says. "But it's getting late. Thank you so much for inviting me . . ."

Penny presses her foot onto mine, hard. My mom looks out from the kitchen, wiping her hands on a dish towel.

"I'll be right there," my mom says. "I need to moisturize as soon as I finish the dishes or my hands get dry."

"Fundamentally, there's no way for us to know," my dad says.

"No," I say, "*this* is what happens. When a time traveler changes the past before they're alive, they become a temporal anchor. Subsequent events fall into place to make sure that they're born."

"Isn't that just a causal loop?" he says.

"No, because when they return to the present," I say, "everything could be radically different. You could be a disgraced genius, mom could be dead, Greta could've never been born, I could be an embarrassing screw-up . . ."

"*John*," Penny says.

"My name could be different," I say. "I could be Tom instead of John but still be the exact same person, I mean, genetically. If I traveled back and then returned to a changed present, the fact of my existence swimming up the time stream would require events to line up in a way that ensures I'm alive to receive my consciousness in the present. I'm the temporal anchor and the ripple effect through time is temporal drag."

I fill a glass with the resiny bourbon. Then, to demonstrate, I pour it into another glass. My dad leans back, engaged but skeptical.

"So, what," he says, "the liquid is supposed to be your mind and the glasses are different realities? It sounds too New Agey for me. Consciousness moving between timelines. Would the version of you in the changed present have your memories from the original reality?"

"Yes," I say, "but he'd think of them as dreams. Or an overactive childhood imagination. He'd have a vague sense of unease, that he doesn't belong here, that this isn't the way things are supposed to be. It would be chalked up as just his personality. Maybe the few people he allows himself to get close to secretly worry he suffers from some social disorder or an undiagnosed coordinate on the autism spectrum. But he seems otherwise functional, even capable in certain ways, so they tamp down those worries and do their best to keep him emotionally connected to them. And it would continue like that until the two timelines sync up at the moment the original version of him, the *real* him, returns from the past. In that moment, the other consciousness would overwhelm his mind and take control. He'd be flooded with memories of another life in a very different world. His brain would feel like it's constantly at war, twin versions of himself wrestling for dominance, each seeing the other as an existential threat. Because it is."

Everyone has gotten quiet. My mom stands in the kitchen door-way, chewing a fingernail. My dad stays very still. Penny stares at the intricate pattern on the tablecloth. Greta sits up on the couch. I finish my bourbon and the empty glass smacks against the table a bit too hard.

"Dude," Greta says, "are you going completely fucking crazy? You can tell us. We love you and we're here to help."

"I'm just talking, like, hypothetically," I say.

"Bullshit," says Greta. "This is all that stuff from your novel. Or what you call your novel. John, do you actually think this is happening to you?"

I look at Greta, and I look at my mom, and I look at my dad, and I look at Penny.

"My name's not John," I say.

86

There's a long, sour pause. I feel spinny from the wine and the bourbon, and the total inappropriateness of my outburst starts to weigh on my chest like a freezer full of body parts, especially since this had been more or less the greatest introduction of a girlfriend to parents in the history of girlfriends and parents.

"You sound like a paranoid schizophrenic," my sister says. "You get that, right?"

"Theoretically speaking," my dad says, "what he's saying is possible. Simultaneous consciousnesses within a single corporeal form, I mean."

"Victor, this isn't an amusing scientific debate," my mom says. "It's our son."

"Sorry," says my dad.

"John," my mom says, "and I assure you that your name *is* John because that's what we called you when you ejected from my uterus, you've had some kind of neurological trauma that the doctors were either too incompetent or too overworked to identify. I should've spoken to Rogier Ames as soon as this happened. He heads the university's Neurology Department and he owes me a favor because of some finicky library acquisitions I assisted him with. Yvette Magwood, too, she's dean of medicine. We'll help you through this, I promise."

I press on my temples with stiff forefingers. *Why* did I say anything? My chair feels like it's bobbing in an ocean of shame and regret and I grip the table for balance.

"Guys, it's fine," I say. "I drank too much. I made a bad joke. This is why people shouldn't drink with their parents. I'm sorry if I worried you. Everything's okay."

"You think I don't know when you're lying?" Greta says. "You're the idiot who taught me how to lie when I was five years old and broke Dad's desk lamp."

"That was *you*?" my dad says.

"I'll call them first thing in the morning," my mom says.

"I have some contacts too," my dad says. "Maybe in Cognitive Science?"

"What if it's true?" Penny says.

There's another pause, but this one's a lot edgier.

"I knew it," says Greta. "I knew you couldn't be so perfect. You're an enabler."

"Penny," my mom says, "you seem like a lovely young woman. Let's not spoil that impression."

"I don't presume to know John as well as you do," Penny says. "I only met him two weeks ago when he walked into my store and told me what is without a doubt the weirdest story I've ever heard. I can't rationally explain any of the things he said to me. But you know what else I can't rationally explain? How he makes me feel. I'm a basically normal person. I've lived a basically normal life. I've had good things happen and bad things happen, but very few crazy things happen. I didn't ask for him to walk into my life. I didn't ask to fall in love with him. But I did. And I haven't even said that to him yet. Which makes it so much more awkward that I just said it in front of all of you. Shit. I've been in love before. I almost got married once. But it's never felt like this. Like I don't know what's up or down."

"It's easy to know what's up and down," Greta says. "You just open your eyes."

"You think I don't know how corny this sounds?" Penny says. "You think I like feeling this corny?"

"I can't answer that," Greta says. "I don't know you."

"Well, it's scary," Penny says. "Especially when he may or may not be completely psychotic."

"He's not psychotic," my mom says.

"Mom, he thinks he's from the future," says Greta.

"Not the future," says Penny. "An alternate timeline."

"What's the difference?" Greta says.

"You should've read my book," my dad says.

"Dad, *nobody* read your book," Greta says.

"I don't want him to be telling the truth," Penny says. "It's weird and it's messy and it freaks me out. But I'm taking it seriously so I can understand where he's coming from. Because, I know it sounds demented, but what if it's true?"

"You're right," says Greta, "it sounds demented."

"Mr. Barren," Penny says, "you're as close as we're going to come to an expert in time travel . . ."

"Exactly," says my mom. "How convenient that his elaborate fantasy world just *happens* to involve time travel, considering his father wouldn't shut up about it all through his childhood."

"You told me to write the book," my dad says.

"I thought you should get it out of your system," my mom says.

"You knew it would humiliate me," says my dad. "And hold back my career. So you could be the successful one and I could be your abashed consort."

"I didn't know it would be a bad book about time travel, Victor," says my mom. "I thought it would be a *good* book about time travel."

"Okay," I say. "That's enough! Everybody stop talking!"

My family looks at me like it's possible I'm about to fly into a berserker rage and murder them with my dessert fork. Penny just looks worried.

"Maybe I have lost my mind," I say. "It feels that way sometimes. But most of the time it feels like the world has lost its mind and I'm the only one keeping it together. And I realize that doesn't make me sound *less* crazy. So, how about this. Mom, you can call your expert friends in the morning. Greta, you can make snarky comments to keep the mood light. And, Dad, you can quiz me."

"Quiz you how?" my dad says.

"Ask me anything," I say. "About time travel and alternate dimensions, whatever seems relevant or, I don't know, even irrelevant. I don't claim to understand everything I've experienced, but I'll do my best to answer."

"What can I do?" Penny says.

"You can marry me," I say.

"What?" she says.

"The fact that you don't immediately think I'm a lunatic," I say, "is only the foyer of the palace that is all the reasons you're the most amazing person I've ever met."

"Oh, for fuck's sake," Greta says.

"Well, this is *exactly* how I imagined this happening," my mom says.

"This has been the most interesting family dinner I can remember," my dad says.

"Penny, I think you should say yes," I say.

"No," she says.

"Really?" I say.

"Okay, *maybe*," Penny says. "I don't know. I can't answer that question right now. Fine, probably. Assuming we sort all this out in a way that doesn't involve you being committed to a high-security mental facility, which is a kind of big assumption under the circumstances, it's possible I may decide to spend the rest of my life with you. But that's not a yes. That's definitely probably not a yes."

"Okay," I say.

"Should we start the quiz?" my dad says.

87

My sister is the one who's supposed to be having the nervous breakdown. My parents weren't concerned about me at all until I collapsed in a torrent of curses in the construction-site mud.

At McGill University in Montréal, Greta did a double major in philosophy and computer science, which required her to field approximately 1,000,000,000,000,000,000,000 lame jokes from lame guys at lame bars. The Venn diagram of datable non-idiots pooled between philosophy and computer science majors was anaerobic, or so claimed Greta to explain why she spent so much of her free time working on a smartphone application, which she eventually pitched to her dual-discipline thesis advisers as her field-integrating graduate thesis, allowing her to then spend *all* her time on it.

Greta has a simple philosophy of life—You Believe What You Do.

Make a list of what you believe in. The top ten most important things to you. Like . . . justice, equality, diversity, sustainability, whatever your politics or religion or morality. Sit down and bullet-point it out. *This* is what I believe in.

But Greta thinks—bullshit. Make another list. A list of what you did today. It doesn't matter what day it is, weekday, weekend, holiday, birthday, the calendar date is irrelevant. Write down all the things that occupied your time on a given day. Woke up, ate breakfast, hit the gym, went to work, surfed the Internet, had a coffee with a colleague, did some work, ate some lunch, did some more work, slipped out to buy new sneakers, clicked around on social media sites, went home, called a parent, watched TV, ate dinner, changed outfits, met someone for a drink, made out with them on a street corner, caught a taxi home, read a book, went to sleep.

That's what you believe in. According to Greta, your belief system is how you actually spend your time every day. She doesn't mean that to be judgmental. She wants people to be more self-aware. Fundamentally, she believes in action. If you believe in a bunch of stuff but never act on those beliefs, they don't matter. She wants people to better know themselves so they can better *be* themselves. This is her philosophy of life and it was also the purpose of her smartphone application.

Called "MapU," it tracked integrated device operations to graph a user's daily activity along a series of programmable criteria. The point was to show you who you are by what you do. If you change your daily activity, movements, and durations, the graphs alter to reflect you becoming more consistent with who you believe yourself to be.

She launched the app for public download the day she graduated and, since it was a school project, gave it away for free. Within a year, 2,000,000 people downloaded it. It was a hit. But it generated no income and the server space needed to store all the data was expensive and growing exponentially as she added hundreds of thousands of new users per month. She coasted for a while on an academic grant, but Greta never meant for the app to be a job—it was an experiment. She just liked tinkering under the hood in a place where design met ethics.

So when she hit 5,000,000 users and got an offer to buy the app, Greta thought it was hilarious. It was a free product. A hobby. A money drain. She named an absurd price and she promptly lawyered up when they agreed to it. Greta assumed the whole thing was a mistake, that eventually someone would run the numbers and realize this was a student project that had somehow caught a minor social media wave and would soon flame out. But there she was, pen in hand, signing a piece of paper that made her spontaneously rich.

It had to be a prank. These people must be morons who deserved to be relieved of their one and a half million dollars. Greta signed.

It took her a week to realize the morons were smarter than she was.

They didn't care about her app and they certainly didn't give a shit about her philosophy. They wanted her data: 5,000,000 people, half a million more every month, voluntarily giving them real-time access to their movements, habits, proclivities, and purchases. Greta had unwittingly built a brilliant machine to parse a human being into the things they can be sold. And that's what the buyer wanted—to sell them things.

She considered unleashing a virus to cook the whole system, but that seemed hokey and adolescent and she didn't want to go to jail. Our parents had spent their careers in academia. Tenure had been a very big deal to both of them. We grew up comfortable but not so insulated from want that the money didn't matter. It mattered.

So, Greta became wealthy and depressed—small-*d* depressed—and hasn't really done *anything* for the past six months except cause my parents considerable anxiety. She was simultaneously the family success story and the greatest concern. Until I made a bold play over dinner for the title of Most Screwed-Up Barren Child.

88

I haven't stayed up all night with my parents since the time Greta got meningitis in seventh grade.

My dad carefully and systematically runs through every question he can think of and I answer in as much detail as I can muster, while Greta sullenly clicks away on a laptop trying to corroborate or, preferably, eviscerate any specifics, demanding the occasional snarky clarification on matters she deems logically inconsistent and then pouting when I turn out to have an explanation. My mom makes a pot of coffee and sits on the couch primly rereading *The Time Machine* with what I guess you could call passive-aggressive literary exasperation. Penny sits next to me and periodically reminds me of an embellishment I'd mentioned to her earlier but neglected under paternal interrogation. Over the course of several hours, the full story comes out.

Everyone simultaneously runs out of steam just as dawn smears across the sky.

"Well," my dad says, "for a schizoid delusion, it's certainly operating at a high level of forensic detail."

The real bonanza turns out to be the Sixteen Witnesses. I remember all of their names and a few of them are still alive. Even those who died many years ago left some sort of an online trail. On her laptop, Greta finds them one by one—Henrik Adell (Skeptical), Norman Driessnack (Awed), Sven Bertelessen (Distracted), Rhys Collins

(Amused), Jerome Francoeur (Jealous), Michel Beaubien (Angry), Susan Lowenstein (Thoughtful), Stephen Modesto (Frightened), Douglas Halliday (Detached), Abe Geller (Concerned), Diane Ortiz (Excited), Frederic Somerset (Nonchalant), Richard Ellesmere (Harried), Barbra Talbert (Weary), Ursula Francoeur (Cheeky), and Rafael Ubitto (Wise).

The only one who eludes Greta's considerable research skills—she took three semesters of information science—is Lionel Goettreider. She can't dig up a single mention of him *anywhere*.

But she does find the Francoeurs.

"Jerome and Ursula Francoeur," Greta says. "They live in San Francisco."

"They're alive?" I say.

"Yeah," says Greta. "No, wait . . . Ursula Francoeur died two years ago. Survived by her husband, Jerome, and her daughter, Emma."

Her tone is matter-of-fact, since she doesn't know these people and thinks I'm using them to prop up my psychosis, but it hits me like a punch to the chest.

I guess I had this idea, ridiculous and romantic, that a consequence of excavating this lost and forgotten past event would be to finally bring Lionel and Ursula together. I have no idea what actually happened between the two of them following the accident, but I imagined—and I should clarify that I didn't spend *a lot* of time imagining this—that after her husband's terrible injury, Ursula would've felt honor bound to stay with him and conceal her affair with Lionel, like, forever. Somehow, and the particulars are hazy and embarrassing to contemplate in too much detail, but somehow my involvement would inspire them to admit the truth, that they never stopped loving each other and that to be truly happy they needed to be together for whatever was left of their lives.

I don't know why I got so invested in their relationship, considering I witnessed it for all of five minutes, fifty years ago—although only two weeks ago in terms of my chronological experience—and for all I know it was dysfunctional and doomed and they were better off without each other. But I don't think so. I saw something in the way they looked at each other, something powerful and connected. Penelope and I never looked at each other that way. But it's what I feel when I look at Penny and she looks at me.

If I hadn't intervened, they both would've died of radiation poisoning five decades ago. But I did intervene. And I was convinced, with zero concrete information except my dull and grasping heart, that my intervention led to their estrangement in separate but equally unhappy lives that they never should've had. Decades of longing and loss between them was my fault, is what I thought.

Except Ursula is dead. And so is yet another of my romantic delusions.

Rest in peace.

89

My mom slaps shut her book. It's a vintage edition, made of sturdy materials, so the cover gives a crisp bark.

"I don't understand," she says.

Everyone in the room except Penny knows that specific tenor to my mom's intonation means she understands with absolute clarity. And Penny catches on pretty fast.

"What do you want?" my mom says. "To go back, is that it? To a world where you're a *mess*, where Penny *doesn't* love you, where Greta doesn't *exist*, where your father is *ruined*, where I'm *dead*? That's what you'd prefer?"

"Who here thinks she wouldn't even be all that worked up about the other reality if she was alive in it and not some self-annihilating retro housewife?" Greta says.

"There is no reality in which I resemble the sad concoction your brother has cooked up in his febrile imagination," my mom says. "I don't know *what* I did to inspire such an offensive caricature of essentially everything I consider worthwhile about myself as a woman, a mother, a feminist, an academic, a . . . well, everything. But clearly I have failed as a maternal role model if that's how you think of me."

"Rebecca, my love," my dad says, "are you sure you're not just mad because I'm the more successful one over there?"

"Over *where*?" my mom says. "In his delusion, Victor? Because it sounds to me like you're a smothering, detached prick *over there*."

"So you were listening," he says.

"Intermittently, yes," she says.

"At least you *exist*, dude," Greta says.

"I understand," Penny says, "that maybe it all seems like hostile character assassination to you, but how does that explain me? I mean, we'd never met before. Why would he construct this elaborate back-story for someone he's never met?"

"You don't know that for sure," Greta says. "Maybe he browsed in your bookstore and developed some loony obsession with you that he embroidered into a fully fledged persona. It's pretty convenient that every single detail about you is different because you're literally a whole other person in this other reality, except you have the same name. Maybe he's not just crazy. Maybe he's also a terrible judge of character."

"So, after everything you've heard tonight, you don't believe him," Penny says.

"I'm in favor of whatever reality I get to exist in, okay?" Greta says. "I'm pro–me existing and anti–me not existing."

"Look," I say, "assuming for a moment that I'm clinically . . . let's call it *nuts*. I've lost it. The other reality is a projection of my damaged brain and those versions of Mom and Dad reflect my sub-conscious way to punish them or whatever. You too, Greta. I deleted you from existence because, I don't know, I'm still mad about the time Dad let us watch *The Blob* and you melted all my G.I. Joes into a single monstrous creature."

"Oh my god," Greta says, "you never even played with those dolls anymore."

"Not dolls," I say. "*Action figures.* And that doesn't mean I wanted you to melt them into a twisted mass that would haunt my childhood dreams."

"I thought you didn't remember *John's* memories," my mom says.

"No, I do," I say. "They're, like, simultaneous with my actual . . . with my *other* memories. That's part of the problem. There are so many memories stuffed in my brain, it feels like it's going to hemorrhage."

"What were you saying, though?" my dad says. "About assuming for a moment?"

"Right," I say. "Assuming I am crazy and this is a delusion, fine, but why would it involve all these people? The Sixteen Witnesses. Ursula and Jerome Francoeur. Lionel Goettreider. How could I possibly know about them?"

My dad gets up and leaves the room. I figure he's going to the bathroom, since he hasn't left the dining room table in about five hours.

"Jerome Francoeur was a big deal, sort of," Greta says. "Science adviser to three American presidents. On tons of boards of directors and science-prize juries. He was the president of Stanford University. Ursula Francoeur was one of the first tenured female physics professors in North America and the first to head the Physics Department at Stanford. She published extensively, more obscure science journal stuff, but a few general public books too. I mean, in the seventies, but still . . ."

"But still *what*?" I say. "How would I know who they even are?"

My dad comes back in, impassive, and lays a book on the table in front of me. It's called *The Atomic Puzzle*—by Ursula Francoeur, published in 1973. On the back of the weathered green fabric cover is a black-and-white photo of Ursula and Jerome and a little girl, Emma Francoeur, with their 1970s hair and 1970s clothes and 1970s smiles.

"I've had this book in my office since before you were born," he says.

"I've never seen that book," I say. "I don't remember it."

"Sweetheart," my mom says, "you don't know *what* you remember."

Penny looks off-balance, strained. She shakes her head, but I don't know what she's saying no to.

"I get it," I say. "I do. But if I'm crazy, I want to know for sure. Because this doesn't feel like crazy."

"We'll get you whatever help you need," my mom says. "Maybe it's psychological, maybe it's neurological or hormonal or even viral. The brain is a complex thing. The point is you need to accept help."

"I will," I say. "Accept help. After we find Lionel Goettreider."

"The man who doesn't exist," Greta says.

"He does exist," I say. "He might be dead, but he definitely lived."

"It's just a bit . . . convenient," Greta says.

"Stop saying things are convenient," I say. "How is *any* of this convenient?"

"I'm not the one hinging my entire lunatic worldview on this one mysteriously nonexistent guy," Greta says. "Everyone else you mentioned, sure, it's *weird* you know the names of all these random old scientists, but I found them online, so you could have too. But this Goettreider guy. Supposedly the world's smartest man. The genius who changed everything. And yet there's no trace of him. *Nothing.*"

"There must be something," I say. "We can go back to where he was born. In Denmark. Find his birth certificate. He lived in San Francisco. There must be records. He had to have a passport, a driver's license. The accident happened. Even if it was swept under the rug, there must be some evidence, somewhere. The experiment was funded with a federal grant. The US government must have, I don't know, a *receipt.*"

"I'm fairly well-read about this stuff," my dad says. "I've heard of Ursula Francoeur. And some of these others, the sixteen, I recognize their names. But not Lionel Goettreider. I've never heard of him."

"Why don't we get you help first?" my mom says. "Then, if you still *want* to, we can look for this Goettreider person."

"If Lionel Goettreider was forty-two in 1965," Penny says, "then he's ninety-three years old now. There's a slim chance he's even alive. But, if he is, who knows how much longer he'll be around."

"Fine," Greta says, "you want to go looking for someone who doesn't exist, go ahead. But speaking on behalf of people who *do* exist, I think you're wasting your time."

"Where would you even start?" my dad says.

"Isn't it obvious?" Penny says.

Penny flips over the book on the table to show everyone the

photo of the Francoeur family. She points at Jerome Francoeur. Smiling, one arm tight around Ursula's shoulders, protective, maybe a bit too protective. His other arm hangs at his side. The sleeve is neatly clipped just below what should be the elbow. The rest of the arm is gone. Amputated.

"Jerome Francoeur is still alive," Penny says. "Or at least he was when Ursula died two years ago. Whatever happened back in 1965, if there's one man in the world who should remember Lionel Goettreider, it's Jerome Francoeur."

I guess I'm going to San Francisco.

90

My dad absentmindedly picks crumbs off the tablecloth and drops them in a tiny pile in front of him. He doesn't look at anyone. One by one, methodical, meticulous, he gathers the crumbs.

"We need to be careful here," my dad says. "Every family has its own . . . dynamic. Its unique way of handling conflict and crisis. A kind of evolutionary adaptation to its peculiar domestic environment. When you get to the point we're at, four adults, experienced with one another's quirks, that dynamic is fairly stable. Otherwise you don't *get* to where we're at. You get divorce. You get estrangement."

He rakes the pile of crumbs with his fingers, forming an equilateral triangle.

"But there are events in the life of a family," he says, "just like there are events in the life of a species. Extinction-level events. Cataclysms. And you really don't know if the dynamic that's gotten you through so much can handle more than just conflict and crisis. That it can handle cataclysm."

He uses the edge of his palm to shift the triangle of crumbs into a square.

"Our family dynamic works for us," he says. "There are jokes and irony and snark. There is occasionally unguarded sentiment. But it's usually layered with jokes and irony and snark in some sort of emotional tiramisu. I just need us to take this seriously. Because there are things even the closest family can't survive. And we are not the closest family. Mostly because, John, you've always held yourself distant. That's not a criticism. It's an observation."

My dad continues his crumb geometry, squeezing the pile from a square to a circle. He runs his middle finger around the edge, evening it into proportion.

"I don't believe in the truth," he says. "I'm a scientist. I believe in questions and the best answer we have right now. That's all science is. A collection of the best answers we have right now. It's always open to revision. Yesterday's fact is today's question and tomorrow has an answer we don't know yet. What I'm saying is, I believe what you're saying. Insofar as *you* believe what you're saying. I just don't want you to do anything . . . rash. To try to prove to us something that seems essential to you. Please don't keep us outside this."

He scrapes the circular pile of crumbs off the table into his open palm. My dad looks at me, nods, and carries the crumbs into the kitchen to throw them in the trash can under the sink.

91

Greta lies on the couch, eyes closed. I figure she's asleep, but she's not done yet.

"I just find the whole concept a little disingenuous," Greta says. "I don't know, I guess I expected more from you."

"More from me . . . how?" I say.

"It's not that I don't get it," she says. "I get it. *We're* the dystopia. We imagine all these postapocalyptic, class-stratified, new-world-order techno-futures. But actually the real world, the world we live in, this is the dystopia. It's not a totally garbage idea. It's funny-*ish*. It's just that fundamentally your so-called utopia is more of the same crap. This idea that we're in control of the world. When, in fact, all of our attempts to take control of the world and make it do what we want it to do have been, like, abject failures. The world didn't become a total shit hole because we don't have enough control over it. It became a total shit hole because we *tried* to control it."

"Greta," I say, "what does that have to do with anything we're talking about?"

"It's the lie we tell each other all day, every day," she says. "If we can *just keep going,* make our technology good enough, we'll solve all the world's problems, we'll be able to clean up the mess we made, and everything will be perfect. No more pollution or war or inequity or blah blah blah. And it's bullshit. The world was not *given* to us to control. We've deluded ourselves into thinking we can control it. But we can't! In fact, our attempts to control it are what have brought life on this planet to the brink of extinction. And it just pisses me off, these fucking sci-fi allegories where, you know, if we just *stick with the plan,* we'll fix it all and live in a futuristic paradise. When, actually, our one chance at saving our only home in the universe is *quitting* the plan. Because the plan is intrinsically flawed. Human beings are incapable of controlling the world, and believing otherwise is making everything permanently worse. So, I'm sorry, I'm not a literary critic or whatever, but I think you should come up with a better idea for a novel."

"So, you think I'm psychotically deluded *and* I came up with a lousy book idea?"

"Yeah," she says.

"You say you know me, Greta, better than anyone, and you probably do. So, you tell me, am I the brother you've known your whole life? Or is something different?"

"Something's different," she says. "And the thing that bugs me the most about all this bullshit is that I really *like* this new you. You're, I don't know, *here* in a way you usually aren't. You're paying attention. To me. To Mom and Dad. You're listening to us. You haven't checked your cell even once. That thing you do when we're talking where your eyes glaze over and I just know you're thinking about work or, I don't even know what, *anything* other than actually engaging with me, I haven't seen you do it once all night. I don't want to like you like this, you dick."

Greta sits up on the couch, glaring at me as she points to Penny.

"And don't get me started on the sexy bookworm over here," she says. "I mean, you finally bring someone home, someone I might even like, and then you sabotage the whole night in the most epic way possible . . ."

"I wish this wasn't how we'd met, Greta," Penny says. "But you should know your whole family is amazing. When my family gets together, we talk about *nothing.* Any thirty-second segment of tonight's conversation would automatically be the most interesting thing my family has ever discussed."

"That's one way of looking at it," Greta says. "Another way of looking at it is that everything I've ever known and loved seems to be teetering on the edge of something dark and cold with very sharp teeth that never let go when they bite. So, I find it a little less interesting and a little more fucking scary."

92

My dad goes to bed. Greta decides to pass out in what was formerly her bedroom and is now the rarely used guest room. Penny goes to the bathroom. My mom takes me by the arm, firm, and leads me into her office, closing the door.

"I suffer from depression," she says. "I'm on medication. Lexapro."

"Does Dad know?" I say.

"Of course he knows," my mom says. "It's not a secret."

"Then why don't I know?"

"Don't change the subject," she says.

"What's the subject?"

"That depression can be hereditary."

"Mom," I say.

"A child with a parent who suffers from it, I mean *clinically*, is three times more likely to have it too," she says.

"I'm not depressed," I say.

"That's what I said for twenty-five years. I have a crossed wire in my brain, John. I've been doing my best to uncross it my whole life. I'm sorry that I gave it to you. But if you feel deep down that you don't *deserve* happiness, you need to understand that feeling is an illness just like cancer and malaria and the flu."

She starts to tear up. And it doesn't matter if I'm a time traveler or a nutcase or just a guy with a headful of bad chemistry—it still hurts to see my mom cry.

"Fine," I say. "I'll get myself checked out. I'll talk to someone. I'll do whatever it is you do when you want to know if you're depressed."

"Thank you," she says.

"After I get back from San Francisco."

My mom closes her eyes and a mosaic of nonverbal reactions flutters across her face. When she opens her eyes and looks at me again, it's with compassion.

"It's normal, you know?" she says. "To feel like a fraud."

"What?"

"I was listening," my mom says. "You feel like a fraud. You've convinced yourself that you plagiarized all your best ideas from another dimension."

"All those buildings that everyone thinks are so bold and visionary," I say, "I didn't come up with any of it. I dreamed it and claimed it as my own. I'm not some genius. I'm a rip-off artist and sooner or later they'll figure it out."

"That's how everybody feels," she says. "You don't think I felt like that when I started teaching? When I wrote my first book? When I became dean? We all feel like frauds. That's the secret of life. Everybody's winging it."

"I know what imposter syndrome is," I say. "This isn't that."

"Okay," she says, "you're not some hotshot architect. You're a phony and a thief. Except you're plagiarizing buildings that don't exist. That have only ever existed in your mind. So, take a moment to consider maybe that's how everyone who creates something new feels. As if they had nothing to do with it. Like they plucked it out of the ether and signed their name at the bottom and none of the credit is deserved."

"No, Mom, this is something else."

"You got a little bit famous. Even a little bit of fame can mess with your head. It's a cognitive disease, you know, fame? It used to only be for royalty and we know what they're like. I'm not much of a Freudian, but something about fame makes the id and the superego devour the ego like anacondas in a cage, right before they cannibalize each other. Fame warps your identity, metastasizes your anxieties, and hollows you out like a jack-o'-lantern. It's sparkly pixie dust that burns whatever it touches like acid."

"Mom, I'm an architect. I'm barely famous. I'm maybe slightly well-known."

"And look what happened," she says.

"What do you mean?"

"You've been slightly well-known for six months and the fact that it coincided with you going kind of bonkers is, what, unrelated? Random happenstance? Do you know what Jung said about coincidence? He said just because we can't see the destination, it doesn't mean that no road goes there."

"I'm too tired to keep talking about this," I say. "Especially if you're going to bring Freud and Jung into it, that's just cruel."

"Then consider this one last thing," my mom says. "There's no way back. This disappointing, moribund reality you're stranded in, we don't have any time machines here. Your home planet is gone forever. You know that, right?"

I shrug. I can't quite say it out loud.

"Maybe it's all true," she says. "Maybe you *are* stealing all your best ideas from your magical fantasyland. But if that world is lost and if, as you claim, you're the one who lost it, then don't you owe it to that world to make this one better?"

"Better how?" I say.

"You have a responsibility," she says. "You're the only one who can show us what paradise looks like. You can build us a future to live in. And I mean that literally, build it in brick and steel and glass. You may not think you're a genius. You may think you're a fraud, a bandit, a world-killing monster. But you're all we have."

I don't know what to say to that. It sounds a little triumphalist to

me, but my mom wouldn't be the first mother with a grandiose per-
ception of her child.

"Chase this mystery to San Francisco if you have to," she says.
"But be safe and come home to us. There's work to do here, in this
world, the world you live in, not the world you dream of. They don't
actually even *need* you. Not like we do."

My mom hugs me, opens her office door, walks down the hall to
her bedroom, and joins my dad inside.

93

Penny and I go back to her place. I've basically been living there since we met because my condo doesn't feel like home. She calls one of her staffers to open the bookstore so we can sleep most of the day. Her bedroom windows face east and the morning sunshine is bright and pushy.

Everything that happened last night rattles around in my head as I try to sleep next to Penny. She's deadweight pressed against my side, wearing underwear and a soft, thin T-shirt, her head notched into that groove where my shoulder meets my collarbone, wisps of her hair tickling my chin and lips. She breathes out, heavy and deep.

I feel lighter, unburdened after telling my family the truth, even if it would've been smarter, probably, to let them think my feverish babbling about alternate realities at the hospital was just a fleeting synaptic glitch.

I forgot to write tonight. Penny suggested that I jot down recollections of my life, a few minutes every evening before we go to bed, a daily routine as a way to hold on to the truth. So I've been doing that, typing on John's laptop, a little bit each night. But the world feels too big and the words feel too small, and turning the slushy tangle of memories into clean lines of text makes them feel *less* real, *more* fictive and faraway.

And what do those memories really get me? Was I happy there? No.

Lying here with Penny, I feel happy. Curled up with her in the bed that feels like home to me, I realize that for the first time I'm intentionally letting Tom go. John is slipping under the door like fingers of smoke from a basement fire, wonderfully calming compared to Tom's constant anxious clamoring. Everyone I care about will be happier when I'm gone. Even Penny. Tom makes everything so hard, so messy, so complicated.

John wouldn't still be awake. He'd realize his whole life had been slightly out of focus and now it's finally in crisp relief—he had an undiagnosed mental illness that quietly cohered in the damp corners of his mind and, when his defenses were temporarily lowered, it tried to seize control. But its moment has passed. The virus that is Tom has no plan of action, just a list of demands. It wanted to be in charge but, like so many aspiring despots, it hadn't projected beyond the coup to the day-to-day grind of running the show. Anyone can overthrow a government. It's ruling that's hard.

Penny shifts in her sleep, turning onto her side. She presses her underwear-clad ass against my hip, pulls the covers up under her chin. I twist onto my side too and she pushes into me. Her hair smells of lemon and rosemary and something else, a scent I'm still trying to place when I fall asleep.

94

I wake up feeling clean. No, cleaned out. Hollowed out maybe, but in a good way. Like a fat tumor was removed while I slept in Penny's bed.

Tom is gone. That whining, miserable, damaged jerk-off is gone. Good riddance.

He haunted me like a ghoul my whole goddamn life. I thought it would be a relief to let him out of his cage but he turned out to be a yawn. All that pointless regret.

I'll give him one thing, he found Penny. Laid her out for me on a silver platter. No effort required. Just lying there next to me, ready for whatever I want. So I kiss her neck until she starts to wake up and then I tug down those panties. She keeps trying to turn around and look at me but I don't let her. Maybe I'm too rough, hard to say sometimes with women, the ways they like to be treated that they can't admit out loud.

After, she's quiet. Asks what's wrong with me and I say I've never felt better. And it's true. My mind has never been so clear. She starts to cry. Asks what happened to Tom. I tell her he's gone and she cries some more.

I grab a shower. Water pressure's crap. Whoever built this dump got ripped off by the plumbing contractor. Shower doesn't even have a rain head. She comes in, naked, staring me in the eye, hard and soft at the same time, hot water spraying down on us, and asks if I'm still in there. I say what does that even mean and she says I'm not talking to you. I'm talking to him. Tom.

I think about pretending to be him for long enough to have her again but I don't even want her anymore. Not worth the hassle.

So I just smile and say Tom's not here anymore and he's never coming back and I leave her in there to cry some more. Hot water was starting to run out anyway. My condo's got one of those tankless heating systems that never runs cold.

I put on the shitty clothes Tom's been choosing for me and head to the office. Can't believe how much he let everything slide. Hiding, running away, apologizing, too scared to make a decision in case it's wrong. I sign a bunch of shit that needs approval.

The concert hall in Chicago is a nice gig. Fat budget, central location, civic pride, all that pressure means they need someone to tell them what to do. Big payday. Need to block out some ideas. I glance at the specs they sent and go to my drafting table.

But not much comes. The way it's supposed to work is I look at pictures of the site and think about buildings I've seen in my dreams and the basic form and scale and texture of the thing floods into me. Not this time.

Makes sense, though. Tom infected me long before he took over. Been inside my head for my whole life. His voice always whispering like an itch in a place I couldn't reach. But now it's gone. Maybe that means all my good ideas are gone too. Whatever, my reputation is set. I can coast off what I got from him for the rest of my life. Make more money doing less fussy versions of this shit anyway. Keep it simple, don't push the limits, let the clients feel edgier than they are, and take them for as much as they're dumb enough to pay. Let someone else change the way the world looks. Or better yet keep it the way it is. Only whiners like Tom think they need to make a difference. The world doesn't care about how you think it should look. The world's only goal is to kill you as fast as possible and use your corpse for fuel.

I did Mom a favor and hired an intern from the Architecture Department at her school and this girl has an incredible ass. Her face is fine but that ass. I should design the concert hall to look like that ass. Tom and his goddamn whorls. Other than me, she's the only one in the office right now, doing who knows what, filing or something. Through the glass walls I can see her at the blueprint cabinet. She knows I'm here, but is she being demure? Or is she bending over at the waist sticking her ass in the air right where I can see it? Don't tell me she doesn't know what she's doing. She knows.

This feels good. Feels right. Didn't even know he'd been holding me back all these years. The doubts. The questions. The hand on my shoulder. The voice in my ear saying, no, don't, it's wrong, just because you want it that doesn't mean you deserve it. That boring whisper is gone and I deserve it all. Wanting it is the same as deserving it.

It's hilarious I thought I loved Penny just because he loved Penny. I'm young. I look great. I'm going to be rich, and even if I'm not, Greta will give me whatever I ask for, she's so screwed up about her money. I'm sort of famous. Famous enough. I never need another good idea in my life. Like Penny could satisfy me when there are interns with perfect asses and the kind of faces that make them drop their jeans for a famous enough man who tells them they could be something one day. Who the hell wears jeans that tight to work? Someone whose main ambition in life is to give herself to me.

Everything is so clear now that he's gone.

I don't know why I'm bothering to write this down. Guess he got me in the habit. And anyway Tom's story needs an ending.

The End.

95

I wake up and I'm missing a day.

Yesterday was Saturday so today is Sunday except it's Monday. I should be waking up next to Penny at her apartment, but I'm in my condo bedroom lying next to a stranger. No, not a stranger, a young woman who interns at the architecture office. Beth. Her name is Beth. She's nervous, embarrassed, her eyes searching my face for evidence that this wasn't a career-damaging mistake, but there's anger percolating there too, held in check, like she hasn't decided if it should be directed at me or herself. She nuzzles her naked body next to mine and I recoil instinctively and I see a wall of self-recrimination slam down over her eyes because of course she sees the panic in mine.

I tell her I need some coffee and I'll make her some too. She tries to kiss me but I act like I don't notice as I skitter out of the bedroom.

I have no idea what happened. My mind is blank.

Something buzzy in my brain stem sends me to check the laptop and there's an entry that I didn't write. As I read it, my body shivers hot and cold like a bad flu.

It's him, John—he somehow took control and did this to me.

She calls out asking about the coffee and I slap down the laptop screen. I make coffee and she pads into the kitchen wearing nothing but yesterday's underwear, too casual, showing herself to me in the morning light. She has a small bruise on each hip. They look fresh.

I feel queasy. The neural scanners aren't supposed to let you wake up into a nightmare. Because that's how this feels, as cliché as I know that sounds, like a nightmare, lucid and crystalline but gummy around the edges.

She asks if I want to go get breakfast and I say I can't, I have to go to the office, and there's this excruciating moment where she makes a joke about workplace sexual harassment and it's supposed to show how grown-up she is about this stuff but it only makes her seem so young, too young, except there's also this steely wire of threat inside the joke, giving it its essential structure, and she sees me get it and she flushes pink, because she's tasting a bit of power and she's not sure what to do with it.

She stands there, stirring milk into her coffee, undressed, a display and a challenge. She wants something more from me, I don't know what, I don't even know if we slept together—I have no memory of yesterday, nothing. But there's a jagged tension simmering in her face, like she's waiting for me to confirm that I've already taken everything I wanted from her and now she's just one awkward conversation away from me never thinking about her again.

I read what he wrote so fast, I didn't get the full picture of what happened with Penny. But it sounds bad. Awful. The kind of awful that maybe can't be fixed.

She asks if she should just go and I say that's probably a good idea. I escape to the bathroom to wash my face and I still have no idea what exactly happened but there's a used condom, *thank god a condom,* in the bathroom trash. I can't make eye contact when she comes out of the bedroom wearing yesterday's clothes, pulling on her shoes, swaying as she balances on one foot, then the other, and in sixty seconds she'll be gone and I can move on to the next phase of this calamity.

But this is not her fault. This is my fault—*his* fault—and even if the last thing in the world I want right now is to prolong this mess, her name is Beth and she matters.

"Wait," I say. "Beth . . . I'm sorry, I'm not good at this stuff. I don't want you to feel like what happened last night didn't . . . mean anything. It's a lot easier for me to pretend it didn't happen and treat you like a stranger at the office. But, I mean, if nothing else we should be able to be honest with each other. Don't you think?"

Beth blinks at me, like she's waiting for something snide or dismissive and when it doesn't come she's sweetly confused and not so sweetly sad. She crosses her arms, tight, guarded.

"You want us to be honest," Beth says.

"Yeah," I say. "Because, uh, I don't totally remember what happened . . . exactly."

"You don't *remember*," she says. "Uh-huh."

"Did we . . . drink a lot?"

"I guess so. Yes. I sure did."

"Okay," I say. "I don't know if you heard I was in the hospital?"

"Yeah," Beth says, "I mean, everybody knows that."

"Right. So, maybe I need to apologize if I said or did anything, you know, inappropriate last night."

"Nothing we did last night was anywhere near appropriate."

"Well, then I'm very sorry about that."

"Why are you being like this?" Beth says.

"Like what?"

"Nice," she says. "You weren't nice last night. You were *rough*. And if you really want me to be honest, it made me feel shitty. It wasn't sex. It was more like you were jerking off into me. That's how you made me feel. Like I was something to *come* in."

She wipes her eyes with her hand and I don't know what to say or do so I don't say or do anything except listen to her.

"You don't even know," Beth says. "I tried to play it cool this morning but I barely slept all night because I promised myself I wouldn't get into a situation like this. Especially not with someone I thought I, like, admired or whatever. The whole point of going to architecture school is to build the world I want to live in and that's how working for you made me feel. Like I could maybe be part of that. And now I wrecked it all."

"Nothing's been wrecked," I say. "You didn't do anything wrong."

"I don't understand," she says. "Last night you couldn't even look at me when we . . . and now you're like a different person."

"I'm sorry," I say.

"You keep saying you're sorry." Beth says. "You weren't sorry last night. You're my boss. You could make or break my career. What we did, it's not the kind of sex I like. I just figured bad sex with an asshole is better than the other way it could've gone. And I'm not threatening you, okay? I know I went along with all of it. I just wanted it to be over. And all night, lying there, I kept telling myself, in the morning just act like it was no big deal and that will mean it really was no big deal."

I'm very aware this is objectively worse for her than for me. I know that. But what am I supposed to say to her? Sorry, Beth, everything you're telling me is terrible and heartbreaking, but it wasn't me, I swear, it was the alternate version of myself I created by shattering reality? I don't know if I have any right to feel devastated by what she's saying, but I do. And roiling under that is the realization that John is not who I thought he was.

The thing is, I didn't *feel* anything. I wasn't shoved to the back of his consciousness, scratching and clawing to come out. I was just *annihilated*. I didn't know I was even gone until I woke up and it was the wrong today.

Maybe it's because I was so tired after staying up all night with my family. I was weak. I lost control. But it's not just that John took over—it's that he took over without any of me left in him.

I didn't understand that until right now. I thought I was like a specter in his dreams. But now I see that I've always been part of him. Not just his imagination—his conscience. Without me, there's no warmth or compassion in him. No human connection. I thought he was better than me, stronger, smarter, more capable. But we were in balance. He was in charge, hands on the wheel, but I was always there, guiding him to a standard higher than his craven drives. I don't know how to make sure I stay in control. I could fall asleep tonight and wake up tomorrow as John and nothing that matters to me matters to him, because all he cares about is what he wants.

"I don't like the person I was last night," I say. "I know I look like him and sound like him, but I don't feel like him and I hope I never do again. It's easy to apologize the next morning when what matters is how I treated you last night. I hope I can find a way to make it up to you or, if you're not interested in my apologies or regrets, then tell me what would make you feel respected. If it's leaving you alone, that's fine. If it's something else, that's fine too. Tell me what I can do and I'll do my best to do it."

"I was probably just going to go home and have a long bath and write an embarrassing blog post about you," she says.

"If that's what you want to do, okay," I say.

"This is really confusing," Beth says. "I mean, I've been interning at your office for six weeks and I didn't think you even knew my name. I'd heard you had some, like, freak-out and ended up in the hospital, but then you give that big speech and everyone's all, like, he's a genius."

"I'm not a genius," I say. "That much must be obvious to you."

"I don't know," she says, "what's the definition of genius? All I wanted was for you to notice me. I came to work on the weekend in case you'd be there. And it worked. You noticed me. I had dinner with John fucking Barren and you actually listened to my opinions about architecture. I was so nervous, I drank way too much, and you kept ordering more wine, and you probably don't even realize anymore how good expensive wine tastes, but I never drank a bottle that cost more than twenty bucks until last night. And you were just all over me and, I mean, it was flattering, mostly. But how the hell did I put myself in this situation? I'm doing my master's degree. I'm trying to build a real career. I'm not the dummy who drinks too much and goes home with her boss."

"I won't let any of this affect things at work," I say.

"I can't tell if you're screwing with me," Beth says. "Like you're pretending to be nice so I don't tell anyone what an asshole you were. Or if you're just kind of screwed up. Like whatever it is that makes your brain spit out the most incredible buildings I've ever seen also makes you a total mess in every other way."

"You have no idea just how much of a mess I really am," I say.

"And I don't want to know," Beth says. "But just so we're clear, this is never happening again."

"I know," I say.

"Okay," she says, "I guess I'll see you at the office. I mean, you are coming back, right? Because people are saying you maybe quit."

"Beth, I don't know what I'm doing. But if you change your mind about any of this, you do whatever you need to do. I'll understand."

Beth walks to the door, her hand on the knob. She looks back at me.

"You're a very hard person to make your mind up about," she says.

"Yeah," I say, "I feel that way about me too."

96

It's common to talk about time as variable. How it can feel radically accelerated or yawningly drawn-out depending on what you're doing. But we don't tend to talk about space that way. Maybe because we gauge it with our eyes, space feels more rigid and fixed. Even though we know inches and feet are just as arbitrary as seconds and minutes, they feel more concrete. But sitting on Penny's couch, telling her everything, everything I *remember*, space feels a lot more liquid. We're less than a foot apart but the few inches it would take for my skin to touch her skin seem impossibly vast.

After Beth leaves, I race over to Penny's apartment. She opens the door, and when she sees me, we both start crying.

"He said you were gone forever," Penny says.

"I'm sorry," I say. "I'll never be able to say sorry enough times. Even if it's the only word I say to you till the day we die."

She tenses at that. I'm right next to her on the couch, but she won't look at me.

"It was like a horror movie," she says. "I woke up next to an alien wearing your face. It was bad. It was very bad."

"I'm sorry, Penny, but it gets worse."

After the torrent of confessions and apologies, there's a long, quiet, kind of achingly domestic moment where we pick up our regular morning routine, minus the unself-conscious physical contact. We make coffee and slice up some fruit and it feels like maybe, not yet, but one day, this could fade into an almost imperceptible stain, like a drop of red wine that's been imperfectly bleached from a tablecloth.

"I get what you're saying," Penny says, "that you never understood your influence on John. How his whole life you were both his imagination and his conscience. But I can't help feel that's a self-serving analysis. It makes you the hero and him the monster."

"I think maybe he *is* a monster," I say.

"But maybe it's not that John lacked any compassionate human qualities. Maybe he was a fine and good and generally functional person until *you* took over."

"What's that supposed to mean?" I say.

"Maybe it's not that you gave him those things, like a gift," Penny says. "Maybe it's that you *stole* all that from him. Because you needed it. And when you receded, for whatever reason, you carried off some important pieces of him with you. And left him without them."

"That's not . . . no, that doesn't make sense," I say.

"Right," she says, "because the rest of this makes complete sense. You said to me last week that you wondered if you were more sexist than you realized because you never grew up with a sister, the way he did. The thing is, Greta doesn't strike me as someone who'd take a milligram of shit from a brother like the man in my bed yesterday morning. I don't have any siblings, so I don't know how blind you can be to their damage. I know everyone thinks he's a bit detached and distant. But that's not the same as what I saw in his, in *your*, eyes. It was angry and cold. Like your evil twin showed up looking just like you in every way except the light in his eyes and the cadence of his speech."

"It wasn't me," I say. "You understand that, right?"

"I understand you believe you didn't do any of the things *he* did," she says. "To me or to that girl. But it was your body. Your body handled me the way he handled me. Your body was with her, doing who knows what, things she apparently didn't like very much but that you conveniently can't remember."

"I'm not trying to minimize what it felt like for you or for her," I say, "but this whole thing feels like a horror movie to me too."

"Well," she says, "that sounds really tough for you, *Tom*."

"Penny . . ."

"No, that's great," she says, "congratulations, you managed to screw your intern, *so original*, and then convince her you're actually a super-nice and thoughtful guy who just has a bit of a twisty dark side when it suits him. And here you are to convince me of the same thing, right? That it wasn't you. It was *him*. You're not responsible. You're pure and innocent and sweet and you say just the right thing and you really listen and you would never treat me like that. It's funny because people say the perfect guy doesn't exist. And yet I found him. Except of course he *literally* doesn't exist."

"I'm far from perfect," I say, "but I'm not like him."

"It's not just what would happen if you were gone forever," Penny says. "It's what would happen if he came back. When I woke up, it really did feel like a nightmare. It had that illogical wrongness to it. You're with the man you love but he's someone else, even though he looks exactly the same and there's no evidence, except for the way he speaks and moves and touches you. After, I thought if I went in the shower with you it would wake me up enough to snap out of it. Like I'd been sleepwalking. I'd look you in the eye and you'd be back and whatever happened in my bed was just a bad dream. But it wasn't. It was him, saying you're gone forever. And now you're here, but how long before he comes back again?"

"I won't let him come back."

"You don't know *what* you'll let," Penny says. "I can't even be sure it's you."

"It's me. I promise you it's me."

"What does that even mean, *it's me*, coming from you?" she says.

I catch myself before I speak because—what *does* it mean? I'm still unclear on what exactly I did to Penny but, whatever it was, it was done with my skin and bones and muscles and nerves, the same lungs breathed the air and the same heart pumped the blood and the same brain that's clogged with staticky dread and guilt for acts I didn't even commit, except that I did, apparently, that same brain set the whole chain of events in motion. I feel like someone whose dog just ravaged a neighbor who strayed too close to his property, except I'm the dog and clearly not the master of anything that matters.

This gap between us, it isn't just empty space. It's a black hole and I don't know that we'll ever escape it. I don't know what's going to happen next. But I do know one thing—I have to find a way to kill John.

97

"Sitting here all day and all night," Penny says, "mostly what I thought about is . . . if he comes back and bad things happen, how *exactly* I'd explain this to, say, the police or my parents or one of the many friends I've been ignoring for the past couple of weeks since you came into my life. Well, you see . . . this guy comes into my store one day and he tells me he's a time traveler from another dimension. And in that other dimension I'm this, like, supercool astronaut. Or I was until I had some neurological episode in outer space and then I trained to be a time traveler instead, but on the side I was really into having unprotected sex with random strangers. And then on the night before the most important day of my life, the day I was going to be one of the first humans to time travel, for some reason I sleep with this guy and he gets me pregnant and I *kill* myself. And this guy is so sad about it that he goes back in time and screws up the past enough to change the entire space-time continuum. Except *he* still exists and so do I. Although I look different. The other me was this toned, stoic sex robot, but I'm just a person. With, like, cellulite and calluses and birthmarks in weird places and breasts that hurt when I run. Oh, and he's handsome and successful and charmingly self-deprecating for someone who's routinely called a genius, at least on the Internet. Because it's not like he's cast himself as this big shot over there who no one recognizes here. In fact, it's the opposite. Here he's kind of a big deal and over there he was a bit of a loser. But, and this is the swoony, magical part, he thinks I'm the most interesting person in the world. Even though I'm just a grown-up nerd with a bookstore. And I've never felt this kind of chemistry with anyone. I get hit on, you know, from time to time, especially by customers and my friends' boyfriends' chronically date-less best friends from college. But this is different. It's electric. He feels electric to me. And it's also so comfortable and intimate with him, it really does feel like I've known him my whole life even though it's been, like, two weeks. I don't read a lot of chick lit but I know what this feels like. It feels like it was meant to be. I meet his parents and they couldn't be more amazing. His mom is a Victorian scholar with an incredible vintage book collection. His dad is a professor who actually wrote a book about time travel, which I *read* because I'm a geek. And doesn't that fit together so well? I have a bookstore, his mom loves books, he's a time traveler, his dad writes about time travel. And there's his sister, smart and sarcastic and suspicious of me because she's protective of him, which gives him this inherent credibility, not that he needs it at this point, because she's the kind of person I'd want to be friends with. It's all so perfect. It's all *too* perfect. Because when you really think about it, actually, this perfect guy sort of sounds like a paranoid schizophrenic. Even his family, the people who know and love him most, they think he's mentally ill. Maybe not his adorably befuddled dad, who is clearly sick of being the least successful person with his last name sitting at the dining room table, maybe *he's* cautiously optimistic that his pet obsession with time travel has been this long-gestating portal to an adventure beyond his most fevered adolescent fantasies. Although even he's worried his son's just crazy. But the *women* in his life, his impressive mom and skeptical sister, they think he needs immediate psychological help because his story sounds *ridiculous* when you lay it out, no matter how many intricate details he's woven into it. But you want to believe him because you love this guy like you've never loved anyone. Like you've waited your whole life to love someone. You're a self-made, self-aware woman, sure, but you still want that.

So you play along with the family summit and tell yourself it'll be okay, even though you never believed it until the day he walked into your store, now you know in your bones that love conquers all. But then, after staying up all night with him trying to explain to his family, who you *just met,* that he really is a time traveler from another dimension, you go back to your place, more tired than you've been maybe ever, and you fall asleep next to him and when you wake up he's inside you. But it's not like before. There's no electricity or connection or love. You try to look at him. To understand why he's shoving himself into you like you're a sex toy instead of the woman he traveled across *cosmic dimensions* to find. But he pins you to the bed and he gets his full weight on you and you can hardly breathe and it just keeps going and going and going and it *hurts.* And so you try to change the narrative in your mind, you tell yourself a little story that he's trying something new, that everyone has weird fantasies they're embarrassed to say out loud, that you have fantasies you haven't told him, and some of those fantasies are a bit weird, you know that, which is why you don't share them with just anyone, but you were going to tell him because you trust him, and so maybe this is what it feels like for someone to trust you so much that they let you see the scary darkness inside them because they believe your love will make it less scary and less dark, and you want to feel that too because you are not without scary darkness, there are parts of you that have always felt unlovable, until you met him and he made you feel like he loved all of you, even the unlovable parts you hadn't shown him yet, and so you tell yourself you can love this too, even though it hurts, because it means he's showing you all of him and there's something inherently good about that even if it feels so very bad. You try to unlock a part of yourself that might even enjoy being roughly screwed like a piece of meat. But guess what? *That part of you doesn't fucking exist.* You can't find it because it's not even one tiny bit of you. You start to panic that it's not even him, because it doesn't feel like him, so what if it's a psychotic stranger who broke in and killed the man you love and attacked you in your sleep? And he finally finishes, but you're afraid to turn around because whatever you see, him or someone else, may define the rest of your life. You hear him start the shower and that's a bad sign because what kind of psycho killer takes a shower right after? You get up and take off the T-shirt and underwear you slept in because you can never wear either of them again. The shower glass is too steamed up to see who it is in there. So you step inside and it's him. The man you love. Except it's not. It's him but it's not him. He looks at you and, let me tell you something, I've had a lot of men look at me in a lot of ways, but never like that. Like a butcher sizing up a steak. I love my body but that look made me want to cut off my breasts and throw them in the ocean. I know you say it wasn't you. But he looked at me with the same eyes that are looking at me now. The same but not the same. And with that mouth that's not your mouth, except it *is* your mouth, he told me you're gone forever. He left and I stayed in the shower till the water ran cold, stood there for, I don't know, hours, just let the cold water pour down on me, hoping it could wear me down to molecules. At some point I got out and I couldn't go back into that bedroom, so I sat here on the couch all day and all night and I practiced my story if I had to tell someone. In case he came back. But instead *you* came back. Unless of course you're still him and he's just really good at pretending to be you."

98

"I don't know how to prove it to you, but I'm me," I say.

"I can't see him again," Penny says. "And you can't promise he won't be here when you wake up tomorrow."

"What can I do?"

"Find proof," she says. "Maybe I'm not as smart as I think I am. Maybe I'm just another girl who falls for the wrong guy and talks herself out of running away because she thinks love matters. Maybe it doesn't matter. Maybe you're crazy and I'm stupid and this ends in a courtroom or a cemetery with everybody I know saying *she seemed so smart, how could she be so dumb?*"

"I know my promises don't mean much right now, but . . ."

"But nothing," she says. "I love you but I can't see you again until you can prove to me you're telling the truth."

She looks me in the eye, wary, checking, and I can tell it doesn't matter which of us I am, not anymore, that everything is different now and has to be.

My father spent his whole life chasing a trail back to Lionel Goettreider and the events of July 11, 1965. And now I have to do the same. His trail was made of tau radiation, but mine is made of something that can be just as malignant—memory.

Penny locks and bolts the door behind me. I go home and book a flight.

99

I'm on an airplane, flying from Toronto to San Francisco, the last forty-eight hours careening around in my head like a windmill that's shredded its bolts and is about to hurtle across the landscape like a gigantic *shuriken*.

I believe Penny and I believe Beth. What I typically *don't* believe in are things like blacking out and hurting people. I don't want to be the kind of person who tells stories to himself that he wouldn't believe if they were told to him. And I also feel like—this is not what I signed up for. You probably feel that way too. This was supposed to be, like, a time-travel romp, you know? I'd make some mistakes but in the end I'd set things right. I fantasized that despite or maybe even because of everything I've done wrong, I'd somehow come out of this a hero. *The* hero.

In principle, I realize that heroism demands sacrifice. But I didn't understand what I'd actually have to sacrifice. Write a list of the things you can't imagine giving up and that's the list of things you'll be forced to lose. Except you couldn't even draw up the list, because they're all the things you take for granted as essential elements of yourself. They don't seem removable from what makes you who you are.

So, I'm sorry this isn't a time-travel romp. I was expecting causal loops and reality fluctuations and branching dimensions and scientifically questionable solutions to ornate space-time paradoxes. I wasn't expecting actual human pain. I didn't ask to question the foundations of my sanity. Wiping someone out of existence because of a time-travel glitch is haunting, but distant and blurry. The woman you love saying that you physically hurt her, even if it wasn't exactly you, isn't distant or blurry. It's heavy and solid. It burrows under your skin to build a nest of poison in which to lay its toxic eggs.

Whether I'm right or whether I'm crazy, the only way through is the path that leads to Jerome Francoeur and whatever he might know. Maybe nothing. Maybe he's just a photo in an old book on my dad's office shelf that I somehow remembered from my childhood and I embellished an opulent delusion out of an evocative detail like the sleeve of a blazer stitched at the elbow.

If Jerome Francoeur has no idea who Lionel Goettreider is, I can't go back to Penny and ask her to trust me, not when I can't trust myself. But if I can't go back to Penny, I don't know where else to go. There's nowhere else I want to be.

100

"Can you do me a big favor?" says Jerome Francoeur. "Can you tell me why the hell you're here? Because you're not writing about my wife. I mean, I like that you went right for the gut there, went *all in* on the dead wife, that's a sharp move. And maybe if I was a little more senile it would've worked. So, cut the horseshit. What do you want?"

I've been sitting in Jerome's house in Palo Alto for about ninety seconds. I stood on the pedimented wraparound porch of the gabled Queen Anne house, staring at the jaunty asymmetrical facade when his daughter, Emma Francoeur, answered the front door, polite, stiff. On the way down the hall, she told me how moved she is that I want to include a chapter about her mother for my book on pioneering women in physics. So I was thinking my lie worked like a charm when she opened the study door, revealing Jerome perched in an antique wingback armchair like a hawk on a branch, his sleeve clipped at the elbow above his missing forearm. Emma pads off to the kitchen to get us coffee. Jerome waits until she's out of earshot before drilling right through my deception.

"Mr. Francoeur," I say, "sir . . ."

"I'm a reasonable judge of character," Jerome says, "and I can see you're about to double down on the horseshit. I have the Internet, Mr. Barren. I know who you are. I read your little speech from the other day. You've got stones, telling all your peers they're worthless, although from where I sit it was a lot of generalities and not a lot of specifics."

"I hadn't prepared anything," I say, "so bravado seemed like the way to go."

"You admit you're here on false pretenses," he says.

"Yeah. I mean, I do have some questions that relate to you and your wife, but I'm not writing a book. It seemed like a good way to get you to see me on such short notice."

"You've got thirty seconds before I call the police," he says. "It's not technically trespassing but we can sort that out at the station."

"I'm looking for a man named Lionel Goettreider," I say.

Jerome's frail, wrinkled face curdles with such force that at first I think he might be having a stroke. But then he bares his teeth, gorilla-like, grimacing through dry lips.

"What do you think you know?" he says.

"I know you oversaw funding for an experiment he conducted on July 11, 1965. I know it failed and it cost you your arm. And I know Lionel Goettreider was, uh . . ."

"What?" he says.

"Close," I say. "With your wife."

"You piece of shit," he says, "coming into my home and dredging all that up, spitting on my dead wife's name, who do you think you are?"

Emma comes in, carrying a silver tray with two mugs, a coffee-pot, sugar jar, and milk jug. She catches the end of Jerome's invective and blanches.

"Is everything okay?" she says.

"Get this asshole out of here before I call the cops."

"I'm sorry if I offended you," I say, "but I need to find Lionel Goettreider."

Emma's grip on the tray gets shaky, the porcelain rattling. Seeing this, Jerome's eyes go glassy and wet. This is a house with ghosts in the walls.

"Why do you need to find Lionel Goettreider?" Emma says.

"Because," I say, "I think he's my father."

101

Okay, yes, that's totally untrue. But Emma's tense reaction sparked a wild guess that this lie would work where the one about the book didn't.

"I'm calling the cops," Jerome says.

But he doesn't reach for the cordless phone next to his armchair. Emma puts down the tray, tugs smooth the front of her shirt, crumpling the hem in her fists.

"Does he know?" Emma says.

Jerome slumps back, looking very much like a man in his late eighties.

"He knows about the affair," he says.

Emma nods. She pours me a coffee, offers the milk and I nod, offers the sugar and I shake my head. It's all very proper. Jerome waves the coffee away, no longer a hawk, more like a turtle that wants back in its shell. Emma pours one for herself, drinks it black.

"I'm not trying to dig up the past," I say. "All I want is to find Lionel Goettreider. I'll be out of your lives forever if you can tell me where he is."

"What do you know about their . . . relationship?" Emma says.

"Not much," I say. "I know it was going on at the time of the accident."

"It was a bad phase in our marriage," Jerome says. "I was distracted. Trying to get my career to the next level. So we'd have the stability we needed to start a family. It ended between them after that goddamn machine of his imploded. You know it could've wiped out half the continent, right? That moron almost caused the apocalypse with his lunatic invention. Harnessing the rotation of the planet. I mean, it was nonsense. I never should've signed off on it in the first place. His paperwork was flawless, though. He said all the right things. Because *she* helped him write what she knew I'd approve."

"What happened to the machine?" I say.

"What happened? He destroyed the lab, almost killed more than a dozen people, and cost me my arm. I had that thing disassembled and melted down, piece by piece."

"And Lionel?" I say.

"I should've pressed charges," Jerome says. "Had him locked up. But she asked me not to. We never talked about what had happened between them. It wasn't how things were done back then. But I understood. Without either of us saying the words."

With his remaining hand, Jerome squeezes the biceps of his amputated arm, massaging it, a nervous habit.

"She was thinking about leaving me for him," he says. "But I saved her life that day. So, the trade was I lost my arm but my wife stayed. And I'd make that trade every day of my life, even now that she's gone. That accident was my defining moment. Whatever came out of that machine, it was a purifying fire. It burned away all of my bitterness and stupidity. When my arm was taken, it took my mistakes with it. Three years into a marriage that wasn't working, Ursula and I got a chance to start again. And we had a happy life together, after that. We changed the story. We had another forty-nine years together. That terrible time in our lives was forgotten."

Jerome's not really talking to me. He's talking to Emma.

"Or maybe not forgotten," he says, "but forgiven."

Tears stream down her cheeks. His too. He massages his biceps, kneads the skin. I sip my coffee, awkward, catalyst and intruder.

"Do you know what happened to him?" I say.

"I can't believe he had the stones to show up at Ursula's funeral,"

Jerome says. "How he even knew she died, I don't know. Creepy son of a bitch was probably stalking her online."

"Wait, you've seen him?" I say. "He's alive?"

"Yeah," Jerome says, "as of two years ago he was."

"Do you know where he lives?" I say.

Jerome shakes his head. He gives a little shudder and his gaze goes slack. His face seems to hang looser, like he's abruptly fallen asleep.

"Grey," he says.

"Sorry?" I say.

"Motherfucker doesn't go by Goettreider anymore," he says. "He's Grey. Lionel Grey. He tried to apologize or some shit but I wasn't interested. I blew him off and went to speak with someone who didn't steal my goddamn arm and sleep with my goddamn wife. Sorry, Emma."

"Was there any even, like, indirect mention of where he might live?" I say.

"No," Jerome says. "And I didn't ask. He's bad news. I could smell it at the funeral, a cloud hanging around him, like when the air gets charged up before a lightning storm. Bad news."

And, with that, Jerome kicks me out of his house.

102

Emma walks me to my rental car. Neither of us says anything but she keeps glancing at me, like she's graphing emotional geometry on the genealogy of my profile.

"Do you really think Lionel Goettreider is your father?" she says.

"Do you?" I say.

There's a lot of pain in the look she gives me and I realize I overstepped, too glib, kicking over stones with complex, shadowy ecosystems growing under them that may react unpredictably to light.

"If you find him," Emma says, "let me know what kind of man he is."

"I don't even know where to start looking. It's a big world."

"You didn't ask me if *I* spoke to him at the funeral," she says.

"Did you?"

"Yeah. It was funeral talk, mostly. I'm sorry for your loss. She was a brilliant woman. That kind of thing. My dad's right, you know? He had this odd smell hanging off him, Lionel Grey or Goettreider or whatever. Not bad. Just odd. Staticky and, I don't know . . . elemental."

"He told you where he lived?"

"He invited me to visit if I'm ever in the area," she says. "I couldn't say anything in front of my father because it's, well, the primal wound of their marriage and he wears it on his sleeve. Sorry, literally. He never talked about it until after she died. It's strange to discover both of your parents are very good at keeping secrets."

"I didn't mean to cause anyone unnecessary pain," I say.

"I don't think it is unnecessary," Emma says.

She looks away and there's something childlike and moving in the way she gives the sidewalk a little punt with her toe, like a kid protesting some magnificent slight.

"My mom and I talked a lot in the hospital," Emma says. "I slept there every night of that final week. My dad couldn't bear it. He took the day shifts. But I captained the night. And the night's when it got bad."

"I'm sorry," I say. "My mother died too. Sort of."

She gives me a look, like, *how does your mom sort of die?* But she lets it lie. She has her own story to tell. In the house, Jerome peers out the kitchen window at us, like a widow in a soap opera.

"The cancer took its time with her," she says. "I watched it gobble her up, but slow, over months, like it wanted to enjoy every morsel of the feast. And then, like a switch had been flipped, it got fast, unbelievably fast. She collapsed in the kitchen. The cancer was suddenly everywhere. We had six days together in the hospital before it took her. She knew this was it, and, so, she told me about *him*. She said she always loved him. She said she always loved my father too. You have to understand that my mother was *not* a melodramatic person. She was tough as hell right to the very end. But she told me that the human heart was as complex and intractable as the thorny physics problems she spent her life trying to unpack. Worse, actually, because physics has solutions and the heart only has questions. She said compared to love, physics was a relief."

Emma wipes her eyes on her sleeve. She gives me an embarrassed smile and I make a wordless gesture that I hope conveys enough empathy.

"My mom told my dad that she never saw Lionel again after the accident. But I know she did, at least once. She went to a conference at the University of Hong Kong in 1968. My dad didn't go, some work commitment. I was born about forty weeks later."

She looks at my face, analyzing the schematic features and comparing them to a mental image of herself that may or may not be wholly accurate.

"As far as I know," Emma says, "he lives in the same place he has for the past five decades. Hong Kong Island."

"I don't know what kind of man he is," I say. "But I know what kind of man he should've been. A great one."

Emma shrugs and goes back into her father's house.

103

On the plane from San Francisco to Hong Kong, I tap through the movie selection on the seat-back screen in front of me, but my brain feels too poached to latch onto anything involving a plot. So instead I watch my fellow passengers, four hundred people staring in blank silence at glowing rectangles.

Where I come from, the storytelling ritual is a private one, because to experience an immersive narrative saturated with your own psychological weirdness is viscerally personal and your body reacts like it's actually happening: laughter, arousal, disgust, rage, terror. Experiencing that in public would be as socially inappropriate as passing gas in an airtight container surrounded by strangers—but then someone sitting near me seems okay with that too.

Of course, most people would consider this *progress*—hundreds of us squeezed into a 750,000-pound metal tube hurtling 35,000 feet above the Pacific Ocean, atomized by headphones and screens, drinking syrupy liquids and ignoring each other's body odors in the bubbles of pseudo-privacy that social propriety carves from this temporary communal space. But what really stands out is how *joyless* it is. The technology that makes it possible to fly through the air, across the planet, inspires none of the honeyed optimism that's at the core of my world's sense of itself.

And I'm not sure that's a bad thing. My sister was talking about this at dinner the other night: The current state of the world isn't because we stopped believing in an optimistic spirit of wonder and discovery, the current state of the world is the *consequence* of that belief. People are despondent about the future because they're increasingly aware that we, as a species, chased an inspiring dream that led us to ruin. We told ourselves the world is here for us to control, so the better our technology, the better our control, the better our world will be. The fact that for every leap in technology the world gets more sour and chaotic is deeply confusing. The better things we build keep making it worse. The belief that the world is here for humans to control is the philosophical bedrock of our civilization, but it's a mistaken belief. Optimism is the pyre on which we've been setting ourselves aflame.

If this was fiction, I'd need to think hard about what message I hope to convey as an alternative to the control myth that's ideologically warped our species into progressive self-annihilation. Fortunately, this is a memoir. And the best thing about a memoir is it doesn't even need to make sense.

I try to rest my delinquent brain by listening to songs on John's cell. I think about what makes music here so different from the music I grew up with. It takes me most of the flight to figure it out—punk and hip-hop didn't happen in my world. So, yes, I admit that this world has the edge when it comes to music.

104

The plane lands and I catch a car service from Chek Lap Kok airport, across Lantau Island, Tsing Yi, and Kowloon, and through the tunnel under Victoria Harbour to Hong Kong Island. I check into a hotel in Causeway Bay and ask the night-shift concierge, Roland, if the information I called ahead from San Francisco to request has arrived. It hasn't, but I slip Roland a grand in US cash for arranging the inquiries on my behalf. I'm so turned around by the time zones that I can't sleep even though it's the middle of the night. I walk down streets lit up so bright with shadowless fluorescence it feels like I'm in a mall with an infinitely high ceiling. I find an all-hours noodle shop, slurp back slippery ropes in a fragrant broth, and on the way back to the hotel I take some stupid detour through an underlit side street and get mugged by a teenager who waves a knife at me, lazily threatening. I'm too out of it to do anything but hand over the wad of Hong Kong dollars I bought at the price-gouging airport currency exchange and let him count his bounty right in front of me. It doesn't feel like my adrenaline even spiked, but when I get back to my hotel room I fall into a dreamless sleep.

A ringing phone wakes me up in the early afternoon. It's the day-shift concierge, Anaïs, letting me know the information I called ahead from San Francisco to request is waiting for me in the lobby, along with a local gentleman demanding five thousand dollars for its retrieval. Groggy from circadian dysrhythmia, I tell Anaïs to pay the guy and have the information brought up to my room by a bellhop, along with some coffee and milk. She takes a moment to run my name through whatever database she has at her disposal and decides to just do it without additional fuss.

Six minutes later I'm drinking not completely horrible coffee with too-thick milk, looking at the view of Victoria Harbour out the wraparound windows and holding an envelope licked shut. When I open it, the adhesive is still damp from a stranger's tongue. Inside is a piece of paper, folded twice, printed with an address.

The car service takes me to Wan Chai, where I discover I'm actually looking for Chai Wan, which seems a bit deliberately confounding but for all I know there's an obvious pronunciation difference and my confusion is culturally insensitive. Wan Chai is west of Causeway Bay and Chai Wan is east so the driver, a paunchy local with a jaunty chauffeur's cap and an Australian accent, backtracks past the gleaming towers and high-end shops of Causeway Bay to the less glittery, more industrial side of the island.

The driver pulls up at the address—a warehouse, huge but unadorned, at the end of a blunt, unpopulated road. It has aluminum siding from top to bottom, flat roof, no windows, and the only visible way in or out is a single heavy steel door. I press a buzzer next to the door. Nobody answers. I try the door. It's locked. I walk the perimeter of the warehouse, which takes almost ten minutes because it's really big. The back and sides look just like the front except without a door. The building appears to be a perfect cube.

But when I come around to the front again, a thick-necked man in a well-tailored suit stands outside the door with a cell to his ear. He barks at me in Cantonese and I hand him the piece of paper, which he crumples into a ball in his fist. His suit jacket hangs open just enough to show me a semiautomatic pistol in a shoulder holster. He murmurs something into his cell, which apparently has a call running, listens, looks at me, and nods. He uncrumples the piece of paper, takes out a pen, and writes another address on it.

I walk away from the man with the gun, and the car service takes me to the new address in Shek O, a peninsula on the scenic southeast-ern tip of the island. The address turns out to be a multileveled mod-ernist mansion perched on a craggy red cliff overlooking the South China Sea. It's sleek but classic, sharp lines, elegant materials, inte-grating local architectural traditions with a confident globalist style. The driver says a house like that on a property like this would cost around thirty million dollars. I think he's expecting quite the tip.

As I crunch along the pebbled courtyard leading to the front door, I notice the stones have two shades, light gray and dark gray, and they form a shape that's ubiquitous where I come from but con-siderably less so here. The pebbled shape is huge, big enough that you could see it from a satellite in orbit. The pilomotor reflex kicks in, every hair on my body raised in its pore. Because—it's a *whorl*.

I knock on the hand-carved wood front door.

The door opens.

When I saw him in 1965, he was forty-two. Which makes him ninety-three now. He still has the long face and crooked nose, although some blood vessels have broken along the bridge. Those full lips are thinner, his face ridged with wrinkles, his curly hair gone white and brittle. But he still has the thick eyebrows over three-colored eyes. He meets my startled expression with an amused grin.

It's Lionel Goettreider.

"Finally," he says.

105

So, Lionel Goettreider is real, he's alive, and he's been waiting for me.

"It's good to meet you, Mr. Barren," he says. "I'm Lionel Goettreider. I assume you're here to talk about time travel."

Since leaving San Francisco, I've been practicing what I might say, on the off chance I actually found him, to convince Lionel Goettreider I'm not a lunatic. I didn't expect that I wouldn't have to explain myself at all. I thought I'd be more nervous meeting him, the towering figure of my world. But I've seen him so many times in simulations that it's like running into the parent of a childhood friend at the grocery store—the main shock is how they've aged.

"It's an honor to meet you, sir," I say.

I reach out my hand and a slight tremor ripples across his face. *He's* the anxious one. He takes my hand and shakes it. I'm shaking Lionel Goettreider's hand.

He gestures for me to follow him inside. I notice he walks oddly, both stiff and fluid at the same time. Encircling his legs are these diaphanous wire-thin bands at six-inch intervals down to his ankles.

"They help me walk," Lionel says. "I won't bore you with the details but it involves subtle electrical stimulation of the muscles coupled with oscillating balance wedges and low-grade gravity manipulation. My own design. Everything here is."

The levels of the house—it's built directly into the cliffside, much longer than it is wide, so each room has an outrageous view of the South China Sea—are connected by rotating escalators with a flexible tile surface, so a man of limited mobility can get around without sacrificing style. We sit on a pair of armchairs that partially deflate and then subtly harden to fit our bodies. I try wiggling around but it's impossible to find a more comfortable sitting position than the one the chair has made for me.

Lionel taps a touch screen on his modal chair and a robot bartender hovers up on a cushion of circulating airflow, pouring us each a drink from one of several tiny nozzles. The bourbon it squirts out is ecstatically good, smoky and sharp. I want to hug the adorable robot. Seeing these nonchalant displays of technology so seamless they're practically magic, I kind of feel like crying. This is the first place I've been since I got to this degraded mirror of the world that reminds me of home.

"Let's get this out of the way, in case you're planning to deny it," Lionel says. "You were there. July 11, 1965. The day my experiment failed. I saw you in the lab, for just a moment, looking more or less exactly as you do right now."

"That's right," I say. "I was there."

Lionel softens, like it's a relief to finally know for sure he's not delusional. I recognize that expression because it's on my face too.

"I've waited to meet you for a very long time," Lionel says.

"How did you know I time traveled to your lab?"

"It was the only reasonable answer," he says.

"You have a different definition of reasonable than most people," I say.

Lionel looks out the window at the sea below the cliffs. He sips his bourbon, squints as the liquor scours his tongue.

"The experiment should've worked," he says. "I had accounted for everything. All possible errors. My calculations were accurate. But something went wrong. Something unaccountable. Something preternatural. Also, I saw you with my own eyes. Even factoring in possible visual or cognitive distortion from the energies released by my device, I knew I was seeing something real. *Someone* real. And then there were the readings. The faintest trace of an unknown type of radiation. I salvaged the detection equipment from the wreckage of my lab and went to work figuring out what it could be. The problem was it didn't exist. Until I turned it on again."

"Turned what on?" I say.

"The device, of course."

"You activated the Goettreider Engine?"

I can see he's about to ask what the *Goettreider Engine* is, but the very fact that I have a name for it seems to answer a long-standing question. He smiles. He's clearly not a man who smiles much.

"I wondered what your people called it," he says.

"My people?" I say.

"The people of the future. Isn't that where you're from?"

"I'm from the present," I say. "Just a different present. Another timeline. One where your experiment didn't fail. In fact, it succeeded beyond even your most expansive projections. Your device, what we call the Goettreider Engine, fueled a technological revolution that transformed the world."

"That's why I built it," he says. "That was my dream."

"Your dream should've come true," I say.

"Yes," he says. "Well, yes and no. The morning after the accident, I left the hospital and snuck back into my lab. I knew once someone had a chance to think clearly, they'd destroy my device and I couldn't let that happen. Not until I understood what went wrong. I planned to substitute an earlier prototype in the wreckage, a decoy no one but me could recognize as a fake. The lab was a ruin, but the device was intact. And the battery, of course. I'd constructed a high-yield battery to store any power generated during the experiment. When I checked, it was full. Which meant that even in failure, my device, what you call the *Engine,* it worked. The building's electricity had been shut off, the whole place closed down. It was only luck that the experiment happened on a Sunday, when the offices upstairs were empty, just seventeen people injured instead of hundreds. But the battery had stored more than enough energy to power up the device. I salvaged as much of the equipment as I could and ran a full diagnostic before turning it back on. I found a serious flaw in the design. It would've caused a radiation surge that may well have killed everyone in that lab if the device *had* operated properly the first time. I worked all day and night to correct it, expecting any moment to be shut down by the authorities. But no one came. They were waiting for test results to ensure the building wasn't dangerously irradiated. It gave me time to fix the device and activate it again. This time, of course, it operated flawlessly. It still does."

"Wait," I say, "the Engine is on? Right now?"

"I switched it on two days after the accident and never switched it off," he says. "It's been running nonstop ever since."

He taps the touch screen and the chair inflates, tilting to gently place him on his feet. An escalator takes us down three levels to a thick steel door that retracts to reveal a concrete room.

Inside it, surrounded by ducts and tubes and cables, is a Goettreider Engine.

A lot of the components have been updated and streamlined, but its familiar design is intact. I can *feel* it working, a dense, undulating field of pure energy that asynchronously rotates around the primary absorption coil. From the side it appears as a sparkly halo, Saturn-like. But I know without needing to see it directly what it looks like from above.

A whorl.

106

The Engine is so glorious it's hard to look away. Lionel stands next to me, vibrating with pride and curiosity.

"Is it amazing?" Lionel says. "Your world?"

"Yes," I say.

"That's what kept me going," he says. "After the accident. After the failure. I don't even know how I managed to avoid a total system meltdown. I've gone through the chronology of events countless times and by my calculations turning off the device midsequence should've been . . . cataclysmic."

"It was me," I say. "You couldn't see me, but I intervened before it was too late."

"You pushed me away?" he says.

"Yeah," I say. "And turned it back on."

"I thought I felt a hand shove me, but it was all so chaotic, it could've been compressed force waves. The energies unleashed were unpredictable."

"Where I come from," I say, "every schoolkid knows the sequence of events from that day. It's the pivot point of human history."

"It's hard to hear what should've been," he says. "Even though, like I said, it's what kept me going. All I ever wanted was to make the world better, but instead I almost ended it. Looking back, I must have shut down some essential part of myself to get through it. But it also gave me the clinical detachment to make sense of what made no sense. Two pieces of data. One, that the radiation signature emitted by the device *after* it was turned on was somehow detectable *before* it was turned on. Two, that I *saw* you there, wearing unfamiliar clothing and clearly not expecting to be seen. I theorized you had an invisibility field around you that was somehow destabilized by the energy spiking from the device."

"That's right," I say.

"But that meant you came from somewhere well beyond the technological capabilities of the time. Only one explanation resolved both data points."

"A time traveler," I say.

"A time traveler, yes. Which meant the experiment was not just a success but a triumph, significant enough to justify coming back in time to witness it. Had my experiment succeeded, my plan had been to leave the device running, conceivably forever, so I assumed you pinpointed the exact moment in space and time by following the unbroken radiation trail from the future to the past."

"We call it tau radiation," I say.

"Tau?" he says. "But it has nothing to do with tau leptons. Or, wait, tau particles weren't isolated until the mid-1970s. If this tau radiation was discovered earlier, then logically the tau lepton would've been given a different name. So, in your world, what do you call leptons that can decay into hadrons if not tauons?"

"I have no idea," I say.

"But aren't you a scientist?" Lionel says.

"Not exactly," I say. "I guess I'm what was called a . . . chrononaut."

"A *chrononaut*?" says Lionel.

"I didn't come up with the name for it."

Lionel looks a bit disappointed, like he expected to be addressing a real peer. This actually relaxes me. I've spent a lot of time in this world being treated with respect I didn't deserve. Disappointment is kind of comforting.

"When I pulled the lever to shut down the device," Lionel says, "it was an instinctive reaction. Shock, basically. If it had been even a few seconds later, the energy flow would've stabilized. But it started to collapse into itself. By turning it back on when you did, you saved hundreds of millions of lives."

"I appreciate you saying that," I say, "but the world lost much more than it gained that day."

"It was a mess," Lionel says, "but it might have been salvageable even with the injuries. Some bruises and abrasions, a few broken bones and chipped teeth, nothing so awful. Except for Jerome. Losing his arm like that, it made me a monster. Still, I could never begrudge him because he saved her life that day. Do you know about . . . Ursula?"

"I was there," I say. "I saw everything."

"When *exactly* did you arrive that day?"

"A few minutes before the others came in. The Sixteen Witnesses. That's what we, uh, call them. You were alone in the lab. And then she came in, Ursula Francoeur."

"You saw us," he says. "Together."

"Yeah," I say.

"How long ago was it for you? That day in the lab?"

"Two weeks," I say. "Two and a half, I guess."

"Ursula used to say that the most complex physics question was a breeze compared to the contradictions of the human heart."

"I've heard that before," I say. "From her daughter."

"You met Emma?" he says.

"She's the one who told me where to find you."

"Did she say anything about me?"

"Do you think you're her father?"

Taken aback, Lionel sags a bit, but his leg joists won't really let him, so he has this weirdly deflated look, like he's been dressed in a larger man's suit, except it's made of his muscles and skin.

"I don't know," he says. "It's possible. No, it's likely. Ursula refused to do a paternity test. She said it was a trade-off. Like Adam's rib transforming into Eve. Jerome's arm would become his daughter.

I tried to joke about it once, that I was surprised someone of her intellect would resort to a biblical analogy, and it was the only time Ursula ever showed me her hard edge. She said this was the deal. The baby was Jerome's or there wouldn't be a baby."

His eyes get watery. He turns away, although I don't think it's because of me. It's like he doesn't want the Engine to see him tear up.

"Does Jerome know?" he says.

"Ursula told him about the affair. He suspects about Emma, but he doesn't know for sure. I don't think he knows she saw you in Hong Kong before she got pregnant."

"How the hell do you know about that?"

"Emma told me," I say.

"She knows?"

"In the hospital, not long before she died, Ursula told her she never stopped loving you. You told her at the funeral you lived in Hong Kong. I think she put it together. It helps that she looks nothing like Jerome and a lot like you."

Lionel smiles at this, just a little.

"We were good at covering our tracks," he says. "Nobody ever knew that our relationship continued."

"Well, Emma's in her late forties," I say. "That trip was a long time ago."

"No. It never stopped. Our affair went on for fifty years. It only ended last week."

"Last week?" I say. "Ursula died two years ago."

"Yes, well," Lionel says, "there's something else I need to show you."

107

A black car waits for us, chauffeured by the same thick-necked thug from the warehouse—Lionel calls him Wen—and I don't recognize the make or model because, of course, the car is Lionel's own design, constructed from a superdense biodegradable compound and running on a battery charged by the Engine. On the winding cliff-edged road from Shek O around the eastern side of Hong Kong Island to Chai Wan, Lionel tells me what happened to him between the accident in 1965 and today.

Lionel Goettreider is still clearly an unparalleled genius, but he's a meandering conversationalist. He doesn't seem to have a lot of people to talk to and there were *many* tangents to explain arcane technical facts even *I* wasn't interested in and, let's face it, this was probably the most important day of my life. Yet I still found myself distracted by the scenery blurring past, steep cliffs crawling with lush foliage, rolling layers of misty green hills, and the cool blue of Tai Tam Bay, while Lionel went into serpentine asides about things like the difference between photons and polaritons—if you actually care, a polariton is a combination of a photon with a dipole-carrying material excitation like a phonon, which is a kind of quasiparticle in condensed matter that involves vibrating elastic webs of interacting atoms and molecules—and if you absorbed more than three consecutive words of that, then, congratulations, you and Lionel Goettreider would get along famously.

The gist of it is, in the aftermath of the disaster on July 11, 1965, all seventeen survivors were quarantined in the same hospital—I know, *so awkward*—because there was a pretty legitimate fear they'd been mortally poisoned with a marrow-blackening dose of radiation. But they were all clean, radiation-free.

I'm not sure how to tell Lionel that everyone in that room, including him and Ursula and Jerome, would've been dead within a few months if I hadn't altered the timeline. He's obviously stacked a lot on the belief that his experiment should've transformed the world, but it's divorced from the fact of their horrific deaths. Theirs was not a fifty-year love triangle. It was an unknown, long-buried secret on which statues to his greatness were erected. Literally—there's a gigantic statue of Lionel Goettreider at the spot in San Francisco where his ashes were dispersed, holding a replica of the original Goettreider Engine that emits its own shimmering whorl.

Following everyone's safe discharge from the hospital—Jerome's arm was cleanly cauterized by the energy plume that seared it off—there was an inquest into the disaster. Overseen by the federal government, it was intensely political and fraught. In July 1965, the US ground war in Vietnam was only four months old and President Johnson was about to announce he was sending 125,000 troops over there, along with more than doubling the draft. He was heavily invested in the "space race" with Russia and achieving President Kennedy's goal of landing astronauts on the moon by the end of the decade. The federal government *needed* a US population aflutter with wide-eyed wonder at American scientific know-how. If word got out that a minor experiment in an esoteric niche field of research had come within seconds of destroying half the continent, that would've been really, really bad for a man who was trying to hold the country together with his bare hands as it wobbled on the razor's edge of a total freak-out. President Johnson had signed the Civil Rights Act into law only a year before—hardly an uncontroversial move. A near cataclysm on American soil that would've made Hiroshima and Nagasaki look like a firecracker going off in an empty parking lot, particularly one funded by the US government itself, was not politically viable.

So, a deal was made. Everyone would shut the hell up about it, forever. Jerome was the wildest card in the deck, what with the amputated arm, but he had a bureaucrat's soul, and a series of rapid career advancements kept him quiet. Plus, he knew it was what Ursula wanted. The other fourteen observers were likewise rewarded for their silence with a well-greased professional track. None of them paid income tax ever again.

And Lionel Goettreider was asked to leave the United States of America and never come back. He had immigrated to the US following the Second World War, as America trawled the planet's ocean of scientific minds to draw all the best brains into its borders. Now he was tossed back out to sea.

Two days after the accident, Lionel snuck into the wrecked lab and salvaged the Engine, substituting it with a lookalike precursor model, fixed the previously undetected radiation surge that should've killed them all, and switched it on. He never turned it off again.

He was supposed to go back to Denmark but instead he went in the other direction, loaded the operating Engine onto a ship, and sailed with it from San Francisco to Hong Kong.

And there, in near total isolation, Lionel Goettreider invented the future.

108

Lionel's being all coy about why we're going back to his warehouse in Chai Wan—I'm sure you've already figured it out, but I'm trying to lean into the whole suspense thing, so I'll defer to his taste for drama.

We get stuck in traffic jammed by a prodemocracy demonstration, creeping forward at a pace that drives Wen to sputter a flurry of Cantonese expletives, the front windshield flecked with outraged spittle.

When Lionel moved to Hong Kong, he had a goal in mind. A goal so technologically advanced as to be absurd. There were countless innovations that had to happen to even get him to the point where he could create testable theoretical models of his goal, let alone construct an actual prototype to fail and improve and fail and improve and fail and improve, and no one else was equipped to do it because no one else had what he had: a working Goettreider Engine. A source of unlimited clean fuel to power anything he could build.

Obviously *this* Lionel Goettreider did not make his revolutionary power source available to the world at large. *This* Lionel didn't have the incentive of assured martyrdom sweeping his future like a lighthouse beam as his body caved in on itself due to acute radiation poisoning from his own defective device. *This* Lionel was rescued from nobility by impotent resentment at the unfair hand dealt to him in his very moment of triumph. It was the vanity of genius I recognize so well from my father.

That was the really messed-up thing about being stuck in traffic with Lionel Goettreider—he reminded me a lot of my father. Not my dad from here, the dotty but warm and careful man who wilted in my mother's shadow. My *real* father.

Once Lionel arrived in Hong Kong, he invented . . . everything. When he needed to alter the trajectory of global technology, he'd set up a shell company to quietly sell one of his inventions in exchange for cash, stock, and zero credit. Through his front companies, he developed secret, one-sided relationships with the titans of the manufacturing and technology industries. His work is everywhere in the modern world. It *is* the modern world. A ubiquitous thread in the fabric of civilization. He is the anonymous polymath wizard behind the curtain of everyday life.

The sick thing is he didn't even sell off his best stuff—it was all the things he didn't need anymore because he'd already moved beyond them. Like how at his home there are no electrical cords, because Lionel invented wireless electricity fields more than two decades ago. Fifteen years ago he dropped electronics altogether and shifted into photonics, which he then replaced with experimental polaritonics five years later. He left humanity to cobble together modern civilization from his discards and trash.

The world I come from isn't quite as lost as I thought. It turns out it was concealed in a little pocket of the planet, conceived and built and nurtured by Lionel Goettreider, and he was profoundly uninterested in sharing it with the rest of us.

109

It's easy to be distracted by Lionel, the layers of ego, resentment, vanity, and expectation roiling and lunging and grappling for dominance in his tone. It's like he wants my approval and my awe but also can't help jabbing at me for taking so long to find him. I can sense this abyss of black terror under everything he says.

I know that terror because I felt it the last time I saw Penny—it's the fear that what my brain is telling me isn't real, that something fundamental is defective inside me, and that everything I think I know is an auroral lattice of self-justification erected to protect me from my own bad wiring. What if I'm a Goettreider Engine with a fatal flaw, but instead of power I generate florid delusions that poison me like a radiation leak?

The thing is, I miss Penny so much. I think about her constantly. I know I sound like a teenager with a newborn crush, but goddamn it, it's hard to focus on anything except her. What we had was so unexpected and now that I don't know if we'll ever have more of it I feel doubled over with longing and loss.

I'm sitting in a super-car with the world's smartest person, the key to everything I've been searching for, and he's taking me to a covert lair full of secrets and mysteries and yet my mind can barely absorb any of it. My graceless disaster of a brain keeps abandoning the present to flit back to moments like the first time I kissed Penny, the precise pressure her lips exerted on mine in that initial contact between our mouths, the seesaw of our jaws as we found the right fit, her top lip, my top lip, her bottom lip, my bottom lip, the stubble on my chin rough on the soft skin of hers.

If Lionel wants to hoard his treasure like a fairy-tale creature, that's up to him. I just want Penny to trust me again.

Anxiety lurches up sticky in my throat because everything rests on this ninety-three-year-old man nattering on next to me, and I'm sorry if that sounds cruel but as he gloats about how he finally deigned to grant the world the technology that enabled cellular networks and global positioning and the Internet itself decades after he first invented them, all I can think is: *What if he's crazy too?* Maybe this is some communal delusion, like religious zealots who writhe on the floor and speak in tongues. Maybe Lionel and I share a unique psychological disorder where we think we rightfully belong to an alternate techno-utopian reality and we're crucial to the true destiny of humankind. What if meeting him doesn't prove I'm right—it just proves we're both wrong?

110

We pull up at the Chai Wan warehouse and Wen locks us in the car while he does a perimeter sweep. Lionel fidgets with a button on his shirt. The thread that binds it has started to come loose.

"I'm sorry," says Lionel, "but something puzzles me. Why do you keep calling it an *engine*?"

"What do you mean?" I say. "That's what it's called."

"But it makes no sense," he says. "Engines turn energy into force. Generators turn force into energy. It should be called the Goettreider *Generator*."

I actually remember a cranky science teacher in high school griping that Lionel Goettreider would be aghast that his legacy had been tarnished with this fundamental inaccuracy. When President Johnson announced the invention to the world in a televised address on August 22, 1965, his science advisers were still arguing over a list of names. Two of President Johnson's special assistants, Jack Valenti and Richard N. Goodwin, both took credit for calling the device "Dr. Goettreider's Engine of the Future"—the cheery appellation that Johnson used in his speech—which was soon informally shortened to: *Goettreider Engine*. The name stuck.

Of course, the reason the invention could be named by a presidential speechwriter instead of its inventor is that Lionel didn't live long enough to see his device change the world. He didn't even live long enough to give it a name. I know I should tell him this, that every moment I don't will only make it more awkward when I do, but it's hard to explain to someone that they should've died in hideous, molten pain five decades ago.

Before I can make a decision one way or the other, Wen gives the all clear and Lionel does his stiff-but-fluid walk to the one door in the otherwise impenetrable box. He makes this conductor-like gesture in front of it and the door opens with the clunk of heavy bolts retracting.

Inside, the warehouse is as unadorned as the outside, blank cement walls, soundproofing insulation, exposed joists and beams. Lionel's home felt like the last refuge of the world I left behind, but his warehouse is just a warehouse. The air in here is cold and astringent, like anything organic has been thoroughly purged.

There are some neat tricks, though. Like no electrical cords anywhere. The overhead lights are spheres of a billowing, iridescent gas. What looks like a solid cement floor turns out to be thinly layered wedges on rotating hinges that move like a conveyer belt, propelling forward at a speed Lionel can modulate with a swipe of his finger in the air. He wears what appears to be an antique spring-and-gear wristwatch that's dense with motion-detecting analytics, which control everything around us.

We pass door after door, segmented metal with elaborate locking mechanisms and sensor panels. They're all unmarked but illuminate invitingly as we approach, like lonely puppies wagging their tails at footsteps on the front porch. Lionel, so chatty in the car, is now all terse. Maybe he's trying to build up suspense for the big reveal, but my mind feels blank, overloaded, so the theatrics are lost on me.

Lionel points to an unmarked door at the end of a hallway and the floor halts in front of it. He makes another gesture and a radiant indigo circle is beamed onto me from an overhead emitter. Every follicle on my body tingles as I'm scanned. He looks at his watch and I see a glint refract off his eyes—he wears some sort of contact lenses that interact with his watch to project a three-dimensional image into his field of vision. The segmented door folds in on itself, revealing a dark room of indeterminate size. Lionel walks in, expecting me to follow. And I do.

He waits for the door to unfold closed behind us, sealing us into blackness.

And then the lights come on. It's a very big room, round, with a domed ceiling seven or eight stories up, lined with thousands of pin-point lights that cast a diffuse, shadowless glow across the vast, sloping space.

In the center of the room is a small blocky device, brushed steel with ultra-black paneling that must have light-absorbing qualities, because the room's ambient glare kind of bends around it. A few flexible pipes lead out of a bulbous chamber in the back, snake off across the floor, and feed into a massive rotating vent at the far end of the room.

In a ten-foot radius, the floor around the device is shinier than it is in the rest of the room, like the concrete has been alchemically polished into mirror.

There's an odd, staticky, salty odor to the air. Not quite sulfuric. Like . . . oceanic.

"What is it?" I say.

"Well," Lionel says, "it's a time machine, of course."

111

Lionel Goettreider built a time machine.

All the technology he spent five decades developing, this was why—to make time travel possible. He didn't care about any of his groundbreaking inventions on their own merits. They only mattered to the extent that they brought him closer to his goal. Some he tossed out his door for the world to gnaw on like a hungry dog with a meaty bone. Some he never bothered to release because he didn't think that anyone who *wasn't* trying to create a time machine required or deserved them.

Like teleportation. Lionel simply felt that humanity had no need to atomically decompose and reconstitute themselves between locations. But he needed to invent teleportation for his time machine to work, so he did. That's what's off-putting about spending time with Lionel—not the noble genius-martyr of my world, the weird old recluse of this world. He's even more brilliant than he was fifty years ago, but he doesn't have the clean-lined personality of a mythic historical figure. He's needy and a bit glum and also vain and abrasive and smug. He regards this retrograde world with amusement and contempt but derives deep validation from his secret role in shaping it, while also resenting everyone for not recognizing his importance, even though he's the one who chose to conceal himself. It's unsettling.

Lionel did have a few things going for him that my father didn't when he invented his version of time travel. Namely, he knew it was possible, or at least had a pretty good working theory that it was possible. The readings that my presence in 1965 fed into his detection equipment gave him the key insight that he could use the energy signature of the Goettreider Engine itself as a radiation trail through space and time.

"Does it work?" I say.

"Yes," Lionel says, "it works."

"How do you know?"

"Because," he says, "I've used it."

112

Before the accident on July 11, 1965, Lionel and Ursula had been seeing each other for just under a year. They'd met by chance in the reception area outside Jerome's office. Lionel had a meeting to discuss the funding opportunities that Jerome was in a position to approve and Ursula had dropped by unannounced to see if her husband was free for lunch. Jerome was tied up or claimed he was tied up and so, intrigued by each other, Lionel and Ursula had lunch together.

This is how the world changes—two strangers experience a crackle of chemistry. Circumstances allow them to explore it in the most hesitant and cautious way. But the kind of immediate, intoxicating connection that Ursula and Lionel felt is a quantum flame. Attention is its oxygen.

Lionel was forty-one. Ursula was thirty-seven. Neither had children when they met. Their work meant everything to them. Ursula and Jerome had been married for only two years but had already settled into a functional comfort that proved useful to both their careers. She miscarried twice in the first year of marriage and they agreed to stop trying for a while and focus on their work. Lionel had spent his thirties looking for a spouse who was his intellectual equal. He wanted a wife who understood everything that he understood. Who understood *him*. He never found her—until Ursula. She dazzled him. He couldn't understand how a man as politically astute but imaginatively dull as Jerome had convinced her to marry him. Lionel didn't grasp that part of what allowed Ursula to trailblaze as a woman in scientific academia was checking all the boxes as a stable, devoted wife. In the early 1960s, the fact that she didn't get married until age thirty-five had been widely noted. To the kinds of people who granted tenure, published articles, assigned classes, and financed research, an unmarried woman in her mid-thirties *implied* something. The ring on her finger made all that go away. Also, and this was by no means insignificant, Ursula *wanted* to believe in her marriage. It mattered to her.

They didn't sleep together right away. It took months for Ursula to trust him. And for Lionel to come to terms with what their relationship would have to be. He didn't think of himself as the kind of man who would have sex with another man's wife, even if he was speedily and irretrievably falling into her orbit. So he had to make some fundamental revisions to his ethical clockwork. But revise himself he did. And come to trust him she did. And so their affair began.

After the accident, they didn't speak for almost three years. They saw each other only once, fleetingly, in the hospital where they were all quarantined until the doctors deemed them unharmed by the unknown energies that erupted during the experiment. Someone had the good sense to keep Lionel lodged away from the others, so even glimpsing each other down the hall that one time was an unexpected bit of luck. Or a cruel twist of fate. Lionel saw it as a bit of both.

In those initial lonely and demoralizing months in Hong Kong, what Lionel wanted more than anything was to simply *talk* to Ursula. But he knew how her mind worked—he had to wait until she was ready, however long that took.

It took two years and ten months. In May of 1968, Ursula showed up at Lionel's lab in Hong Kong, unannounced. He didn't even know she knew where he was.

That day, she set her terms. She couldn't bear to never see him again. But she'd never leave Jerome, not after he lost a piece of himself saving her life. So, this was the deal—they'd see each other when they could, but never where either of them lived. When one or the

other was going to an appropriate location for a legitimate professional reason, they'd get in touch and, if the timing worked, they'd
meet. In the interim, however long that might be, they would not
communicate. If at any time either of their feelings about the other
changed, they'd both accept the decision to end it without question
or argument.

Of course it was always up to Ursula.

The truth is they both figured it couldn't last. Eventually Ursula
would get over Lionel, or she'd fall back in love with Jerome, or Lionel
would meet someone else, or he'd get over Ursula, or they'd simply
tire of the contorted logistics and the affair would run its course.
Instead, it went on for decades. Usually it was one weekend a year.
Occasionally twice a year. There were stretches when they didn't see
each other for more than a year, sometimes two, once even three.

Every time they met, Ursula said this should probably be their
final encounter, that it was getting to be too much for her, the stress,
the anxiety, the split heart. They treated each time together as if it
was the last. It was nothing like the everyday intimacy of a marriage.

It's not that Lionel never got involved with anyone else. He did,
briefly. But none of them could possibly compare to Ursula. He tried
not to dwell on the fact that she was someone else's wife. Ursula
once tried to explain to Lionel that sex with Jerome was a different
biological act from sex with him—that it was friction and moisture
and whatever pleasure she felt came from its speed and uniformity.
Sex with Jerome was math. Sex with Lionel was physics. Jerome was
self-conscious about his stump and insisted on the lights being off so
she couldn't see him, but that meant he couldn't see her either. She
told Lionel if her head was cut off in a grotesque accident, she
doubted her husband could identify her naked body on a coroner's
slab. While Lionel knew every part of her, surface and depth. She
lived her life behind a mask that came off only when she was with him.

Lionel felt the opposite. He structured his life to be available at a
moment's notice, so when he'd get an out-of-nowhere message from

Ursula to meet in Prague or Buenos Aires or Tokyo on such and such a date, he could always be there. When he was with her, knowing each encounter could be the last, he was his best self, never letting down his guard or being anything but attentive, romantic, spontaneous. But when he wasn't with her, the mask came off and Lionel spiraled into increasingly dubious ethical terrain with his experiments.

He spent three-and-a-half decades doing two things—working on his time machine and waiting for Ursula to call. He fostered no other meaningful relationships. He let Ursula be everyone for him, but that also meant his intimate connection was limited to a few days a year. As the decades passed, this provisional arrangement turned into his whole life.

Until one day it all changed. Because his time machine was finally ready to test.

113

The greatest scientific experiment of all time happened in total obscurity.

On February 2, 2002, at 2:02 A.M., Lionel turned on his time machine and prepared to send himself sixty seconds into the past. He didn't know what might happen if he materialized in the same physical space as himself a minute earlier—and he didn't want to find out since it was probably nothing good—so he'd built a vacuum-sealed pod as a safe arrival point in his Shek O mansion seven miles away.

It worked. He spent one minute in the past and returned to the present, one minute after he'd left. He traveled from his lab at 2:02 A.M. to his home at 2:01 A.M. and then reappeared in his lab at 2:03 A.M. The full minute gap was intentional—to keep him aging chronologically. He was one minute older but had spent that minute in the past. There were no observers or recordings.

Afterward, he had a tinny déjà vu sensation, like trying to remember the address of a childhood home. There was a staticky, salty smell in the air, one he could never seem to wash out of his hair. But otherwise, following this culmination of his life's work, he felt unchanged. He'd built something unbelievable, the greatest invention in human history. But now he was stuck, because Lionel's ultimate plan required the one element he couldn't simply invent—me. He was waiting for me to show up at his door.

Like a lot of high-functioning technical geniuses, when Lionel had a plan he could accomplish the impossible. But when he didn't have a plan, when all he could do was wait with no end in sight, he started to think about the *possible*. For example, all the things you could do with a time machine.

For thirty-four years, Lionel let Ursula contact him. On a whim, for the first time he contacted her instead. They arranged to meet at a picturesque inn outside Naples. He understood the look on her face when he opened the door to the room—this really was it. She couldn't do it anymore. She came to say good-bye.

And so, as they lay in bed together, the late afternoon sun glowing through the open window, he told Ursula about his breakthrough. Together, they came up with a plan.

Ursula's main anxiety was that Jerome would find out about the affair and use it to destroy her relationship with Emma. Her daughter was the great unspoken between Ursula and Lionel. They talked about pretty much everything except the obvious math underlying Emma's parentage. Ursula led a double life, caught between twin realities, dedicated wife and mother versus torrid, intellectually star-crossed lover. But in Ursula's mind it required Emma to be Jerome's.

Time travel solved a number of structural challenges with managing an affair between two hemispheres. This is how they did it—Ursula would go somewhere private, it didn't matter where, and she'd turn on a signal-frequency beacon that Lionel made for her. If there were no interruptions for an allotted time, say, three hours, she'd turn off the beacon and send Lionel a message with its spatiotemporal coordinates.

As soon as Ursula sent the message, a memory would surge in, like it had temporarily slipped her mind—she had spent those hours with Lionel. He had appeared as soon as the beacon was activated. It could be anywhere. A hotel or an inn, but also her office, even her own bedroom. As long as they were careful and precise, they could have time and time and time. They were both scientists, so careful and precise came easily.

They had more than a decade of this arrangement, seeing each other several times a week, the happiest years of Lionel's life. Occasionally he considered visiting himself in the past to help develop the technology sooner, so he could have more time with Ursula when they weren't so old and didn't need so many pharmaceutical inducements to enjoy each other's bodies. But that seemed unwise. Dangerous and foolish. He was still a scientist, careful and precise.

And then the beacon wasn't turned on for a whole week. Then two. Three. Before the time machine, a year or even two could go by with no contact between them. But now he was used to seeing her almost every day.

Still, Lionel was good at waiting. He'd waited most of his life.

It took just over a month before he found out that Ursula was dead.

114

Lionel lapsed into a deep depression. It all felt pointless. He began to doubt I'd ever show up. Maybe the time traveling he did to be with Ursula had corrupted his reality. Maybe he was waiting for someone who would never come.

After six months webbed into a restless lethargy, Lionel came up with a new plan. It was bad science, the opposite of genius, but he didn't care. With Ursula gone, the mask he wore in her presence, the best him, that man was gone too. All that was left was who he was without her.

The last time he'd seen Ursula was the day before she collapsed in her kitchen and Jerome rushed her to the hospital. She died six days later with Emma at her bedside.

Lionel had an existential decision to make. He could use the beacons Ursula had set for him in the past to go back and try to cure her cancer before it took root. But it would mean remaking experiences of Ursula's that he'd already revised. The results would be unpredictable.

Until this point, his trips back in time had been consistent and seemingly without consequence. This was different. This was tying the space-time continuum in knots. And the effect could be profound—he might save the life of the woman he loved.

So he did what you do when you're heartbroken and have a time machine—something stupid.

115

It was the time travel that did it to her.

I don't know how much more patience you have for semi-lucid explanations of time-travel physics, but I need to make something clear—Lionel's version of time travel wasn't the same as my father's. Both of them figured out how to send a person backward in space and time, but they went about it in categorically different ways. Two separate roads to the destination.

A crucial distinction is—I went back to before my own birth and accidentally caused a new timeline to branch off from that point, but Lionel was traveling within his own lifetime to other locations on the planet. Which meant he existed simultaneously in two places at the same moment in time.

So it took him a lot longer to realize what I learned right away—time travel is bad for the human brain. Your body can handle it, more or less, but your mind struggles with the cognitive dissonance.

At first, it seems okay. Your brain is very good at managing cognitive dissonance. Arguably, it's your brain's main purpose. Your senses absorb a calamitous frenzy of information every moment you're conscious, and your brain has to streamline it all into coherence so that you can function. It lets you focus, shunts unnecessary stimuli to the periphery, and parses huge gulps of perceptual data with dazzling heuristic tricks.

Like movies. You know how movies work, right? What you see as a moving image is actually a series of sequential still frames that your brain interprets as movement thanks to persistence of vision and the stroboscopic effect. Your brain's prodigious capacity to cohere data is why a painting can look gorgeously lifelike from a distance but, up close, degenerates into globs of pigment on canvas. Or how the individual instruments of an orchestra gel into a symphony.

Lionel's version of time travel didn't ask his brain to hold simultaneous memories of the same time *at* the same time. He experienced his trips to the past as present-tense events. He always returned to the present after the same amount of time he spent in the past—if he left the present at 8:00 P.M. and spent two hours in the past, he'd return to the present at 10:00 P.M. The reason for this time management was so he could age properly, but it also meant his brain was never required to double up on its experiential intake. When he got back to the present, his memory of the past didn't *feel* like the past. It felt like he'd teleported to another location in another time zone. It's just that the time zone was in the past. So his memories maintained accurate chronology.

But Ursula's didn't.

Lionel wasn't overwriting his own experiences, but she was, and it destroyed Ursula's mind. The conflicting timelines gnawed at the structural integrity of her neural barriers. They were just trying to protect her marriage by using only the hours they already knew would be safe, but each time Lionel went back to see her Ursula's brain mapped a new memory over the old one.

The immediate effect was negligible. The cumulative effect was devastating. Her brilliant, expansive mind, the thing that most attracted him to her, that made her who she was, came undone. No human being had ever experienced this before, having small parcels of their memories revised, again and again and again. To cope, her brain, as a biological organ, began to secrete neuritic plaques to scab over what it interpreted as damage to the gray matter, similar in protein structure to the abnormal neurofibrillary tangles of Alzheimer's disease.

As their time-travel romance continued over the years, these neu-ritic plaques, unique in human neurology because her situation was unique in human history, curdled into a coarse poison—malignant cancer cells buried deep in the memory centers of Ursula's brain. They didn't affect her everyday activity, until they outgrew their nest and went looking for new real estate.

Ursula knew she was losing it. She could feel her sharp, complex mind collapsing in on itself like a neglected backyard shed. For the preceding months, she'd kept their encounters brief and carnal to conceal the truth from Lionel. She never told him that she'd started chemotherapy treatments. She was worried about what he might do.

She knew him well.

116

It's the middle of the night on the other side of the planet, and between the trip to San Francisco, the flight to Hong Kong, and the shuffled time zones, Penny's had a few days to think about everything that happened. What is she doing right now? Did she open the store, greet customers, shelve returns, order stock, act like nothing's wrong? Is she sleeping peacefully or not at all? Is my absence making things better or worse? How can I prove to her incontrovertibly that John will never come back?

I need answers but what Lionel is giving me is just information. I expected the Lionel Goettreider who died in 1965, the selfless genius-martyr, his mistakes and failures and heartbreaks retroactively bronzed into biographical trivia. But here, in this world, they're just mistakes and failures and heartbreaks. His face is not the face of a statue. It's the face of a man worn down by time. And the more he talks, the less I trust him.

Maybe Penny would know how to respond to his confessions. Maybe she'd show the right mix of compassion and respect and curiosity. Maybe Penny would trust him. At least the Penny who existed before I showed up in her life. That morning with John, maybe it created a new version of reality, just like my time traveling did, one in which Penny is as different from the woman I met in the bookstore as I am from John.

You don't need time travel to smash apart a world.

But it helps.

117

Unfortunately, this is not the story of how Lionel Goettreider cured cancer. It's the story of how the smartest person who ever lived failed to save the love of his life—and what that failure did to him.

Lionel was a physicist and an engineer, not an oncologist, not a geneticist. His genius had limits. He spent the next eighteen months trying to cure cancer or at least slow its progress. He couldn't do it. Maybe if he'd attempted it a few decades earlier. But even his great insights into the mechanics of time travel happened in his forties and fifties. The subsequent decades were about solving the logistic barriers. He finished building his time machine in 2002 and had spent the past dozen years sleeping with Ursula and self-medicating to be physically capable of sleeping with Ursula. His best years were behind him. Still, he tried.

His most effective notion was nanotechnological hybrid bacteria that eat cancer cells. The problem was getting them, once unleashed, to distinguish midfeast between corrupted cells and the healthy cells adjacent to them. Sometimes the nanites just kept eating once they got a taste for human flesh, so they had to be carefully monitored.

Lionel went back to his final visit with Ursula. He didn't want to be in the same place at the same time as himself, so he used the out-point of the beacon as his in-point. To Ursula, it was like he disappeared and instantly reappeared looking two years older.

She immediately understood what Lionel's plan to save her life really was—and she didn't want it. Her mind was gone and it wasn't coming back. She was uninterested in a mindless life. She begged him not to go back any further. Even if they figured out the exact moment the cancer first appeared in her hippocampus, lodged deep in her medial temporal lobe, it was several years earlier. She needed her happy memories. She didn't want to trade years' worth of them for memories of his desperate and probably fruitless attempts to cure her. She wanted to die peacefully with whatever was left of her once-magnificent brain, lying in bed reminiscing about their times together. His body and her body, connected in a way that gave her life meaning, even if it was a secret meaning, a hidden meaning, a shameful meaning. If he were to take those memories away from her, it would be a far more devastating amputation than what happened to Jerome all those decades ago.

Lionel promised her he wouldn't go back any further. They cried, they kissed, they said good-bye.

As soon as he returned to the present, he went back again. And again. And again. And again and again and again and again. He lost count of how many times he went back to that exact same moment. It's not just the promise he made to her—there are technical reasons why he couldn't go back any further than that last day together. But, each time, he tried a different way to convince Ursula to let him attempt to cure her. Each time, she refused. Each time they cried and kissed and said good-bye and each time he tried again.

He went back and forced her to take the treatment and the treatment failed and she died anyway, her final memory of him one of betrayal and anger. He tried again and forced her again and it failed again and she died in his arms, her brain consumed by out-of-control nanites, Lionel frantically trying to deactivate them before they ate her whole and infected him too. He tried again, failed again, tried again, failed again, and each time Ursula got worse, more confused, more disoriented, less present, less herself. Her husband and daughter just thought it was the ravages of her disease. To them, locked into linear time and unaware of Lionel's chronic resetting of Ursula's experience, it just seemed like she got very sick, very fast.

And so, for the first time in his life, Lionel Goettreider gave up. He went back one last time and Ursula was a wreck, because he wrecked her, and so he just held her and told her he was sorry. They cried, they kissed, and they said good-bye.

This time, he stayed in the past. Ursula collapsed in her kitchen the next day and Jerome rushed her to the hospital. She died six days later with Emma at her bedside.

Lionel went to the funeral, spoke with Emma for the first time, tried to apologize to Jerome, and when it was over he returned to the present. Before that, his longest time in the past had been about three hours. His final trip was just over a week.

You love someone for fifty years and then they die. People talk about grief as emptiness, but it's not empty. It's full. Heavy. Not an absence to fill. A weight to pull. Your skin caught on hooks chained to rough boulders made of all the futures you thought you would have. How do you keep five decades of love from souring into a snakebite that makes your own heart the threat, drawing the poison up and down the length of you?

Goddamn it, I don't want to but I can't help thinking about my father. And what it felt like for him when my mother died. Because of course I never asked.

I remember, a week after her death, finding a dozen grilled cheese sandwiches discarded on their kitchen counter with a single bite taken out of each one. I tossed them in the organic dissolution module and shook my head at my father's self-absorption—he can unravel the mysteries of time travel but he can't work the food synthesizer.

Now I understand. It wasn't waste. It was longing. He was trying to re-create a meal his wife made him for thirty years. But the machine couldn't get the flavor right. And so something as banal as a sandwich becomes fraught with sadness.

My father spent his life in Lionel Goettreider's shadow and I spent my life judging him unworthy of the comparison. It took until now to see him for what he *didn't* do. He didn't use his time machine. He didn't go back. He didn't save her. Whatever pain he felt, he *lived* with it. He had an inner compass that eluded Lionel. And me too.

When my mother died, my father was four months away from the scientific triumph he'd worked on his whole life. I was all he had left. Even if it doesn't matter, even if it never happened, even if the only place that pain still exists is in my memory, it turns out my father finally taught me something about love.

118

Once, over dinner in a small bistro in the countryside outside Clermont-Ferrand, after a day spent hiking the cinder cones of the Chaîne des Puys volcano range, Ursula ate dessert and explained to Lionel her conception of reality. According to her, reality isn't concrete. It's loose and gelatinous, like the crème brûlée she was midway through. The surface is crystalline, but it's just a hard, thin crust that keeps the soft insides held in place. When pierced, it cracks into jagged shards as the innards spill out.

Lionel admits to me he fears that what he did to the timeline has precipitated a systemic failure in reality itself. It started because two people wanted some time together. But it ended with one unable to let the other go. Returning to the same moment in time over and over again is like repeatedly tapping a spot on a mirror with your fingernail. Is it enough to break the mirror? Probably not. But how do you even tell if it's doing something imperceptibly damaging to its structural integrity?

What happens if the hard skin of reality punctures? What comes out?

I know there is a better version of this world because I lived there and saw its wonders undreamt of. But that doesn't mean there isn't a much worse version of this world standing in the yard hoping someone leaves the back door unlocked.

Am I being too coy? Let me be more plain—terrors undreamt of, that's what comes out when the hard skin breaks open.

If a single mistake I made five decades ago can create a whole new reality, what did all of Lionel's mistakes on all of his trips back in time do to the world? And to *me*?

I have a question that's been clawing at me since Lionel started explaining all of this. It's one of those questions you have to ask even though you know the answer.

"The last time you went to the past," I say, "when *exactly* did you get back?"

Lionel checks a readout on his watch. He tells me he returned five days ago, in what would've been the early morning of last Sunday in Toronto.

Already knowing the answer doesn't stop the icy burn from gripping my muscles and organs. When Lionel traveled back to see Ursula that final time and stayed until her funeral, he was gone for much longer than ever before. A week in the past isn't like tapping the mirror with your fingernail. It's like hitting it with a hammer. It cracked open the hard shell and something slipped out—*John*.

Sunday morning was when John woke up in Penny's bed and I was gone.

I didn't lose control the way I thought I did. Lionel's time machine did it to me.

119

This feels all wrong, too murky, too dark, too compromised. Lionel Goettreider invented time travel and used it to have an affair. I'm not a physicist or a philosopher, I'm only an architect in name, I'm not anything in particular, and this is way over my head. I want to be in Penny's bed, lazing away the morning, cajoling each other into being the one to make a coffee run, contemplating if I'm physiologically able to have sex again without using the bathroom first. I don't want to be here. I want to go home.

And now I can go home—I needed to prove to Penny I wasn't crazy. Okay, well, Lionel Goettreider is alive and, sure, narcissistic and weird, but brilliant enough to invent a time machine. So, mission accomplished.

I'll say a polite but heartfelt good-bye to Lionel and make plans to pick up this conversation again soon. I'll go directly to the airport, pay as much as it costs to fly back to Toronto right away, and spend the flight rehearsing exactly what to say to Penny to regain her trust. I'll talk to my family and agree to get whatever psychological help they think I need to stop worrying about me and, I don't know, maybe that'll help keep John away and, yes, I'm aware this sounds vague and shaky but I don't care—I got what I came for and now I'm done.

"Thank you for showing this to me," I say. "But I think it's time for me to go."

"I agree," Lionel says. "There's no point delaying any further.

Your genetic scans have already been integrated into the transmission matrix and all systems are activated."

"What are you talking about?" I say.

"Sending you back," Lionel says.

"Sending me back where?"

"To reset the timeline. Put things back the way they're supposed to be. I know I've caused minor ripples by using it for personal reasons, but you're the one who started it. You made the first crack in the shell of time. My experiment should've worked. Ursula should've chosen me. None of this should've happened and you can fix it. You can stop yourself from ruining everything."

"Lionel," I say, "I'm not going anywhere except home."

"But you *have* to," he says. "You owe it to the world. You owe it to me. This is not my life."

"Look," I say, "I should've told you something right away. Your experiment should've worked, yes, and it should've powered the future we never got to have. But you didn't live to see it. You, Ursula, Jerome, and everyone else in the lab that day in 1965, you all died within weeks of the experiment. That radiation surge you found and fixed after the accident? In my world, it killed you. It killed Ursula too. You don't get a happily ever after. You never see each other again."

"So this is it?" Lionel says. "This is the best I get? My reward is to waste my whole life waiting to see her? No. It's not enough. I'd rather die knowing my work changed the world."

"I get it," I say. "I've thought about how I could set things right. Go back to the accident and stop it from going wrong, then return to my timeline just one day earlier and make a simple, different choice. I could even sleep with her and, as long as she didn't get pregnant, everything would be okay. I know that makes no sense to you, but what I'm saying is I understand that when you have the technology . . . change haunts you. It's so clean and easy in your mind. Alter this one little thing and the rest will work out. But it won't. It's messier than you think. You have no control. You can only destroy. Well, I'm done destroying. I want to *make* things now. I know it's selfish to keep the world I come from lost forever. But no more selfish than, I'm sorry, the fact that you've kept all your inventions locked up in this mausoleum when you could've changed the world. I mean, don't you see that? You could already be everything you think you should've been. In my world, you've been dead for fifty years. You release all this stuff you've been tinkering with, it won't get us everything we could've had, but it's a hell of a start. And time travel won't make it better. It will only ever make it worse."

"I'm very sorry to hear you say that," he says.

"Even if I thought it would fix anything, which I don't, I can't give up my family. My mom and dad and sister. And Penny. I can't trade Penny for anybody. I won't."

"I'd hoped it wouldn't come to this," Lionel says. "But please keep in mind that you're the one who is making this about four people out of seven billion."

He touches his watch and, with a fluid motion, taps the air in my direction. And just like that it all falls apart.

120

A flat square hovers in front of me, showing a grainy green image of Penny asleep in her bed. Standing in the room are two women, their faces covered with leather balaclavas and chunky night-vision goggles. They hold axes, like for chopping wood.

A third masked woman sets the video camera on the dresser. She carries some sort of canister and I see her fumble with the spigot while the other two watch Penny sleep, silent, gripping their axes.

I don't have a plan, just abject panic, so I charge at Lionel, but I don't get near him. He makes another gesture in the air and suddenly I'm pressed against the cold concrete floor. I can't move. I can barely breathe.

"Localized gravity field," Lionel says. "Similar to the system in my leg braces. I walk in three-quarters Earth gravity. What you're feeling is quadruple Earth gravity. Don't bother trying to move. At these gravitational levels, blood won't flow properly to your muscles and brain. Even if you get some leverage, your ligaments can't handle it. Your limbs will shear right off and that gets very messy."

I try to talk but my tongue is a dumbbell in my mouth. All I manage is to drool.

The floating screen repositions itself into my field of view, down at floor level. Two more screens appear, also showing greenish shots of bedrooms, one of my parents asleep together, the other of Greta asleep alone. The cameras sit on stationary objects, three masked and goggled women next to each bed, two holding axes, one holding a canister, just like at Penny's.

The intruder with the canister in Greta's room turns the spigot and some sort of gas leaks out. I can tell because the cloud of molecules causes distortion in the night vision, so it sparkles like a pixie sprinkling magic dust on a sleeping child. Except these pixies wear gimp masks and carry lumberjack axes. The same thing happens in my parents' room, glittery gas floating over their bed.

"It's a tranquilizing agent," Lionel says. "No cognitive damage at these doses but they won't wake up until they're here in Hong Kong."

But something's not going according to plan in Penny's bedroom. The gas canister isn't operating properly and the woman struggles to crank open the spigot. There's no audio with the image, so I can't hear what it is that wakes Penny.

The three intruders look at her in unison. Judging by her open mouth, it's because she's screaming. I feel a surge of pride as Penny lunges into action like a goddamn champion. She's up and out of bed, grabs a lamp, and launches it at the intruders. But the lamp is plugged into the wall, so it rebounds back without hitting anyone. They flinch, though, and that gives Penny a second to hurl herself at the wall, her shoulder smacking into the light switch. If that was her actual plan and not dumb luck, it's a good one because they're wearing night-vision goggles and the abrupt burst of light blinds them. The greenish image tweaks into full color as Penny stares wide-eyed at the three crazily masked figures in her bedroom.

She makes the shocking, ballsy decision not to run, which I assure you is what I would do in this situation. Instead, she yanks the heavy-framed antique mirror off the wall and smashes it across the head of the closest axe-woman. She goes down in a spray of jagged silver as the other two pull off their goggles. The one with the canister fumbles with the spigot, trying to stick to the plan. The other axe-woman is between Penny and the door, but she's caught behind the one Penny hit, who flails around with broken shards lacerating her skin.

The second axe-woman must assume Penny's going to go for the door, so she responds slowly when instead Penny dives for the bed-side table. She swings her axe. Penny ducks and the axe blade pierces the wall, snagging in the drywall, which is I guess why people generally don't fight with axes.

While the axe-woman tries to yank her axe from the wall, Penny rears back and punches her in the stomach as hard as she can. The woman doubles over, retching as she throws up. She struggles to pull off the mask so she doesn't choke on her own vomit.

The first axe-woman sheds the mirror frame, her skin raked bloody, and comes at Penny with her axe.

But Penny's already pulled a pistol out of the bedside table drawer.

I've been in that drawer many times, fumbling around for condoms and once or twice borrowing a pair of her too-small socks, so I know there was never a gun in there. I guess until she met John.

Penny pulls the trigger. It's hard to miss at such close range and the first axe-woman's shoulder erupts in a flood of gore. She pitches forward, smacks her head on the sharp corner of the bedside table, and collapses at Penny's feet, deadweight.

Even without sound, watching on the floating screen, it's clear the gunfire changes the tenor of the room. Penny fires at the axe-woman who puked into her mask and her kneecap just kind of explodes. She drops like a marionette with its strings cut.

The third woman stops screwing with the spigot and throws the heavy metal tube at Penny. She blocks it with her arm, but it clearly hurts like hell and, more devastating, it distracts her for the moment it takes the woman to lunge across the room and punch Penny in the face.

Dazed, Penny tries to aim the pistol, but the third woman twists her arm until she drops the gun. She slams Penny to the floor, knee jammed into her back to pin her down.

I can't imagine anything worse than watching the woman I love soundlessly scream for help that I can't give her because even if I could move I'm 7,800 miles away. But I'm about to find out exactly what's worse.

The woman with the shattered knee stands, balanced on her good leg, the ruined one dragging behind her. She hefts up her axe and heaves it, blunt edge down, onto Penny's head.

The lights go out in Penny's eyes. She goes limp.

There's no sound, but the silent impact of solid steel meeting hair and skin and bone is like a cloud of razors whirling through my arteries and veins. I try to scream but all I manage is a raspy, guttural moan. I am fear and hate. I am violence and revenge.

The woman lifts the axe for another blow, but the other woman says something that stops her. They both look at the camera on the dresser. She checks Penny's pulse and gives the camera a thumbs-up. The other woman turns it off.

The screen goes wispy and pixilated. The other two screens show my mom and dad and sister, unconscious, being hauled out of their beds and carried away. I can feel tears well in my eyes but the intense gravity screws with their internal structure. They inflate weirdly until they burst from my eyes like water balloons on pavement.

"I apologize for that," Lionel says. "No one was supposed to get hurt. These operatives are from a rather peculiar Japanese apocalypse cult, and while they're eager to please, they can be hard to control. Something a bit too fatalistic in their essential worldview to be truly successful employees. Fortunately, everyone is alive. They'll be on a private jet to Hong Kong within the hour."

Clarity rinses out my mind. The fear is gone. The hate is gone. I have no violence, no revenge, no goals, no plans, no hope. It's almost a relief, knowing that I don't have to make any more decisions—I just have to do whatever Lionel says.

121

Gravity returns to normal but I can't seem to peel myself off the floor. Lionel fires up his time machine, gesturing emphatically like the crackpot conductor of an invisible orchestra. He doesn't seem at all concerned that I might leap up and beat him to death. And he's right. My whole body is numb, and even if it wasn't, I won't do anything to further endanger my mom and dad and sister and the woman I love.

"This is what's going to happen," Lionel says. "You're going to go back to July 11, 1965, so you can stop yourself from sabotaging my experiment. The timeline will return to its proper track. All of this, the last fifty years, will be set right."

He looks down at me, baffled that I'm still lying on the ground.

"I dialed your gravity back to normal," he says. "You can stand now."

In fact, I feel like I could jump high enough to touch the curved ceiling seventy-five feet above me. But I don't. I just sit up.

"All I want is for you to fix your mistake," he says. "Every human being on the planet, including the four people you're so concerned about, is living the wrong life. Once things are the way they should be, their lives will be moot. As well as their deaths. Because in the *correct* timeline they'll have another life and another death and this life and this death won't even exist. If they have to be sacrificed to make you do the right thing, it would hardly even be murder. You can't murder fiction. And everyone on this planet is living a terrible fiction that has to be rewritten. By you."

"I just expected so much more from you," I say.

"The feeling is mutual," Lionel says. "You seemed so much smarter before."

"What, two hours ago," I say, "when I thought you were the greatest human being who ever lived instead of the asshole who kidnapped everyone I love and warped the space-time continuum so he could bang another man's wife?"

"No," he says. *"Before."*

He reaches into his pants pocket and takes out an old Polaroid photograph with a crinkled edge. He hands it to me.

It's a photograph of me and Lionel. But not the Lionel who stands in front of me. The Lionel from 1965. And me—I look just as I do right now. I'm even wearing the same clothes.

"This picture was taken on July 13, 1965," he says. "Two days after the accident, I turned the Engine back on for the first time. And you appeared."

122

I stare at the photograph. Obviously it could be faked. I'm wearing exactly what I'm wearing, but he did scan me earlier. Lionel built a time machine—he could manufacture a phony Polaroid. But it doesn't feel fake. It *feels* old. It feels like a photograph taken fifty-one years ago.

"You'll go back to July 13, 1965, at 4:38 A.M.," Lionel says, "the moment I turned the Engine back on. My earlier self will follow your instructions to help you jump the last two days back to July 11, 1965, moments before the accident. My device can manage smaller gaps in time even without the dedicated radiation trail to follow. But it also has a secondary fail-safe, a detection matrix to track any of the radiation still in the atmosphere from your initial trip back in time. You'll make sure that my experiment succeeds and you'll return to the present, the world restored."

"So, I bring you the technology you need to send me back the final leg of my journey and the *you* in 1965 just goes along with it?"

"I'd already theorized that the person I saw in my lab that day was a time traveler," he says, "so your appearance just confirmed my impossible hypothesis. You also seemed like you knew what you were doing and, frankly, in the wake of my life's work collapsing around me, it turned out I could use some direction."

"Maybe I go back and kill you with my bare hands."

"Well," says Lionel, "you don't appear to be as intelligent as I'd expected, but you seem to grasp enough about causality to realize that would have unpredictable consequences. What if my death in 1965 meant Penelope were never born?"

"I feel like this is a good time to tell you to go fuck yourself."

"If it will help us move on," he says, "then by all means."

"Go fuck yourself," I say.

"Are you ready?" he says.

"Right now?"

"No time like the present," he says.

I pick up the time machine, which is surprisingly light.

"I had to make it easy enough to carry," he says. "And easy enough to operate. Even for someone as ignorant about time travel as the man I used to be."

Lionel explains how it works and it really is simple. Dangerously simple. Black thoughts churn in my mind. Going back to make sure Lionel Goettreider is never born. Or stopping myself from knocking on his door just a few hours ago. Turning around and flying home and finding another way to rebuild Penny's trust. Except of course I see now that Lionel had been waiting for me, prepared to go as far as necessary to get me to do what he wants. And there's the photograph. I know it's perverse but I can't help it—the loop demands to be closed.

A section of the floor retracts and a platform rises. On it is another Goettreider Engine—or, actually, as Lionel explains, *this* is the original one. The device I saw at his house is his backup. This is the original prototype, the one that's been running constantly since 1965. I can see that its components look much older than the updated one back at the house. Robotic arms connect the Engine to the time machine, and Lionel hovers next to them, checking their work like a doting kindergarten teacher.

If I appear inappropriately calm, it's only because I'm paralyzed by the adrenal gleam of terror. I keep picturing Penny on her bedroom floor, the axe's blunt end hitting her skull. She could already be dead. Even if I figure out a way to save her, how can she ever forgive me now? And if I don't do what he asks, Lionel will kill them all, my mom, my dad, my sister, my love, and I'll have no reason to live in this world anyway.

It's too painful to think about Penny and my family, the impossible choice between letting them be killed or letting them be erased, so instead I think about the world he wants me to bring back. Flying cars and robot maids and food pills and Deisha and Xiao and Asher and teleportation and Hester and jet packs and Megan and moving sidewalks and Tabitha and ray guns and hover boards and Robin and space vacations and moon bases and my father. Am I really qualified to judge which world deserves to exist? If all goes according to Lionel's plan, that world will be mapped over this world and all that will be left is my memory of a reality that was never supposed to be.

But I know a thing or two about flawed plans.

Lionel is so much smarter than me and he's had so much more time to think this whole thing through. I assume he has a good reason to put his time machine in my hands and trust me to use it the way he expects. But once I'm back there—if a better solution presents itself, I'll take it, even if I don't fully understand the consequences. Let's face it, I never have.

123

Lionel's time machine is compact and unembellished. There's a simple control panel on the lid, which opens to reveal its microscopic innards, but otherwise it's seamless. Lionel had no financiers to impress, no customers to awe. He didn't need his device to look cool. It just has to send a person back in time.

Lionel runs a final diagnostic and I start to undress. He looks at me, bewildered.

"What are you doing?"

"Don't I have to take off my clothes?" I say.

"No," he says. "What kind of pervert would make you time travel naked?"

"My father," I say. "Where I come from, he's the one who invents time travel."

"The professor? Interesting. So he wasn't able to solve spatiotemporal transmission of nonorganic matter. There are implications to doing so, of course, it *slows* the journey considerably, but it would resolve the problem of instantaneity . . ."

Lionel touches his watch and gestures emphatically in the air, noting something. I could explain the skin suits to him, but I don't feel particularly cooperative right now.

"*My* father was paranoid," he says. "I mean clinically. Most days he was a pleasant, fussy, attentive man. But occasionally we'd come home from school to find a muttering lunatic who would sit me and my brothers down in the kitchen and debate with my frightened mother if it would be more humane to kill us all rather than let us be hunted by who knows what nefarious shadows. My mother may have been the only Jew in Europe who was relieved when the Nazis marched in. Finally my father's paranoia was entirely justified. And yet despite a lifetime to prepare for persecution, he handled it badly. His plan was foolish and he got everyone under his protection killed."

"But you survived because you trusted the king of Denmark," I say. "I know the story. Everyone knows the story."

"The *king*? It was my *father* I didn't trust. He was delusional and I was judicious enough to say no. Why would you think it had anything to do with the king?"

"Because that's what you told an old classmate at Niels Bohr's funeral. He wrote a book about it. Everyone you ever spoke to about anything wrote a book about you."

"Showing up uninvited at his funeral was vanity. I was young and too easily impressed. Bohr had some insights, some ideas, but did he ever *build* anything? No. He liked to see his name in the newspaper. He certainly didn't remember my name. Some student he once taught. Some life he once saved."

"Lionel, I get that you have nobody else to talk to. But since you're threatening to murder my family and the woman I love, I don't really feel like listening to you."

"The woman you *love*?" he says. "Is that a joke? You met her two weeks ago. Do you really think I wouldn't bother to learn everything about you? I've been watching you for thirty-two years. Waiting for you to become the man who came to me in the past. To even use that word with me after the life I've lived because of *love*. You've never spent more than a month with any woman. You keep your family at a distance. You have no friends. You have the grudging respect of your employees because of your talent. Your talent is what gave me hope. That one day I'd be free of this wrong life."

"And where are your loved ones, Lionel? Where are your family and friends? In fifty years, the only person you could find to care about you was someone else's wife."

"You don't know a goddamn thing about it. Who have you ever loved? Who have you ever lost? Your life is buildings. You don't care about the people inside them. I risked everything for her. I crossed time and space for her. What could you possibly understand about that kind of love? That kind of loss?"

Considering he's a towering genius and all that, I'm a bit confused by how utterly wrong Lionel is about me, until I realize—of course, he thinks I'm *John*.

Even if Lionel surveilled every second of John's life, he could only observe what happened in *this* timeline. Everything he knows about my world is conjecture.

In the past three weeks I lost the woman of my dreams and my unborn child, stole a trillion-dollar piece of technology, became history's first time traveler, witnessed the experiment that began the modern world, broke reality, plunged humanity into dystopia, caused billions to never be born, ruined my father, resurrected my mother, got a sister that shouldn't exist, met the love of my life, became the planet's most brilliant architect, found the smartest person who ever lived, and discovered the secret history of global technology, but it took until this very moment for someone to finally *underestimate* me.

I know love. I know loss. I know the grief that chews and swallows you whole.

But Lionel doesn't know any of that. He's been wasting his time watching *John*.

My name is not John. My name is Tom Barren and I've already changed the world once. I can do it again.

124

As the only person to ever try both kinds of time travel, I can tell you that Goettreider's version wasn't at all like my father's. And the son of a bitch definitely didn't prepare me for what was to come.

I stand there, holding the time machine, and Lionel looks me in the eye.

"I hope that by the time you arrive at your destination," he says, "you will understand why I did what I had to do."

Then Lionel says something genuinely strange—halting unintelligible noises that sound rehearsed but make no sense.

"*Yrros ma I*," he says.

And, with that, Lionel sends me back in time.

I assumed it was going to feel more or less the same as it did when I used my father's time-travel apparatus and, at first, I have a similar sensation of falling back into a drawn-out moment between balance and gravity. But the mind-bending, body-inverting sensory swirl that I anticipated never comes.

Instead, Lionel stands in front of me making these off-puttingly jittery movements as his hand retracts from the device's control panel. His eyes meet mine and he opens his mouth, his jaw flexing oddly when he speaks.

"*I am sorry*," he says.

I want to tell him that his apologies are meaningless to me but I'm paralyzed. My mouth won't move. My eyes won't blink. All I can do is stare straight ahead.

"*Od ot dah I tahw did I yhw dnatsrednu lliw uoy, noitanitsed ruoy ta evirra uoy emit eht yb taht epoh I,*" Lionel says.

It takes me a moment to realize he's speaking backward.

Mostly I'm confused, like, is this Lionel's idea of a prank? He apologized in reverse on purpose, like a clue. But right before that—"*by the time you arrive at your destination*"—what did that even mean? With my father's time machine, the traveling part was instantaneous. There was no *time to arrive*. You were immediately *there*. What could I possibly come to *understand* in a trip that happens in microseconds?

Except it wasn't happening in microseconds. It was happening in regular seconds, one by one, ticktock, but in reverse. I see the twitchy motions and hear the wobbly alien phonemes that Lionel and I make as we speak in the moments before he activated the device. That's when I start to get it, not all of it, not yet, but the very beginning of shocked comprehension—Lionel's time machine turns back the clock, literally.

A raw terror creeps up and I try to mash it back down because this isn't going to happen in real time, right? This is going to accelerate, any moment now, any moment now, any moment now, any moment now, any moment now, any moment now.

It doesn't.

This is what Lionel neglected to mention—I'd go back fifty-one years and experience *every second* of it. Although it doesn't take long for concepts like seconds and minutes and hours to feel like nothing but the abstract human constructs they are.

I watch Lionel and me talking in the domed room, our herky-jerky movements and reversed dialogue. But I'm not paying close attention because I'm waiting for everything to speed up into a dizzying wormhole velocity that instantly propels me to 1965. So I miss what turns out to be the last sight of myself that I have for five decades.

The platform that the Goettreider Engine sits on lowers into the windowless underground chamber from which it powers Lionel's operations. And I follow it down, frozen in the position I was in when the time machine engaged, tethered to the Engine, invisible, immaterial, immobile, holding the device like a courier bringing a package to someone's door. I'm not following *myself* back in time. I'm following *it*—the Goettreider Engine. A reverse path into its own history, winding up the thread of its tau radiation trail like an unspooled yo-yo.

I don't see anyone for what feels like months. It turns out Lionel doesn't visit the Engine too often. As long as everything runs properly, he has no reason to. He checks the machinery once or twice a year, but his visits are abrupt and banal, eyes darting across the readouts, nodding, and leaving. And Lionel is the only one who comes in, not trusting anyone else, which makes sense when you have the most valuable piece of technology in history and don't want to share it.

I would've lost my mind within a week if not for Penelope.

Not Penny—*Penelope*. It was that thing she told me, how she'd master a training module by breaking down each technical procedure into discrete tasks and counting them down by the second. It was a way to take control of something as vast and liquid and riotous as time. It's what kept me sane in that first decade. Or as sane as can reasonably be expected in a circumstance for which the human mind is not fit. And so Penelope Weschler did for me what I couldn't do for her: She saved me.

The system is automated and through careful observation I come to know the precise, rhythmic sequences that comprise the seconds, minutes, hours, days, weeks, months, years. The Engine is never turned off, so the radiation thread is never severed.

I stand there. I hold the time machine. I wait.

Seconds into minutes into hours into days into weeks into months into years into a decade of standing there, of holding the time machine, of waiting.

This is probably what it was like for Lionel, wondering when I'd knock on his door and set this sequence of events in motion. Maybe he did this on purpose, to punish me, torture me, teach me what it was like to be him and why he did the things he did.

And even if that wasn't his plan, it works. I get it. When you spend more than fifty years waiting for something to happen, everything else erodes into meaninglessness. You have one goal and whatever doesn't help you achieve it is just in the way. Morality seems very small and wet and delicate, a bug you find in your boot.

In the early years, I think about my family a lot, frozen like me in a moment of peril, but it's hard to maintain a state of primed anxiety for that long. Besides which, I'm already doing the best thing I can to help them, and they're not in *more* peril—they're in the exact same amount of peril, tiptoe on the point of a long, sharp knife.

And Penny. The acuteness of her, despite my determination and focus, can't help but fade. She starts to feel, increasingly and then maybe irrevocably, like someone I knew long, long ago for a very, very brief time. I want to save her, but it's also sort of like being asked to risk your life for someone you met once as a child. You want to be the kind of person who would sacrifice everything for the one you love, but as the years stretch on and you're imprisoned, static, in a dark, whirring room it begins to feel like, what, *her*, that woman I knew for a few weeks ten, twenty, thirty, forty, fifty years ago? That's who I'm willing to die for? No, I hope she's okay but that's not what this is about anymore. This is bigger than that, more crucial—it has to be or no amount of counting time will keep me from going mad.

It becomes obvious that I can't let the world continue to suffer in a technological and social wasteland just because I have emotional connections to four individual human beings. To squander global civilization and the fundamental welfare of the planet itself because I like my family better and Penny likes me better is selfishness at its most cruel and idiotic. Really, who is the greater monster, Lionel, for a few threats and manipulations in pursuit of a better world, or me, for resisting it when so much good was undone by my folly? Me. *Clearly* me. It only takes, like, ten or eleven years for me to let go of every last vestige of my egotism so I can genuinely accept it. By around 2004, I've fully committed to resetting the timeline to its original path. Rather than, you know, trying to get revenge on Lionel and rescuing Penny and my family.

Fourteen years in, Lionel finishes his time machine. It's ready to test.

And that's when my true education begins. I have the privilege and the curse of watching Lionel spend nearly forty years trying to build it. His workshop is in a corner of the same underground bunker where the Engine sits—a man with any imaginable resource, financial, technical, and intellectual, who deliberately chooses to work in what is essentially a prison cell. If he's aware that I'm an inmate here as well, he never acknowledges my presence. I'm as much a ghost as I was that day in 1965.

What I witness is—failure. Entire decades spent failing. The farther back I go, the more failure there is. This is how you discover who someone is. Not the success. Not the result. The struggle. The part between the beginning and the ending that is the truth of life. Whether or not he intended it, this is Lionel's gift to me. Respect him, despise him, judge him, absolve him, marvel at his achievements, plot his demise, I came to know Lionel Goettreider better than anyone. Hunched over his worktable, scribbling calculations with a chewed yellow pencil, tinkering with equipment, running simulations on a computer of his own design, day and night, weekends, holidays, every day, he worked. He was trying to make something no one else ever had. Just like my father.

I can't say I forgive my father for his distance through so much of my life, but I finally understand what he was doing all those years, in his study, in his lab, around the dinner table, giving a speech to his peers, ordering around his employees, tuning out while my mother spoke to him, leaving the room when I walked into it—he was failing.

Watching Lionel, I learn something about success I never did in a lifetime as my father's son. You keep working. You keep trying. You keep failing. Until one day in the distant future, that for me is the

distant past, the failure ends. That's all success feels like. It's not tri-
umphant. It's not glorious. It's just a relief. You finally stopped failing.

You can do a lot with fifty years of nothing but thinking.

I consider what Deisha once said to me in an abandoned town in
a lost world. Do something. Be something. Make something. And
what that actually means.

I come up with a plan for what I'll do when I finally arrive at my
destination. Not just one linear plan, a continuity of plans, every po-
tential contingency unpacked, considered, fit into the lattice of even-
tualities.

Whatever anger I felt for Goettreider dissipates over the decades.
It feels like an ancient family grudge, one I know should matter, but
it was all too long ago to bother with. Besides, his is the only face I
ever see and as I watch him decompress from old age, unfolding into
the man I first saw back in 1965, I can't help but feel affection for
him. Seeing him walk straighter, his face smoother, his body looser,
his hair thicker and darker, his eyes brighter, more keen, I empathize
with him, isolated, brilliant, lost. I did this to him. That's something
that echoes through me as I watch him become the man he was: I
was the toxin that unmade him. I told him to wait, that I'd come to
fix what went wrong, but I didn't understand what the waiting
would do to him.

Or maybe I did. After all, I haven't told him to wait yet. The me
trapped for five decades is the one who will make that decision. Is it
to punish him for doing this to me, a loop of pain that neither of us
can escape until it's run its course? Or did fifty years of nothingness
inure me to the agony of an endless wait?

Eventually, there are no more plans to make. I know what to do,
what to say, everything he could possibly say in reply and how I will
respond, a branching nest of words and actions that can lead only to
their proper resolution. So I move on from plans.

I turn inside. I figure out who I am, what parts of me are Tom,
what parts of me are John, where they overlap and why they differ.

We reach an understanding—John doesn't even mind receding into the deepest folds of our shared mind as long as I give him something to think about.

Together, John and I design every building in every city on the planet. We draw a blueprint of the world and it is magnificent. All that John accomplished before now was the aimless doodling of a child. Together we build a new hull for our civilization.

I write this book, chapter by chapter, memorize the words in sequence so I can assemble it at will. I remember composing this chapter. It was some forty years into the process, the mid-1970s judging by Lionel's appearance, although of course by then I'd long stopped caring about dates.

I try to hold on to Penny, I do. It's not just that two weeks out of fifty-one years is a wisp of time. Lionel made his life about Ursula and it brought him equal measures of happiness and pain. But he got to refill that tank in occasional gasps, their intermittent reunions tightening the bolts and scrubbing away the rust of their perpetual emotion machine. All I had were memories. Sunlight in hair. The pitch of her deep-throated laugh. An elusive scent that might have been her or might have been the other Penelope or might have been someone else or might have been nothing at all.

I considered going into more detail here, trying to convey what it feels like to live through fifty-one years of inverted chronology. How by the time you get to them, events you thought you'd be thrilled to witness—Lionel first setting up his worktable in the corner of the room, opening the first of hundreds of notepads, chewing the first of thousands of pencils—feel stale because you've projected so many different versions of them, reverse-engineering what occurred from what you've already seen, that when they happen it's just a shrug: *yeah, that's how I figured it went.*

And what's the point? The vast yawn of time can't be described the way I experienced it. Shouldn't be.

After five decades without breathing or blinking or talking or smiling or screaming, the months pass like hours, the weeks like minutes, the days like seconds. When things start to happen, I'm so beyond noticing physical events that I almost miss it as the thread winds up tight on its spool. The Engine is unhooked from its nest of wires and tubes, loaded on a truck, driven to a dock, hoisted by a crane, packed into a crate. It's in the cargo hold of a ship. It's at the Port of San Francisco. Seagulls. Gasoline. Cigarette smoke and pop songs on a staticky radio.

I see myself appear—disappear—with Lionel Goettreider looking more or less as he did when I first saw him. It must be July 13, 1965, just after he turned on the Engine and I materialized with the time machine I've been carrying for five decades. I watch us talk in the off-kilter glottal breaths of reversed phonemes, which I understand because somewhere in the late 1980s I spent a few years teaching myself backward language. I hear everything we say in inverted real time so that even this, the ultimate moment I've been waiting for, the climax of this interminable journey, becomes flat and predictable. By the time I merge with myself at the moment I appear in this timeline, I've already experienced it in reverse. I know everything I'll say and do and everything he'll say and do and so all that's left is to replay my part the right way around.

125

I materialize in Lionel Goettreider's ruined laboratory in the basement of the San Francisco State Science and Technology Center
on July 13, 1965. I'm standing right in front of Lionel himself, jar-
ringly close, his hand releasing the lever that he just pulled to switch
on the Engine for the first time since the accident.

He freezes, shocked, speechless. There's an open blister on the tip
of his nose from the skin-peeling heat that blasted from the Engine
as it prepared to melt down. His eyebrows and eyelashes are just
wispy, singed remnants. He wears leather gloves and I remember
that his palms nearly burned off in the moments before I was able to
shut down the Engine. It must hurt like hell.

The lab is a mess. Jagged cracks across one half of the ceiling, the
other half collapsed, machinery from the lab upstairs in a broken
pile. The consoles warped and shattered. Steel support beams melted
like modern art sculptures. Fire-blackened holes in the walls where
the plumes punched through. There's a dusting of ash on the floor—
what's left of Jerome's incinerated arm.

As I open my mouth to speak, despite so many decades practicing
for this very moment, I almost screw it up by speaking backward.

"Lionel," I say, "my name is John Barren. I'm here from the
future. I know you saw me in this lab two days ago and I know
you've already theorized that I was a visitor from another time. I
know these things because you're the one who sent me back here."

"It's true?" he says.

"It is," I say. "And the less you say the better. You designed the time machine to follow the radiation signature of your device as far back as it could, to this moment. Now that it's on, you must never turn it off. Do you understand?"

"Yes," he says, "but . . ."

"I need your help to make the last small jump to just before the accident," I say. "The unidentified radiation traces you noticed, you've hypothesized they're from the device itself, paradoxically detectable before it was even turned on. That's correct. And I am the paradox. The time machine is designed to follow the remaining traces in the atmosphere back to the moment the experiment took place."

I realize I'm still holding the time machine, like my hands are bolted to it. I really want to put the piece-of-shit thing down after carrying it for five decades but can't quite let go, not yet.

"You're actually a time traveler?" Lionel says.

"Lionel, you already know this. Please don't waste time. You sent me here to fix what went wrong. To put the timeline back on track."

"So the experiment should have worked," Lionel says.

"Are you done stating the obvious?" I say. "I need power to make the final jump. You designed the two devices to be compatible. Hook them up."

Lionel hesitates. He looks like he might cry. It's sort of sweet and sad, but I have no interest in sympathizing with him right now.

"Is this the life you want?" I say, gesturing to the ambient destruction around us. "Or do you want the life you're supposed to have?"

I don't mention that in the life he's supposed to have he'll soon be dead.

"Ursula?" he says.

"She stays married to Jerome for the rest of her life," I say. "Unless we change the timeline."

She stays married to Jerome for the rest of her life in the other timeline too—it's just that her life lasts only nine more weeks. But, whatever, it gets Lionel to start hooking up the time machine to the Engine. After fifty years, I feel no ethical qualms about lies of omission.

"You will build this time machine," I say. "It will take a long time. It will seem impossible because it is impossible, but you are Lionel Goettreider and *impossible* is a meaningless word to you."

That seems to cow him. Maybe this bullshit pep talk is what corroded him through the decades, but it's what I already heard myself say when I saw this play out in reverse.

"You said I'm the one who sends you back here," he says. "But from when?"

"I understand why you'd balk at being told your future is predetermined, but take solace in the fact that you're the one who determined it. This is *your* plan. To set right what went wrong."

"But aren't *you* to blame for what went wrong?" he says. "If you hadn't appeared when you did . . ."

"And if you hadn't panicked when you saw me, yes, we both made mistakes. Which is why I'm here. I can apologize, or I can fix the timeline so neither of our mistakes ever happened."

"Or you could do both," he says.

He flashes me a slick little grin, like he's over the initial shock and now kind of enjoying the lunatic charge of this historically insane situation. I appreciate his calm under pressure, even though he still turns into the devious old asshole who threatens to kill everyone I love. Which leads me to the part of my plan I'm most leery about, because it's shaky and contrived, but I have to at least try it on the off chance it actually works.

"Are you paying attention?" I say.

"Yes," he says.

"My name is John Barren," I say. "My father is Victor Barren. My mother is Rebecca Crittendale-Barren. My sister is Greta Barren. In the future, you will find them and you will keep track of them, but you will never interact with them in any way. Do you understand? In *any* way. If you do, it'll ruin everything. But you'll be ready. When I show up at your door, you'll know it's time to act. You will send operatives to take them into custody. By force. You'll need this for leverage over me."

"What are you talking about?" he says. "You want me to kidnap your family?"

"In the future," I say, "I won't be inclined to help you. I need to be compelled. But you will never harm them. It'll be an empty threat."

"There's got to be another way," Lionel says.

"There will also be a woman," I say. "Her name is Penelope Weschler. Your operatives will take her as well. But something will go wrong. She will try to escape. There will be a physical altercation and she will be terribly injured."

"I'm a scientist," he says. "The whole purpose of my work is to create unlimited power for the world. To make life better for everyone. I can't *hurt* people."

"And you won't," I say. "It will all be fake. It will look real to me, but it will be a simulation. Designed to only *look* authentic. Nobody will be harmed."

"I don't understand," he says.

"You will safely transport the four of them to your base of operations in Hong Kong," I say.

"Wait, why Hong Kong?" he says.

"I'm asking you to do this because it has to be done. To close the loop. It's your responsibility to keep them safe but *appear* to threaten their lives."

"If you change the past," Lionel says, "why does it matter what happens in a future that will never occur?"

"It matters because it's my consciousness," I say.

Even with fifty years to think about it, I'm not sure that convincing Lionel to *fake* kidnapping my family and injuring Penny will work. But after decades spent weighing the options, my best chance to protect the people I love, without completely dismantling the timeline that got me to here, is this coy psychological gambit. It all has to fit together.

"Fine," Lionel says.

"Where's your Polaroid camera?" I say.

"What Polaroid?" he says. "I don't have a Polaroid."

"Yes, you do," I say. "Go get it."

Lionel's about to reply when he stops, something occurring to him. He steps over a pile of rubble and reaches into the nook where the consoles meet. He pulls out that famous leather rucksack. Inside it is the birthday gift with the bow on top. He tears off the wrapping paper. The present is a brand-new Polaroid Automatic 100 Land Camera.

"It's a gift from my aunt in Copenhagen," he says. "My only living relative. It's not even my birthday. Her memory is going. She mixes me up with her brother, my father. June 29 was his birthday. I've been carrying it around for two weeks. I thought it would be too depressing to open it."

"Are the devices linked?" I say.

"Yes," he says.

I fire up the time machine and its detection matrix pinpoints the remaining tau radiation traces from my original trip back to July 11, 1965, mapping out a knotted, looping, fractal thread to the moment in space and time where it all went wrong.

Lionel loads the Polaroid with a cartridge of instant film and I stand next to him. He aims the lens at us and snaps a picture. I don't bother to watch the image emerge from the photochemical glaze. I already know what it shows.

"I don't understand how any of this works," he says. "How am I supposed to build a time machine? And even if I somehow figure *that* out, I mean, how long do I have to wait for you?"

"Good-bye, Lionel," I say.

I activate the device. And I'm gone.

Let him wait.

126

Radiation is made up of three particles—alpha particles are positively charged combinations of twin protons and neutrons, beta particles are negatively charged electrons or positrons, and electrically neutral gamma particles are high-energy photons. The initial surge of tau radiation that erupted from the Goettreider Engine when it was switched on is still circulating through the lab when I arrive there on July 13, 1965, and the time machine's detection matrix is programmed to find the remaining traces and follow them back to their origin two days earlier, July 11, 1965.

I quickly discover that chasing a degraded cloud of energy in reverse real-time chronology is extremely disorienting—I feel like a gyroscope banging around inside a clothes dryer strapped to a roller coaster caught in a tornado. It's hard to even think straight. I grasp moments as they skitter by. Goettreider tinkering with the prototype to fix the very radiation leak that I'm following. The dust settling, but it's in reverse so the dust rises from a prone state into an excited fog. A tumultuous crash as the half of the ceiling that lies in rubble rises from the floor and knits itself back into place over the lab. As the ceiling uncollapses, a dozen men in 1960s-era gas masks and hazardous-material suits, rubber gloves sealed around their wrists with elastic bands, scurry backward out of the room for safety. Before that, they inspect the wreckage with yellow Geiger counters, waving the metallic sensors around, tapping the glass panels over the indicator gauges to confirm the readings are correct.

Paramedics carry off the witnesses too injured to walk. The rest limp and crawl out of the lab. Goettreider is roughly hauled to his feet. A paramedic inspects his wounds as he sits against the wall in a daze, bleeding from the tip of his burned nose, staring at the machine, flayed palms open on his lap.

Firefighters pull away wreckage to clear a path to the door. They pry Ursula from Jerome as she screams and reaches for him. Ursula sits on the floor, cradling Jerome's head, sobbing, while he shudders and twitches, clutching his cauterized stump.

The Engine stops spinning, slows, Goettreider powers it down, he runs a safe shut-down procedure, his hands scorched and raw, he stumbles to the instrument panel, he rises from the spot slumped against the wall where I pushed him right before I switched the Engine back on and ricocheted to my own time.

By the final seconds of this rewound thread, as I sync up to the point when I first arrived at this moment in time, my mind is utterly scrambled. I see the events I already experienced, but frenetic and unlatched, like a stream of all the right words laid out with all the wrong syntax, off-kilter and half-deranged.

127

*D*isappears Tom, worked act final desperate his if knowing not. On back Engine the turns and safety to Lionel shoves Tom, apparatus travel-time the of circuitry the fries meltdown the as. Burns and blisters Lionel, Engine overheating the to closest. Out way no there's but, escape to try observers the of rest the. Off seared arm his has and plume a from away Ursula pushes bravely Jerome. Apart lab the tear destruction of spires fiery. Meltdown into shudders which, Engine the off switches abruptly Lionel, panicked.

Lab his in standing figure ghostly a sees Lionel. Field invisibility his disrupts and Tom hits plume a until. Harmless but dazzling, room the through wildly arc light glittering of plumes. Energy of amounts massive in pulls and speed to up gets Engine the.

Engine the activate to lever the up pulls he and concerns Lionel's overrules pressure social. Him from coming is radiation the realizes Tom. Radiation of type unknown an up pick instruments Lionel's. Jerome, husband Ursula's including, arrive observers other the. Affair an having are Ursula and Lionel that learns Tom so and alone they're think they. Francoeur Ursula by interrupted is curiosity Lionel's.

Goettreider Lionel of attention confused the drawing, environment his with interacts accidentally Tom, immaterial not but invisible. Engine Goettreider the activates first Goettreider Lionel before minutes just, 1965 to 2016 from travel to machine time prototype father's his uses Barren Tom, idiocy and, anger, grief, shock by fueled.

128

If you want to remember what happened the last time I visited July 11, 1965, go reread chapters 44 to 54. I'm so disoriented I miss everything up to about chapter 52.

My plan was that, on arrival, I'd take control of my own consciousness in 1965 the way I had John's consciousness in 2016—two versions of me simultaneously inhabiting the identical point in space-time, my current mind steering my earlier self to trigger the emergency return function on the time-travel apparatus before the Goettreider Engine is even turned on.

But the plan immediately goes sideways. I arrive, yes, inside my own body, but I'm woozy and addled. I can't think straight, let alone stop myself—the Tom I was on my first trip to 1965—from making the exact same choices in the exact same sequence as last time. I don't know if it's because I'm inside my *own* earlier mind, but I can't seem to grip the cognitive wheel. I can only observe my actions, unable to alter them.

Did I live through fifty years of stasis just to watch myself make the same disastrous mistakes? If I fail, I know my sanity can't survive another try. I'll come undone. I may have already come undone.

I'm trapped in my own mind, watching myself blunder forward in time, unable to stop him, me, us.

I guess this is probably how John feels about me.

There's a reference in those earlier chapters to a "tickle" in the back of my mind telling me—Tom, the *previous* Tom—to stay concealed behind the crowd instead of repositioning to get a better view. Now I realize that "tickle" was me—the *current* me, goddamn it's hard to get the pronouns right—straining with all my cognitive power to seize control of Tom's—the *other* Tom's—consciousness before he slips from his hiding spot into Lionel's line of sight. And there's not much time. Lionel is moments away from turning on the Engine.

I've got to get myself out of the path of the energy plumes that are about to erupt from the Engine and disrupt my invisibility field, triggering the whole chain of events I came here to stop. But I can't. I'm a powerless observer in my own mind.

Picture a room. Four walls, one with a big, wide window through which you can see the outside world. The room's walls are made of memories, layered over each other like panes of stained glass, an infinitely dense story of a life. This is Tom's mind in 1965.

Now drop an identical room into that room. This is my mind returning to 1965 for the *second* time, inhabiting the same body. The walls are made of *my* memories and there's another big window, but this one looks out at the first window.

And there's a third room *inside* the second room inside the first room—John's consciousness inside my consciousness inside my *earlier* consciousness, like nesting dolls. That room is made of John's memories and, for now, he's locked in there.

I'm simultaneously trying to get my scrambled mind back on an even keel, keep John locked away, and take over my earlier consciousness before the disaster I'm here to prevent plays out in its original sequence.

The bad news is it's not working.

The good news is I spent five decades trapped in my own mind, so I've developed an array of cognitive tools with which to maneuver *my* consciousness to the forefront.

I see Lionel pull up the lever and activate the Engine. In a few seconds those glittering plumes of energy will spike out across the room, dazzling the witnesses and disrupting my invisibility field.

My best chance, probably my only chance, to grab hold of this mind and get us out of here is while Tom is distracted by the experiment. The timing will have to be perfect, but I think I can do it . . .

Which is when the whole back wall of the room—it's a metaphor, sure, but it's also how it feels when it happens—explodes in a frenzy of brick and plaster, and something thick and black gushes in, threatening to drown all of us in dank, oily memories that I've never known before but which stick to everything they touch and burrow in roots of alarming solidity.

They're a stranger's memories, but this mind is their home too. These memories belong here just as mine do. Memories of a timeline where things go much, much worse.

129

This is how the apocalypse starts.

On July 11, 1965, Lionel Goettreider tests an experimental power source for a group of colleagues at a research laboratory in San Francisco, California. But while the device is gearing up to full operation, he is startled by the inexplicable appearance of a ghostly observer and abruptly switches off the machine, causing it to malfunction. Destructive energy erupts in fiery plumes. The lab is wrecked. Goettreider and his sixteen colleagues are incinerated. The observer—sorry, I don't know why I'm describing the events as if I'm not part of them, but the memories flood into my mind with such velocity that it's easier to be detached and reportorial about them than it is to absorb their sheer propulsion—the *observer*, me, I'm flung into a brand-new future as the time-travel apparatus overloads.

But the meltdown continues. A crater 2,000 miles across is carved into the Earth. It burns so hot the bottom is crystalline glass a mile thick. Since San Francisco is on the coast, half of the crater gets punched into the Pacific Ocean, causing tsunamis and earthquakes that decimate vast tranches of the eastern coasts of Asia and Australia. California is gone. Oregon, Washington, Idaho, Montana, Utah, Wyoming, Nevada, Arizona, New Mexico, Colorado, South Dakota, most of North Dakota, Nebraska, Kansas, Oklahoma, and about half of Texas, three-quarters of British Columbia and the lower halves of Alberta and Saskatchewan, Baja California, Sonora, Chihuahua, Sinaloa, Durango, and Coahuila de Zaragoza are seared into a rough arc of emptiness that quickly fills with seawater. Hawaii is obviously gone. Fiji, Tonga, the Cook Islands, gone. Japan is gone. Taiwan is gone. Papua New Guinea is gone. The Philippines are gone. Indonesia is gone. Malaysia is reduced to a quarter of its landmass. The North Island of New Zealand disappears but the South Island survives. Costa Rica and Panama more or less disintegrate. Earthquakes destabilize countless cities as tectonic spasms rend the planet's surface.

The massive redistribution of global ocean levels, plus some warping effect on the Earth's magnetic fields thanks to the unprecedented energy release from the meltdown, causes a polar shift—basically, a radical repositioning of the magnetic poles. The magnetic South Pole shifts a little under 1,000 miles to the middle of the Indian Ocean. The magnetic North Pole ends up in Hudson Bay. What's left of Canada and the northern United States is sealed in a tomb of ice half a mile thick. The land under Antarctica is suddenly livable, virgin territory, desolate but untouched. So of course everyone invades it to claim it as their own.

That is, everyone who isn't lobbing volleys of nuclear missiles at one another. The United States descends into a second civil war following a military coup that seizes the country's nuclear arsenal and fires on the Union of Soviet Socialist Republics under the belief, despite contrary evidence, that the San Francisco explosion was the first strike of World War III. The Soviets claim innocence, but with a third of the United States vaporized and another third encased in ice, no one's thinking clearly. Both the United States and the USSR are rendered uninhabitable for generations.

With the global weather system in chaos due to the polar shift, entire ecosystems collapse. Desperate survivors mass-migrate, trying to escape the undulating hurricane clouds of radioactive ash spreading across the planet. China seizes what's left of Asia, insisting they're uniquely poised to manage the cataclysm. Europe and Africa collapse into dozens of civil wars within individual countries. Australia tries to sit the whole thing out but that just makes them an easy target when China comes for them. South America declares an emergency political unification and ends up as the closest thing to a haven of stability, although nobody's safe from the rancid clouds wafting down toxic ash.

But I still show up in 2016 with a crazy story about time travel.

Temporal drag is in full effect—my existence in 1965 demands that I'm born in 1983 to receive my consciousness in 2016. My mom's parents were from northern England and survived World War III. My father's parents never moved from Austria to Canada, so he grew up in the ruins of Vienna. They met in a hospital in Geneva. My father had lost both legs trying to stop a suicide bomber at the Voltaire Museum and my mother had gone blind after irradiated ash dusted her eyelashes while she hid out in an Alps ski resort that had been crushed by an avalanche and abandoned. She was halfway through *Great Expectations* when her sight winked out. A clerical error assigned them to the same room and they got to talking. My father offered to read my mother the rest of the novel out loud. It took three days to finish it. Afterward, they made love.

She never knew what he looked like. He died the next day because the sex was strenuous enough to dislodge a wedge of shrapnel in his aortic valve. My mother named me Victor and took me to Argentina to start a new life. Or she tried to anyway. She died on the ship, somewhere in the Atlantic Ocean—cancer, everywhere.

Orphaned at sea, I was quasi-adopted by the ship's captain, a man named Hathaway, because he thought his wife back in Australia could use some companionship. She was a sweet lady, Marigold, and I have some nice early memories of her before she was murdered by raiders when I was nine.

My semi-feral adolescence in the Australian outback really wasn't too bad, considering the planet's ecosystem was in free fall. Everything in the ocean was dead. Reptiles were doing okay but birds and large mammals were extinct. The soil was toxic. When it rained, you had to hide under something sturdy because the drops burned your skin. The moon was starting to look like a reasonable option for resettlement. Except with the global economy dismantled and all functioning nations in a state of perpetual war, nobody was building spaceships.

At age seventeen I enlisted in the New Pacific Army, a strained military pact between China and Australia, who shared control of Antarctica and used it as a stable base to launch skirmishes against the South American Republic. The New Pacific Army was big on rigorous testing to determine every individual's place in the social machinery and I was directed to Research and Development, which meant I got to study science and engineering instead of just learning efficient ways to kill people. I mean, the end goal was to innovate more efficient ways to kill people, but still—books were involved.

I was enjoying a steady rise up the ranks when I collapsed on July 11, 2016, cursing and seizing up. When I came to, I spouted off a lunatic story about traveling back in time to witness the original accident that triggered the apocalypse.

Scientific inquiry in the New Pacific Army was reasonably open to inexplicable phenomena, which I guess happens when your world is devastated by an unexplained phenomenon, so my superiors dutifully sent my story up the chain of command. A politically powerful general, Antares Liong, was intrigued—he thought time travel could be a way to defeat his enemies before they became his enemies. I was assigned to a clandestine group tasked with building a time machine.

Eventually, my colleagues were all executed for failing to invent time travel. My status as the visionary who inspired the program saved me from a bullet, but I got another kind of death—I was frozen in a cryogenic chamber until time travel could actually be invented. I assumed this would be *never*, so as the cold pulled me into a dreamless sleep, I considered it about as happy a death as the world could offer.

Did someone eventually figure out time travel, thaw me into consciousness, and send me back to 1965? I don't know. That part isn't in the memories that are swallowing me whole. I could've been on ice for a week or 10,000 years. All I know is that everything I believe to be true is under siege by a new reality insisting with volume, clarity, and force that what's supposed to happen is—Lionel pulls the lever, the device switches off and goes into meltdown, and *I don't stop him.*

The apocalypse already happened. Someone sent me here, not to prevent the end of the world, but to witness its beginning.

130

Now I understand. It's always been a causal loop.

The plan was for me to reset the timeline back to my 2016 by ensuring that Lionel's experiment succeeds as it should have. But what I tried to explain to Lionel before he sent me here, what he refused to accept even after everything that happened with Ursula, is that time travel is very bad at fixing mistakes. What it's very good at is creating even worse mistakes. My world can't be brought back. When I traveled to 1965 the first time, I erased it, permanently. That reality is gone forever and there's no time to mourn it. The only thing that matters now is making sure the Goettreider Engine doesn't malfunction and destroy half the planet.

So I have a very simple goal—stop the apocalypse.

And my only chance is to act *exactly the same way.* In fact, any attempt to act differently will cause the horrific timeline that's currently sluicing into my brain. Lionel's experiment must fail, but fail *safely.* When he panics and turns off the Engine, I have to be ready to switch it back on before it goes into meltdown.

I thought *John's* reality was the worst-case scenario. But *Victor's* reality is so much worse, devastatingly worse. It turns out John's 2016 is the best I can hope for. And its likelihood is dwindling by the second.

I have to take control of this body. But even with fifty years to prepare, I didn't plan for this—for Victor.

We're in this brain together, so I know what he wants, just as he knows what I want. Victor gets to be born only if the apocalypse happens. In his timeline, nobody prevents the Engine from melting down. I need Tom to pull up the lever—and Victor needs to stop him from doing that. Whoever succeeds gets to exist.

Right now, in this moment, both timelines are equally possible.

Fuck.

I feel like I'm swimming through a corrosive sludge of memories and impulses and beliefs, Victor's mind flooding mine the way the Pacific Ocean filled the glass-bottomed crater that the meltdown scooped into the Earth. Sorry, *will* scoop into the Earth in . . . just under thirty seconds.

Lionel has already activated the Engine. I've already moved my position to get a better view. In a few seconds, the energy plume will hit me. My invisibility field will fail. Lionel will see me and pull down the lever, switching off the Engine. It will overheat, the harmless energy plumes turning destructive. The observers will scream as the room around them is destroyed. Jerome will save Ursula but lose his arm. I will shove Lionel to safety and pull up the lever, just as my damaged time-travel apparatus triggers the emergency function that sends me back to the future.

All of that has to happen in the next twenty-one seconds.

Which means I have twenty seconds to save the world.

131

Twenty. The first energy plume erupts from the Engine's absorption coils. The Sixteen Witnesses react in shock, delight, fascination. Tom doesn't know the rest of us are in his mind, but because he's distracted by the Engine I have an opportunity to wrench away control. But before I can take over, Victor attacks, pulling me into the layered walls of memory. They look solid, but they're gummy and pliant like a membrane and we fall into one, a quicksand portal to another time.

Nineteen. The second energy plume bursts out. This is the one that disrupts Tom's invisibility field, but he's too busy being dazzled by the glittery whorls to realize his camouflage is gone. I'm in Robin Swelter's bedroom. She screams as her brother punches me in the face. But this is dream logic, greasy and unstable, so it's Victor's fist that sends me sprawling into another memory.

Eighteen. Lionel is stunned to see Tom appear out of nowhere in his lab. I land in a chair in the conference room at John's architecture office. Victor lunges across the epoxied maple table at me, the junior associates mute and staring. Everything is sticky and elastic, a land of melting wax.

Seventeen. Tom freezes when he realizes Lionel can see him. But it's not just inchoate panic. It's a mess in here, multiple consciousnesses jockeying for cognitive control. To Tom, his thoughts are a stuttering echo of clashing imperatives that he mistakes for fear. I'm on the front lawn of the housing unit, my mother reading her novel on the grass, my father working at his desk, the lemon tree guarding his office window. Victor pilots a hover car, veering out of formation, but he's not aiming for my mother—he's aiming for me. When I try to dodge, John grabs me tight. I thought he was safely walled away, but once John understood his prison was viscid and loose he broke out. I pull free just in time and the impact hurls the two of them away.

Sixteen. I manage to get control of Tom just long enough to make him reset the invisibility field, so he winks out of sight. John and Victor pull me into another memory. There's something *familiar* about Victor that I can't quite place. I thought of John as a worse version of me, but what if I'm just a better version of him that never realized there could be a rival whispering in his other ear, cunning enough to stay hidden until now?

Fifteen. Lionel asks the confused observers if anyone saw what he saw. John and Victor loom at me in the Hong Kong alley where I got mugged. They don't just want to take control of Tom. They want to wipe me out. I'm not a fighter. I'm a runner. So I run.

Fourteen. Jerome looks suspicious of Ursula's familiar tone with Lionel. As I race down the alley, the walls of the buildings blur into thickets of close-pressed trees, an impossibly tall forest, the ground underfoot springy with fallen pine needles. John chases me, but Victor uses this moment to seize the reins of Tom's mind.

Thirteen. Tom wants to trigger the emergency return function and blast out of the past. But it's actually Victor guiding Tom, trying to evict him from the present so nobody can stop the meltdown. I run through the forest, unsure if John is even still behind me.

Twelve. Lionel panics and yanks down the activation lever to shut off the Engine. This is the point of no return for all of us. The forest floor is no longer littered with pine needles—it's decaying books, each one a hardback edition of *Great Expectations,* open to the page my mother was reading when she died.

Eleven. The Engine shudders and spews jagged fingers of energy.

No wonder Tom's frozen—there are three versions of him churning in his mind. I'm in the abandoned library and growing from the heap of moldered books are lemon trees just like the one that saved my father's life. I follow an instinct to dig through the rotting books with my hands, clawing through the pages, ink staining my hands, the words tattooed onto my skin in nonsensical syntax.

Ten. The previously harmless energy plumes turn a fiery blue, destroying the control console. Victor flexes his will, keeping Tom paralyzed. All he needs is to stop Tom from doing anything while the Engine overloads. I tunnel through the ceiling of John's condo and fall to the floor. Victor and John take positions to attack me. I look for somewhere to run, a door, a window, but they're blocking any escape. Victor directs John to corner me . . . and that familiarity I couldn't place smashes into focus. The day I was annihilated, the day John did those awful things—*Victor was there.* Because that was the same day Lionel broke reality's shell. It wasn't John that slipped through. John was already there. It was Victor. He's the one that made John do what he did. And now he's controlling John again, trying to eliminate the only obstacle to his existence—me. I feel his desperation, he just wants his ruined world to live, but that means killing billions of people. I can't let it happen. I won't. I feel a current charge through me, like a dull metal filament that suddenly flares incandescent. It's not anger. It's not fear. It's simpler than those impulses, calm and ready and true. It's *resolve.* I guess I finally found a fight I can't run away from.

Nine. Ursula screams at Lionel to get back. And there's something in that scream. Something I'm not yet grasping, a word on the tip of my tongue. No, not a word. A *feeling.* Until now, I've been on the defensive, so Victor doesn't expect me to launch him through the wall of framed pulp anthologies. We land in Tom's place on the 184th floor of the octagonal complex, hover cars darting past the windows, careening into each other in fiery, silent explosions. Victor lashes out, fierce, and it's clear he's too strong to beat in a fight. But there has to be another way. Something I have that he doesn't. Something that Victor wouldn't even perceive as a threat. And that's when I see it. On the bed. A strand of Penelope's hair. And it hits me—none of the memories we've been fighting through involved *Penny*. She's the key. No, not the key. The *lock*.

Eight. The next blue pulse comes right at Ursula, but Jerome pushes her to safety, his outstretched arm vaporized below the elbow. I plunge into the murky swamp of my mind, not even sure what I'm searching for—until I find something buried in all the soggy, elastic memories, something *hard*. The memory is pale and brittle, but solid. It's the restaurant where Penny and I ate breakfast the morning after our first night together. I don't know what we talked about or what we ordered, but the feeling is there—possibility. When I wedge this fragile memory into the syrupy web around me, it holds its place. It's not enough to stop Victor. But it's not my only memory of her.

Seven. The remaining observers panic en masse as another plume slashes open the ceiling. I build a structure from my memories of Penny. Some are so thin they crumble at the edges when I pick them up. A taxi ride in the rain, city lights blurring vivid like wet paint in a halo around her profile. But some are as strong and thick as bricks. Her bookstore, Penny reading a novel on a stool, too absorbed to look up at the customer who just showed up to change her life. My family home, the dinner that started so well and ended so badly. The auditorium where I gave my speech, ready to risk anything because I walked in holding her hand. Her apartment door, the look on her face as she realized John was wrong when he said I was never coming back. That one is almost too heavy to lift. The night we met, her kitchen, our first kiss. That memory could bear any weight. Victor is a soldier and he knows how to fight. But I'm an architect. I know how to build.

Six. Lionel's hands blister, the hair on his face catches fire, the tip of his nose burns. When I slam the structure around Victor, he lunges at it expecting to push through with brute force. But these memories are made of something different.

Five. Ursula cradles Jerome as he goes into shock. While I'm busy trapping Victor, John takes command of Tom and I have no idea what he'll make him do. I keep adding memories to Victor's prison, as many as I can find, and he can't figure out how to break through them. Because Victor has no Penny. He doesn't know what it does to you to love someone the way I loved her.

Four. This is the moment I was so proud of, when I displayed cool under pressure. Except now I know that it's John who snaps Tom's cognitive paralysis and animal terror. Which makes sense. Tom was never brave. He was reckless and, in certain circumstances, reckless-ness can appear courageous. But Tom was never the kind of guy who'd pull it together in the clutch and save the day. I don't trust John, but he's the one who gets Tom moving.

Three. Tom shoves Lionel away from the Engine. Or, really, John does. Victor goes ballistic with rage. But why isn't John pulling the lever and ending this? Why is he relishing the deranged adrenal surge that gushed in when he shoved Lionel? And then, because we're all in this mind together, I get it—John doesn't care about stopping the meltdown. He just wants to hurt Lionel for what he did to our fam-ily. I didn't realize John felt that kind of intense, protective loyalty. But if I don't stop him, he'll murder Lionel Goettreider in the past so he can never become the man who threatens our loved ones.

Two. A plume hits Tom dead on, frying the time-travel apparatus and triggering the emergency return protocol. I have one second left to pull up the lever. And I finally understand what I have to do. Tom's crime, erasing a whole world and everyone in it, is incalculably worse than anything Victor or John ever did. I can never forgive myself for that. Even now, it presses down on me, the mountain of regret. I don't want *any* of them in me. I don't want Victor's vicious-ness and desolation or John's arrogance and detachment, but I also don't want Tom's glum passivity and callow nonchalance. I want to be purged of all of them. I want there to be nothing in me that isn't light and pure and good. But of course that's not real. That's what happens when you're a statue in a city square, stripped of any human adornment that can't be cast in bronze. What knits together all my memories of Penny is the overwhelming feeling that there's someone who doesn't need me to be anything except who I am. That's what love can do for you, if you let it—build a person out of all your broken pieces. It doesn't matter if the stitches show. The stitches, the *scars,* just prove you earned it. And so I stop trying to keep all these versions of myself apart. Instead, I make us whole. I let Victor out, but instead of fighting him I pull us together. John doesn't see it coming until it's too late and he's already been drawn into us. Tom has no idea what's happening in his head but we don't need him to. We're in control.

One. We pull up the Engine's activation lever just as we're boomeranged back to the present. The only present there will ever be.

132

I get a frigid spear of anxiety that I'm going to wake up in the hospital, having just collapsed on John's building site, and be forced to relive this entire sequence again and again and again in an endless loop. But I'm spared that particular existential horror. This final trip through time is with my father's instantaneous apparatus, so I'm not thrust into fifty more years of paralytic self-examination. With a sharp flash of light and a thrumming whoosh of sound, I'm back in 2016. It took until just now to truly appreciate my father's genius in comparison to Lionel's.

From the perplexed expression on Lionel's face, standing right in front of me, it's clear that almost no time has passed. Everything is just as it was when I left, except I'm not holding the time machine.

"It didn't work," Lionel says.

"It worked," I say.

"You went back?"

"Yes."

"But I'm still here," he says.

"That's right, Lionel. We did it. We saved the world."

I embrace him. His body goes rigid as I press myself against him, enveloping him in my arms.

"No," Lionel says. "You'll try again."

Obviously I didn't hug Lionel because I missed him. I did it to get close enough to pinch a nerve in his elbow, sending spikes of radiating pain up to his neck, while I tear the device from his wrist that he uses to operate the facility's systems, drop it to the floor, and stamp down on it, smashing its delicate circuitry under my heel.

There must be a built-in alarm because as soon as it's off his wrist the security door hurls open and Wen, the thick-necked driver, hurries in with his semiautomatic pistol drawn.

I whirl Lionel in front of me as a human shield and give him a little shove in Wen's direction, so he takes a wobbly, involuntary step forward to keep his balance. Wen flinches, unsure if his primary source of income is about to pitch face-first into the floor.

I use the moment's hesitation to lunge at Wen, sideways to make a smaller target. I have no idea how I know to do that. Wen shifts his aim, but it's too late for him.

My hand grasps his hand on the gun's grip, twisting the weapon away from me, breaking his trigger finger, while jamming an elbow into his nose, crushing the cartilage.

My other hand wraps around to the back of Wen's neck and, with a sharp twist, I cut off muscular access to his spine.

Wen's legs give way and, conscious but temporarily paralyzed, he collapses to the ground, leaving me with his pistol. Blood pours from Wen's broken nose, but he can't move anything below his shoulders, so he just twitches like a trapped spider.

I place the muzzle of the pistol against Lionel's forehead.

The whole thing takes, like, two seconds and, even though I'm the one who did it, feels impossibly badass.

It turns out that integrating Victor into my consciousness gives me access to his feral postapocalyptic survivalist military training. Which opens up some interesting possibilities in terms of my future life choices, but right now I care about only one thing—making sure Penny and my family are safe.

I have my shoe on Wen's neck, the gun pressed firmly enough against Lionel's forehead that it's leaving a mark.

"Wait," Lionel says. "It was your idea. Do you remember? You told me to make it look like I'd kidnapped them. You said you'd need the motivation. They're safe and unharmed. Even Weschler, the woman, Penelope, it was fake. I hired a Hong Kong action director to shoot the whole thing. He thinks it's for a Japanese reality show."

"The other timeline is gone," I say. "Permanently. I barely saved *this* reality."

"No," he says, "this can't be my life."

"It is," I say.

"But I wasted it all," Lionel says.

"You built a time machine, Lionel," I say. "You're the greatest scientific mind that ever lived."

"I didn't build it," he says. "I copied it."

He gives a cautious nod to a small alcove in the wall. I twist my shoe into Wen's throat until he loses consciousness, and then I gesture with the gun. Lionel hobbles over—that wrist device monitors proper operation of his leg braces, so without it his steps are shaky and off-balance. Inside the alcove is a small metal case with a genetic scanner that opens only for Lionel.

Nestled inside it is the time machine.

"You left this with me on July 13, 1965. I don't know if you meant to but . . . you did. I understood that I couldn't just use it myself. That it would be catastrophic for reality as we know it. But I was in no position to build a time machine from scratch. It was *impossible*. So, I took this one apart. Piece by piece. And I figured out how to fabricate all the components. I did my best not to cheat. I didn't manufacture any of the pieces until it was technically feasible with contemporary science. When I hit an impenetrable obstacle, yes, I guided the world's technology to where I needed it to be. That's why I sold my inventions when I did. Not for money. Out of necessity. You never told me how long I'd have to wait for you."

"You never told me how long it would take to travel back. Fifty-one years, Lionel. I was trapped for fifty-one years."

"Yes," he says, "well, I suppose we both could've given the other a bit more information. To avoid some pain."

"So the loop is closed," I say. "And we never open it again."

"No, if you won't try again," Lionel says, "I will."

"You don't know how close we came to destroying everything. *This* life you think you wasted, this is what saving the world looks like."

"But I didn't do anything," he says. "I copied myself. I'm a fraud."

"My mom once told me that's the secret of life," I say. "We all think we're frauds. Everybody's winging it."

"I spent most of my life trapped in an ontological paradox and I'm supposed to just live with that?"

"Yes," I say. "For the rest of the world."

"What do I care about the rest of the world?" he says.

"Then just care about you and Ursula," I say. "This is the best you get. Is a lifetime of loving each other, even if it was messy and secret and hard, is that really worse than no time at all?"

"At least in that other world I got to be a hero."

"Lionel, you still can be."

He doesn't understand, of course. But I'll show him. And then we'll show everyone.

133

Look, I've never written a book before and I apologize if I did it wrong, especially here at the end. A lot more happens, but I feel like I've already asked for a lot of your time, so I'll wrap this up as efficiently as my limited talents allow.

I let Lionel revive Wen and the guy seemed remarkably nonchalant about the whole thing. Maybe when you're a chauffeur and bodyguard for a reclusive genius billionaire that's just in the job description. We drove back to Lionel's house and made some preparations for the arrival of my mom, dad, sister, and Penny from the airport. A typical flight from Toronto to Hong Kong takes about fifteen hours, but of course Lionel's private jet was built to do it in a quarter of the time.

A change had come over Lionel. He seemed *relieved* he no longer had to enact his elaborate master plan, but he also seemed kind of lost without it. He was surprisingly malleable, ready to follow wherever I led him. Which was weird, for sure, but of course *I'm* also the one who gave him the elaborate master plan in the first place. I told him what to do back in 1965 and he spent the next fifty years doing it. He's showing his age, too, like his single-minded pursuit kept his body in check and without it something vital sloughed off of him, leaving behind a very tired ninety-three-year-old man.

My family and Penny were brought to the house still unconscious and revived with some colorless, odorless vapor that counteracted whatever gas knocked them out. True to Lionel's word, they were unharmed, including Penny.

There was some confusion and upset when they woke up on the other side of the world. Greta felt very strongly that she should be punching someone in the face but wasn't sure whether it should be her brother, the stoic bodyguard, or the old guy. My mom wanted to call the police or the consulate or whoever had jurisdiction over international kidnapping. My dad had a lot of questions about how they got all the way to Hong Kong so fast. Penny said nothing at all.

I introduced them to Lionel Goettreider.

That got their attention. Lionel and I gave them a brief rundown of what had happened since they last saw me. They did their best to follow along but, as I'm sure you're all too aware, trying to keep this time-travel crap straight in your head is a chore, particularly since in the end my big heroic accomplishment was keeping the world exactly as they've always known it to be. It's tough to get worked up about what might have been when all you know is what already is.

The key was Lionel's house itself—it proved that the techno-utopian world I'd described to them wasn't just a lingering adolescent fantasy filtered through a nervous breakdown. It was real and it was all around them and it was pretty cool.

Lionel showed my mom and dad and sister his many outrageous inventions, but I could see Penny's interest waver. She doesn't care much for gadgets. She likes books made of paper and glue, pillows stuffed with feathers, chairs built with wood and nails, fruit grown in velvety earth, kissing the one you love.

We stood together at a wall of windows looking out over the rusty cliffs to the sloshing, white-peaked South China Sea. And we talked.

That's another thing Penny likes—talking. And listening. Thinking things through. Considering points of view. Trying to understand.

I lost a lot in the decades I spent traveling to the past, especially what it feels like to connect with another human being. It got buried deep, sealed in concrete, shut in a steel box, shot into outer space, frozen solid, asphyxiated, drawn into the burning heart of the Sun. It felt gone forever.

It took ten seconds with Penny to find it again. She looked at me and there it was.

134

They do some pretty nice sunsets on Hong Kong Island and this one was dappling pinks and oranges across the water down below.

"I believe you," Penny says. "For what it's worth."

"It's worth a lot," I say.

"But I don't know if it's enough," she says.

"Is it at least a start?"

"It's at least a start."

"Okay," I say.

"Of course," she says, "it's possible that this is all an elaborate hoax you've painstakingly cooked up to trick me into falling back in love with you. But if it is, I mean, points for creativity."

"When you say falling *back* in love with me," I say, "does that mean you fell out of love with me?"

"Yes," Penny says. "Well, I don't know. Most of the way."

"And now?"

"And now it's more complicated," she says.

"I can't change what happened. I have access to a *time machine* and I still can't change it. Plus, I mean, it would require me to explain how reality is like a crème brûlée and I don't think that'll help my case. I believe that part of me is gone, but I understand if my assurances aren't enough. I can apologize until the day I die, and I will if you'll let me, but the best way I can think of to get back what we had is to show you every day of our lives that something like what happened to you will never happen again. But if you really feel we can't go back, that what we had is lost forever, I'll accept it. I will. Just knowing you're safe and alive will have to be enough for me."

"Yeah," she says, "that's not what I meant by *complicated*."

"Okay," I say.

"I'm pregnant," says Penny.

"Like with a baby?" I say.

"Yeah. Pregnant like with a baby."

"It's funny," I say, "because I just single-handedly saved the space-time continuum, human civilization, and reality itself, and yet this is the best thing that's happened all day."

Penny stares out the window. The sun is already half swallowed by the horizon, the hot disk melting into the cool sea—going, going, gone.

"I should've been there when you found out," I say.

"You were pretty busy saving the world."

"Reality itself," I say.

"Don't let it go to your head," she says. "Nobody outside of this room even knows it happened. In fact, all you really did was *not* screw up reality even more than you did last time. So, maybe let's ease up on the time-traveling savior thing."

"You know, in another reality I'm this, like, badass apocalyptic warrior."

"Do you want to keep it?" she says.

"I've never wanted anything more," I say.

"I kind of feel the same," Penny says.

"Penny, I'm sorry."

"I'm sorry too. And don't say *for what*. Because, trust me, I doubted you to my core. I had some shitty, vengeful, dark thoughts about you. And it's hard to wipe them all away and act like they never happened. But I'd like to try."

"Me too," I say.

I'm nearly done telling this story and I'm still nowhere near strong enough a writer to convey what it feels like to kiss the straight-up uncontested love of my life after fifty-one years, so I'll try to keep it simple—it feels really good.

Here's what Penny doesn't say. What she'll never say. What we'll never discuss, not once, not ever. She doesn't know exactly when we conceived our baby. We were newly infatuated and casual about the whens and wheres of our intimacy. It could've been one of two or three or four occasions. And it could've been that time with John. Genetically, it's irrelevant. Psychologically, I have no idea. Maybe it doesn't matter. Maybe it's something wonderful that came out of something awful. Maybe that's a self-serving way to frame it. Maybe I'm an asshole for even thinking that the fleeting, elusive moment of conception of something as momentous and everyday as the beginning of a human life could have any influence at all on who our child will be. Maybe I should just shut the hell up and enjoy it. Maybe I will.

135

This is how the future starts.

My dad will exhaustively explore the technical specifications of the Goettreider Engine and what he finds will blow his mind. Even though, you know, I already *told* him what it can do. The difference between his possibly psychotic son's suspect delusions and the actual machine emitting zettajoules of clean energy will turn out to be unsurprisingly vast. My dad will feel we have a responsibility to announce it to the world as soon as possible, since it's one of the great scientific breakthroughs of human history.

As a group, we will decide on a more judicious approach.

We will form a company. Me, Penny, Greta, my mom, and my dad will share 50.1 percent, so 10.02 percent each, and Lionel will take 49.9 percent, which will transfer to Emma the day Jerome dies. Even though Lionel will want nothing more than to assert his paternity, he will respect Ursula's wishes that her husband never know the truth. At least not for sure.

Greta will argue that the world in which Lionel graciously made the Engine open-source technology for anyone with the wherewithal to build one is a world long gone. With corporate control and political corruption five decades more entrenched in global civilization, we will have to handle the introduction of this epochal technology with a lot more care than the other Lionel did on his deathbed back in 1965.

Greta's been reading a lot since her previous company was taken from her due to her excess of self-entitled superiority and lack of business acumen, qualities she's been working very hard to reverse. She's particularly taken by a French philosopher named Paul Virilio, who writes about the Accident—the idea that every time you introduce a new technology, you also introduce the accident of that technology, so you have a responsibility to anticipate not just the good it can do but also the bad it can wreak, not just the glory but also the ruin.

I've mentioned this notion before, but where I come from it was otherwise attributed. Maybe no idea is ever lost. Maybe it just waits somewhere in the swirl for somebody else to think it.

Lionel's warehouse is equipped to mass-produce Engines and we start doing that immediately. All the components are in place, but of course we don't want any catastrophic malfunctions. They'll have to be flawless right away. Fortunately, Lionel had a long time to perfect them.

My dad will use the manufacturing and testing period to write a book, his first since his much-maligned, pun-embellished time-travel primer—which he'll be delighted to discover Lionel actually read, and they will spend many late nights caught up in arcane, impenetrable discussions about both the theoretical science and its practical applications. The book will be about Lionel, his life, his work, how the Engine came to be, and what it means for the world. He'll leave out a few key personal details. We'd like to change the world without hurting anyone. It will be among the bestselling biographies ever published. There will be very few puns.

The goal of the company will be to make the technology open-source, available to all for free. But Greta will convince us to be at least initially cautious. There are too many out there who will perceive what we're doing as an existential threat. So we will have to take them off the board.

Greta will have a plan. She believes that money is arbitrary in that it has power only because people collectively grant it power, like a mass hallucination that's come to life, a golem of infinite zeros. We will embrace that arbitrary power and use it—to buy up any company that could threaten us. This will require several trillion dollars. But a machine that produces unlimited energy is also a delivery system for unlimited wealth.

Greta will turn out to be a visionary bare-knuckle bruiser of a corporate CEO. As we prepare to launch the Engine, she will work out the kinks in her long-term strategy by delivering to market a steady flow of the designer trinkets with which Lionel equipped his home.

My mom's interest in all of this will be political. She will have a simple outcome in mind—no more war, ever. She will see the Engine not in terms of unlimited energy or unlimited money, but as a machine for unlimited peace. She wants every person on the planet free to feel what she feels, curled up in an armchair on a sunny afternoon reading a novel written in another age—to have no cares. She will strive to turn this age into another age, a bad dream from which humanity finally woke up.

She will become our driving political operator. You might not think a career in academia would prepare her for that, but it turns out that academics are goddamn crazy and getting anything done in the university environment is so convoluted and asinine and theatrical that my mom will find actual politics to be kind of relaxing in comparison.

Lionel will have no interest in further involvement. He will care about only one thing—spending whatever time he can with Emma Francoeur. He will outlive Jerome by eighteen months and die with Emma at his bedside. I will never ask her how she feels about it all. She is very private and it will be none of my business anyway.

Lionel will live just long enough to hold his Nobel Prize.

Penny and I won't have much of a role in any of this. We won't want one. Penny will give birth to our child and we will raise him together. With our share of the Engine's limitless financial resources, we will buy a building and tear it down and rebuild it. And then we will buy another building and tear it down and rebuild it. And we will do that again and again and again, for as long as the money keeps coming, which means forever.

I don't believe I can ever be forgiven for erasing my friends from existence, but the best way I know to honor them is brick by brick by brick. Every time we pour the foundation of a new building, I will write the names of those I lost in the wet cement. Deisha. Asher. Xiao. Hester. Megan. Tabitha. Robin. Penelope.

We will remake the world, Penny and I, one building at a time. Penny likes things that she can touch and I will find I do as well. I will discover that what makes me happiest, beyond Penny and our child, is to make things. A building. A family. A life.

It won't be fast, changing the world. But we have time.

136

As I've mentioned *many* times, I come from the world we were supposed to have. But lately I've been thinking about that a lot. Whether or not it's true.

When I consider it now, despite my breathless descriptions of its multivalent wonders, I'm struck by how recognizable it all was. What I mean is—people lived in buildings, had jobs, bought things that were advertised to them, followed fashion trends, enjoyed entertainment projected on screens, ate food, drank liquids, had sex, fell in love and broke hearts, made babies and raised them as they saw fit, voted in elections, sometimes broke laws, and tried to contribute meaningfully to a civilization they believed was always open to improvement but fundamentally worth propagating. The whole enterprise, top to bottom, would've been immediately, intuitively understood by anyone from this 2016. Or, and this is my point, our common 1965.

The world I come from was an accelerated version of the human civilization that developed through the twentieth century, hinging on the calamities of the Second World War, and rocketing ever faster on a track laid in the two decades between 1945 and 1965. And then it just kept on going, the technology getting more sophisticated, more seamless, more comprehensive, more integrated, more . . . more. But it wasn't *imaginatively* different from the future dreamed up in the wake of Pearl Harbor, Normandy, Stalingrad, Auschwitz, and Hiroshima.

It was in fact specifically those dreams made real. If the technology had existed for neural scanners to map a virtual projection of humanity's most fervent hopes, to give them something glittering and buoyant and comforting to wake into following the grisly pandemonium of the wartime nightmare, it would've looked exactly like the world I come from. And it did—activated by Lionel Goettreider on July 11, 1965.

It was like our collective imagination stopped revising the idea of what civilization could be, fixed a definitive model in place, and set to work making it happen. It was the world we were supposed to have. And so there was no reason to consider any other world. Another pretty good working definition of ideology.

So, okay, what's the alternative? If the world *isn't* supposed to be a dazzling acceleration of the postwar generation's techno-utopian fantasies, then . . . what? Between futurist manifest destiny and apocalyptic ruin, is there another way?

We sit around the dinner table, Penny and I and my mom and my dad and Greta and Lionel and, following Jerome's death, often Emma too, and talk about this. Is it possible to think outside the box of your ideology? Or is *ideology* the box and you just have to work at opening it? Maybe it's too late for us and the best we can do is to raise a generation less shackled by outmoded dreams, free to imagine something . . . else. Penny and I are working on that too.

We need new futures.

137

I wrote all this down for two reasons.

The first reason is John. This is the novel he wanted to write. I took over his life and he never came back, at least not yet, so it seemed correct to do this last thing for him.

Why do I even care about doing right by John? Because of Victor. Imagining me and Victor as an angel and a devil on John's shoulders, like in an old cartoon, it's comforting. Because it means the life I'm inhabiting in the world I saved isn't irrevocably contaminated. Maybe, like any life, it could go either way.

Morally, emotionally, ontologically, I'm not sure it matters who was really to blame for the unforgivable things John did. I have to take responsibility because I'm the only one left. If Victor is a tumor I excised, it means it was a problem with a solution. He's gone, so the people I love are safe. We all have problems we'd like to believe have solutions. We all have parts of ourselves we'd like to cut away.

I know novels shouldn't state outright what they're about. But this isn't a novel. It's a memoir. So, I hope it's okay to admit there's a general point to all of this. I never claimed any wisdom, pretty much the opposite every step of the way, but here's what I think this book is about—there's no such thing as the life you're supposed to have.

Of course, I'm mostly an idiot who has only impossibly brief judders of hazy insight, so by all means feel free to think it's about something else entirely.

It's about what you need it to be about.

The second reason is you, Tom.

I want you to know why your mother and I gave you the name we did and what really happened, in case for whatever reason I can't tell you, or don't, or won't. I finished this when I could, a little every night, sometimes with you asleep in my arms while your mother stole a few minutes of rest between feedings. I tried to capture what it felt like at the time, so it would be interesting enough for you to read, not an obligation or an embarrassment, although my limitations as a writer have probably made it a bit of both.

And it's fine, it's truly fine if you don't believe a word of it, if you think even this final chapter is a weird affectation, another of your father's odd jokes, pretending a novel is a memoir when it's obviously the most absurd fiction. Tell your friends your parents named you after a character in a half-baked story your father once wrote down because of a dream he had that he couldn't shake—but that he refused to admit it, that he always took the joke too far, that he insisted to the end that every word of it was true.

The thing is, I saw you come out of your mother and it changed my life. All the other moments that changed my life seem so clean and orderly in retrospect. This was messy and loud, sweat and blood and tears and a whole new life with its eyes, your eyes that already looked like her eyes, squeezed shut, and its mouth, your mouth that already looked like my mouth, wide open, and Penny squeezing my hand and looking at me and me squeezing her hand and looking at her and both of us knowing it was finally starting. The world we were supposed to have. It was you.

All along, it was you.

ACKNOWLEDGMENTS

"*We must suffer fools gladly, otherwise how can we help them to stop being fools?*" is inspired by something my mother, Judith Mastai, used to say. And, more to the point, how she approached her work and her life. She died on February 17, 2001, and so she never got to find out what kind of people her son and daughters would become. This novel is dedicated to her memory.

The concept of the Accident is influenced by the writing of Paul Virilio, particularly *Open Sky*. Greta's critique of science fiction is influenced by the writing of Daniel Quinn, particularly *Ishmael*.

There are few people in one's career who do exactly what they say they're going to do. My agent, Simon Lipskar, is one of them and I'm grateful for his indispensable guidance. Thank you to Maja Nikolic, Katie Stuart, Celia Taylor-Mobley, Taylor Templeton, Joe Volpe, and everyone at Writers House for their efforts on my behalf.

This book was written with zero expectation that it might actually get published, but because of a number of people at Penguin Random House that expectation was thwarted.

Thank you to my American editor, Maya Ziv, who was the first to acquire this book and—with great wit and even greater patience—helped me to make it better. Thank you as well to Ben Sevier, Christine Ball, Amanda Walker, Alice Dalrymple, Eileen Chetti, and everyone at Dutton.

Thank you to my Canadian editor, Amy Black, for her thoughtful guidance in refining this novel. Thank you as well to Kristin Cochrane, Val Gow, Susan Burns, Melanie Tutino, Christie Hanson, Tracey Turriff, and everyone at Doubleday.

Thank you to my British editor, Jessica Leeke, for her incisive observations and ardent support. Additional thanks to Alex Clarke for his editorial input. Thank you as well to Louise Moore and everyone at Michael Joseph.

Thank you to the publishers and translators bringing this book to so many other languages and countries. I hope my travels allow me to meet you all in person.

I'm grateful to Frank Wuliger, Greg Pedicin, and Karl Austen for their years of friendship, advice, and hard work. I am a better writer for knowing them.

Conversations with Jonas Chernick, Ron Cunnane, Jonathan Feasby, Zoe Kazan, Anna Levin, and Ziya Tong helped shape certain ideas in this book. I thank them. Martha Sharpe and Jonathan Tropper offered much appreciated advice to a first-time novelist. I thank them too.

Being a high school English teacher can be a thankless job. But Muriel Densford of Sir Winston Churchill Secondary School in Vancouver inspired me to see books, and myself, in a different way, and I hope mentioning it makes the job slightly less thankless.

Thank you to my family—Moshe Mastai, Galit Mastai, Talia Mastai, Bill Morris, Mary Morris, and basically anyone with the last name or married to someone with the last name or related to anyone with the last name Mastai or Morris.

Thank you to my wife, Samantha Morris Mastai, and my daughters, Beatrix and Frances. Because of them I am a husband and a father and because of that so many things about this life finally make sense.

In my grandparents' house there was a low shelf lined with battered old science-fiction anthologies from the 1950s and 1960s. As a child, I would carefully slip them out and stare at the brittle covers, thinking about the futures these artists and writers imagined, already fixed in my distant past. My grandmother, Leonore Freiman, died in 2004 and my grandfather, Milton Freiman, died in 2006. That collection of anthologies is now on a shelf by the desk where I wrote this book. I still look at the covers sometimes.

ABOUT THE AUTHOR

ELAN MASTAI was born in Vancouver and lives in Toronto with his wife and children. He writes movies. This is his first novel.